GREENSLEEVES

Also by Eloise Jarvis McGraw

GREENSLEEVES

ELOISE JARVIS MCGRAW

SKYSCAPE

Original copyright © 1968 by Eloise Jarvis McGraw
Skyscape copyright © 2015 Eloise Jarvis McGraw

Published by Skyscape, New York

www.apub.com

Amazon, the Amazon logo, and Skyscape are trademarks of Amazon.com, Inc., or its affiliates.

ISBN-13: 9781477829165
ISBN-10: 1477829164

Cover design by Regina Wamba

Library of Congress Control Number: 2014956298

Printed in the United States of America

Contents

Introduction

ELOISE JARVIS MCGRAW—who was born in 1915 and died just before her 85th birthday, in 2000—published *Greensleeves* in 1968, in the middle of her long, productive, and very successful career as a writer of books for children and teens. She's best known, though, for the fiction she wrote for middle grade readers. In fact, quite remarkably, three of her books—*Moccasin Trail*, which was published in 1952, 1961's *The Golden Goblet*, and *The Moorchild*, which came out in 1996—were Newbery Honor Books. Multifaceted as a writer, in 1978 McGraw's *A Really Weird Summer* won an Edgar Award for the best juvenile mystery of the year.

But the novel of McGraw's that I've always been fondest of is *Greensleeves*, which explores issues that teenagers—especially teen girls—can and do identify with. Actually, given my own experience of reading *Greensleeves*, maybe you don't have to be a teenage girl to enjoy it. I first became acquainted with Shannon Kathleen Lightley, the main character and narrator, when I was in my twenties. I loved the novel then, and, having just reread it for the third time in two years, I love it still.

McGraw's greatest strength as a writer is her ability to develop plots that keep readers turning the pages to find out what happens next; but even more important, she creates three-dimensional characters whom we come to care about as we would a member of our own family. And with the creation of Shannon Kathleen Lightley, she hit the jackpot.

Here's how Shannon describes her life before we meet her in the opening pages of the novel:

When you've spent your tothood in London, your six grade-school years in Mary's Creek, Oregon (pop. 4,741), and that gruesome period between ages eleven and seventeen playing hopscotch all over the map of Europe, swapping parents and personalities with every change of headquarters, it results in fairly total confusion on all fronts.

After graduating from high school in small-town Mary's Creek—where she was, disappointingly and against all her expectations, greatly unhappy—Shannon, with a world-famous actress for a mother and a theater producer stepfather, and with a globe-trotting writer for a father, seems to have lost herself. Shannon has no idea what sort of person she is, or wants to be, or what she wants to do in the next few years (college, or not?), let alone with the rest of her life.

And then Shannon gets the opportunity to leave that old life, with all its expectations, behind. She changes her hairstyle, the way she talks, and how she dresses; moves into a rooming house; and gets a job as a waitress in Portland, Oregon. For a whole summer, she can invent a new way of being, leaving Shannon Kathleen Lightley behind and becoming Georgetta Einszweiler Smith from Morton Center, Idaho. The most important question Shannon grapples with over the summer is whether altering all the externals about herself has any effect on the person inside—her real self.

Despite the fact that few if any of the original readers of *Greensleeves* in the 1970s—or even the contemporary readers who are just discovering the novel in this new edition—have a background similar to Shannon's, I know from talking to teens, including my two daughters, that Shannon Kathleen Lightley's dilemma of who and what she wants to be and do with her life is something with which they can totally identify.

That's the beauty of a novel like *Greensleeves*: it might have been written almost half a century ago, but its heroine, and the choices she faces, are totally modern.

These days, the number of fantasy novels being published for teen readers far outweighs what can be called "realistic" fiction for the same age group. This is a sea change from the situation found in the latter part of the last century. Then, publishers generally offered only a few fantasy or science fiction novels aimed specifically at teens (especially teen boys, who were seen as the target market for authors like Robert A. Heinlein and his works such as *Red Planet* [1949] and *Space Cadet* [1948]). Certainly these titles didn't constitute a large part of any major publisher's business plan. In fact, when I look back at the books I read as a teen myself, or suggested to my teenage daughters or those teens I helped at libraries or bookstores, off the top of my head I can think of only three fantasy titles whose authors seemed to have young female readers in mind: Madeleine L'Engle's *A Wrinkle in Time* (1962), Sylvia Engdahl's *Enchantress from the Stars* (1970), and Elizabeth Marie Pope's *The Sherwood Ring* (1958). I still recommend these novels to teen readers who want fantasy novels without werewolves, vampires, and the like.

Of course, there are wonderful examples of realistic fiction being written and read today. Four excellent writers come immediately to mind—John Green, Rainbow Rowell, Laurie Halse Anderson, and E. Lockhart—but there are many others. If, after reading *Greensleeves*, you want to try some other realistic novels, take a look at the "Further Reading" section at the back of this book for a list of some great suggestions.

But in the last half of the twentieth century, when *Greensleeves* was published, it was one among many, many examples of its type. Writers such as Betty Cavanna, Rosamond du Jardin, and Adele de Leeuw were all writing realistic fiction. I wish we could bring back into print all of these authors' titles, and I am so grateful that a new generation of readers will now be able to experience the great pleasures of *Greensleeves*.

Nancy Pearl

For Lynn
who taught me much I needed to know

1

The Beginning of June

1

Last night, about the middle of the night, which is the time I do a lot of my worrying, the idea struck me to write the whole thing down, just as it happened—that whole summer. My theory is that if I really explain everything, as if I were talking to somebody else, it might begin to make more sense to me. Of course, it might make less sense; one never knows. Still, I'll have a go at it. And though that summer's nearly two years back, there'll be no glossing over any little awkward bits I'd as soon forget about—because I've that old journal now, and I'll use it, word for word if necessary, to pin me down to facts.

I came across that journal again only yesterday. What happened was this: before I changed for dinner, I went downstairs to the luggage storeroom to track down my last passport. It's expired, and I'll need a new one if I join Dad and Jeanne this summer, and to get a new one, you have to let them borrow your old one for a while. I had a feeling I'd put mine in my biggest suitcase somewhere, so I dragged the case down and started going through the pockets. Well, I found a whole little treasure trove—an assortment of lint and bobby pins, of course, and three Austrian *Groschen*, and half a bar of Dutch chocolate that looked about thirty years old, and a British airmail stamp, and *two* passports—the one I wanted and an even older one. With them was a red leatherette-bound notebook I recognized instantly. The very sight of it gave me an indescribable little jolt. I put it on the floor beside me—gingerly, as if it contained explosives—while I dealt with the other things.

The chocolate I consigned to the trash basket without a pang, but when I started to send the earlier passport after it, I found myself hesitating, riffling through it. Every page was crammed with stamps and scrawls and *turista visums*—even I find it hard to believe anybody could have crossed the Swiss border that many times from that many different directions in only five years. On the first page was a picture of me, Shannon Kathleen Lightley, at age eleven—product of Ed's Foto Shop in Mary's Creek, Oregon, as I well remember. Aunt Doris got me out of school that morning to go have it taken. A revolting vision, all tooth bands and that un-pulled-together look one has at eleven, but grinning ecstatically because I was about to go back to Europe to live with Dad and Jeanne—they'd just got married a month before.

The photograph in the other passport, taken in Switzerland when I was sixteen, caught the rigid, no-comment expression I wore like armor through my entire six years at Madame Fourchet's Academy in Lausanne.

Well, that later one was the passport I wanted; I stowed it in a pocket to take upstairs. I threw the earlier one in the trash—then after a moment I fished it out again and slipped it back in the suit-case pocket. One doesn't just chuck away the story of one's life, however much one wishes it had read differently. I must say mine's been remarkably disjointed, with never a permanent address or a rationally organized family, in fact, nothing but passports—and parents advancing and retreating in relays, two by two. Dad and Mother, Aunt Doris and Uncle Syd; then Dad and Jeanne, Mother and Nevin—and Uncle Frosty, thank heaven, always popping in and out of the wings. When you've spent your tothood in London, your six grade-school years in Mary's Creek, Oregon (pop. 4,741), and that gruesome period between ages eleven and seventeen playing hopscotch all over the map of Europe, swapping parents and personalities with every change of headquarters, it results in fairly total confusion on all fronts. Take for example the fact that I speak French with a Swiss accent and German with a noticeable Viennese one. Even my English is schizophrenic—half British Isles, half U.S.A. People never can *place* me. I've never really placed myself. This sort of thing, plus some others I've had to complicate my life, can get to one rather badly after so long a time.

The journal was still lying there on the storeroom floor, daring me to look inside. I finally picked it up, then had to pick up a lot of odds and ends that promptly slithered out of it. Most were newspaper cuttings—such things as Dad's award-winning story about the Berlin Wall, and Jeanne's long-chance shot of an air crash that's been reprinted in everything from *Life* on down, and a *London Theatre Review* picture of Mother as Lady Macbeth. There was a snapshot of Franz Bach, too, aged about thirteen, that I took in Paris one day when we were killing time together as usual, waiting for our fathers to get through with some press conference or other. It's a jolly good thing Franz and I got on well; we spent half our school holidays for six years in each other's undiluted company. Now that I think of it, he's the reason my German sounds Viennese—and I suppose his English has turned out half American, like mine. And there was a London *Times* interview with Nevin Drake, who's been married to Mother since I was five years old and produces all her plays.

My mother, I may as well say right now and get it over with, is Rosaleen O'Leary, the British actress. This is usually the first thing people find out about me, and often it's the last, since from then on they'd rather talk about her, what she's "really like" offstage and all

that. Everybody knows already what she looks like—a sheer staggering beauty, classic black-Irish, with wide blue eyes and skin like gar-
denia puree, and a round high forehead adorned with those winglike
dark eyebrows that have become her trademark on two continents.

Dad is a hawk-nosed, red-haired, black-eyed man, all bones
and intensity. Guess which one *I* took after.

Well—let's be as charitable as possible. I inherited those eyebrows, if not the face to go with them, and my nose isn't *quite* as
large as Dad's—though the most charitable adjective I can think of
for my profile is "striking." Unquestionably, red hair is striking,
too. And Nevin says I *move well*, a comment I have never found
very comforting, since I never see myself move, and anyway what
about all the times when one is just standing there? Especially right
next to one's mother? . . . Well, Mother is one of those other things
I've had to complicate my life.

I put the snapshot and the cuttings in one of the suitcase pockets, wrestled the case back onto its shelf, and went upstairs to my
room. I took the journal with me. After dinner I read it, all the way
through. And in the middle of the night I had my idea, about writing that whole summer down.

And now I'm wondering how one starts. I guess I'll just start—
with that morning in Mary's Creek, in early June almost two years
ago, when I was trying desperately to reach Uncle Frosty by phone
in Portland before I left for there myself. That was the beginning
of that summer. I was *back* in the States, you understand. Madame
Fourchet's was a closed book, I was eighteen years old, and leaving
Mary's Creek *again*.

Why was I back there in the first place? Because I'd begged and
nagged and argued until Dad finally gave in and sent me back,
that's why. Nobody to blame for it but me. All I'd wanted in the
world, ten months before, was to be released from servitude at
Madame Fourchet's Academy and sent home to beloved Aunt Doris

and Uncle Syd, and the little town and the big old house where I'd
spent the best six years of my life—what seemed to me then the
only good ones. I wanted to have my senior year at Mary's Creek
High with my long-lost classmates from grade school, then go on
to college at the University of Oregon, to live in the States forever
and turn into the American my passport said I was, instead of the
mongrel expatriate I could feel myself becoming the longer I leap-
frogged around Europe after Dad.

I'd never dreamed it would be hard—that it simply wouldn't
work, that it was years too late already to come back to a place like
Mary's Creek, Oregon, and expect to fit right in as a local girl.
Local curiosity was more like it. Local freak. I've never spent a more
miserable ten months. And two days after I graduated from Mary-
High, I was standing in Aunt Doris's front hall with my luggage
around me, trying to reach Uncle Frosty to say good-by. I'd tried
ringing his home in Portland the night before, but Mona said he
wouldn't be back from San Francisco until morning. So I called his
law offices at nine sharp—only to be told by Miss Jensen that his
train was late. So that was that. I asked her to tell him I was leaving
for London at noon from Portland airport and that I'd write. Fifteen minutes later I was on a Greyhound bus, trying to hang onto
myself in the face of what seemed a complete dead end to my life—
a trap I'd got myself into and saw no way out of, ever again.

It's hard to believe, now, that on that morning I'd never even
heard of Mrs. Elizabeth Dunningham and her will. And harder to
believe how close I came to never hearing of them.

2

It was eleven-fifteen when I climbed out of the limousine at Portland airport, dragged the camel-bag out after me, and pointed out my two big suitcases to a porter. A red-faced man, who had been staring at my hair rather too approvingly all the way out from town, now stared at the bits of European hotel stickers on my luggage. "Well, little lady," he said jovially. "Looks like you've racked up some travel time already. Where you off to now?"

I gave him a blank smile and said in Portuguese, "I have no English"—hoping he had no Portuguese—and made a hasty escape into the terminal.

I was at once drearily at home, a goldfish back in its bowl. The vast, long room was full of noise and motion; people hurried here and there carrying airline bags and children, or stood about in impermanent little clots. The usual small boy slid hilariously on the polished floor; the inevitable garbled voice issued from the loudspeaker. Back to normal, I thought as I crossed an acre of marble paving toward the Pan Am desk. No use to struggle, this is where I belong, it's the only place I do belong—in transit.

The porter had added my suitcases to the shorter of the two Pan Am queues. I paid him off and from long habit sat down to wait on the camel-bag, which is very good for sitting on in queues. It's my favorite, though most eccentric-looking, piece of luggage— a pouch-type affair made of camel hide, all buckles and pockets outside and apparently limitless space within, which I got years ago in Cairo and have been hard to separate from since. I'm the impulsive type—I tend to buy large, awkward objects on the way to the plane, or abruptly decide to take my ski boots—and I've never exhausted the camel-bag's capacity. In Zagreb once it managed to swallow four extra books, a large Turkish coffeepot I'd suddenly acquired, and Jeanne's mohair lap-robe, on top of its usual load.

There were only two ahead of me in the queue. I wished it were twenty. For a moment it seemed inconceivable—just pure nonsense— that I should be in Portland airport, sitting on my camel-bag in another Europe-bound queue. It was pure nonsense. But there I was, and all I could do was try not to think about it. I'd already endured an eighty-mile ride by bus and limousine in the nerve-racking company of my own thoughts, after a leavetaking in Mary's Creek that still ached like a tooth. Uncle Syd had been sad, upset about not driving me to Portland—though he hasn't tackled city traffic for twenty years—Aunt Doris barely restraining tears . . . I too numb to say good-by to her. When the time came, she looked so bewildered and—I don't know, *bleak*—standing there at the bus door in her little squarish knit suit with the Garden Club pin on the lapel, that all in a rush I felt I couldn't bear to leave her, wished desperately I weren't going, and couldn't speak at all. It remained to be seen whether I could control my present untidy mess of mixed emotions until I could make it onto the plane.

"Excuse me," said a porter, politely doubling himself to the level of my drooping head. "Are you Miss Annie Mae Johnson?"

"No. Sorry." Oh, I *was* sorry—sorry I was not Miss Annie Mae Johnson, or the porter, or anybody else on earth except me, with anybody else's set of problems. Quit *thinking*, I told myself in disgust. You'll live. Recite German declensions or something. Count every pair of white shoes to walk in through those doors . . . The queue moved up a notch. I shoved my bags forward, sat back down, and fixed my eyes on the doors.

Three seconds later a tall man walked swiftly through them and stopped, silhouetted against the brilliant sunshine outside. It was a silhouette I knew well, topped by an unmistakable white crew cut, and it had never looked so good to me.

"Uncle Frosty!" I cried, springing off the camel-bag and waving my arms. Several people turned to stare at me, but I didn't care— he'd spotted me. His long legs covered the distance between us, and a moment later his arms went around me in a tight, hard hug. "Oh, Uncle Frosty, I'm so glad to see you," I gabbled against his shoulder. "With your train late and all—how did you ever *do* it?"

"Drove eighty," he said calmly. Uncle Frosty is not an emotional type. Incidentally, he's not my uncle, either; he's Charles Frost, a lifelong friend of Dad's and a sort of ex-officio parent of mine since I was five years old. He disentangled himself from my arms and hair and handbag, and pushed me far enough away to peer into my face. "Well, Shan? How are things?"

"Oh—all right," I quavered. I pulled myself more or less together. "Quite all right. Don't look so worried."

"Your telephone message wasn't exactly soothing. Isn't this departure more than usually sudden, even for you?"

"Yes. But I guess it's more than usually sensible, so that's that." I attempted a bright smile. "I *am* glad you got home in time to say good-by."

"I wish I'd been in time to chauffeur you up here this morning."

I suddenly realized I wasn't sorry. Eighty miles with Uncle Frosty, who really knows me, and I'd have been all to pieces. It wasn't even quite safe to have him turn up now—the only thing gluing me together was the determination not to think, just to make it somehow onto that plane. The loudspeaker crackled out some announcement. I shouted over it, "How was San Francisco? Enjoy your trip?"

"Not much. It was just business."

"Oh? I didn't know you had clients in California."

"I don't, but an old law-school buddy has kindly saddled me with one of his. I did enjoy seeing old Newton again. He's completely bald," Uncle Frosty added with deplorable satisfaction.

I smiled and began to feel infinitesimally better—just because he was there, sounding sane and normal and as if the world were right side up instead of upside down. He went on, in the same even tone, "Shan, I called your Aunt Doris before I came out here. She seemed a mite upset."

"Yes—well, her usual farewell dither. She—"

"I got the impression it was a good deal more than that. She said *you* were upset."

"Oh, no. I mean, naturally I hated to leave her and Uncle Syd—"

"She told me, very forcefully, that she was sure you didn't want to leave at all."

"Uncle Frosty, she can't comprehend *anybody* wanting to leave Mary's Creek, once they've achieved a state of grace and got there. *You* know Aunt Doris." . . . Poor, dear, warmhearted, exasperating, indomitably provincial Aunt Doris, pattering about her comfortable old kitchen in a fragrance of cookies and fried chicken, trying desperately to understand what was the matter with me, arriving at all the wrong conclusions, doing all the wrong well-meant things.

"Then," Uncle Frosty persisted, "you are *not* harboring some secret longing to stay on in Mary's Creek?"

"My word, *no*."

"You are, in fact, overjoyed to be going back to Europe?"

I struggled to say "yes" so we could drop the subject, but it came out "no."

Uncle Frosty's left eyebrow, which is an individualist and slants upward, lifted a trifle higher. After a minute he said, "That seems a remarkably unsatisfactory situation."

I didn't contradict him. I didn't have to answer, because suddenly the one man between me and the counter departed, and there I was, scrabbling in my bag for ticket and passport.

"*Good* morning!" said the beaming young man behind the counter.

I pushed my documents across. I do find aggressively cheerful people hard going, especially when I'm in a totally uncheerful mood.

"Let's see . . . Lightley, Miss Shannon Kathleen. Off to London, are we?" he added, scribbling things on my ticket and flipping papers about. "How'd you like to slip me in your suitcase, hm?"

There was more of this fingernail-on-the-blackboard sort of badinage, mercifully cut off by another reverberating announcement over the loudspeaker. Then the young man got busy talking on his little phone to whoever it is they always talk to, and I turned back to Uncle Frosty, who was regarding me speculatively.

He said, "If you don't want to stay in Mary's Creek but don't want to go back to Europe either, what do you want to do?"

"I've no idea."

"Don't give me that. I've never seen you yet without an idea— usually half a dozen. You must have tried to break this deadlock."

Feeling unutterably tired all of a sudden, I said, "Oh, I had some notion of going to business school somewhere this summer. But Aunt Doris—and Dad—scotched that."

"Business school?" echoed Uncle Frosty, squinting at me.

"Well, you can't get a job just by knowing how to talk French and German and act in plays. So I thought a business course, maybe here in Portland . . . but you should have heard Aunt Doris."

"What did she say?"

I sighed, remembering all we'd both said, and enacted Aunt Doris for a minute. "'Shannon *Lightley!* A girl your age? Why, Sugah, *how* could I let you start off by yourself to live in a big place like Portland, with goodness knows *what* kind of . . .'—and so on. I keep forgetting how dangerous the world looks to Aunt Doris. But really, Uncle Frosty, considering that since I was eleven years old I've been 'starting off by myself' and frequently ending *up* by myself in Paris, Berlin, Belgrade, Rome . . ."

"She keeps forgetting *that*," Uncle Frosty said gently. "Didn't you write your dad?"

"Yes, three weeks ago. For permission, for tuition money—and explained everything *clearly*. I thought. He just sent a plane ticket to London and said quit being quixotic and come on home."

Uncle Frosty drew a deep breath. "Ever since our kindergarten days there've been times when I longed to punch Greg Lightley in the nose for a sheer, pigheaded fool. In our kindergarten days I used to do it."

I couldn't help smiling. "Did he punch you back?"

"No. He always sat down very earnestly and thought things over again. It's why I've never been able to stay mad at him."

"He won't think this over. He considered my whole idea of coming back here quixotic in the first place."

"And was it?" Uncle Frosty attempted to meet my eye.

"Yes," I said, avoiding his. "So I just—phoned and got my reservation."

"Not even a cable of protest?"

"Oh—cables from me scare Dad. He always thinks I'm dead or something. And being scared makes him angry. And . . ." I let it trail off, thinking bitterly, I should have cabled in the first place. Instead of writing. No explanations. *Neck broken, send hundred dollars.*

"Shan," Uncle Frosty said, in a voice that suddenly put me on my guard. "There's one thing you haven't even touched on. What happened to—"

"OK, all set I guess, Miss Lightley," cried the young man, tossing his phone on its hook and diving down to tag my luggage. "Departure 11:55, Gate 17, Concourse B . . . These three bags everything?"

"I'll carry the little one," I said, snatching the camel-bag just in time as he slid the others onto the conveyor belt. I stood frozen, watching my two cases toddle irrevocably away from me, as if on their own little legs, and vanish one after the other through a pair of leather curtains and beyond recall. I was as good as on the plane.

The young man banged his stapler and handed over my papers, asking cheerily, "Don't suppose you're any kin to that Gregory Lightley comes on the TV news sometimes at six o'clock?"

"I don't suppose so," I mumbled. I can do better when I have my wits about me, but at the moment I was witless. I turned away so hastily that I almost ran Uncle Frosty down. He sidestepped, took the camel-bag and my elbow, and propelled me around a passing wedge of people and luggage.

"I was about to ask," he said firmly, "what happened to your plans for college?"

I knew he'd been about to ask that. "Oh—they—sort of evaporated," I muttered.

He glanced at me, then stopped and faced me. "Shan, one of your primary reasons for coming back to the States was to have four years of American college. The University of Oregon, because it was typical, and you said—"

"I know what I said!" I could hear myself saying it, in eager, impassioned tones, to him, to Dad, to Aunt Doris, to anyone who would listen—ten months ago. "But I've changed my mind. You couldn't pay me to go to the University of Oregon. I don't want to go to any college. I'm sick and *tired* of school, I—"

"Not even a European university?"

"No! I am absolutely dead set against a European university. The very idea makes me simply—" I took a breath and shut up until I had my voice in hand. "That's not to say I won't end up in one, of course. Dad'll talk me into it. He can always sound more reasonable than I can." I shrugged. "It doesn't matter."

"Doesn't it?"

"Well, it won't in forty years. So I turn out mongrel expatriate after all. So what's the difference?" The loudspeaker drowned me out—fortunately, since I might have talked nonsense for quite a while—and I suddenly realized what it was saying. "That's my flight," I said in a strangled-sounding voice.

"Still fifteen minutes." Uncle Frosty studied me gravely. "Time for a cup of coffee."

"No thanks. I— Look here, Uncle Frosty," I said, making a desperate attempt to smile carelessly. "Why don't you just run on? I hate long-drawn-out farewells, don't you? And I'm all right now, I'm perfectly fine—"

"You're perfectly miserable. You're in a state."

"No, really. I've just been *telling* you—"

"Old dear, I know what you've been telling me. But the performance wasn't quite up to your usual standard." For a minute we stood looking at each other. He added, "Would it help if I wrote your dad?"

"No. Nothing would help." Abruptly, I felt large, revolting tears of self-pity welling into my eyes. In a panic I said, "Uncle Frosty, once I'm on that plane I'll be all right. But I'll never make it unless you go away. I mean it. Please. Just leave. Leave the *airport*. Get in your car and drive to town."

He drew a long breath. "All right, Shan. Good-by. Write." He jerked around, walked rapidly to the nearest doors, and went out.

Just in time, too. I snatched up the bag and headed blindly for the ladies' lounge, where I sat on a stiff leather sofa getting myself under decent control until he'd had ample time to get a mile or two away and the reiterated announcements for my flight were beginning to sound final and urgent. Then I fished my ticket out and hurried down the long vista of Concourse B.

In Gate 17's boarding area, my fellow passengers were already forming into an untidy queue beside the ramp; the plane was visible out the wide rear window. Two latecomers were still at the ticket barrier—a thin man and the inevitable fat one. There is always a fat man just ahead of me as I board a plane, I don't know why. I could remember standing behind one in Zurich, in Milan, in Athens, in Vienna—my future stretched out clearly before me, translated into a long line of fat men, all exactly alike except that one smelled of garlic, one of beer, one of schnapps, one of *eau de cologne* . . . Just three more minutes, I told myself. Hang on three more minutes and it'll all be over.

I closed my eyes, feeling very peculiar. The loudspeaker blared something—it sounded louder than usual. Then somebody said, "Your *ticket*, please." I blinked, saw the fat man struggling through the turnstile and the official extending a hand to me.

"I don't want to go," I heard myself saying in an odd, high voice. The official stared, said, "Miss, you'll have to hurry"—and all at once I felt quite normal, in fact, preternaturally composed, like a duchess at the vicar's tea. I stepped up to the desk and looked the official in the eye. "I'm not leaving," I informed him. "So sorry to be a nuisance, but I find I can't get away. Could you tell me about turning back my ticket and that sort of thing?"

I have no idea what he replied. He said something. Quite a number of somethings, I expect. I dimly remember assuring him that whatever he suggested would be quite all right. I then withdrew. My stately calm lasted about halfway back to the lobby, then changed to wild exhilaration. I ran like a hare up the stairs leading to the roof, burst out into the sunshine, and for the first time noticed that it was a glorious day. Still clutching the camel-bag, I stood on the parapet with the wind whipping my hair, watching a big Pan Am plane taxi slowly into the middle distance and glorying that I wasn't on it. It then occurred to me that my suitcases *were* on it. And that Dad and Jeanne were flying back from Stockholm especially to meet it. And that Uncle Frosty was now somewhere between this and downtown Portland, thinking me gone.

Everybody thought me gone. My wardrobe was on my back, except for whatever odd bits might turn up in the camel-bag. I had about $47 in cash, one probably unredeemable airline ticket, all the same unsolved problems, and no plans. I hadn't even an idea what to do next.

The impulsive type. Quixotic. And in top form today.

I threw a last dazed look at my erstwhile transportation, now poised for takeoff, and crept back downstairs. Consequences settled on my mind like ravens. I'd have to cable Dad. Face that awful, cheery young man again and do something about my ticket. Explain the inexplicable to everybody and sundry . . . Well, I couldn't do any of those ghastly things, not yet.

The loudspeaker broke into my near panic with the information that the limousine to downtown Portland was departing in five minutes. Before the echoes had died away, I was hurrying toward the nearest doors, terrified that I might miss it. What I would do in downtown Portland was immaterial—my only thought was to get away from the airport. Dodging people and baggage carts, with a guilty eye on the Pan Am desk, I made it to the doors, banged through them, and found myself face to face with Uncle Frosty.

I regarded him in silence. He smiled faintly, probably at my expression, and remarked, "My hunches seem to be in good working order today."

The scream of a jet engine cut through the last words; a large shape streaked past the terminal building, lifted, climbed steeply, and diminished into a silver flash.

"There goes my plane," I said, in somebody else's voice.

"Yes, we'll have to phone your dad." He glanced at his watch. "Within a couple of hours, or we'll get him out of bed. I'll do the talking."

"But what will you *tell* him? What is there to—"

"I'll tell him I've taken our favorite puzzle home with me until further notice, if it's all the same to him—and it's going to have to be." He reached for the camel-bag. "Come on, you can have your hysterics in the car."

3

One way Uncle Frosty differs from all my other parents is that I never have to cope with him. He copes with me. He's been at it since I was five, when Dad brought me to the States right after the divorce. He's the only thing I remember about my first day in America—a tall, tanned man, white-haired already at twenty-eight, standing in an echoey place full of people (Portland airport, I suppose), smiling down at me and saying, "Well, Greg, I'd know her anywhere." Then he offered me a large, firm, reassuring kind of hand and said, "Come on, I've found out where they keep the ice cream in this place. Let's go get some." Dad says I never even looked back.

Another thing about Uncle Frosty—he never tries to do me out of a good hard cry. He just minds his own business and lets me rip. About a mile from the airport I said, "Sorry. This is almost over."

He smiled, remarked that it sounded about six months overdue, and waited till we reached the freeway before he said, "Shan, I'm loaded with questions. I don't like to pry into your private life, but—"

"I don't have a private life. Too many parents."

"All right, then—I think you'd better tell me what's been going on this year. Why didn't you tell me long ago?"

"Oh—I suppose I kept thinking it might get better." Actually, I'd spent the first awful month refusing to face facts, the other nine grimly saving face. "It's just been a disaster, start to finish. But I'll tell you if you like." So I told him, for several miles, about the Siberia that was Mary-High, the strangers my old friends had turned into, the innumerable In groups who agreed on only one thing: I was Out. "If I could just have been anonymous—plain Shan Lightley. But no. I was Greg Lightley's daughter. My word, how I wish Dad had never begun that TV freelancing! When I was little, nobody knew or cared what he did for a living. Now every time you turn on a newscast there he is, standing beside the Elysée Palace or somewhere, being madly intelligent and interesting, and *impossible* to live up to . . . Or else I'm Mother's daughter! People hear about that, and then they *look* at me. With utter incredulity." An odd sound escaped Uncle Frosty, and I added, "Laugh if you like. It's a very mixed blessing to have a mother who looks like mine."

"Well, old dear, I know. So what did all those peerless beauties at Mary-High do about it? Make scathing remarks?"

"Oh, no. They talked only to each other. I could sit in a whole room full of girls I've known since grade school and never be directly spoken to once. I mean it. Uncle Frosty, it makes you feel *inanimate*, like a chair. Of course, I had nothing to say to them, either. I suppose I never acted natural." I stared out the car window, wondering what *was* natural. For years I'd simply acted as various people expected me to act. Mother wanted a naive schoolgirl, the younger the better. Madame Fourchet took for granted a gawky American with an A average and a personality like an ingrown toenail. Dad and Jeanne expected a congenial companion who could talk newspaperese, figure a tip in *dinars*, and get herself from Lausanne to Helsinki with a minimum of fuss. Aunt Doris only wanted back her happy little hoyden, but that was hardest . . . And I was tired of adapting, switching languages and attitudes, memorizing American slang—oh, I'd tried to adapt to Mary-High, too, early on when I was still trying anything. But it was like trying to adapt to a family party. I said, "No telling how I acted. I know I smiled until my jaw ached. All I could think of to do. Smiled and smiled and *smiled*."

"'The foolish face of praise,'" Uncle Frosty quoted. "'. . . the forced smile which we put on in company where we do not feel at ease, in answer to conversation which does not interest us.'"

"Who wrote that?" I asked in astonishment.

"Emerson."

"Well, it's a speaking likeness of me anytime this ten months."

"You did speak sometimes, then."

"Yes, and always regretted it." I turned to him in real bewilderment. "Uncle Frosty, *do* I have a British accent? Mother keeps complaining that it's American!"

Uncle Frosty cleared his throat. "Well—let's say it's not pure Mary's Creek. And you do tend to forget that lorries are trucks here, and lifts are elevators—"

"Oh, *that* lot. And nobody here says 'frock.'" I brooded a moment. "I hold my knife and fork wrong, too—did you know that? Wrong for America, right for everyplace else in the world. My word! Why do I have to learn to *eat* differently to get on with people? Why do I have to keep changing myself, wherever I am, whoever I'm with?"

"You don't," Uncle Frosty said patiently.

"I can't." I suddenly felt desperate. "Don't think I wouldn't. I'd trade lives with anybody, tomorrow morning. But you *can't* go back and not live places you've already lived, or unlearn things you know, or pick different parents—you can't get out, you're just trapped inside yourself!"

"Shan, old dear. There's no need to get out. Give yourself a little time—"

"I don't *have* any time. Uncle Frosty, I'm eighteen years old—
I've got to find someplace to live, something to do with myself! I
don't belong anywhere. Except airports. In Europe, I thought I was
American—I thought that was my *trouble*. But people *here* think
I'm European. I'm just nothing, nobody identifiable. *Basically.*"

"Oh, there's not a thing on earth wrong with you basically."

"Something must be, or people would like me better. Wouldn't
they? And I'd find people *I* liked. Aunt Doris says I'm too critical
of the Mary-High lot—maybe she's right. Or maybe Dad is—he
says I close my mind against Europe. And Mother says . . . Oh, I
don't know. Whichever parent I'm with, I decide that one's probably right. Until I get away from them. I've got to find my own
answer. Some kind of *new* one."

"The University of Oregon would be new, wouldn't it?"

"No! It'd be just a larger version of Mary-High, and I'd loathe
it. And everybody'd loathe me, as usual."

Uncle Frosty sighed rather lengthily. Presently, we swung off
the freeway and stopped at a traffic light. He said, "Let's back off
from this whole thing a little. What do you actually want out of
life, Shan, anyway? What sort of thing would you like to do, or be,
or have, before you die? Now don't just say something—think
about it before you answer."

I thought about it, but all I came up with was what other people wanted me to be or do. Aunt Doris hoped I'd marry some nice
steady boy and live forever in Mary's Creek. Mother thought I
should stay in London and try for the stage—when she found a
moment to think about it. Dad, of course, was bound I'd go to
college—somewhere, anywhere, though he failed to mention what
I was to do with all this education once I'd got it.

"I don't know," I told Uncle Frosty irritably.

"Oh, sure you do. Everybody does, at least vaguely. Just sort of
squint your eyes and see what shape your inner man—inner girl—has

been gradually assuming for eighteen years. For instance, you used to write stories—remember? You were going to win the Pulitzer Prize."

Oh, I remembered. At one time I was going to be a U.N. interpreter, too. And later a prima ballerina, and later a film star. I'd had dozens of fervent ambitions, and they'd all worn out faster than my shoes. "Uncle Frosty, my inner girl hasn't any shape at all; she's just a mass of protoplasm. If you want to know, I'm bored stiff with her. What I'd really like is to start fresh, be somebody else altogether, and never hear my name again."

He didn't answer—understandably enough. I sighed and stared at my hands. Long fingers, rectangular nails a bit paler than the tanned skin around them—I'm the odd redhead who gets a tan. Good hands for the stage, Nevin had told me once. Great. I wasn't going on the stage. My head was beginning to feel queerly detached—as if it were floating somewhere just above my shoulders. I reached up to sort of steady it, saying, "I do keep feeling so odd."

"You probably need some lunch." Uncle Frosty glanced at his watch. "Holy smoke. I should think so." He turned sharply, backtracked a block or two, and we came to rest in the parking lot behind a restaurant. "You know, Shan," he said as we left the car. "I may be having an idea about you. It's just a-borning. Give me a few minutes—I'll tell you as we eat."

4

It may have been that statement, or it may have been the aroma of charcoal-broiling—or maybe just the aftereffects of soul-baring and a good cry. But by the time we'd ordered, the world began to seem a slightly brighter place. I kept thinking, *at least I'm not on my way to London—and I'm not in Mary's Creek.* I was still in the States, though, and from my brief but wild exhilaration on that parapet, I knew I wanted to be. I had no idea what came next, but I hoped Uncle Frosty was about to tell me.

He thought it over until we'd got our hamburgers and begun on them. Then he said abruptly, "See here, Shan, would you be interested in a little bargaining?"

I felt a bit suspicious of that. "What kind of bargain? If it involves college in any form, I wouldn't."

"No, it specifically does not involve college—that's its point." Uncle Frosty gave me the mustard and a slightly exasperated glance. "You and your dad! You're exactly alike. Both want everything settled right this minute—and settled *your* way and no other. Neither one of you thinks he's human and might change his mind. Well, I think you both are. In my opinion no decision at all ought to be made just now. About college or anything else."

"But one's got to be! I can't just—"

"Wait. I'm about to take off on a flight of fancy." He ate a bite of hamburger, staring past me. "All right, now listen. Suppose you were to stay right here in Portland, for the summer. You don't go to business school, you get a job. You earn your own keep, mind your own business, run your own life. Everybody you know, especially parents, stays strictly away from you and out of your affairs. You needn't even give anybody your address—you're incommunicado. All this goes on for three full months." He waited while I absorbed that—felt trap jaws opening, bricks lifting off my head. "Well? What does that sound like?"

"Heaven," I quavered.

He smiled. "I thought it might. Well, Shan, I'll undertake to arrange those conditions—as my part of the bargain. Here's yours: in return for all this let-aloneness, you shelve the whole question of college for those three months. You refrain from making up your mind one way or the other—in fact, you try hard not to think about it at all. Then at—well, say at the end of August—we take another look. If you still say no, all right. It might be for better reasons."

We sat for a moment, not speaking. Then I said tremulously, "A breathing space. A sort of three-month Nirvana. Do you mean it?"

"I do. If you think you can do your part."

I could feel myself beginning to bubble internally like a bottle of champagne. "Well, you're on! I'll be so *glad* not to think about it. I'd even considered a job, you know. But Aunt Doris—"

"I'll handle your Aunt Doris. And your dad."

Dad. I swallowed, and the bubbles began to subside. "He's going to thunder and lightning. He'll say I'm not trained for any job. It's true." I gnawed my lip, then brightened. "D'you think anybody'd want translating done? Or—"

"I think somebody might easily want envelopes addressed or telephones answered."

"Oh." The brightness dimmed a bit. "Or dishes washed."

Uncle Frosty grinned and said it might not come to that, and to get on with my lunch. He went on with his own, adding, "The chief thing is to get busy enough with something else to quit thinking about yourself for a while. That's the crux of my idea. And while you're going through the want ads—well, you can do a job for me."

"For you? No. That won't wash, Uncle Frosty. I don't want made-up work."

"This is a bona fide job. With pay. The fact is, I badly need somebody to go rent a certain room and occupy it for about three weeks, at near-starvation wages. If you agree, you're hired."

I stared at him over my lifted fork. He seemed quite serious. "Well—jolly good, then. But what an odd thing to need. What happens after three weeks? The room turns back into a pumpkin?"

"No, my pet detective gets free from another job he's on and takes your place." Uncle Frosty pushed aside his plate and explained the problem. The boardinghouse this room was in was quite near Fremont College, and while the room was empty now, it might soon be snapped up by some student arriving for the summer session, which would begin shortly after the present term ended. "In three weeks, my sleuth can take over; then you can move to better quarters. Our guest room, if you like. Strictly under the terms of the bargain, naturally. Mona and I will behave as if we didn't know you."

"Yes, all right—but tell me why you're suddenly involved with what sounds like cloak-and-dagger fiction? I thought you only filed lawsuits and wrote wills and that sort of thing."

"This is that sort of thing. There's a will—one you'd never believe if you saw it in fiction—and there'll probably be a lawsuit. Depends on what my man finds out."

"Why wouldn't I believe in it? The will, I mean?"

"Because the thing is twenty-two carat oddball. Wouldn't your credulity be a little strained if you read about a bequest of $50,000 to be granted in scholarships solely to students who want to study subjects of no practical value to them?"

"*No* practical value?"

"That's right. And there's a bequest of $7,500 to a man named Kulka, specifically for the establishment and maintenance of a weed garden."

I put down my cup and stared at him. "Uncle Frosty, where did you *get* this will? You never drew it up, surely?"

"Heaven forbid. The whole thing was dumped on me just last week in San Francisco. By Newton, my now-bald buddy from law school." He explained: Newton had come around to his hotel, bringing a Mrs. Lorna D. Watson of Oakland, who wanted to contest her mother's will. Since her mother had moved to Portland four years before and died there the previous spring, probate and the suit—if any—would be in Portland, and Mrs. Watson needed an Oregon lawyer. Uncle Frosty had agreed to take the case. "For auld lang syne. *Before* I'd read Mrs. Elizabeth Dunningham's will. That'll teach me to be sentimental."

"But you're joking, aren't you? She didn't actually say *weed* garden? Right in the will?"

"She did. What's more, she left one fellow $10,000 to go fishing."

"Why, she was crazy as a bedbug, wasn't she?" I said in awe.

Uncle Frosty said he suspected it. "That's no help to me in trying to break the will, though. Being crazy as a bedbug isn't legal grounds for contesting."

"Not even if she was *obviously* dotty and you could prove—"

"Not even if she'd spent the last fifty years in a mental institution and left her entire estate to establish a home for indigent mice. She could still have a valid will." He reached for the check and dug in his pocket for a tip. "We'd better get home and start proceedings on that transatlantic phone call. Feeling better?"

I was feeling remarkably better. As we walked to the car, I took a deep breath of warm June air and marveled at how good I felt. He's right about me, I thought. I've been in an egocentric rut a mile deep. A job is what I need, a good hard one, something to get my *mind* on . . . Just now I couldn't get it off what he'd been saying. As we turned away from midtown traffic and started winding up into the west hills toward his house, I said, "Uncle Frosty, *is* her will valid?"

"Mrs. Dunningham's? I've no way of knowing yet." He glanced at me, smiling. "You seem very interested in that will."

"Well, my word! Who wouldn't be? Can you imagine anybody wanting a weed garden?"

"I can imagine somebody wanting $7,500 with no very binding strings attached."

"Oh!" I pondered that a moment. "You think it's all a plot of some kind? To get her money?"

"I don't know what I think yet; I've barely had time to read the will, so far."

"But that's what you suspect? That she sort of fell among thieves?"

"It's certainly one possibility. She'd never set eyes on any of these legatees until she moved up here four years ago. Her daughter—this Mrs. Watson—hasn't set eyes on them yet. Then there's another"—Uncle Frosty jammed on the brakes to let a bus thunder across our bows—"odd fact. All the legatees live within one square block of 1234 College Street—that's the boardinghouse where the old lady lived in Portland, and finally died."

"You mean the *neighbors* ganged up on her?"

He shrugged. "Could be. She already had a perfectly good will, dated a week after her husband's death—that was about five years ago. It left everything to her only child, Mrs. Watson. In the new will, Mrs. Watson isn't even mentioned. And the new will's dated just a couple of months before her death."

"My word!" I said with relish. It scarcely took a lawyer to catch a whiff of fish in that. We'd driven the last two blocks and were turning into the driveway before it occurred to me to ask where the detective came into this. "And what's that room I'm to rent got to do with it?"

"Everything. That's the room Mrs. Dunningham lived in for four years, and died in last March eleventh."

"It's *what?*"

He grinned as he cut the engine. "Well, I'm not sure it was her room, but it's the same boardinghouse. And presumably the same neighbors are still around. Do you begin to see my devious methods? Come on in the house. Mona's still at Symphony Committee meeting, but you know the way to your room."

We went in, and I took the camel-bag up to the guest room, wondering what I might have thrown in it when I packed yesterday. I didn't open it to find out, though. I stood a moment pondering Uncle Frosty's devious methods, then went back down to find him. He was in his study, just pushing the phone aside. I said, "Look. Let me see if I have this straight. You're planting a spy in the thieves' nest, is that it? To see if they'll give themselves away in an unguarded moment? And I'm to be substitute spider in the middle of this web until the real spider takes over?"

"You make it sound awfully sinister, but yes, that sums it up."

"And what if the web gives a promising jiggle or two while *I'm* crouching in it?"

Uncle Frosty laughed. "If you see or hear anything incriminating, by all means phone headquarters. Though not from the boardinghouse! I meant to warn you—you'll have to be careful not to mention any connection with me. The legatees have no idea yet that the will might be contested. It's my secret weapon."

"Oh, lovely!" I sank into his easy chair, enjoying this more and more. Then a thought struck me. "My word! I shouldn't even be seen with you, should I? And we might already have been seen—at lunch." Automatically, my hand went to my hair. "You know, that's a problem. People remember me; I've often noticed it." I broke off as my mind began to work at this.

"Now, Shan—" Uncle Frosty was watching me uneasily. "Don't take the bit in your teeth. There's no need whatever for any false moustache, or whatever you're cooking up. This isn't a spy movie. It's a perfectly prosaic—"

By then I had the answer. "How soon do you want me in that room, Uncle Frosty? Would tomorrow evening be soon enough?"

"Oh, any time in the next few days. Spring term doesn't end for a week or so; we're safe till then."

"Good, that gives me plenty of time. I'll get a dye job."

"You'll *what?*"

"Have my hair dyed. Black, maybe. That would—"

Uncle Frosty exploded—almost like Dad. I was surprised at him, and told him so. He informed me it was times like these he felt great sympathy for Dad, and if I dyed one hair of my head, I'd lost my job, and no, he would *not* listen to reason. So I had to give in on that. Of course, I knew I'd think of something else. I'd begun trying to when suddenly the whole thing collapsed on me—I couldn't believe in it at all. "Uncle Frosty, none of this is actually going to happen, is it?" I said dismally. "We're just making it up. A week from today I'll be on that plane to London."

"I don't see why you should be."

"Dad, that's why. He'll say I got my way last year, and look what happened; now he'll jolly well get *his*. The minute you get that call through—when is it going through?"

"Within an hour, they told me."

Within an hour. The day was no longer glorious, the job and the bargain were idle fancies, my trap was still tight around me, and my head ached again. I said, "I wish I hadn't asked that."

"Don't stew about it, Shan—it'll be all right." The front-door latch clicked, and his head turned toward the sound. "There's Mona. Go tell her she has a house guest."

This seemed only fair, and I gathered myself together again. I don't know Mona well—never will. Uncle Frosty was a bachelor until age forty, then surprised everybody by his choice. Mona is a handsome woman, cool, chic, imperturbable, and to me impenetrable. Uncle Frosty told me once that he was aware Mona was hard to know—and added that he had found the effort supremely worth his while. I must say she's always been perfectly gracious to me. I went into the hall to say hello to her, then on upstairs to dither in private about the phone call, to wonder what anybody could want with a *weed* garden, and to see what fate had allowed me in the way of a summer wardrobe.

Not much. I found the usual mad jumble of odds and ends that always winds up in the camel-bag—underwear, toiletries, my gray seersucker frock but not the jacket, my blue cotton but not its belt, a paperweight, a couple of wash-and-wear shirts, my *winter* dressing gown, an elderly cardigan lacking two buttons, an old journal I hadn't written in for years, a skirt or two, a frightful raincoat I got once in Petticoat Lane for ten-and-six, a bottle of ink, a shoehorn but no shoes. I was wearing my sleeveless yellow linen and my white pumps, and to keep down air weight, I'd carried my winter coat, an Irish tweed about right for Poland in December. Oh, well. I'd probably be going straight to London anyway.

I abandoned all that and went back downstairs to pace the floor. This I did for the next half hour, making nervous conversation with Mona, who returned tranquil replies, and looking at my watch and the phone so many times that Uncle Frosty finally escaped into his study with a book. I even got on my own nerves. But underneath all, my mind was still playing with that improbable will, like a cat with a catnip mouse, and five minutes before the scheduled hour was up, I suddenly had a quite brilliant explanation for that weed garden. Dazzled, I rushed into the study and announced it to Uncle Frosty, who emerged from Marcus Aurelius and frowned at me uncomprehendingly.

"What do you mean, it's a euphemism?"

"Pure double-talk. *Marijuana* is a weed!"

He looked startled, then amused. "So it is. You're postulating a College Street crime ring? I suppose it's possible. Have you figured out how the scholarships fit in?"

"Well, no, I've only just this minute—"

"Or the doctor's time-machine visit to ancient Greece?"

"The *what?*"

"Didn't I mention that? I guess there are several bequests you don't know about. Why not read the will? Open that briefcase and ferret around in the right-hand side. You'll find a carbon in there somewhere."

I'd just located it when the phone went. It was the overseas operator. I dropped the carbon, forgot the weed garden, and fled. An unconscionably long ten minutes later, Uncle Frosty peered into the sunroom, where I was staring through the big window at Portland spread out below, and came over to me, saying calmly, "It's all right."

I let out my breath and turned. "Really all right? The whole plan?"

"Yes. He saw my point about the necessity of a time-out for both sides in the tug-of-war. Reluctantly, but he saw it. And he agreed."

I could scarcely believe it. "Was he very angry?"

"Just badly worried, under the surface fireworks. He loves you, Shan, and hates to see you follow a course he thinks a mistake.

That's all. Now start forgetting the whole thing—that's your end of the bargain." I nodded shakily, smiled even more shakily, and he added, "You look bone-tired. It's been quite a day—in fact, quite a ten months, hasn't it? Go up and stretch out a while—I'll call you for dinner."

It struck me as the best idea anybody'd ever had. I was suddenly so done in that I wondered if I could even make it upstairs. "I don't want any dinner," I told him as I started the long trek. "All I want in the world right now is to sleep a week."

2

Shannon

1

I awoke, for the first time in ten months, to a perfectly silent house. In Mary's Creek there were always the turtledoves in the eaves outside my dormer window—then Uncle Syd's shaver whirring from the bathroom, then the percolator thumping in the kitchen below me, and Aunt Doris pattering about. I used to long for those sounds in Europe when I woke to taxi horns or chattering foreign voices instead. But then, in Europe I started off every morning homesick.

I started this one off puzzled—couldn't think where I was. Then I remembered, and it brought me bolting out of bed. I'd slept eighteen hours instead of a week, but I felt wonderful anyhow, hungry as a navvy and eager to start planning my day. I nipped downstairs in my dressing gown and found the house empty—Uncle Frosty gone to his office, and Mona probably at the Crippled Children's Hospital or out raising funds for something. It's not a house I feel much at home in—all polished and smooth, like Mona, with pale carpeting and professional draperies—so I went straight through, devoured some buns and milk in a glacially tidy kitchen, and afterward stopped by Uncle Frosty's study to get the carbon of that entrancing will. Reading it would have to wait; I took it back upstairs with me and tucked it into my handbag. Then I faced the looking glass and considered. Regardless of Uncle Frosty's staid remarks about false moustaches, I'd no intention of going to College Street as I was. Too prosaic by half. Besides, the ideal spy, as I understand it, is either so well disguised that he could fool his own wife, or a creature so colorlessly just like everybody else that nobody remembers him ten seconds. I had handicaps on either count.

Clothes were not one of them; I put on my gray seersucker, which was completely forgettable without the missing jacket. At the moment I couldn't think what to do about my alleged accent— except fake a different one or try to hold my tongue. There remained my hair. For years I'd worn it very plain, just brushed off my forehead and caught with a silver sidecomb Dad found once in an Istanbul bazaar. But it was half a yard long and, from the back, about as inconspicuous as a red flag. Something had to be done about that.

I caught a bus to town, the will in my handbag, and got off down among the big shops. After a bit of searching, I discovered a doorway on a side street labeled The Poudre Puff Salon of Beaute, went in, and asked the woman at the desk what could be done right away about transforming me. "I don't care how. I just want something to make me look like somebody else, as nearly as possible."

"You mean something like a bleach job?"

I had an exhilarating vision of golden tresses, then a dampening one of Uncle Frosty's face when he next saw me. "No," I said reluctantly. "More like cutting a lot of it off. But I want to look quite different."

"Well—I couldn't arrange a *cut* until tomorrow." The woman, whose own hair was a rich ash-lavender, thumbed dubiously through her appointment book, then studied me. "I tell you, honey—whyn't you let us just restyle it for you? You'd be surprised how different that'd make you look. Opal's free now; she's a nawfully good stylist. Let her create something real unusual, why not?"

"Yes, all right, why not? If you think it'll work."

The woman assured me it would and touched a bell.

Opal was a tiny, brisk blonde with a towering coiffure and white-gold bangs that nearly hid her bright-blue eyelids. She was remarkably pretty under the overemphasized makeup, expressionless as a kitten, and completely self-assured—just the type that makes me feel all legs and misgivings. I trailed her across the busy workroom like a daddy longlegs towed by an ant, and feeling homelier than usual, subsided before the looking glass in her cubicle. She picked up a strand of my hair and let it drop, then studied my reflection dispassionately, chewing her gum.

"How d'you want it?" she said.

"I don't really care, just so it's as different as possible from this. The lady at the desk said—"

"You like mine?" Opal asked, switching her gaze to herself and giving a disciplinary yank to a cheek curl.

Surprised into automatic hypocrisy, I assured her it was very smart.

Without comment and before I'd comprehended that we'd reached an agreement, she enveloped me in pink plastic and went to work. After a steel-fingered shampoo that left me wondering if I'd ever really been clean before, she reinstated me in the cubicle and announced that she'd have to cut some bangs. I said, "Yes, all right," but it would have made no difference what I said. Opal's hand was firmly on the controls. She combed a wet veil over my face and cut a window in it, then began winding my head full of rollers, jabbing clips home with machine-like precision and occasionally snapping her gum. By this time I was far too fascinated by her to care what she was creating.

"Quite a decent day out, isn't it?" I remarked, hoping to get her talking so I could find out what she'd say.

She glanced up in mild surprise, as if the wig form on her shelf had spoken, then murmured "Mm-hm," and went on chewing gum. I tried again. "My hair's frightfully heavy. I expect you find it rather a nuisance to handle?"

She didn't look up this time, just said, "Hmp'mm," and stabbed in another clip. After a silence I couldn't think how to break and she wasn't trying to, she added suddenly, "George's is lots worse'n this, and longer besides."

"Oh, is it?" I faltered, my imagination boggling. "Did you say 'George'?"

"Mm-hm. My sister, Georgetta. That one." She bobbed her head toward the shelf in front of me. On it, flanked by the wooden wig form and a bouquet of combs, were two diplomas from the State Board of Cosmetic Therapy Examiners. One was made out to Shyrle Opyl Dagweiler, the other to Jorjetta Dagweiler Jones.

"Oh," I said, trying over possible pronunciations of "Shyrle" in my mind. "Your sister works here too?"

"Only on my day off. She can't spare the time to it any more— she's married and got three kids. Tip your head, honey."

"Three children? She must be a lot older than you."

"Hmp'mm. Just easier to please," said Opal—Opyl—without the slightest change of expression. "Why, gee, she took the very first fella that came along. But you can't tell *her* anything. Only time she ever listened to me was about her name."

"About her name?"

"Mm-hm, Georgetta. She never could stand it, always said it sounded like dress goods. Of course, what's it matter—everybody calls her George anyhow. But I says, if you feel that strong about it, whyn't you spell it a little different? Like with j's? And sure enough she took the hint. Was I surprised."

"Well. I think it's quite distinctive," I said truthfully.

"Mm-hm. Gives it a little more zing." She dabbed a bit of glue or something on a side curl and stuck it to my cheek, then began coiling up stray locks at my nape and skewering them.

"Have you just the one sister?" I asked, wishing she wouldn't work so fast.

"Hmp'mm, I've got four. One brother. Say, is *he* spoiled. You don't come from around here, do you? You talk kinda different."

I murmured something about the East.

"I thought there was something. I'm from Kansas, myself." She plastered my bangs to my forehead with a strip of scotch tape. "What's your name, honey? If you don't mind me asking?"

"Oh—it's Shannon."

"Hm." Opyl snapped her gum thoughtfully as she crowned her labors with a pink ruffled hairnet. "Can't do much with that." Then, to my deep disappointment, she led me off to the dryers.

My forty-five minutes' imprisonment passed almost without my noticing. For a while I was busy inventing names for Opyl's other three sisters and watching her flying fingers and pretty poker-player's face as she worked on other customers. But finally I got the carbon of the will out of my handbag and plunged into the trackless jungles of legalese.

Pruned of whereases and a rich undergrowth of relative clauses, Elizabeth Dunningham's will was better entertainment than a lot of novels. It began by naming one Henry Bruce executor, and granting him a fee of $2,000 for his services. Then came seven bequests: (1) $3,000 to Wynola Jackson for lessons in sky diving. (2) $5,000 to Dr. William Edmonds for a journey to ancient Greece. (3) $7,500 to David Kulka for the establishment and maintenance of a weed garden. (4) "Enough money" (no special amount named) to buy Mrs. Sarah Hockins a plastic canopy that would cover one-quarter of an acre. (5) $4,000 to Emma Heater, in payment of a debt. (This sounded quite ordinary at first. Then I began wondering why Mrs. Dunningham would have run up a debt if she had all that money? And why make the repayment posthumous?) (6) $50,000 to be wisely invested and the yearly income granted to a student who wished to study subjects of no practical value to him. The first scholarship was already earmarked for one George Maynard Sherrill. Thereafter, grants would be made by the Scholarship Committee, who would also make and manage those wise investments. And guess who formed the Scholarship Committee. None other than Henry Bruce (already the generously rewarded executor) and Dr. William Edmonds (already a major legatee).

Then the grand finale: the "rest" of the estate was for Brick Mulvaney—to go fishing.

It was certainly a refreshingly original will and testament, and I could see why the daughter wasn't holding still for it. Also I had a strong notion that Dr. William Edmonds, Mr. Brick Mulvaney, and Mr. Henry Bruce, who looked suspiciously like the masterminds behind the scheme, were going to wish they had never met Uncle Frosty.

I put the will away and sat blinking in the arid gale of the dryer, speculating about what Mrs. Dunningham *could* have been like, how she'd reasoned, even in her craziness, to hit on such very odd things to bestow on people. Or why the legatees had hit on them, if it were all a plot. People really are so queer and fascinating. Never what you expect.

I forgot all about what real unusual creation my hair might be drying into. It therefore came as a shock, when I was back in the cubicle and freed from my trappings, not to see my forehead looking its accustomed size and shape. When a few flicks of Opyl's comb had loosed the full glory of my bangs, my eyebrows vanished, and as she teased and piled and built the rest of my mane into a sort of Albert Memorial tower, all semblance of my normal appearance and expression vanished, too. My face shortened, my neck lengthened, my cheekbones widened. I watched, electrified, while she chewed her gum and put the finishing touches on a stranger I scarcely recognized as myself.

"Ooo, *nice!*" the woman at the desk said when I walked out, dazed with my success, to pay my bill. "Opyl's so clever, isn't she? And you certainly look different."

I certainly did. Moreover, I *felt* different, with the full weight of my hair on top instead of hanging. As I moved toward the door with my head poised on my new bare neck like a heavy tulip on its stem, I could even feel my walk adapt to the altered balance.

There was a brisk breeze blowing when I stepped outside. It didn't ruffle a hair of my coiffure, which had been petrified into its baroque architecture by Opyl's lavish use of hair spray. I stopped to study my reflection in a shop window. Well, I thought, that's what you wanted, wasn't it? To look like somebody else? All right; you're a reasonable facsimile of Shyrle Opyl Dagweiler—maybe of Jorjetta Dagweiler Jones, too. Only thing missing is the gum.

I went in and bought some at a quick-lunch place, peeled a stick, and examined myself in a weighing-machine mirror, chewing. Something lacking still. Blue eyelids, that was it. I headed for one of the big shops.

I was beginning to wish mightily for Franz Bach, who is the only person I've ever known who's as ready as I am to follow impulses just to see what happens. I suppose it was all those hours and hours we spent together prowling aimlessly about foreign cities waiting for Dad and Herr Bach and Jeanne. Just putting in time like that, in big cities where you know nobody, you think up quite mad things to do. Once, in Lisbon, Franz and I bought his whole new summer outfit while pretending we were both deaf and dumb.

I think it was missing Franz that suddenly gave me the notion of extending my reasonable facsimile of Opyl to include more than

looks. Imitating her flat Midwestern vowels and voice would be no
harder than adopting some thick European accent and improvising
whole nonexistent families and life stories, which Franz and I did
often to enliven a long tram ride.

I found a big shop and bought my blue eye shadow, using the
glass at the cosmetic counter to put it on, meanwhile trying out my
performance a bit on the clerk. She apparently noticed nothing
wrong. I bought some largish pearl earrings, too—the hairdo
seemed to need ballast—then remembered that I needed shoes anyway, and after some window-shopping found near duplicates of the
ones Opyl had been wearing: white flats with gold leather bows.
There were alternate buckles and ornaments available, which you
could substitute for the bows as the spirit moved you. I thought,
Why not?—and bought several, still practicing my gum-chewing
and expressionless expression. Then some remnant of common sense
told me I'd better quit buying things. It was now past one o'clock. I
waited at the nearest bus stop till a behemoth labeled COLLEGE
STREET—FREMONT PARK came rumbling up to me. Then, feeling
perfectly secure behind my bangs and gum, I climbed aboard.

2

As soon as I got off the bus, I spotted the boardinghouse, across the street and half a block down. The "Room for Rent" sign was still tacked on one of the white wooden pillars of the porch, right under the big numerals, "1234." The house itself was big and old, painted a fading but decent gray. It was one of a row of similar houses, all old and decent and fading, like retired governesses living in reduced circumstances. They stood well back from the street and high above it, had a near-vertical scrap of lawn apiece, and lots of concrete corseting—retaining walls to hold up the lawns—and sloping front walks that turned into long flights of steps descending to the sidewalk. Behind the roofs you could see the tops of trees, but the concrete and the street had won out—they, and the buses wheezing by, and the traffic lights, and the tired-looking little grocery on the corner, with a sign like a big milk bottle revolving lethargically on its roof. There was a chiropractor's sign in the window of a house on my side of the street; the ground floor of another was a photographer's studio. Directly across from me, a shiny little café with neon scrawled across its windows had been built at sidewalk level, jammed up against the knees of the dim old granny of a house behind it. The neighborhood had lost its battle with commerce. Very likely Fremont College, which was only two blocks away, would eventually buy the whole row of houses and build a dormitory.

Meanwhile, here they still were, rather less interesting than most houses—in fact, unrelievedly ordinary—and there was no point in standing on the sidewalk gaping at them any longer. I wondered what I'd expected, anyway. Suddenly, I was convinced none of this was going to be the least bit of fun. If there's anything I loathe, it's an anticlimax.

However, I could scarcely climb on the next bus and head tamely back to town—incidentally leaving Uncle Frosty in the lurch. Reluctantly, I started across the street. At once my life was brightened by the sight of an ancient parked car with a rain-washed message straggling across its side: "Butch is a goo"—the rest was illegible. It reminded me of a very different announcement I'd once seen chalked in schoolboy capitals on a London wall: "Colin is a lackey's lackey." London was a long, long way from College Street. At least, I thought, I'm here, not there. And I'm not going to leave this place until I've seen *something* interesting.

I saw it as I was passing the little café—the Rainbow Café, according to the pink neon on one of the big front windows. Under the improbably vivid rainbow painted on the glass, there was neat gold lettering. It read: "Owner and Proprietor, H. G. Bruce."

Henry G. Bruce? Executor of the will, chairman of the Neighborhood Masterminds? It could be nobody else. I'd scarcely finished the thought before I was opening the door to go in.

The place was a bit larger than I expected, but it was all visible at a glance, and I failed to spot anybody who looked as if he might be Henry G. Bruce—unless it was a habit of his to sit at his own counter wearing his hat and eating a hamburger. Behind the counter was a gloomy-looking blonde of the Brünnhilde type, resentfully excavating for ice cream. Two women who should have been sternly slimming were eating banana splits at the table by the farther front window, and college boys filled the back corner booth. Otherwise, the room was empty, except for the disembodied spirit of a singer moaning from a juke box as elaborately lighted as Trafalgar Square at Christmas.

I walked over to the counter, chewing my gum, and asked Brünnhilde if Mr. Bruce happened to be around.

"Just left," she said.

In a way, this was a relief, since I had no idea what to do with Mr. Bruce if she produced him, but it was a disappointment, too.

"He'll be right back," she added. She turned away to hook a milk shake into the mixing gadget, which immediately began to compete with the moaning singer. "He's just gone home to change his shoes. His feet give 'im trouble." She snatched two slices of toast from a toaster, slathered on mayonnaise, clapped cheese and lettuce between, cut the sandwich in two, and had it on a plate with a pickle and an olive with the speed of prestidigitation. "Mine give *me* trouble, too," she added. "But changing shoes wouldn't help, unless I could sit down an hour after I'd done it. Say—you wouldn't be after the job?"

For an unreasoning instant I thought she must know exactly who I was and all about me—then my panic vanished as I noticed the sign taped onto the long mirror behind the counter. It said, "Waitress Wanted," and inspired me with another impulse. I could be interviewed—that's what I could do with Mr. Bruce.

I murmured, "Mm-hm," and casually adjusted my bangs in the glass.

"Boy, I hope you get it. I can sure use you." She was making a chocolate soda by this time. "Sit down and wait, why don't you? Had your lunch?"

I certainly hadn't, and the mélange of food smells was making me forcibly aware of it. Sliding onto one of the stools, I said, "I'll have a sandwich, I guess, if you've got time to make one."

She remarked that I'd never get one if I waited till she had time, and approximately thirty seconds later slid a grilled cheese and a Coke across the counter. "Fall to. He won't be ten minutes."

Ten minutes. I reached for the Coke, suddenly feeling a bit dry-mouthed under my air of Opylescent calm. Even five minutes was a long time for an impulse to hold up, not to mention my nerve. Besides, it had belatedly occurred to me that a spurious job application might not be the best beginning for my three weeks' stay in the neighborhood. Think of it from Mr. Bruce's point of view. He interviews a girl, he turns her down, and she immediately moves in next door. Not the most logical behavior. Or would he merely assume that I needed a room as well as a job? Maybe he wouldn't think about it at all. On the other hand, maybe I'd better bolt my sandwich and get out of here.

All this jumpy conjecturing took no more time than to chew a bite or two. "He must not live very far away," I said to Brünnhilde, who was scooping ice cream into another milkshake container.

"No. Right behind here, in the old house. It's practically the same building. The restrunt kitchen used to be the garage or something . . . OK, I'm *com*ing!"

This last was aimed at the college boys in the corner booth, who were shouting for her to hurry. She unhooked the milk shake, hooked the second one in, and made another soda, grumbling under her breath. Just as she assembled the order on a tray and started for the booth, the hamburger customer got up to pay, the banana-split ladies waved for her attention, and two more people came in. It was clear she needed help.

About all there was to the café was the long soda-fountain counter, some booths and tables, and lots of color. The "rainbow" idea came through loud and clear; it only missed being garish because the walls of the room were natural maple. Everything else was either lavender, pink, green, or yellow, even the wide mats around a row of big flower prints on the side wall, and the seats of the counter stools. Brünnhilde's uniform-frock, of which I could see little under her starched white pinafore except the voluminous gathered sleeves, matched the yellow of every fourth stool. The swinging doors to the kitchen were upholstered in plastic—one pink, one lavender—and the upholstery tacks were green.

I was just blinking at them, reflecting that Brünnhilde was now going to think it rather eccentric behavior if I *didn't* apply for the job, when the lavender door opened and a tall, somehow odd-looking man in a shirt striped to match the decor came in from the kitchen.

"There he is," said Brünnhilde, striding back with her empty tray. "Good luck. Oh, Mr. Bruce, here's somebody about the job."

She snatched the hamburger customer's check and started stabbing at the cash register, and I slid off my stool to go meet Mr. Henry Bruce.

He gave me a grave, courteous little bow and led me back through the lavender door to a little office off the kitchen, where he waved me to a seat on one side of a desk, sank into the swivel chair on the other, and unhurriedly looked me over. I looked him over, too, chewing my gum and reminding myself reassuringly that my eyelids were bright blue. He was a quiet, impassive sort of man—tall and neat, with a round bald head and a round face that looked as if it ought to belong to a fat man, which he wasn't. It gave him the odd appearance of having swapped heads with a friend. He didn't fit my idea of a crook, though, except perhaps for his eyes, which were fog-gray and unsurprised, and looked older than the rest of him. I hoped uneasily that they couldn't see right through my collar, which he was studying, and decipher the London label underneath.

"You're interested in becoming a waitress?" he asked finally.

I murmured, "Mm-hm," but it came out so nearly inaudible that I added in a rather shaky voice, "Well, I'm interested in a job."

"Have you done this sort of work before?"

Now, steady on, I warned myself, and said "Hmp'mm" in a nearer approximation of Opyl's tone.

He moved a paper on his desk. "Of course, the work isn't very difficult to catch onto. It isn't very highly paid, either. The salary is fifty-two eighty a week. Plus tips, of course. The girls say they amount to another twenty or so usually."

"Mm-hm, that'd be OK," I said. I was fatalistically beginning to enjoy this.

"Have you any references?" Mr. Bruce said, picking up a pencil.

"Hmp'mm. I mean, I would have, but my last boss went bankrupt. In fact, he died."

"I see." Mr. Bruce put the pencil down. "Where was the job?"

"Idaho," I improvised. "A five-and-dime, in Idaho. I clerked in the ribbons." I held my breath, realizing I'd said "clarked," the British way.

Apparently he hadn't noticed. "You've just recently come to Portland, then?" he asked, leaning back in a relaxed way.

"Mm-hm."

"Well. I hope you'll like it. A pleasant city. Where did you live in Idaho?"

I gave him a small smile while I tried in vain to remember the name of even one town in Idaho—even the capital. "It was just a little bitty place. You wouldn't have heard of it." That sounded so unconvincing that I added, "Morton Center."

Morton Center, I thought in disgust. Surely I could have done better than that. It ought to have been something vaguely Indian. Skallamaloosa. Wawkanap.

Mr. Bruce suddenly leaned forward again and reached for the pencil. "Well, suppose we say your hours will be eleven to seven. That's the lunch-and-dinner shift. You'll eat in the kitchen, whenever there's a lull. There'll always be somebody else on duty with you—I employ three waitresses and try to stagger the shifts so you're all there during rush hours but only two of you between. There'll be a lot to learn at first, but Rose will teach you." He opened a drawer and took out a form sheet of some kind, while I stared at him in utter disbelief.

"You mean—you're hiring me?"

Mr. Bruce gave me a mildly interrogative glance and said, "Oh, yes, I think we'll try you." He pulled the paper toward him, glancing up at me again. "Unless you find the terms unsatisfactory?"

"Oh . . . no . . . they're fine." This was pure surrealism. I located my gum and began to chew.

"Good. Your name, then, Miss—"

"Georgetta Einszweiler Smith," I heard myself, as in a dream sequence, saying.

It seemed not to surprise him. I wondered if anything had ever surprised him.

"Address?" That stumped me long enough for him to glance up. "Where do you live, Miss Smith?"

"Nowhere. I mean, I don't actually—"

"Haven't found a room yet? There's one for rent a few doors down the street, if you're interested. We can fill that in later. Last position—salesgirl." I watched his pen wiggle across the sheet, realizing I should have said that, instead of "clerk." "Former residence— Morton Center, Idaho. References—unobtainable. Social security number?" He glanced up, then back to his paper. "We can fill that in later if you don't remember. Let's see—I expect your age is around eighteen . . ."

He went right on calmly filling out that unbelievable paper with all those unsatisfactory answers. How *could* he want to hire me—no references, no experience, less than no personality? Maybe he was thinking I'd do for the scullery work, anyway, or until he could get somebody better. Actually, I couldn't tell what he was thinking. First Opyl, then him; it seemed to be my day for meeting inscrutable people. When I left a few minutes later, I'd learned less about Mr. Henry Bruce than he'd learned about Georgetta Einszweiler Smith. In fact, I did not know one thing about the man except that his feet hurt—and that I was supposed to start working for him the next morning.

Out on the sidewalk again, in the sane, ordinary light of day, I could scarcely believe I'd let things get so out of hand. But there it was, and I began to feel remarkably silly and guilty about it. To let myself be hired for a job I had no intention of working at— what could I have been thinking? Answer—I hadn't *been* thinking, I had just idiotically been saying "Why not?" to everything that came up. Now I'd have to slog through the embarrassing aftermath—either ring up Mr. Bruce and tell him some plausible lie (I hate lying when it's not for entertainment) or go back and confess flat out that I hadn't meant a word of it. And wouldn't *that* be fine inconspicuous behavior!

It was the first time all day that I'd felt trapped. But the only alternative I could see was simply to take the job.

Simply take the job.

Why not? said a little voice inside me.

Now, stop that, I told it. There'll be a phone in the grocer's shop—go use it to get yourself out of this.

But why? That's what I want, a job. Why not take this one? And then very logically go rent the room in the boardinghouse? And just carry right on all summer in this common, ordinary, lovely

College Street, where nobody knows me from Adam, and learn to make milk shakes?

And also carry right on being Georgetta Einszweiler Smith?

I was in front of the grocer's by now, staring feverishly at a pile of oranges in the window. Not *Georgetta*, my word! I thought. It does sound like dress goods or something. Mary E. Smith maybe— oh, never mind that now. I've got to *examine* this . . . I'd better walk around the block.

I walked around the block, examining, and I couldn't find anything wrong with it. All I asked was to be kept occupied and solvent. What did it matter what my name was, so long as it wasn't my own? When the detective showed up, I could find some other room to live in. Or . . . the little voice piped up again, but so out-landishly that I shushed it on the first try, or thought I did.

After a short deliberation on ways and means, I ended up after all in the grocer's phone booth, where I rang up Uncle Frosty at his office and told him where I was and that I'd found myself a job and was just about to go rent his room, so he needn't give me another thought until late August.

I guess he was still picturing me at home in bed. "You're *where?*" he said in a confused voice.

"Half a block from 1234 College Street, at a grocer's with a milk bottle on it. Listen, if you won't interrupt for five minutes, I'll explain all about today."

It took me ten. He didn't interrupt. When I finished, there was a long but busy silence.

"Georgetta Einszweiler Smith?" he repeated, as if he were try-ing hard to believe it.

"Well, I didn't plan the name—it just came out, like a hiccup. I mean to change it to something more—wearable."

"But you mean to stay incognito? All summer long?"

"Why not? I was going to be incommunicado anyhow. And I'll be earning my own money and working hard and keeping my mind off college, and our bargain still goes, so why not?"

"Why not, indeed?" Uncle Frosty said, after another pause. "There must be some reason why not, but I seem too rattled just now to find it. Have you got any money?"

"Well—I will have, after I've worked a week. I've enough to rent the room—I think."

"You'd better catch a cab and come on down here for a short conference."

"First I'm going to get that room, before somebody else does. Then I'll have to go out to your house to fetch the camel-bag. After that I'll stop by."

"I'll be using the time to adjust," said Uncle Frosty, sighing.

3

The door at 1234 College Street had one of those bells that grind
out a quavering ring when you twist a knob. The woman who
answered it was stooped and iron-gray, with a frame too big for her
sagging flesh. Her eyes and eyebrows were still dark, and she looked
up at me sideways from under them and just waited, without a word.

At first I was wordless, too, but as I was starting a nervous
swallow, I discovered my gum and chewed instead. "I saw the sign.
About the room for rent," I said.

"Thirty-two fifty. Forty with board."

Another inscrutable type. I said, "Think I could see it?"

The woman opened the door just enough for me to get in, then
started along the dim, long hall. There were closed doors to right
and left; the only light came from thick beveled-glass panels at
either side of the front door, and from one yellowish wall bracket
with a fluted-glass shade that may once have been a gaslight. The
whole place was haunted by the frail but persistent ghosts of
Cabbage Past, Cabbage Present, and Cabbage Yet to Come.

There were stairs at the back of the hall, facing the front door,
but the woman went past them and along an even darker passage

to a door near the back of the house. She fished a bunch of keys out of her sweater pocket and presently threw the door open.

For a minute I just stared. Then I walked into the middle of the room, still staring, and said—remembering just in time to remain expressionless—"Seems nice enough."

"It's got a private bath," the woman remarked.

She needn't have bothered with all the salesmanship. I nodded and said I'd take it.

"Full board or just the room?"

"Well, I'll be working at the café down the street, and I'm supposed to eat lunch and dinner there, so I guess—"

The woman gave a resigned nod, then added grudgingly, "You can make your breakfast on the plate there. Last tenant did."

She jerked her head toward a little electric hot plate just visible behind a cretonne-covered folding screen near the bathroom door. I wondered if the last tenant really had been Mrs. Dunningham. There was no way to know.

"That'll be a week in advance," said the woman.

Nothing of the little old chatty, impractical widow-woman type about *this* landlady. I'd probably heard my last word out of her, except a bulletin about when next week's rent would be due. I counted out money with a silent prayer that I had enough, found I could keep one dollar and two cents for my very own, and handed the rest to her.

As she took it, she said, "Your regular rent day'll be Mondays." Then she put the money in her pocket and surprised me. "Towels and bedding are furnished. There's a mailbox on the corner. Grocery store up the street. Laundromat around the block. Pay phone's in the hall. My room's t'other side of the kitchen and up the back stair, if you want anything. Here's your key. I'm Mrs. Jackson."

Dazzled by this spate of words, I answered automatically, "How do you do. I'm—" I stopped, then hurried on. "My name's Smith."

"Will you be moving in today?"

"Mm-hm. I'll have to fetch my bag. It's at"—where was it, where was it?— "the bus station."

She was starting to leave, but she hesitated, turning to look at me with her dark eyes peering up sideways under her dark eyebrows, and there was actually a kind of little smile on her face—though it looked a bit creaky from disuse. "From out of town?" she asked.

I told her Morton Center, Idaho, which I seemed to be stuck with, adding that I felt real lucky to get a job my first day in the city.

"I used to live in a small town myself," Mrs. Jackson said. "Blue Falls, Wyoming."

"Well," I said, somewhat inadequately, but I couldn't think just how I was supposed to react to this news. Mrs. Jackson was already heading toward the hall again, apparently not caring whether I reacted or not.

I closed the door behind her, hoping I could remember all these bits of information I kept having to improvise. And I had to settle on a first name. But what? I'd already told Mr. Bruce Georgetta. Deciding I'd think about that little problem later, I turned to explore my room—which might have been Mrs. Elizabeth Dunningham's.

Clearly, it was somebody's besides Mrs. Jackson's, whose personality struck me as more akin to the decor of the front hall. However, this room had the natural advantage of three big windows, two at the back and one at the side. They let the light in, and the old-fashioned white ruffled curtains and buttery yellow wallpaper reflected it; the whole room looked full of sunshine even on a gray day, like today. Most of the furniture was the sort secondhand shops are full of, but painted white like the woodwork, it was unobtrusive. The things one noticed were a wonderful old carved highboy, rich and dark against the yellow walls, and a fourposter walnut bed, and the bands of color formed by books under the side window, and a cuckoo clock, the third dark, rich, carved object in the room.

I happen to love cuckoo clocks—a *gemütlich* taste my dad finds incomprehensible. I'd had one in my room at Madame Fourchet's all the years I was there, and still missed it; I don't know anything with a better sense of humor than a cuckoo clock. I hoped this one would still run. The weights were off its chains, but I spotted them lying on the sill of one of the wide back windows. When I walked over to get them, I was caught by the view outside. There was a garden—a striking contrast to the concrete and traffic lights on the street, for it was green and countrified, with lilacs and a tall tree or two, and rosebushes planted in a stiff rectangle in the middle where a person could get at them to spray and prune. There was a gardener or somebody in a battered old hat and chinos working around them now. The area was actually four gardens in one, including those on either side of Mrs. Jackson's and the one behind, which belonged to a house facing on the next street. Obviously, my unknown neighbors were an uncommonly chummy group.

The gardener or whoever it was straightened up and started toward my window, dragging a length of hose. He was a dark, youngish man, with a hard-jawed, sallow face and a certain kind of somber black eyes—heavy-lidded, with sparse lashes and brows— that reminded me exactly of something, only I couldn't think what. Renaissance paintings—that was it. All those Madonnas and Medicis and people. I'd just identified it when I realized that the reason I was having such a fine leisurely look at his eye structure was that he'd stopped to light a cigarette and was staring straight at me. I quit staring straight at him and stepped back from the window, first snatching the weights so I could wind the clock.

It was working fine. I'd no sooner weighted the first chain and pulled it up than the cuckoo popped out to inform me shrilly that it was thirteen o'clock, though the hands pointed to half after four and my watch said ten past two. That cheered me immediately— not that I needed cheering—and for a bit I kept him busy popping out, yelling, popping in, and slamming his door, while I moved the hands around where they should be. By the time I'd finished, the cuckoo had corrected his arithmetic, so I set the little pendulum going and went to wash my hands before starting for Uncle Frosty's house. The gardener had lost interest in my window; he was walking down the length of the lawn toward the house that faced the other street, where a woman in a pink apron was doing something to a flower bed.

The bathroom startled me by being enormous—a desert of white-tiled waste space guaranteed to give a good architect hysterics. A high, dignified tub with claw feet stood at one end of the grand vista, a washbowl as important-looking as an altar at the other. Two small, thin towels hung midway between, unreachable from either one. I washed my hands, gazing fascinated at my new self in the glass, then remembered that the afternoon was getting on and tore myself away. As I passed the window this time, the gardener was talking to the woman in the pink apron—and they were both staring my way.

It gave me an odd feeling for a moment. I wondered if the Neighborhood Cooperative Society was already hoping for another rich old lady to fleece. If so, I was going to be a disappointment.

4

When I walked into the law offices of Milligan, Frost and Turnbull at about three-fifteen, carrying the camel-bag, Uncle Frosty was in the outer office talking to Miss Jensen. He glanced up, stared, then wordlessly led the way into his private office, closing the door after us.

"Holy smoke," he said in tones of genuine awe.

I was delighted. "Do you see now why I feel perfectly safe?"

"Safe?" He seemed to be weighing the word in his mind, examining it as curiously as he was examining me.

"Secure. Relaxed. Free."

"But why should just looking different make you feel all those pretty profound things?"

"It isn't just looks." I gave him a sample of Georgetta's flat vowels and overdone r's and underdone t's. "It feels a bit like Halloween. Nobody knows it's you under that Indian suit, so you can go ahead and soap the windows."

"You mean you have some nefarious plan in mind?"

"No, just a holiday from Shan Lightley. Can't you see, Uncle Frosty? When I don't look or sound like myself, I needn't feel like myself either. I've told two people I'm from Morton Center, Idaho. If I don't know what to say to somebody, I just chew my gum."

"Morton Center, Idaho," Uncle Frosty repeated as if fascinated. "What else do you know about Georgetta Einszweiler Smith?"

"Not much. I'm just making it up as I go along. She sold ribbons at a five-and-dime. Her boss went bankrupt and then died. I suppose I'll have to invent a family, eventually."

Uncle Frosty studied me a moment, then drew a long breath and shook his head.

"What's the matter?" I demanded.

"I'm only wondering if you may have saddled yourself with a sort of Sorcerer's Apprentice. Isn't all this going to be pretty hard to sustain all summer long? And control? Once you get acquainted and involved with people—"

"I'm not going to get involved with anybody."

"No man is an island," he remarked. However, he didn't argue or voice any more doubts or give me any sound advice, which is one thing I love about Uncle Frosty. He just tacitly turned my summer over to me and began to ask about practical matters, such as what he was supposed to do with the allowance checks Dad would be sending, and whether Miss Smith would have a bank account, and how I felt about accepting a small avuncular cash advance, in case I might like to eat before payday.

"Yes, I'll take it. Oregon banks stay open till five, don't they? I'll go open an account right now—I want to buy a new suitcase anyhow."

"What's the matter with that one?"

"The *camel-bag*? My word, it looks too—Egyptian. Besides, I can't get those bits of hotel stickers off. Georgetta has never been out of Morton Center, I feel sure."

The bank was just downstairs, and in the next block I found a cut-rate luggage place, at which I spent a minimum of time and money in exchange for a suitcase emblazoned with my new initials in stamped silver. On the way back to the office, I saw a newsstand, and after a moment's careful consideration of Georgetta's character, I bought two movie magazines and a copy of *Hair Glamor* to strew around my room for atmosphere.

All this time the little voice I had shushed an hour ago was chattering away at me again. I really did try to ignore it, although maybe not very hard. But while I was transferring my odd collection of belongings to the new suitcase—which at second glance proved to be made of plastic-coated cardboard—it started talking right out loud.

"Uncle Frosty," it said. "What will your sleuth be doing, exactly, after he takes over the spider web? I know he'll be getting information, but how will he go about it? Is it all something madly technical and abstruse that requires years of experience and that sort of thing?"

Uncle Frosty, who had been swiveling gently in his chair, studying me, said, "Oh, no, he'll chiefly just keep his eyes and ears open, I expect. And get on friendly terms with the legatees, so that he can slide a couple of wily questions into the conversation now and then."

"I see," I said. And the little voice added recklessly, "Well, why couldn't I do that?"

"You? Oh, you can, of course. We already agreed that if the web jiggles promisingly during your three weeks—"

"I don't mean that. I mean why can't *I* be your sleuth? All summer?"

Uncle Frosty blinked.

I hurried on. "Unless there's more to it than you say. It doesn't *sound* complicated. And there I'll be, all established in the room, with a perfect camouflage and a perfect reason for being there—in fact, taking that waitress job was really an inspired notion, don't you think so? I've even met one of the legatees already—Mr. Bruce—though I must say I didn't find out much about him. But on the other hand, I hadn't much chance—I'm sure to do better when—"

"Hold on just one moment. Let me get my breath and think about this," said Uncle Frosty. I held on—in fact, held my breath—while he presumably got his and sat reflecting. Finally, he said, "Well, all right. No reason why you shouldn't try."

"*Really*? My word, do you mean it?"

"I guess so," Uncle Frosty said as if listening to his own words in mild surprise. "If it doesn't work out, we can always revert to the old plan. I'll give you three weeks' trial, how's that?"

"Fair enough!"

"Then we'll call that loan your sleuth salary for three weeks."

"Oh, I don't want *pay*!"

"A professional wouldn't call that pay," Uncle Frosty said with a grin. "But I warn you, I expect results. I've got to find out if I've a legal leg to stand on in this case."

"Yes." I swallowed. "Of course, I'm not quite certain I'd know a legal leg if I saw one."

"You will when I've briefed you, which I'll do as soon as you've quit messing with those bags." I hastily stuffed the last items into my new suitcase, snapped the catches, and sat down. "All right, pay attention," he said. "I'm about to give you a five-minute law course. There are only two ways I can break this will, if it's breakable. One is to prove the absence of testamentary capacity in Mrs. Dunningham. The other is to prove there was undue influence on her."

"Undue influence means the plot?"

"Yes—if there was one. But I think the weakest spot in that will is the fact that she didn't even mention her daughter's name. If you ever plan to disinherit your children, Shan, be sure you remember to call them by name as you do it—that proves that at least you know you've got them."

I promised. "Is that testamentary capacity?"

"That's half of it—'recognizing the natural objects of your bounty' is the legal term. The other half is 'knowledge of your property'—which means being reasonably clear as to whether you have five dollars or five million to give away."

"Surely she was clear about that!"

"Well, it's hard to tell. Remember the bequest to that fellow to go fishing? It's actually worded, 'I leave *the rest*' to what's his name 'to go fishing.' Sounds as if she thought she were disposing of a few odd dollars. It turned out to be ten thousand. You could go fishing at the South Pole on that."

"Still, it's possible the South Pole's what she had in mind, is that it? In which case she'd have known she meant ten thousand and had knowledge of her property, and the will's good?"

"Right. So what Georgetta must find out for me is whether Mrs. Dunningham ever mentioned her daughter after she left San Francisco, whether she was noticeably vague about money, and whether it was her own idea or somebody else's to leave all those peculiar bequests to people. You can't read minds, but you can probably spot a slip if those legatees make one." Uncle Frosty stood up and came around his desk. "Think you've got it straight?"

"Yes, quite. That's all?" I asked in surprise.

"That's all. School's out."

"Well. At least the law course was a snap. Though I've still to prove Georgetta's a good snoop. Do you want your reports in invisible ink? And how soon?"

"There's no hurry. I can't get this suit onto a docket before fall. Let's see—Mona and I are going to Mexico in August. Come see me the last of July. Unless you get bored with this and want to call it quits after three weeks."

"I won't want to. I've been less bored today than any time this last three years!"

"Well—fine," Uncle Frosty said, just a shade uneasily, I thought. He reached to open the door for me, but hesitated with his hand on the knob, looking from the new suitcase to the new me. "You know, I always liked Shan Lightley pretty well," he remarked. "I trust you won't forget her altogether."

"I wish I could. But don't worry."

"Oh, I'm not worrying—I guess." He smiled, dropped a quick kiss on my cheek, and opened the door. "Well, good luck, Miss Smith. If you find out anything of real interest about your neighbors, sneak out to a phone booth and let me know."

But the first consideration, I reflected as I walked to the bus stop, was to prevent the neighbors from finding out anything of real interest about *me*. Remember, I warned myself, you're not Shan Lightley, from this moment. You don't know any lawyers or any foreign correspondents, you've only seen Rosaleen O'Leary in films, you've never been near Europe, you don't speak a single language except American English—and by the way, that lorry's a truck, and films are movies, and a hoarding's a billboard, and petrol is gas, and remember to say "OK" a lot, and "pleased to meet you," and—

The bus arrived.

5

For all the lugging about of suitcases I've done in my life, I've never learned to carry one so that it doesn't bang me about the legs. My new one wasn't heavy—one advantage of cardboard —but it was awkward like all the rest. As I carried it from the bus stop toward the boardinghouse, feeling like an ant with an especially cumbersome crumb, I heard brisk footsteps on the sidewalk behind me. When I started toiling up the first flight of steps, they suddenly got a lot brisker, and a cheerful little man bounded up beside me. He looked about sixty, a bit old to bound, but he beamed as if he'd never felt younger and said, "Excuse me, young lady! May I relieve you of that? We seem to have a common destination."

"Oh. Mm-hm, thanks!" I relinquished the suitcase and immediately had to hurry to keep up with him.

"Haven't rented our corner room, by any chance?" He had a fine, deep voice that sounded as if it ought to be coming out of a much bigger man, and he said everything heartily, as if he were congratulating you. When I admitted I lived here now, he boomed, "Good! Too nice a room to stay empty so long. Allow me to extend a welcome. I'm perhaps the oldest living settler—aside from Mrs. Jackson, of course. I've been here thirteen years this month."

"My! You sure must like it."

"Yes, it's handy to my work. By the way, my name's Edmonds."

"Oh. How d'you—pleased to meet you. Mine is—" And here was that little problem again, the one I was going to think about later, only here it was later and I still hadn't thought about it. "I'm Georgetta Einszweiler Smith," I said, casting the die.

He set my suitcase down on the porch, where we were by now, and shook my hand. An instant later his name registered on me. Edmonds. The Dr. Edmonds in the will? "Are you a doctor?" I asked incautiously. "I mean—that is, Mrs. Jackson mentioned—"

"Not the kind that cures measles. A mere pedagogue, I'm afraid. Raised in captivity and quite tame. I teach math and physics at the college yonder." He beamed again, opened the door for me, and reburdened himself with my suitcase, adding, "I'll just see you to your room."

"Oh, don't bother—"

"No bother at all. Tell me about yourself, Miss Smith. Are you newly arrived in Portland? Or just moving from another house?"

I told him I'd just arrived. In the few moments of walking along the dim, musty reaches of hall and passage and fumbling in the gloom for my keyhole, he had my whole Morton Center routine out of me, and my lucky-to-get-a-job routine, and an additional fact or two about my Idaho relatives and home life that I hadn't known myself. It was a bit like finding yourself onstage, speaking lines, before you're quite sure what the play's about. "Well, thanks a lot," I said in relief as I finally got my door open.

"You're entirely welcome, Miss Smith." He stepped in just far enough to set my bag down and smiled. He had a quick, warm smile and beaming dark blue eyes that were the only thing you noticed about his face. "I hope you'll soon feel quite at home. We'll do our best to help—we other lodgers."

"Well, thanks a lot. How many other lodgers are there?"

"Just Miss Heater and Mr. Kulka, besides myself—and of course Mrs. Jackson and her daughter. It's a small group, but we find ourselves quite congenial—remarkably so, I may say."

You certainly may, I thought, as I recognized two other familiar names. I couldn't help staring a bit at this blue-eyed, cheerful little man and marveling that crooks could look so much like anybody else. At that moment the cuckoo burst out of his little house to shriek about its being five o'clock. Dr. Edmonds' eyes flashed to it, and a curious, complicated change came over his expression.

"Oh. You've wound her clock, I see."

"Her—?" I said.

"It belonged to the previous tenant," he murmured. "Well, I must run."

He was gone before I could say another word. I closed the door and inspected the room all over again. "Her" clock, was it? I made a small bet with myself that he was referring to the late Mrs. Dunningham. It was probably "her" marvelous old highboy, too, and her bed—maybe even her books. I went at once to the bookshelves under the side window. Sometimes you can tell a lot about a person just from the books he owns.

Not this time. *Grimm's Fairy Tales*, Moore's *Héloïse and Abélard*, *French Made Simple*, Priestley's *The Good Companions*, Edith Hamilton's *The Greek Way*, a rhyming dictionary, *The Wizard of Oz*, Shelley's *Collected Works*, a book about elephants and one about cheese, a couple of very fat old tomes about archaeology, a *Guide to the British Isles*—nobody could have deduced anything from such a mixed-up collection. I gave it up and started to unpack.

It was quickly done because I certainly hadn't much, but half the lot was wrinkled from its two days in the camel-bag. I was just wondering if I'd have to buy an iron when there was a timid little knock at my door. I opened it to find myself face to face with a stack of skimpy towels like the ones in my bathroom, two plump, tanned hands holding them, and a lot of bushy dark hair showing above them. Below was the rest of what appeared to be a very large girl.

"I've brought the clean towels," she said in a very small voice.

"Oh. Why, thanks, honey," I said, vowels carefully flat. "Shall I—sort of take them?"

"Mom said I was to put them away for you."

"OK. Come in."

She came in, still hiding behind the laundry, and headed for the bathroom in a sort of cringing hurry, as if she'd found herself on the street without her skirt and was trying to get inside again before anybody noticed. It made my teeth hurt, just to watch her. I've been stiff and self-conscious in my day—my first year at Madame Fourchet's, for instance—but never like that.

"My, that's a fine supply. I'll be able to take lots of baths," I babbled, mainly to fill the silence. "You Mrs. Jackson's daughter?"

"Yes," the girl whispered, achieving the bathroom door and scuttling out of sight.

"Well—d'you think your mother'd let me use her iron?"

"There's one for the boarders, in the util'ty. I'll show you." She emerged reluctantly from the bathroom, and I had my first look at her. She was about fifteen, and no taller than I, but she outweighed me by a good four stone. As far as I could tell, there was nothing much wrong with her features, but they were lost in the middle of that moon face and bushy hair, and she wore a shapeless tan dress, white ankle socks with big black loafers, and carried her head ducked between her shoulders. She did have nice skin—smooth and clear and brown, with a faint rose flush over the cheekbones.

"I'll get my things," I was saying as I took all this in. "I'm Georgetta Smith. What's your name, honey, if you don't mind me asking?"

"Wynola."

"Oh! Well—I won't be a minute—" I went on talking at random, this time because I was startled. Plain "Mrs. Jackson" hadn't registered as one of the significant names, but "Wynola Jackson" did. *This* girl was supposed to take sky-diving lessons? Three thousand dollars' worth? I found Mrs. Dunningham's sense of humor difficult to grasp.

While I collected my ironing and my key, Wynola just stood in one spot wishing she were invisible—oh, I could tell, I could *remember*—and looked at anything but me. I couldn't help trying to put her more at ease, not that I accomplished it. I was in the act of wondering whether it wouldn't be more merciful to stop my chatter about Idaho and just ignore her, like a chair, when she exclaimed, "The clock! You've started her clock to going!"

"Yes, shouldn't I?" I asked, turning to see if she were going to look queer, too.

She only mumbled, "Oh, sure, it's yours now," and I couldn't see how she was looking because she already had her back to me and was starting for the hall. It was the last word I got out of her; she led the way to the utility room, waved toward the ironing board, and vanished through the nearest door.

Now if I were a real detective, I thought, I'd already have drawn some brilliant deduction from people's reactions to that clock.

The cuckoo was announcing five-thirty when I got back to my room, reminding me I hadn't much time to get in groceries for breakfast. On investigation, I found a makeshift but workable kitchenette behind the cretonne-covered screen in the corner near the bathroom door. I'd inherited half a tin of Earl Grey tea, too, presumably from Mrs. Dunningham, and I instantly put the kettle on to boil. Tea in the late afternoon is a habit I find very hard to break. I drank a cup while I scribbled a brief list, then walked down to the little grocer's to fill it. Coming back, I met Dr. Edmonds striding along to the mailbox. He saluted me cheerily, then jammed on the brakes and swung around, asking if I planned to take my meals at Mrs. Jackson's. I explained my arrangements.

"Oh, yes, I see. Well—we lodgers usually gather in the living room for a half hour or so before dinner. Why not drop in anyway, on your way to the Rainbow? I'll introduce you to the others."

Nothing could have suited me better. So at six-fifteen I was being ushered hospitably into a furniture-crammed lounge off the front hall. After a few pleasantries, Dr. Edmonds escorted me to a flowered wing chair near the big window and introduced me to Miss Heater, whom I hadn't noticed—partly because she wasn't the noticeable sort, partly because the room was so full of chintz and ruffled lampshades that it would have taken a while to notice an elephant in it.

Miss Heater was a faded, wispy little woman with glasses and a thin pink nose. She gave me a strained little smile and a little bird claw of a hand, then took them both back quickly and became very involved in wiping the nose with a minute pink handkerchief. She gave me several similar strained little smiles during the next fifteen minutes but scarcely said a word. I'd come in meaning to say scarcely a word myself, but lifelong training in decent manners is awfully hard to eradicate. Besides, there are questions to which "mm-hm" and "hmp'm" simply will not work as answers, such as "What's the country like up around Morton Center?" Dr. Edmonds, obviously an expert at drawing people out, was full of such questions. I found myself describing a little town set among potato farms, and a big old house (like Aunt Doris's), and a Wawkanap Creek where my lot always swam and picnicked. I invented a cousin Sam who'd cut his knee there last summer on a submerged log, then went on adding bits of autobiography and uncles and best friends that I knew I'd better take notes on soon or I'd be forgetting them myself, and was quite enjoying my performance when Mr. Kulka came in.

Guess who *he* turned out to be—the gardener. Only he was really an artist, Dr. Edmonds explained, and merely gardened for his rent. (Where the weeds came into this I couldn't fathom.) He lived at the top of the house, in a big attic he'd turned into a studio.

"My, an artist!" I said, gazing up at him in an impressed way as I chewed my gum—though he looked more like a tough than an artist in his old corduroy pants, and his faded brown shirt that wasn't tucked in, and his black hair falling over those Bronzini eyes. "What kind of pictures do you paint?"

He muttered something about drawings and etchings, and stared at me somberly while I told him I didn't know much about art myself, but I knew what I liked, and that my Aunt Eugenia used to paint lovely pictures on plates. Well, naturally I was just practicing my accent and hadn't expected him to greet these tidings with much enthusiasm, but neither had I expected him just to sit down in the middle of one of my sentences and pick up a magazine, without a word. That's what he did, though, leaving me gaping at empty air. It took me a second to find my wits; then I lost my temper, abruptly and completely. It was all I could do to keep from slapping him. I did spin around with my back to him, though I doubt if he noticed. Fortunately, Wynola came in just then to announce dinner, and I escaped.

Serves you right! I told myself as I stalked down the concrete steps and along to the café. Hereafter, chew your gum and let the small talk muddle along without you.

I was beginning to get sleepy again as I worked my way through the Rainbow's southern-fried chicken—no relation to Aunt Doris's—and Mr. Bruce detained me afterward to issue me three uniforms and to remark that he'd see me at eleven in the morning. But when I plodded back to my room, I went dutifully, though wearily, to dig out the old red-bound journal I'd transferred from the camel-bag with everything else. There were all those notes to make on my mythical relatives, and it had struck me at dinner that I'd do well to take daily notes on the legatees, too—just jot down impressions and snatches of conversation while they were fresh in my mind. For all I knew, they might be full of significance, which Uncle Frosty might spot later if I couldn't now. I read the first lot over when I'd finished, but if some vital clue lurked there, it escaped me. By then I was too sleepy to care much about anything but falling into bed. It had been an active day, and I suspected that tomorrow— my debut as a waitress—might be more so.

Courage, Camille, I told myself. You can't detect everything in the first eight hours. Relax and lie still, or you'll wreck that hairdo— then where'll you be?

6

I did rather struggle with my coiffure the next morning. My hair is the slippery, heavy sort most susceptible to the law of gravity, and by now it was showing a decided tendency just to hang down and behave like hair, the way it had been doing for eighteen years. Obviously, I was going to have to renew Opyl's stern disciplinary measures. They began with ruthless backcombing—that much I remembered. Then somehow she'd scooped and swooped the resulting mass into its tower, using the hairbrush gently as a butterfly's wing just on the surface, so as to leave the tangles intact beneath. I imitated this technique as slavishly as I could, feeling as if I were sweeping crumbs under the rug, and achieved a fair copy of the original after about half an hour's effort.

Then I fetched one of my new uniforms out of the closet and had a look at it. It was just the frock—the starchy white pinafores were issued us daily, fresh-laundered, at the café—and it was really quite pretty, with a full skirt and extremely full sleeves caught in at the elbow. But unfortunately, mine was not yellow, like Brünnhilde's. I should have known—the waitresses matched the decor. I was to be grass-green, a peculiarly penetrating shade, which with my hair and bright-blue eyelids turned me into a kind of rainbow all by myself. I decided the color-conscious Mr. Bruce ought to like me fine.

When I walked in at eleven, he was behind the counter, polishing glasses in a dignified manner, while the waitress on duty—a dark girl in pink—carried coffee to some customers in a booth. As soon as he saw me, he abandoned his labors for some menial to finish later—probably me, I thought—and ushered me through the upholstered swinging doors to the kitchen. At the big stainless-steel sink, a bitter-looking party in a cap and long white apron was chopping vegetables as if he hated them.

"Oh, Malcolm, this is our new waitress," Mr. Bruce said. "Our cook, Mr. Ansley, Miss Smith."

I turned Opyl's brisk smile on and off again and told Mr. Ansley I was pleased to meet him. He shot me a suspicious glance around his shoulder, then went back to his carrots without comment. Wondering if he and David Kulka might possibly be related, I followed Mr. Bruce into the linen room off the kitchen. "Your cook's quite a chatterbox," I remarked, with what I thought considerable restraint.

Mr. Bruce, who was opening one of the big linen drawers, stopped and looked at me consideringly and gave me a surprise. "Mr. Ansley has sound reasons for despising the human race," he explained. "He prefers to limit his contact with it. Don't worry," he added quite kindly. "It needn't have anything to do with you." Before I could close my mouth, he went on, "Now, the pinafores are in this drawer. Table linens in these. We use tablecloths only at dinnertime. One of your duties will be to reset the tables each day around five o'clock, matching the cloths to the tabletops, please. Number five is your locker; here's your combination." He found a slip of paper and gave it to me, along with another of his considering looks. "Now, don't feel you must learn everything in one day," he said earnestly. "We'll soon ease you in. Just report to me when you've put on your pinafore."

Five minutes later I was behind the counter, polishing those glasses.

The luncheon business hadn't begun, apparently; there were coffee drinkers in two booths, and the counter was deserted except for one college boy who brooded over a book and an empty cup down at the far end where it curved parallel to the front window. While Mr. Bruce was explaining that the regular dishwasher arrived at eleven-thirty and that Miss Madison would show me where things were, a trio of coffee drinkers got up to leave. Mr. Bruce stepped to the cash register to ring up the check. A minute later the brunette in pink came back with the empty cups, gave me a quick look, and edged past me to the sink.

"Oh, Miss Madison," Mr. Bruce said as he closed the cash drawer. "This is Miss Smith, our new waitress. Please help her learn her way around, will you? Miss Madison is a student at the college," he explained to me, and drifted away across the room.

"Pleased to meet you," I told Miss Madison, who was trying not to stare at my coiffure. "Fremont College, did he mean? You must be real smart. I hear it's awful hard to get into."

I hadn't heard any such thing—it just came out when I opened my mouth—but all unwittingly I'd set the keynote of our relationship and established the pecking order, in my first dozen carefree words. Miss Madison's smile was a study in gratification shading rapidly into condescension.

"Oh, perhaps not that hard," she said. "I'm glad to know you, Miss uh—"

"Georgetta Smith," I said, squashing my vowels. "Or George, if it's easier. That's what my boyfriend in high school used to call me, so I'm used to it. What's your first name, honey, if you don't mind me asking?"

"Well—just plain Helen. My . . . special friends, even back in high school, never seemed to go in for nicknames." Miss Madison smiled down at her fingernails, contriving somehow to suggest a throng of dark-browed, intense admirers who went in for things like Proust or Zen. "Are you in college somewhere, dear?"

I widened my eyes and giggled, "Oh, not *me*!"—an answer she so obviously expected that it would have been a shame to disappoint her—and added that it was hard enough to get through Senior English. Then I was sure I'd overdone things and waited for Helen to tell me to come off it.

I just didn't know Helen. She gave me a forebearing little smile as her eyes flicked from my shoe bows to my hairdo, plainly lowering my status and elevating her own with every flick, and I could see her deciding that she was going to be Completely Democratic about me. "I think you're wise to be so sensible about it," she told me—"it" doubtless referring to my sharply limited mentality—and tried to exchange a Speaking Glance with the boy at the other end of the counter, who unfortunately was still buried in his book.

It was already obvious to me that Miss Madison was the sort I instinctively want to kick. I gave her my expressionless expression instead, accompanied by an accidental but quite effective snap of my gum, and said, "Want me to wash those cups?"

"Yes, dear, do that," she said, abandoning the cups with pleasure. "It's time I got things organized for the noon rush. Let me see now . . ." She strolled toward the refrigerator, which was about midway along our narrow alley behind the counter, calling to the boy at the far end, "You want some more coffee, Sherry, before I get busy?"

He looked up briefly and said, "No, thanks." Then, having caught sight of me in the background, he looked again.

"You positive?" Helen urged, swinging winsomely on the refrigerator door. "How about some lunch? Be glad to fix you a sandwich before our mob of colleagues arrives."

However, the boy had apparently recovered from the slight shock my coiffure and Christmas coloring had given him, and he seemed impervious, or maybe just inured, to Helen. He merely said, "No, I'm leaving in a minute," and went back to his book. Helen turned off the magnetism and got tomatoes out of the refrigerator.

"Now I'd better explain some things, dear. You see, we make all the sandwiches here on this big breadboard. And the pickles and relish and so on are in these little containers. I'm telling you now because I *really* won't have time to answer a lot of questions later. In about thirty minutes half the college will be in here. Oh, horrors, here comes the first batch already," she added happily, as the door opened to admit three large youths, indistinguishable from the ones I'd seen yesterday in the corner booth, except that one of these was very good-looking. "Tell you what, dear," Helen said. "Why don't *you* slice the tomatoes and just finish washing those dishes when you have time. It's a little tricky to take people's orders until you're used to it." She wasted an irresistible smile on the boys, who weren't looking at her, and handed me her paring knife. "These are rather particular friends of mine, anyhow. Vince is in two of my classes—my hardest ones."

"What are those?" I asked obediently.

"French and trig. Trigonometry," she explained carefully, so I wouldn't be out of my depth.

"My," I said. Then, because I simply couldn't resist it, I added, "Let's see, is trigonometry kind of math or something, or is it like science? I never can remember."

The bookworm at the end of the counter slowly raised his head.

Helen smiled at me tenderly and said, "It's a branch of mathematics, dear." I managed not to trip her as she went past me to the three boys, wreathed in jaunty little smiles and twinkles. "Well! Aren't *you* the early birds today!"

"Hi, Helen," one of the boys said good-naturedly. "Ham on rye and a chocolate shake, please. Hi, Sherry."

The bookworm removed his gaze from me, said, "Hi, Charlie," then nodded to the other two and went back to his book.

"Sherry's just leaving—when he gets through another hundred pages," Helen said fondly. "He thinks this place is the Libe. Relish on your hamburger, Tom? Vince, you want the Main Hall Special as usual, I suppose."

"No, cheeseburger and milk," mumbled the good-looking boy in a discouraging sort of voice that didn't discourage her at all. She laughed musically, shot him a mischievous glance, told him he just liked to keep her guessing, and would have tapped him with her fan if she'd had one. "Say, did you catch the French assignment?" she added, leaning cozily on the counter beside him. "I had to leave for the A.A.C.O. meeting, and—"

"Subjunctive of irregular verbs," Vince said.

"Subjunctive! *Mon bête noire*," sighed Helen, giving me a clear idea of how good her French was. "Honestly, I think I have a *block* on subjunctive. Like somebody was saying in that O.M.A. meeting the other day—there were a lot of N.R.G.G.O. members there, and this psych major stood up and said—"

She'd lost her audience; the bookworm had apparently developed automatic earplugs over the months and was peacefully reading; Charlie and Tom had started discussing tennis rackets. She had Vince trapped, though. He stuffed his hands in his pockets, glanced longingly at his notebook, on which Helen's elbow rested, then past her at me, and I decided to come to the rescue.

"This enough tomatoes, honey?" I asked, remembering to call them tomaytoes. "I better start frying hamburgers, hadn't I?"

"Oh, no, dear, I'll do it." Helen returned to the dreary workaday world with a bravely stifled sigh—and a glance toward Mr. Bruce that caused her to start moving pretty fast. "You set places for these nice men, would you? Knife and spoon on the *right* side, and fork on the left."

I blinked and said, "Gee, at home we always just put 'em all together, in a bunch." I should have refrained; it made the boy at the end of the counter raise his head again. But Helen wouldn't have doubted me if I'd said we always just stuck them in the water glass or tied string around them and suspended them from the ceiling. She merely smiled democratically and said to be careful not to touch the tines of the forks with my fingers.

"Oh, before you get the silverware, dear, you might just scoop the ice cream for Vince's milk shake," she added, daintily shaking hamburger patties onto the grill and removing the wax paper with her little finger crooked. "And then you might make Charlie's ham-on-rye, and then—" She went on down quite a little list of things I might just do before I did anything else, adding, "I certainly hope there won't be much of a crowd today, with me so busy."

"Where's Brünnhilde?" I asked absently as I peered around for the ice-cream scoop. Out of the corner of my eye, I saw the boy at the end of the counter look up again—he seemed to be losing interest in his book—and it made me realize uncomfortably that Georgetta probably shouldn't know a Wagnerian heroine from Mickey Mouse.

Obviously, Helen didn't; she said, "Hilda? You must mean Rose. She'll be late today, she had a dentist appointment. Just when I need her worst!" To ease the strain, she told me something else to do.

For several minutes I was extremely active, while Helen shifted her weight to the other hip and turned a hamburger. Two new customers sat down near the three boys as I was starting that way with a handful of silverware, and she added that I might just take those ladies' orders while I was there. I succumbed once more to temptation and asked her nervously if she didn't think it would be too tricky for me. She gave me a fairly sharp glance, but said only, "You have to learn sometime, dear, and I *do* have my hands full right now."

There were simply no thin spots in Helen's skin of complacency, and if there was a limit to what she'd swallow, I couldn't find it. I decided I'd better quit trying to; I was attracting a bit too much notice from the bookworm. As I laid the places for the three boys, I reverted to my gum chewing and poker face, responding to Charlie's amiable comments on the weather with bland stares and monosyllables. Then I turned casually to face the bookworm, hoping the latest sample of my conversation had switched his attention back to his book. It hadn't. He'd even closed the book and was sitting with his chin propped on his hand and his eyes fixed on me. The chin was long and spade-shaped, the eyes long, grayish-green and mild under quizzical eyebrows, and the expression one of baffled enjoyment.

I suddenly wished he'd leave—he made me nervous. "Ready for your check?" I hinted.

"No indeed. I'll have some more coffee, please." He lowered his voice to add, "I don't want to miss any of the performance."

I retained my poker face, but with such an effort that I could feel my features congealing into what was probably the most simpleminded expression I'd yet achieved. "Performance?" I repeated.

"Your act. It's very good," he assured me. "I don't think a soul but me has caught on yet. But what's it all about?"

I said, "Sorry, I don't follow you. I have to take an order," and fled without bothering to get his coffee. Nobody else had heard the exchange, I was sure, but it had rather taken my breath, and there was no knowing what he might come out with next, or in how loud a voice. Cursing Helen—and myself for not letting her alone—I paused in front of the two women to scribble "2 hambgr, no mstrd," in a handwriting that looked like Arabic, then went on, as far down the counter as I could go.

Now, get busy thinking of something to do to convince this Sherry person you're nobody but Georgetta, I told myself sternly. And after that, mind your fences. And hold your tongue.

The trouble was, I was already frightfully busy being a waitress; Helen's noon rush was upon us by this time, and there was nearly as much strenuous dashing about to do as she'd predicted. I couldn't do a thing about Sherry except try, unsuccessfully, to forget him. Every time I glanced in his direction, I found him watching me, sometimes with a puzzled squint that made me hope he'd decided he was all wrong, but more often just watching, the way you'd watch TV. I wondered if by some ill luck we'd actually met before, for instance in Mary's Creek, and he'd remembered me— but I knew we hadn't, because I'd have remembered him. Not that he was remarkable-looking. His hair was medium dark, that rough kind of wiry hair that tries to curl even around the ears where it's clipped closest, and his complexion was medium fair, and his nose straight and his cheeks thin, and his mouth just a mouth, with a rather gentle, inquiring curve to it. Still, you'd remember his face, if only for that dreamy, quizzical expression.

The dreaminess was obviously pretty deceptive. Never mind, don't get rattled, I told myself. Just ignore him, and he'll go away.

About twelve-thirty, long after I'd extended my dashes into the kitchen to fetch Mr. Ansley's hot lunches, Rose arrived and instantly began to be worth three of Helen and me put together. Even so, my feet were developing a throb and my shoulder a sore spot from banging through the kitchen door with loaded trays, and now and then I wondered where those lulls were, during which we menials were supposed to eat. Still my faithful observer sat on, forming a spot of meditative silence in the bedlam of clattering forks and crockery the café had turned into. I couldn't ignore him any more than you can ignore a mosquito in the bedroom.

By the time the noon rush thinned out a bit, he was making me so nervous that I had to *show* him I was ignoring him—always an unwise move. I went down his way to clear some dishes, noticed with spurious surprise that they were his, and told him I thought he'd left ages ago.

He didn't even pretend to believe it, merely smiled benevolently and narrowed his eyes at my hair—as if he wished he could pull it to see if a wig came off—and remarked that I'd get used to him in time. "I hang around here a lot. Too much, I guess, but it's a good place to study."

"To study? In this noise?"

"Oh, I don't mind a nice homogenous din like this. Drowns out the one usually going on in my head," he said cheerfully. "Very rackety place, my head, it's always full of scraps of music and little voices reminding me to get my hair cut, and questions about this thing and that—for example the new waitress."

I gave him an opaque stare as I chewed my gum, and remarked that he was quite a kidder. "Like all that about the act." I laughed tolerantly, told him that was pretty good, that was, and started to turn away with his dishes.

No use. He said, "Oh, I wasn't kidding. In fact, I'm a pretty serious fellow, Miss—Miss Greensleeves. What is your name, by the way?"

"Georgetta Einszweiler Smith. Just call me George."

"*George?* I certainly will not."

"You got something against my name?" I asked truculently.

"Not a thing, but it just won't do. That's my name—George."

"Why, I thought it was Sherry."

"It's George Maynard Sherrill," he said patiently.

A small thunderclap resounded in my mind. I didn't know I was staring at him until I realized he was staring at me.

"What's the matter?" he demanded.

The first scholarship must go to George Maynard Sherrill, my memory was repeating for the third or fourth time, as if its record were stuck. "Hm? Nothing," I told him, setting down his dishes. "I just remembered I forgot your check."

"Check, my eye. You recognized my name. The one nobody ever calls me," he said wonderingly.

With great dignity I said, "It merely sounded kinda familiar for a minute."

I tore off his check, slapped it down on the counter, and walked swiftly away, but not before I'd seen from his expression that I was going to have to think of a better explanation than that. He really was curious about me now.

I went back to work, feeling quite dazed at the speed with which I'd managed to complicate Georgetta's life in the space of one lunch hour. But it was hopeless to try to sort things out until this day was over and the pressure off. Some of it went off a few minutes later when George Sherrill paid and drifted out of the café, to my intense relief. Soon after that the worst of the crowd had gone, and so had Helen, who got off at one-thirty. She'd be back at five, Rose warned me, but the respite was wonderful anyway. I got on fine with Rose, who told me all about her dental problems and said I looked real cute in my pinafore, and that I was more help than Helen already, and that if she (Helen) didn't watch it, I'd be stealing all her college boyfriends—to which I replied sincerely that I didn't believe I wanted them.

After we'd had some lunch ourselves—finally—she concentrated on teaching me how to make milk shakes and sodas and things, and I attempted to concentrate on observing Mr. Bruce, and we both concentrated on staying off our feet as much as possible. I drew a blank with Mr. Bruce, because between two-thirty and five he simply went home and stayed there. By the time he was back, Helen had arrived, too, and so had the time to set the tables with those matching cloths, and light the little colored hurricane lamps, and memorize the kinds of pie we were offering for dinner, and begin to serve the first customers—and soon I was too busy again to think about sitting down.

George Sherrill drifted back in at six-fifteen, with a couple of other students. I tensed up at first glimpse of him, because I was so fagged by now that I didn't see how I could take him on, too—but the three of them went to one of the back booths Helen was serving, ordered dinner, and minded their own business. So I minded mine, which was certainly all I had strength enough for at that point. Sherry and Company had just left when seven o'clock finally came. Thankfully, I headed for the kitchen, shed my pinafore, and got my handbag from my locker.

Three minutes later, when I limped out onto the sidewalk, my Nemesis straightened up from a waiting posture by the door. His friends had vanished.

"Ah, there you are, Miss Greensleeves," he said, and came welcomingly toward me.

7

Well, I cut him dead and walked on, but of course it didn't work. He merely took a couple of long, lazy strides to catch up and fell into step beside me. He was taller than I'd thought.

"Where you going?" he asked cheerfully.

"Home," I snapped. "My feet hurt and I'm tired."

"Can I just walk along? I want to talk to you a minute."

Since there was very little I could do about it, I gave my grudging permission, along with a chilly look out of the corner of my eye.

He gave me one of his slow, benevolent smiles in return, asked me where I lived, and raised his eyebrows when I told him. "At Mrs. Jackson's? You took that back room that's been vacant? Why, that's nice—we're next-door neighbors. I live just beyond there, at Mrs. Moore's." I muttered that I was just born lucky, and he grinned. "Oh, come on, don't be mad at me. I'll quit prying into your secrets if that's the way you want it."

"I don't even know why you think I've got a secret."

"The ambiguities, Greensleeves. You're just full of ambiguities and even contradictions."

"Lot of big words," I muttered crossly.

"Plus a few anachronisms," Sherry added. When he looked directly at you, narrowing his eyes like that, they seemed lighter—less green than gray. They also seemed less dreamy and much more penetrating. "That Greensleeves nickname suits you much better than 'George.' You know the song?"

I hesitated, remembering my Wagner-Brünnhilde blunder. "That's a folk song or something, isn't it? I might've heard it on TV."

"It'd be a wonder if you hadn't," he remarked, making me very glad I'd decided against playing ignorant. I'd known "Greensleeves" since the days of a certain nursemaid who wore garnet earrings and used to sing me to sleep, but I thought of it as rather specially Olde Englishe, like a Morris dance, and perhaps not well known in the States. Which just shows how ignorant I was about the States. Sherry went on, "If you've only heard some folk singer doing it on TV, you haven't really heard it. They murder it, most of them—pretty up the dissonances, even change the key—so they can chord it easier on a guitar, I suppose. That's cretin, like correcting Chaucer's spelling. The song's just right as it was written. C minor. Kind of moves in and haunts you," he added dreamily.

"That where I come in? I'm some kind of spook or something?"

He grinned. "It's just that there's been a rumor around since the sixteenth century that Henry the Eighth wrote that song and that the girl in it was Anne Boleyn. He just called her My Lady Greensleeves to hide her identity. See? That's where you come in. Ambiguities and secrets."

I heaved a sigh and stopped to face him. "For the last time, I don't *have* any secrets. I'm an open *book*. I'm—"

"Oh, come on. Nobody but Helen would buy that Tobacco Road routine you were giving her."

It was too true. "Oh. That," I said, and began to chew my gum in a more amiable manner as I strolled on. "I *was* kidding Helen a little. She's so stuck on herself. Just because she goes to college. Why, gee, I could've gone to college if I'd wanted to. A beauty college in Boise, Idaho. Supposed to be the best in the state."

Sherry studied me a moment out of the corner of his eye. "You come from Idaho?"

"Mm-hm, Morton Center. It's real little—you wouldn't have heard of it . . ." I went ahead with my Morton Center speech, and my Wawkanap Lake speech, and a new best-friend-who-went-to-beauty-college speech . . .

"But you didn't think you'd like it?" Sherry put in as I paused for breath.

"Well, I didn't think I'd like the *career*. Just one dirty head of hair after the other, all day long—that's what my sister Charmeen says. Once you think about it that way, it kinda loses its glamor."

Sherry nodded reflectively. From his expression, he was trying to label these various tidbits true or false, and so far couldn't—but I suspected he was beginning to believe in me. We'd reached the boardinghouse steps by now, but he made no move to go. "Do you have any other sisters besides Charmeen?"

"Mm-hm, four others. And a brother. Say, is *he* spoiled!"

"He's the youngest?"

"Next to Shyrle—she's only in sixth grade. Bud's in high school. He's going to work in my dad's filling station this summer, though. Do him good to get his hands greasy—that's what I say." I smiled blandly at Sherry, feeling that Franz—maybe even Nevin—would have been satisfied with my performance. At that instant my subconscious produced a magnificently valid explanation for my worst blunder. "Say!" I exclaimed. "I know why your name sounded familiar! One of the boarders here mentioned you yesterday—a teacher." I was sure he'd know Dr. Edmonds because of the will; and I saw right away that my logic was a success.

"Oh. Dr. Edmonds," Sherry said. "I suppose he might have."

"You taking one of his classes or something?"

"No, just some private work. I'll start one in summer session, though—integral calculus." Sherry smiled. "That'll get my hands good and greasy."

"Sounds awful. You're not going home for the holiday? Where do you live, anyway?" I added, deciding it was my turn for a bit of information now.

"Bell Landing. Ever hear of it? Well, don't feel bad—nobody else has either. It's about eighty miles northwest of here, a little place kind of hiding behind some fir trees on the side of a mountain."

"You don't like it?" I ventured, thinking of Mary's Creek.

He looked surprised. "Sure, I like it. Why shouldn't I?"

"Well—you know. Little hick town. Same old 4,741 faces day in day out—"

"Oh, Bell Landing's bigger than that! We've got 5,958 faces, and a mayor and a high school." Sherry smiled, watched me a minute, and eased himself down on the cracked concrete steps, motioning me down beside him. "I take it you've got no use for little hick towns."

"Well, I don't know much about any other kind," I said hastily. "But a big city—like Portland—it's got a little more zing. I like variety. Different kinds of people."

"My dad says you can find out more about human nature from knowing 5,958 people as individuals than you can by knowing five million as just a crowd on a subway. Of course, he spent ten years in New York, so maybe he's just embittered."

I reflected that maybe I was just embittered, too—only for the opposite reasons—and decided it might be best to change the subject. "It's too bad you've got to take that math this summer, instead of going home," I remarked.

"Oh, I don't have to take it. I just want to."

"Want to?"

"Sure. I'm signed up for a couple of other courses, too. You find that eccentric or something?"

"Well, I can think of more relaxing things to do in summer than study integral calculus."

"But I couldn't fit it into my schedule last winter. And I sure can't next winter—I'll be a senior."

This didn't clear up why he wanted to take it in the first place, but I just asked why he couldn't fit it in.

"Because it's got nothing to do with my major. That's the heck of wanting a degree. After your first two years, you've got to cut out darn near everything except just what you're majoring in. Lousy system. It's like being led into a candy store and then told to eat your spinach."

And integral calculus was the chocolate creams? I gave it up and said, "What's your spinach? I mean major?"

"Commercial art. Advertising, packaging, and so on." He glanced at me and smiled. "Yes, I ought to be in an art school instead of Fremont. But that'd be too logical, Greensleeves. Besides, I wouldn't have got *any* candy at a place like that—just spinach and more spinach, and rutabaga on top of it."

"Well, my w—goodness, if you don't like this sort of thing, how come you're majoring in it?"

"Because I can do it." With one of his lazy motions, he reached for a sheet of paper he'd been using as a book mark, plucked a pencil from his shirt pocket, and in a few seconds blocked out a box design for Pot O' Gold Oatmeal, complete with jolly, fey little leprechauns and Gaelic lettering. He handed it to me and said, "People pay you a living wage for that sort of thing. Eventually."

"My!" I said in my most impressed voice. In fact, I was rather impressed and couldn't think why I was also vaguely disappointed. The box would catch one's eye on a grocer's shelf, and both sketch and lettering were slickly professional. Obviously, a certain offhand skill with a pencil came as naturally to Sherry as curly hair. "How come you don't like to draw?" I asked. "Seems like it would be fun."

"I do like to—but not that way."

"What way, then?"

"Oh, just a way I've always drawn. Before they taught me how." Sherry smiled, produced the pencil again, and worked carefully for a few moments on the other side of the paper. "Cartooning, I suppose you'd call it. Sort of."

He finished, studied what he'd done, added a very small, precise touch somewhere, and handed me another leprechaun—an utterly different one. This one was drawn with a thin, wavering line that possessed a sort of questioning quality all by itself. It traced the figure of a leprechaun who was neither fey nor jolly, but merely rather scrubby, with patched shoes and a resigned expression. The style was odd, unlike anything I'd ever seen. The whole sketch was as intensely individual as a signature.

"Now, that's good," I muttered, before I remembered that Georgetta's tastes weren't mine. Still, there was something at once funny and bleak about this little figure that would appeal to almost anybody.

Sherry remarked, "I'd never sell oatmeal with it, though."

I thought he might sell opinions with it—being my dad's daughter, I'd immediately thought of political cartoons—but I didn't mention that of course, just handed the sketch back.

Sherry tucked it into his book with a shrug. "Anyway, cereal-box art as a lifework . . . well. As your sister Charmeen would say, just one dirty head of hair after the other."

"Must it always be cereal boxes?"

"No, it can be pictures of refrigerators for the Sunday papers."

There was something very odd about his attitude. He seemed to have written off his whole career as wasted motion before he even got started on it—yet he sounded neither resentful nor bitter, only mildly bored. There must be better reasons than he'd told me. "Is your father a commercial artist?" I asked him, probing.

"Dad? Oh, no. He's a professional failure."

My eyes widened of their own accord. "Well! That's a pretty impolite way to talk about him."

"I'm only quoting him. He says people who practice one difficult skill for upwards of twenty years are known as professionals—and people who never get promoted are known as failures. Well, for upwards of twenty years, he's been very skillfully not getting promoted, though it's been very difficult. Ergo, he's a professional failure."

I couldn't help grinning at that. "What is this work that he's so dead set against promotion?"

"He teaches English at Bell Landing High School. Promotion would boost him right out of teaching and into administration. He doesn't want to administrate; he just wants to teach English." Sherry smiled comfortably and rested his elbows on the step behind him. "They outmaneuvered him last year and made him head of the English department, and he darn near quit. He says it's a blot on his otherwise unsmirched record of getting absolutely nowhere."

I was beginning to like Sherry's dad. And Sherry, too. "He sounds very sure of himself," I said, feeling envious.

"He is. He was designed by God specifically to teach English, and he knows it. He believes in people doing what they're fitted for. He says it's the whole trick to living." Sherry hesitated, then added, "So I'm majoring in commercial art."

"It's not quite the same, is it? He likes what he's fitted for, and you don't."

"Oh, I only dislike part of it. He didn't like all his training, either. He says get your tools, then build something you do like with them. It's not clear yet what I'm going to build." Sherry smiled a bit grimly. "Still, there's a good chance Dad's central theory is all right. It's worked for him."

It had worked for everybody I knew—all three sets of parents, Uncle Frosty, even people like Auguste at Pension Algère, who must certainly have been designed by God to be a Paris concierge. I stared absently at the old car across the street with its straggling "Butch is a goo"—and considered my inner girl. "What if you don't know what you're fitted for?" I muttered.

After a reflective moment, Sherry said, "That's a good question, Greensleeves."

As he spoke, he turned and looked at me, with such complete comprehension in his eyes that I felt we'd somehow discussed the subject exhaustively. In fact, for just a second I was irrationally convinced that in some previous conversation I couldn't quite remember we'd talked about everything on earth, including our autobiographies and what we liked for breakfast. It was a queer sensation—a kind of flash of recognition—and gone in an instant, leaving me feeling idiotic and slightly rattled. I decided it was time this tête-à-tête came to an end. I couldn't even remember if I'd been flattening my vowels this last few minutes or saying "Gee" and "OK."

"Gee, I better go in now," I said, standing up abruptly. "I'll see you tomorrow or sometime, OK?"

"OK, Greensleeves." Sherry stood up, too, lazily scooped up his books, and stood watching me with that quizzical half-smile as I ran up the steps. When I glanced back again from the porch, he was drifting on down the sidewalk toward the house next door.

An odd sort, I reflected as I went into the dark, cabbage-haunted hall. *Un type*, as Madame Fourchet would say—but all the same, *très sympathique.*

Since I'd spent ten months in America without finding a single person of my age *très sympathique*, or even talkable-to for as long as I'd sat out there talking to Sherry, this reaction of mine was worth a bit of surprised mulling over, which I gave it as I shucked off my green uniform and waited for that enormous tub to fill. Then I stepped into the bath and quit thinking about anything except how good hot water feels to weary feet.

Before bedtime, though, I spent half an hour with my journal, noting down all I knew so far about George Maynard Sherrill—who was after all a suspect—and all the various new bits I'd invented about Georgetta Smith.

3

Georgetta

1

It's an odd document, that old journal. I started it one year at Madame Fourchet's, but after some meandering accounts of skiing and ballet lessons, mingled with bitter complaints about German declensions, I'd abandoned it in disgust because nothing diary-worthy ever seemed to happen to me. Next come the College Street entries, but halfway through that summer they break off, too—for the opposite reason. My life got so eventful that I couldn't keep up with it. At first the entries were pedestrian enough. I was just scrawling memoranda about Georgetta's family or about the lega-tees, or talking to myself. Here are some excerpts, beginning the evening of my second footsore day as a waitress and covering roughly the next three weeks.

8th June . . . Believe I put paid to Sherry's suspicions yesterday. When I got to work this morning, he was already occupying his regular pew down at the end of the counter, and he stayed through lunch, but he kept his word and didn't do any prying or staring. I think he's convinced I'm nobody but Georgetta, though he insists on calling me "Greensleeves." . . . Rose says my feet will harden to this job in time. I devoutly hope so.

10th June . . . My chief daily irritant (next to Helen) is obviously going to be that dishwasher—a boy of sixteen, name of Milton, who looks twelve and acts ten . . . Autobiographical notes: Georgetta is the only redhead in the Smith family; sister Charmeen was May Queen her senior year at Morton Center High; Charmeen's boyfriend's name is Al. I invented all this for Sherry's benefit today.

11th June . . . I needn't have worried an instant about my name. Everybody's adopted "Greensleeves," even the customers—except for Mr. Bruce, who goes right on calling me "Miss Smith," and Helen, who goes right on calling me "dear," and of course Dave Kulka and Mr. Ansley (the cook), neither of whom bother to call me anything . . . Wish I could get somebody talking about Mrs. Dunningham. It's remarkably hard, since I'm supposed to be ignorant of her existence.

12th June . . . Spring term at the college ended today. Hear, hear. Now maybe Helen will stop being tragic about her simply *awful* exams. There'll be a week's hiatus before the summer session begins—which means, judging from today, that the Rainbow will be jammed continuously instead of just at noon . . . Dr. Edmonds is writing a physics textbook. Says he plans to spend all his free time this summer revising it. Dreary prospect . . . My feet finally are getting a bit better.

14th June . . . Today was gorgeous—Riviera weather, exactly like Villefranche in April. Actually it's been remarkably fine (for June in Oregon) since before I left Mary's Creek, only there I was in no mood to notice . . . I must remember not to ask people if they want their coffee "black or white." They always look rather blank for a second. Maybe it's one of those Britishisms. Sherry overheard me say it today and got a sudden very interested gleam in his eye, which gave me a bad moment—but he didn't mention it later, when he walked home with me. He must be a very good student—got A's in every course but one, and that was a spinachy one that bores him. I told him he'd better mind what he's about—he might end up a success and disgrace his Dad's profession. He just said, "Dad told me to get whatever I want out of college. His sole requirement is that I want *something*. Reasonable enough. I've decided to want five cups of coffee per forenoon." He does have a quite engaging grin.

16th June . . . Tried to start a conversation with Miss Heater this morning when we met at the mail table, but no luck. Every time I see her, she just smiles in that mousy sort of way, and murmurs something inaudible into her little pink handkerchief, and vanishes through a door . . . Rained today—just when I was boasting about the weather.

17th June . . . I've been trying to work out just what it is I like so much about that song, "Greensleeves." It keeps running through my head lately—no wonder, with people shouting "Greensleeves!" every time they want a napkin—and Sherry's right, it does rather move in and haunt you. I think it's that plaintive little minor strain weaving in and out of the melody, and the rhythm—like children skipping—and those strange key changes or whatever they are, shifting about like colors in a dream, so that you keep feeling intrigued and diverted because the next chord or interval isn't the one you'd have expected, and neither is the unresolved chord at the end. That's it, I guess—the medieval flavor of the thing. Now that I think of it, nearly all medieval music sounds that way, happy and sad together, with that inconclusive, rather drifting end. Always brings to mind a vision of the old, small, wooden London with gates you could close at night, and mummers and minstrels and rowdy torchlit taverns, and laughter and ale and the Globe Theatre—and though you knew the plague was in Stepney and a footpad might cut your throat between here and home, that was all part of life, too, part of what you were singing about in that minor key . . . Of course, a spoil-sport musician (that BBC friend of Nevin's) told me once it all has to do with the twelve-tone scale or some such thing—but I like my notion better.

18th June . . . Sherry is certainly a fixture in that café. I've got so used to seeing him up there at the far end of the counter, always buried in one of those intellectual-looking paperbacks, or doodling his wavering, baffled-looking little cartoon creatures, that the place wouldn't quite seem furnished without him . . . Must remember that I told him Georgetta's room at home (she shares it with sister Charmeen) is done in pink and purple. I can't think why I had to invent that revolting detail. I'm getting a bit tired of inventing things—or, anyway, of trying to remember them all. I've been avoiding Dr. Edmonds, rather, so as not to be drawn out. I seem maddeningly unable to draw *him* out, at least about Mrs. Dunningham. Nobody seems to want to talk about Mrs. Dunningham—for some not so strange reason! But I've got to get some kind of information soon, or I'll have nothing to tell Uncle Frosty at the end of my three weeks.

19th June . . . Mr. David Kulka does *not* like sugared doughnuts, so he informed me today in his least endearing manner. Really, the man is impossible! I don't see why Helen can't wait on him once in a while. Scared of him, I daresay. Well, I'm not. Exactly. I've written him off as a source of information, though—I don't even *want* to talk to him. He doesn't come in often anyhow, just for lunch sometimes, or with Dr. Edmonds for coffee. Actually, I don't see much of any of the legatees, except Sherry, and he is an eel for avoiding certain subjects. Mr. Bruce is around all day, but I never saw a man so hard to detect anything about. He's always the same—courteous, grave, even-tempered, unapproachable, and unreadable. The more I see of him, the less I know of him, the "him" who's underneath that whatever you call it—cover-up—he wears. Domino, that's the word. That kind of dark, long medieval-friar cloak that characters in Regency novels are always wearing to masquerade balls. Handy things. You could put one on right over your clothes, pull the hood up, and go to the ball looking so anonymously like all the other people in dominoes that nobody would ever guess you were a duke. Or a pickpocket.

That's what Mr. Bruce reminds me of, a man in a domino. Only who's underneath?

Only twice so far have I heard him say anything unexpected. Once was that first day at work, when he surprised me with the little speech about Mr. Ansley and the human race. The other time was yesterday. The noon rush and personality kid Milton were both going off duty, having combined in a really special effort to drive me mad. I'd just stepped on my own toe to avoid Milton's parting towel flip and was standing on one foot, rubbing the other and longing to choke him, when somebody—Rose, I thought—came up behind me. I said, "Who does that cove think he is, anyhow, a human being or something?" Instead of Rose, Mr. Bruce answered, in an apologetic sort of voice. "I don't believe he does—not yet. He still needs to pretend he's several inches taller. But his father's tall. And Milton's still growing. Be about a year more before we can tell." Before I could think of anything to say, he added, "I know he's a trial," smiled dimly, and wandered on into the kitchen.

Today I asked Sherry if he knew Mr. Bruce very well. He said, "Not very, why?" I said I just wondered, and that Mr. Bruce sure was reserved, wasn't he, and that I couldn't figure him out. "Never mind, he's probably got you figured out by now," Sherry said. I don't think he meant anything in particular by it, but at the time it made me drop the subject fast and start casually wiping my way down the counter away from him—still without having found out a thing about Mr. Bruce. Sherry merely lowered his nose into one of his formidable paperbacks and went on reading. And that got me wondering which of us had dropped the subject after all.

20th June . . . Thursday—my second day off. Naturally, it rained, though not very seriously. Didn't know quite what to do with myself. Took a walk around the college, came back in time for the mail (nothing for me), took a bus to town and renewed my hairdo and my acquaintance with Opyl—whom I found *entirely* different from the Georgetta I've been creating, but I guess it doesn't matter— and wound up dining in lonely spendor at an American version of a Lyons' Corner House, then seeing a film. I think the film might have been good if I'd had somebody to laugh with; as it was, I left in the middle and came home and poked around in Mrs. Dunningham's bookshelves for something to read. Not much choice except things I've read half a dozen times already, or things I was in no mood for, or that *Guide to the British Isles*, which is redundant to say the least. I did find out one thing—the books are no secondhand lot of left-overs, they were hers. Her name's on the flyleaf of most of them, in a little spidery old-lady script.

I wonder what Sherry does with his evenings? He often walks home from work with me, sits on the steps and talks, but never sug-gests doing anything later.

24th June . . . Here it is Monday of my third week and I *still* haven't found out one useful thing about that dotty, elusive old lady, though I know her cuckoo clock's character like the palm of my hand. It's not that I don't try. In fact, this afternoon I abandoned all subtlety and asked Sherry straight out if he'd known the lady who used to live in my room. Here's how the dialogue went:

SHERRY (*placidly stirring his coffee*): Mrs. Dunningham? Yeah, I knew her. Why?

ME: Oh—well, nothing. I mean, can't a person ask a simple question? (*Merry laugh, business of twisting my side curl.*) I just got to wondering what she was like, that's all.

SHERRY: Oh, what she was *like*. But that's not a simple question.

ME: I don't see why not.

SHERRY: Well, she was a very complicated person. You can't ask a simple question about a complicated subject, Greensleeves. Now you take electronics. If I asked—

ME: If it's all the same to you, I don't *want* to take electronics. All I said was—

SHERRY (*quickly*): OK, we'll approach the whole thing from another angle. Now if I asked you what time a certain Pan-Am flight gets into London airport, that would be a very complicated question, because right off you'd have to know whether I meant what time was it *here* when the plane got there, or what time was it *there* when the plane got there—and that would bring up a lot of allied matters such as daylight saving time and the Greenwich Observatory, and it might take you half an hour to give me a real answer. But if I merely asked, "What time is it?" you could merely tell me, see? That's a simple question. Let's try it once. What time is it, Greensleeves?

ME (*resigned sigh, glance at my watch*): Five after two. *Why?*

SHERRY: Now, I'm glad you asked that. It— (*Grabs my wrist to look at my watch himself.*) Holy smoke, is it really that late? Well, whaddya know, I've got a class five minutes ago. (*On his feet, swallowing coffee.*) To be continued in our next. So long. (*Slaps dime down on counter, scoops up books, launches self toward door, then stops in mid-launch and turns slowly back. Picks up my wrist again, then releases it and gives me extremely odd look.*) Mighty nice watch you have there, Greensleeves.

Well, he was gone before I'd got through staring at my wrist myself, in a perfect panic. It certainly is a nice watch; I don't think they even *have* this sort outside of Switzerland. And Georgetta's dad, who as I remember runs a petrol station, would not by the maddest chance have just dashed impulsively over to Zurich to buy it there—a point Sherry has no doubt been pondering all afternoon. So now what kind of story do I invent? Or should I just ignore the whole thing, pretend it's a brand they sell at the five-and-dime, and hope he'll forget it?

And I still haven't learned anything about Mrs. Dunningham.

25th June . . . Sherry never even glanced at my watch today or behaved as if anything had happened. Tempest in a teapot. Thank heaven.

26th June . . . A drizzly day. Very much like England, this climate, but rain doesn't seem to depress me here as it used to there. Anyway, it cleared off about sundown, and now the garden is shining in that pale summer-evening light. Our Mr. Kulka does a superb job on the garden. I'll give him that—he and the tall, elderly lady from the house on the next street, the one I saw from the window my first day here. Mrs. Greenthumb, I call her—don't know her name. Every day, rain or no, she's out there snipping and grubbing and pruning. Even this morning when it was wettest, there she was in raincoat and boots, mucking about the rosebushes with a pair of clippers or something. She's a real gardening buff—or else as dotty as Mrs. D.

This afternoon I was laughing at some remark of Sherry's when without warning he leaned forward, peered at me interestedly, and said, "Well, what do you know! I didn't think girls had dimples any more—haven't seen one in years." !!! Sticky few minutes. He was nice afterwards, though . . .

I daresay that last entry needs explaining. I do have a dimple, a lone, asymmetrical one, which after years of trying I've learned to forget. My mother has two, and on her they're enchanting, flashing in and out of those full cheeks of hers—but then, my mother's the midnight-and-gardenias type on whom anything looks enchanting. I'm rather more the sunflower-at-high-noon sort, like my dad. Let somebody remind me of my dimple, and I instantly feel like a cart horse with a bow behind its ear. Sherry's remark had the usual effect—just curled me into a tight little wad inside, like a threatened sow bug. I muttered something about getting back to work and beat a retreat down toward the ice-cream bins.

Sherry lounged to his feet—he never appeared to be moving fast—and a second later was leaning on the counter opposite me. "I'm sorry, Greensleeves. Did I step on a toe or something?"

"Hmp'mm. Time I got busy, that's all."

"No, that's not all," he observed, but he didn't pursue it, just studied me thoughtfully, then began talking about something else. A few minutes later, just before he gathered up his books and drifted out, he bent toward me confidentially and whispered, "Greensleeves, I don't want to argue, but I *like* your dimple."

What with his hanging about the Rainbow so much, Sherry and I were getting rather well acquainted. That is, I was getting acquainted with him. He was only getting acquainted with Georgetta—a small fact that gave me some large headaches later.

I finally did have a bit of luck with my sleuthing, later that same afternoon. I was drying coffee cups and staring idly at the six big flower prints that hung in a row over the booths across the room. They were remarkably interesting, the colors delicate and the line crisp, and the subjects weren't the usual roses or camellias—they seemed to be some kind of wildflowers. Wondering if they might be reproductions of sketches by somebody famous, I went over to look at them more closely, and discovered they weren't prints at all, but pen-and-ink drawings touched with watercolor. I couldn't see any signature, craning up at them like that, and I still couldn't identify the flowers. One was a plume-shaped affair, actually seedpods; another looked for all the world like the dog fennel Aunt Doris is always eradicating from her flower beds. Dr. Edmonds came in just then and saw me looking.

"Like them?" he said as he slid into the booth by the front windows. I said yes, but I guessed I didn't know much more about flowers than I knew about art, because that one kept looking like dog fennel.

"It is dog fennel," he announced. "And that next one's Queen Anne's lace. And the third one's burdock." (That was the plume-shaped thing.) "They're weeds, all of them. That's Dave Kulka's passion—weeds."

Naturally, my ears came up like a terrier's. "Dave *Kulka* did these?" I said.

"Yes, indeed, He's done hundreds—chiefly pen-and-ink like these, but lithographs too, and a lot of etchings. It's cheaper to buy copper for etching plates than lithograph stones of the proper quality, he tells me. He's allowed to use the presses over at the college—after class hours, of course. It's quite an involved process . . ."

I didn't care about the process, because I wanted to get back to Dave Kulka and the weeds, but I heard about it anyway, in a concise, professorial little lecture.

"Yes, Dave's an expert in his field," Dr. Edmonds wound up neatly, making me feel that the class bell was about to ring. "He's probably made at least a pencil sketch of half the varieties of weed in this part of Oregon. Finds a lot of hidden beauty in them, doesn't he?"

"Um-hm. But where does all this fit in with his gardening? Those *neat* flower beds—"

But the lecture was over. Dr. Edmonds shot out his wrist to consult his watch. "Yes, no weeds allowed there. The fact is, it *doesn't* fit, just at present. Well, Miss Greensleeves, I've a class in eleven minutes, but I think I can work in a little nourishment first—say, coffee and a maple bar?"

So that ended that. Of course, I cornered Dave Kulka himself the minute I got a chance, which was a day or so after. It was easy to bring the subject up—all I had to do was tell him how zingy I thought his flower pictures were; but it wasn't easy to get an answer more informative than "thanks." In fact, that's all he said, "Thanks," and the word was curt and final, accompanied by a glance that reminded me rather less of Renaissance Madonnas and rather more of Renaissance Borgias.

I said, "You're welcome," stared back at him with a defiant snap of my gum, and went away. Obviously, I'd never find out anything from Mr. Kulka.

It was discouraging. It was infuriating, because my three weeks' trial period would be up the next day. I sat thinking about it that night in Mrs. Dunningham's big old armchair and simply lost my temper. I liked my job, I liked my room, I liked my cuckoo clock and being Georgetta Greensleeves Einszweiler Smith, and neither Dave Kulka nor anybody else was going to make me give them up. I stalked over to the desk that minute, found some note-paper, and wrote belligerently:

Dear Uncle Frosty:

Dr. William Edmonds is a math professor at Fremont College. George Sherrill is a student in his junior year. Wynola Jackson is the landlady's daughter. Miss Heater is a mouse with a pink handkerchief who lives in the room above mine. David Kulka is an artist-gardener with an incomprehensible passion for weeds and the world's surliest manners. The books in my room all have Mrs. Dunningham's name in them.

My cuckoo clock used to be hers, too. I can't find any clues in either books or clock. I don't yet know who Mrs. Sarah Hockins and Mr. Brick Mulvaney are, or whether they're alive or dead or moved to Tasmania. I don't know a thing more about Mr. Bruce than I did when I last saw you. In fact, I don't know anything at *all*, but I *intend* to before I'm much older, and I'm *staying right here*, so forget about hiring a detective, because I'm It.

Yours truly,
G. Einszweiler Smith

I walked down to the corner and mailed it before I went to bed.

2

The more I got into my stride at the Rainbow, the more I found evenings hanging on my hands. A good time to get chummy with the lodgers, I kept telling myself—only they never seemed to be around. When I got home from work, they were still finishing dinner, and by the time I'd bathed and changed, they'd vanished. They were chummy enough with one another; several times I heard conversation and laughter from Miss Heater's room, which was just above mine. But I was never invited to these *kaffeeklatsches* or whatever they were. My evenings were strictly my own and the cuckoo's, and so were my days off.

It was on one of these, the last Thursday in June, that I found out who Mrs. Greenthumb was. Since it was pouring, I just pottered about doing my nails and catching up my journal; didn't even get dressed until noon, and made myself another breakfast instead of going out to lunch. Then, keeping a movie magazine handy to snatch up in case anybody came in—unlikely chance—I once more combed through Mrs. Dunningham's peculiar library. I had to read *something* and hadn't dared bring in any other books, reasoning that

Georgetta would be the sort who always intended to read but never had the time. I'm the sort who has to mind what I'm about, or I never have time for anything else.

I settled down with one of the books on archaeology, reflecting that spinach was good for you, whether you were mad for it or not, and, in fact, was learning some rather interesting bits about Stonehenge when I heard a key rattle in my door and Wynola came in with a stack of towels. Naturally, she'd thought nobody was home, and when she saw me there, reading my movie magazine— I was by then sitting rather breathlessly on the archaeology book— she stopped, as horrified as if she'd interrupted the Duchess of Windsor in her bath.

"Come in, it's OK," I told her cordially. "Want me to get rid of those for you?"

"Oh, no. Thanks. I'll only be a minute," she said in her little tiny voice, and scurried toward the bathroom.

"Gee, take your time, honey. Here, I'll move that screen."

I got up to conceal my kitchenette, trying to think of something to talk about so she'd linger and perhaps be coaxed to impart a bit of information. While I was there near the window, I glimpsed Mrs. Greenthumb in her raincoat, snipping away, and for lack of anything else, I said, "Our neighbor sure is a bug on gardening, isn't she? Out in this downpour. You'd think she'd catch her death."

"Who?" Wynola emerged, looking flattered to be spoken to, and followed my glance out the window. "Oh, Mrs. Hockins. Yes, y'would. But I guess she never does."

"Mrs.—what did you say her name was?"

"Mrs. Sarah Hockins. She's a widow—she lives in that house back there. She was a real good friend of . . ." Sharp pause, followed by unintelligible mumble.

"Of who, honey?" I said with an innocent smile.

"Oh—just the lady who used to—have this room. Mrs. Dunningham. Well, I better run along."

"Oh, stick around. I'm not doing anything."

The rose color came flushing up under that pretty, clear olive skin, and Wynola threw me a glance that seemed as pleased as it was scared, but she was backing toward the door at the same time, saying, "Thanks, I couldn't. I have to—I have ironing. Thanks." Next minute she was gone.

I stood surveying the closed door, thinking, Well, nice try, anyway—I suppose. I glanced at my archaeology book half under the chair cushion, then out the back window at the steady rain and Mrs. Hockins out in it. Then I sighed, told myself I hoped I knew where my duty lay, and struggled into my raincoat.

The garden was just as soggy as it had seemed from inside my nice cozy room, but I went out anyway, trying to look as if it were quite normal to stroll about admiring roses in a downpour. It was at least as normal as to prune them under such conditions, which was what Mrs. Hockins was doing. She had a big basket half full of unwanted bits, and was so busy collecting more that she didn't hear me come up behind her.

"My, those pink ones sure are pretty," I said chattily.

She turned to stare at me, not unnaturally. "Oh. Good afternoon."

"Not very, I guess, is it? But they say Oregonians are half duck."

She gave me a quarter-inch smile and murmured something polite but baffled. I could scarcely blame her. Obviously, she had no notion who I was or where I'd sprung from, felt little enthusiasm for bright-blue eyelids and none for conversation at the moment.

I took a long, desperate breath, eased around with my back to the direction the rain was driving from, and asked her what kind of roses those yellow ones were, then what kind the big white ones were, then said didn't roses have funny names sometimes though, and she said yes, or maybe it was just that they were named after funny people. Of course I laughed merrily, to encourage her, but she only smiled another quarter of an inch and looked at a dead bloom nearby and at the clippers in her old, fragile, veined hands. I said roses must be quite a hobby with her. Then I couldn't think of another solitary thing to say about roses, and Mrs. Hockins asked if I weren't getting my feet awfully wet out here. I said I always had liked to walk in the rain, which she didn't believe any more than I did.

I had one more go at it and told her where I lived. "The room that used to be Mrs. What's-Her-Name's—Dunningham's. Wynola says you knew her pretty well."

Her face changed a bit at that, but she seemed to draw even further into herself. "Yes. Yes, Mrs. Dunningham was my friend." She looked past me toward my windows, turning the clippers over and over, slowly, in her hands. "I've often had tea in that room, winter afternoons. I miss her."

"I'm sure," I murmured. I wanted to say, Come have tea with me sometime—but I simply couldn't bring myself to it. She was being civil enough, but she wanted my company about as much as she wanted mildew on her roses. Suddenly, I felt frightfully sorry for her, without knowing just why. I uttered one or two other inanities, to which she responded patiently, while her eyes wandered back to the roses. She couldn't resist just clipping one dead bunch that had been worrying her. So I let the conversation die its natural and overdue death, wandered on to stare at some other flowers while my feet got even wetter, and finally returned to the house, feeling frustrated and discouraged and queerly snarled up inside. On my way down the back hall, I met Dr. Edmonds and Dave Kulka emerging from the kitchen, talking animatedly. Dr. Edmonds said hello and gave me one of his brisk, bracing little nods; Dave Kulka glowered scornfully, as usual. Both of them walked straight past me to the stairs.

I went into my room, shed my soggy shoes and raincoat, and eyed my reflection in the glass. "To what, Miss Smith," I asked it, "do you owe your overwhelming popularity? Your magnet-like attraction for people of all ages, who keep following you about in clusters, eager to tell you the story of their lives? Would you mind describing for the *Courier*—"

I dropped that and put some dry shoes on and found my place in the archaeology book. But I couldn't put my mind to it now; I kept looking out the window at Mrs. Hockins puttering about her roses, or thinking how brightly impersonal Dr. Edmonds' friendliness was beginning to seem. The truth is, I was fighting off a kind of panic. It looked as if Georgetta were turning out as friendless as Shan Lightley, and knew just as little what to do about it, and were just as incapable of getting next to people, much less sleuthing. When the cuckoo flung himself out to remind me I'd spent a full half hour getting soaked for absolutely nothing, I came near hurling a shoe at him.

Instead, I went out to the front hall to see if the mail had come and found a letter from Dad, sent on by Miss Jensen in a discreet white envelope to cover the British postmark and stamps. He said Charlie Frost had baldly ordered him to leave me alone to work something out by myself for once, and that he would—having been presented with a *fait accompli* that left him precious little choice. But might he say one thing—that a girl like me without a college education was like a fiddler without one hand. If I would just believe that, this incomprehensible balkiness of mine—mere matter of adjustment, probably—would vanish, and I could get on with things. Then he quit grumbling and muttering and said he hadn't a doubt I'd work things out and do it well, since I succeeded at everything I tried.

I stared a moment at that last remark, wondering if it were possible Dad had sort of forgotten whom he was writing to, just for a minute. Or if he'd just wanted to make encouraging noises and hadn't noticed how peculiarly unsuitable these were. Or if he could possibly, conceivably, have failed to grasp any better than that what I was all about. Of course the irony of the remark's coming at this precise moment was pure coincidence. But just what Dad might mean by "succeeded"—my high marks at school, maybe?—I couldn't imagine. The whole thing was as unaccountable as if he had forgotten my name.

I gave it up and read the rest of the letter—eagerly, because it seemed a long time since I'd heard. He said he and Jeanne were in London, along with half the rest of the international press, because of the Cabinet crisis (which he assumed, erroneously, I'd read all about), that Jeanne had a new camera, that they'd just lunched with Harlan Manning of the *Chicago Trib*, whom I would probably remember . . .

Whom I would *probably* remember, I thought incredulously. I was dumbfounded again at how little Dad seemed to remember about *me*. Had he forgotten my thirteenth birthday, when he and Jeanne were delayed ten hours in reaching Copenhagen, and Harlan took me to Tivoli for the day? Had he forgotten who finally found my passport that time in Rijeka? Who once taught me how to say "scram" in fourteen languages? Who . . . well, obviously he had. But I had not.

"And, Shan, Willy Bach is here, out of the hospital at last. He says Franz was six-feet-one last time he measured. Jeanne sends her love and asks if you want her to send some of those shoes from Harrod's—I assume you'll know what she's talking about. I phoned your mother just now to see if she had a message for you, and she did—you must absolutely catch her new film when it comes to Portland. I'm sorry, Shan, she's just that way, nobody can do anything about it, though God knows I tried. Well, so long, Luv, we're going to run down to Beckenham to Ann and Kingsley's for the weekend, and it's time to get moving. Love and lots of it, Dad."

I came out of the letter slowly, the way you come out of an anesthetic, and looked about the stranger's room where I was sitting and wondered what I was doing there, anyway—what I was doing in Portland, what I was doing in the States. For a minute I was so shocking homesick to see Dad and Jeanne, or Harlan or Franz or even Ann and Kingsley Benton-Jones, whom actually I can't stand, that I thought I'd just break down and howl. I'd even have settled for Mother, right that instant, and if the film had been in town, I'd have gone to it.

However it wasn't, so I folded the letter and went over to hide it under my underwear in the dresser. As I shut the drawer, I caught sight of Georgetta in the glass—hairdo, eye shadow, rhythmically moving jaw—and instead of howling ended up laughing. I don't know why, but it cheered me up—particularly when the cuckoo popped out at that moment to say exactly what I was thinking. Moreover, the rain had stopped, and there was even a feeble ray of almost-sunshine glimmering out there in the wet garden. And Sherry, at least, seemed to like my company, even if he *didn't* ask me out. One of these days I might even find the nerve to invite Mrs. Hockins to tea.

I slung on my cardigan humming, ". . . merrie sing cuccu"— now there was *one* thoroughly cheerful medieval song—and went out and walked hard for an hour and breathed a lot of damp fresh air. By the time I got back, my morale was up to normal. The day hadn't really been wasted. I'd identified Mrs. Hockins, thanks to Wynola. I'd identified all the legatees now, except the elusive Brick Mulvaney. I wondered if Wynola might know him, too. At that point I had a brilliant inspiration—I'd ask *Wynola* to tea on my next day off.

3

My next day off happened to fall on July 4, but I had no other engagements (as I scarcely need mention), and if Wynola did, she broke them.

She put on her best dress to come to tea. It was rose-colored linen, exactly the shade of that tint along her cheekbones, and it was well cut and slimming. In spite of her bushy hair and large black oxfords, the overall improvement was considerable, and my admiring comment was quite sincere.

"Oh, thank you. Do you really like it?" she breathed, and became almost pretty for a minute.

"Mm-hm. Where'd you buy it?"

"Well, I—it was a present. Mrs. Dunningham—" She stopped, flushed, and subsided into a chair as if she wished it would go on through the floor with her.

"Mrs. Dunningham what?" I asked carelessly, on my way to the kitchenette.

"Nothing. She gave me the dress, is all."

"Well, how nice!"

There was a small silence, which I filled with cup rattling and a chummy smile over my shoulder. Wynola was clenching her hands together and looking as guilty as if she'd stolen the crown jewels. I decided that now was the time to break this conspiracy of silence and asked straight out what Mrs. Dunningham had been like.

"Oh, I'm *sorry*," Wynola burst out in a desperate but still tiny voice. "I didn't mean to *mention* her, even. We all said we wouldn't."

"You did? But why?"

"Well—because of you. Mom and Dr. Edmonds . . . I mean, *everybody* thought it'd be—just better. If we didn't talk a lot about her in front of you."

This was going incredibly well. What a job lot of crooks—and they didn't seem like crooks at all, really, especially Dr. Edmonds. Or old Mrs. Hockins. Or *Sherry*.

All of a sudden the whole thing simply revolted me—what they had done, what I was doing. I wished I'd never heard of College Street, never met any of these people, and were on my way to Madagascar. I jammed the lid onto my biscuit tin, plastered a smile on my face, and carried the tea tray over to the little table between the two chairs.

"Well, gee, why shouldn't you talk about her?" I asked brightly. "I been kind of wondering why her stuff is still here, and all. You'd think her relations would come get her things."

"She—she wanted her things to stay here. To belong to this room. She gave them to my mom."

"Hm! That's funny. Most people would want their own family to have their things. If they *have* any family." There. I'd slid in my dratted wily question.

"Yes," Wynola said uninformatively. She took the cup of tea I handed her and added, as if she couldn't stop herself, "She wasn't like most people."

I thought this an understatement, but I merely smiled encouragingly and passed the sugar.

"Oh, I quit using sugar. I promised Mrs. Dun— I mean, I can't." Wynola sank back, crimson, and folded her lips, whereupon the conversation dropped dead. No matter what I did, I could get nothing out of her but monosyllables accompanied by small, agonized smiles intended to show me how much she was enjoying herself. And suddenly I just couldn't pump her any longer—I felt too sorry for her. I started talking about my sister Charmeen, and she began to relax a bit. Once she actually laughed, and I was feeling quite successful—though not as a detective—when I got some unexpected help from the cuckoo, who popped out to announce that it was three o'clock. I said, "That bird is always telling me I'm crazy. And at the most appropriate moments."

Wynola's whole face lighted up. "Oh, do you feel that way, too? That's why Mrs. Dunningham liked cuckoo clocks—she said they kept a person reminded of the ridiculousness of the human race."

It was so obviously a direct quote that I felt the old lady's ghost had sailed right in the window and joined the conversation. I said involuntarily, "She sounds like fun."

"Oh, yes, I—she—" Wynola was heading for her shell again.

"Look, honey," I said. "I wish you'd just cut loose and tell me all about Mrs. Dunningham. You want to talk about her, and I want you to. I can't see why anybody'd tell you not to."

"Because—it might make you feel bad."

Whatever I'd been expecting, it wasn't that. I said blankly, "Make *me* feel bad? How could it?"

Her face cleared; she was practically glowing all of a sudden. "I *told* Mom you weren't like that. But she said she knew how it was to come from a small town and not to know anybody, and if we all kept talking about Mrs. Dunningham this and Mrs. Dunningham that, you'd think we were always *comparing*. But we wouldn't have been, only she was just so wonderful, and—"

"Wait a minute," I said. "You mean—the idea was not to *hurt my feelings*?"

"Yes," Wynola said simply.

I felt as if I'd sat down on a chair that somebody had just removed. Then in a second my brain got working again, and I realized this was just what they'd told Wynola, who obviously believed it and knew nothing about the swindle. But then I remembered Mrs. Jackson's remark to me about coming from a small town herself—but *then* I tried in vain to imagine Dave Kulka being delicately solicitous of my sensitive feelings—and, well, I was very busy thinking for a minute. Meanwhile, I held out the plate of macaroons and muttered, "Have another biscuit." Wynola looked a bit startled, and I came out of my trance in a hurry. "Cookie, I mean," I added with a tossed-off little laugh.

"You know, in England everybody calls cookies 'biscuits.' Mrs. Dunningham told me when she came home," Wynola said, gazing at the macaroons hungrily but not taking any. "Thanks, but I'm supposed to be on a diet. Mrs. Dunningham said I'd be a different girl if I lost twenty pounds. I did lose six, but after she died—well, I kind of gained them back."

"She went to England? You mean while she lived here?"

"Yes, last summer. Not by herself, she knew she was kind of—well, old—to go alone, so that's why she took Sherry along, to look after the—"

"She took who?" I said in a thin high soprano.

Wynola looked mildly surprised at my surprise. "One of the college students, George Sherrill. I thought you might have met him over at the Rainbow."

"Oh. Mm-hm, I have," I said, collecting myself and making an upper-case, underscored mental note to grill Sherry about this at the first opportunity. Meanwhile, I saw another opening. "I was only thinking it was funny she wouldn't take one of her own relatives."

"I guess she didn't have any," Wynola said without much interest. "At least, I never heard her mention them. Maybe they'd all died or something." She thought a minute, while I was awarding myself a small medal for having finally got a definite statement on this subject, then she added, "That must've been it. Because she said once she'd been waiting fifty years to see Stonehenge, and she'd just realized there was nothing stopping her. You know about Stonehenge? It's a queer kind of—"

"I've heard of it," I said cautiously.

"There's a whole book here about it that she used to read me out of. She used to read me *Grimm's Fairy Tales*, too." Wynola glanced at me defensively. "You might think I was too old for those, but *she* read them herself, all the time. She said fairy tales were good for people."

"Good for people? How?"

"Well—*she* said, 'Same way helium is good for a balloon.'"

I was beginning to be delighted with Mrs. Dunningham, dotty old lady or not. I filled Wynola's cup, remarking, "This is her tea we're drinking—I found it on the shelf."

"Oh, I know it's hers. I recognized the taste." Wynola smiled tremulously, let her eyes wander around the room, and said it seemed so natural to be sitting in this chair again, drinking this tea out of these yellow cups, and that Mrs. Dunningham used to say it was the best way to get acquainted with somebody, over a teacup. "I don't know why she wanted to get acquainted with *me*," Wynola added as if she'd never ceased to be dumbfounded about it. "Nobody else ever has. But she used to invite me to tea just like a grownup and ask me what I thought about things and all, just like she was really interested. Mom used to say, 'Watch out you don't get hurt. People are nice just so long as it suits them and no longer,' and that's right, I guess. But Mrs. Dunningham was always nice. I guess it kept on suiting her."

"What was she like, Wynola? What'd she look like?"

"Oh, she was a real *little* lady. I'd of made five of her," Wynola said in a wistful voice that made me suddenly wish I were over-weight myself, just to keep her company. "But she never did make me feel big and fat and clumsy like most people do. She made me feel like I was just about her size. She even made me feel—" Wynola stopped and gave an embarrassed laugh. "Oh—I don't know what I started to say. Anyhow, she was real tiny, and she had brown eyes, and—you know, white hair—I can't describe her."

I thought I knew what she'd started to say. That Mrs. Dunningham had even made her feel she could be attractive if she'd lose that twenty pounds and gain some confidence instead. The more she talked—and she was fairly launched, now—the clearer picture I got of a lonely, self-conscious, homely girl getting her first taste of hope from this queer but kind old woman, who had made her feel she could do what she liked if only she believed in herself and tried. I also gathered—from frequent quotes of what Mom Always Says—that Wynola's mother had taught her just the opposite. Maybe she was trying to protect Wynola from the sort of lumps she'd had to take herself; anyway, she'd warned her over and over not to expect any luck in life, not to expect anything.

"Mom always says a person who sets his heart on something is just stupid. She says if you don't want anything, you don't mind when you don't get anything. I guess she's right. But—"

"But you've got your heart set on something anyway?"

"Well—yes, but it's silly." Wynola glanced at me and blurted it out. "An airline stewardess. I always did wish I could be an airline stewardess. But gee, they've got to be so slim and pretty and all and have a lot of training, and—"

"So get slim and take the training! There's no rule that says you've got to be a raving beauty." Wynola looked at me big-eyed and swallowed, and I couldn't help it, I went on. "Besides, you might look entirely different once you lost that weight."

I suddenly realized I wasn't talking much like Georgetta, but Wynola was too hypnotized by what I was saying to notice how I was saying it. "*Entirely* different?" she repeated.

"Well, different enough," I said, resuming my Midwestern twang. "You ought to've seen my sister Charmeen before *she* got slim. You couldn't even find her waistline. Besides, her hair was all— Say, have you always worn your hair that way?"

"Oh, I know it's awful." Wynola's hand flew self-consciously to her hair as she glanced admiringly at mine. "I don't know how to do hair. Not even after I finally got my permanent. And that's nearly grown out now anyway, so—"

"I don't think you ought to have permanents," I told her, trying to envision her without the frizz. "Say, come over to the mirror a minute—let me try something."

I know it was idiotic. I should have ignored Wynola's beauty problems and got on with my detecting. But I couldn't resist finding out how she'd look with that whole bushy mass cleared away. I brushed and brushed until I'd tamed the top, then pulled the rest back into a ponytail and kept it there with a rubber band. The tail part now closely resembled a thorn bush. But the effect from side and front was good and revealed the fact that she had a nice turn to her chin. The severity only needed softening and her forehead covering.

I said, "I bet you'd look good in bangs."

Wynola was staring, fascinated, at her reflection. "Cut some and let's see," she breathed.

"Me? Oh, I might ruin you. Besides, you ought to have the back cut, too. Real short. With just a little dab in front of your ears."

"Cut it. Go on. I don't care if it ruins me or not!"

– 129 –

Our eyes met recklessly in the looking glass. I said, "OK, but for heaven's sake get it trimmed up later at a hairdresser's."

"I will, I promise! Go ahead."

I did—I couldn't resist her. Well, I'm no Opyl. Naturally, I hacked up the back something shocking, but I left enough so that it wasn't beyond professional rescue. And even rough, the effect was a good one—clean and simple and off her neck, which immediately looked less thick. She did not turn into a beauty. But when you've a lot of pounds, you simply don't need a lot of hair, and any pruning would have improved her. She was tremendously excited—less about her hair than about the fact that I was fussing over her, I think. Her eyes had begun to have a worshiping expression when they turned my way.

As soon as I noticed this, I began to feel uncomfortable; then guilty because I'd fooled away another half hour of spying time on beauty counseling and undoubtedly needed *my* head examined. While Wynola helped sweep the clippings off the floor, she chattered happily about how surprised everybody would be, and how wonderful I was to take so much trouble, and how sure she was that she'd lose ten pounds by mid-July—and I tried to get back on the subject of Mrs. Dunningham. Suddenly, she did it for me.

". . . and then maybe I'll have those sky-diving lessons, only I don't see how I could ever learn to do that—it's so—"

"What kind of lessons?" I said, so abruptly that I rattled her.

"Oh—nothing. I probably won't get to do it—" She laughed self-consciously and started backsliding into the old Wynola, but I caught her before she got there, and soon she was telling me all about it. "Well, Mrs. Dunningham and I saw this *exciting* thing on Miss Heater's TV once—these people would dive out of an *airplane* just like you'd dive off a diving board. Only lots more gracefully . . . I don't know, they sort of *flew*, and soared, and—it was like sea gulls.

Then their parachutes would open, and they'd float down, and it was just *wonderful*."

I gathered this was a performance by experienced instructors she'd seen; both she and Mrs. Dunningham had been entranced. Later they'd seen a follow-up program about the students these instructors taught—ordinary nonacrobatic people, who'd *still* behaved like a lot of gulls, and this had not entranced Wynola—it had depressed her. *She* couldn't even dive into a swimming pool. She was fat. The kids at school thought she was a creep. She *was* a creep. She couldn't do *anything*. And so on. Mrs. Dunningham had said, "Nonsense, you never know what you can do until you try. You could do this sky diving if somebody taught you and you practiced." Wynola had said no she couldn't, either; she was too fat and clumsy, and anyway she just couldn't. Mrs. Dunningham had said she probably wouldn't *be* fat if she took up sky diving in earnest, but of course nobody could do anything if they wouldn't even try.

"And I said did she think sky diving would really—well, *do* something for me, if I tried. Make me more interesting," Wynola told me earnestly. "And she said no, not the sky diving. But the *try-ing* would. Do you think that's so, Georgetta?"

"I don't know. Maybe so." I was too startled to think it through. "Was that all she said about it?"

"That's all, she never mentioned it again. But—she left me some money, in her will. For sky-diving lessons. Maybe she was just—sort of joking. Anyway, Dr. Edmonds said I mustn't count on that working out. And Mom says—" She was frowning and studying her fingernails. Suddenly, she stood up. "I better go. I've got to string the beans for dinner." She touched her shorn head and smiled, in an odd, wistful way. "I sure do thank you. For cutting my hair and—just *everything*."

I couldn't get her to stay or say another word about the will. But just as she was leaving, I said, "How did Mrs. Dunningham happen to turn up here, anyway? To rent this room, I mean?"

"Oh, that was just so *lucky*. Mr. Mulvaney just brought her here one day."

I nearly shrieked, "Not *Brick* Mulvaney?" as if he were a long-lost chum of mine, but I restrained myself and asked carelessly who that was.

"He lives down the block a ways; he's a taxi driver. Haven't you ever seen him around the Rainbow? Great big, with red hair—only not like yours, more carroty. Well, 'by, and I sure do *thank* you."

I closed the door, flipped rapidly through my mental pictures of people who came often into the café, and found Brick Mulvaney. At least, I found a great big man—not tall, but bulky—with hair more carroty than mine and a round, jovial face that he was always mopping as he walked in taking off a—yes, a taxi driver's cap. So he'd brought Mrs. Dunningham here in the first place? I'd better ask *him* to tea.

I washed the cups and then sat down with my feet up and just thought for quite a while, about Mrs. Dunningham and Wynola. There was a lot to think about, and when I was finished, I understood some things but was more mixed up than ever about some others. However, I didn't believe Wynola's legacy was a joke—not any more, I didn't. I believed it was a challenge. It looked to me as if that old lady had known she was going to die soon and had searched for some good death-defying way to go right on prodding Wynola to try, to have some gumption, to believe she could do things. It might have worked, too.

The trouble was, Wynola was almost certain not to get that legacy. In a way, it was a shame.

4

It was nearly six o'clock when I finally came out of my trance and took my feet down. I'd had a go at a lot of questions, including Sherry's trip to England with Mrs. Dunningham, and though I'd found no answers, merely having some facts to think *about* gave me a nice brisk feeling of accomplishment. The sole item I never gave another thought to was Wynola's haircut, which says precious little for my woman's intuition.

The day had held good, in weather as well as in my devious little private affairs. Mrs. Hockins was out cutting roses in the fine late sunshine, and two girls in Sherry's boardinghouse next door were dressing to go to a fireworks display that evening—I couldn't see them, but their voices floated out their open windows and into mine. I hoped Sherry wasn't going anywhere except to the Rainbow for dinner as usual, because I wanted a little chat with him about that English trip.

I freshened up a bit and walked down the hall to the front door, where I met Mrs. Jackson coming in with the evening paper. She stopped dead, looking up at me sidewise from under her dark brows, and totally ignored my greeting.

"What right *you* got to cut Wynola's hair?" she demanded.

The attack was so sudden that it caught me unprepared. In fact, I had to scramble about mentally to think what she meant; then I was further off balance because I had no answer. What right *had* I to cut Wynola's hair? Obviously, none whatever.

"Wh—why? Don't you like it?" I said in a slightly shaky voice.

"Never mind. Took her months to grow all that hair! It was a permanent, too. Cost me eight dollars. All cut off now. Just throwed in the wastebasket!"

She was furious. That shook me as much as anything else; I'd never seen her exhibit emotion about anything before.

"I'm terribly sorry," I said, forgetting all about Georgetta's furry r's. My lips felt as stiff and unmanageable as a couple of tongue depressors.

"Lot of good that'll do. Sorry don't put the hair back, does it?"

"No, it doesn't." Suddenly, I was angry, too. "Wynola doesn't want the hair back. And a good job, too—she's a hundred percent better-looking without it."

"None of your business to say whether she is or isn't."

"That's perfectly true," I told her coldly. "I'm saying it anyway. Wynola loved it. It made her *feel* better. More—more hopeful."

"What's *she* got to hope for?" Mrs. Jackson flung at me.

"Whatever she wants to hope for—same as anybody else!" I flung right back. We were both talking rather loudly by now. "Hope doesn't cost anything, does it? Neither does looking and feeling a bit prettier."

"Pretty, with all that hacked-up stuff on her neck?"

That knocked the props from under me. "Of course it'll—it'll have to be evened up by a professional," I faltered.

"*That'll* cost something."

"Well, I'll pay for it! Oh—Mrs. Jackson, didn't you ever cut *your* hair when you were a girl?"

Whether this touched any chord I don't know; she had no ready answer for it, but on the other hand her face didn't change nor her eyes soften. She just seemed to look through me, instead of at me, for a minute.

At this point a light, nervous little laugh sounded from the living-room door just opposite us. "I'm sure I did, many times," Miss Heater said gaily. "My mother despaired of me, I know, but then it's a girl's privilege to change her mind, as everyone admits!"

This little speech failed to hew very fast to logic or even to good sense, but I've seldom been more grateful for anything. We both turned to Miss Heater, who stood, fluttering and beaming, in the doorway. She blinked and nodded and did her best to twinkle reassuringly at both of us as she added, "And really, Mrs. Jackson, Wynola's hair looks quite stylish short, I think. She came and showed me."

"Oh, I'm *so* glad you liked it, Miss Heater," I said fervently.

Mrs. Jackson said nothing, but her hackles more or less subsided, and she turned abruptly and went off, muttering, toward the kitchen. This left Miss Heater and me standing there—rescuer and rescuee—feeling rather close-knit and tremulous about each other, but not knowing precisely how to talk about it. I was still upset and showed it, which probably saved the situation.

"Mrs. Jackson gets a bit cross sometimes. You mustn't worry," Miss Heater said in a comforting undertone. "She only acts this way about Wynola."

"She acts like a dog with a bone about Wynola!"

"Yes. She does, doesn't she? You're quite right."

"No, *she's* quite right," I said distractedly. "I hadn't the least business cutting her hair, even if she doesn't treat her as she ought to. I shouldn't have let her talk me into it."

Wisely making no attempt to sort these pronouns out, Miss Heater advised me again not to worry about it—and I began to realize I hadn't flattened a single vowel during the entire little fracas.

"Well, thanks a lot for sticking up for me," I said, climbing hurriedly back into my characterization.

Miss Heater told me it was nothing and asked me if I were going out to celebrate the Fourth. When I said no, only over to the Rainbow for dinner, her colorless eyebrows lifted in surprise. "Not going to the fireworks display? My, I thought all the young folks were attending that."

"I guess I didn't know about it," I said, feeling awkward. "Probably it'll struggle on without me, though."

I smiled and was backing toward the door when she startled me by stepping forward and putting a hand impulsively on my arm.

"I wonder—would you care to come up to my room later on and watch some fireworks on my TV? It's a special program, *The Glorious Fourth*. Nine o'clock. That is, if you haven't anything else to do, or—"

She appeared to feel a bit awkward herself and broke off with a nervous smile, which changed to a relieved one when I said I'd love to come. "Till nine o'clock, then," she said, and fluttered a hand at me as I left.

Well, what do you know, I asked myself. Miss Heater feels sorry for me.

5

Sherry was in the Rainbow as I'd hoped, studying the menu—can't think why, because he invariably ordered shrimp or steak. I wasn't sure how I meant to invite myself to join him and was too upset to think it out. I simply walked straight over and asked him why he wasn't at a Fourth of July picnic like every other self-respecting, red-blooded American college student.

"Got rid of my self-respect, finally," he answered, lounging to his feet and giving me a welcoming smile followed by a rather penetrating glance. "Why aren't you? Just can't stay away from this place, hm?"

"I'm having dinner, if I can find a place to sit down," I said, looking at the other bench in his booth and not around the café, which was almost deserted. Sherry grinned, dusted the bench with a flourish of his napkin, and I sat down and appropriated the menu. "Are you having shrimp or steak?"

"Chicken," Sherry said gently, just to prove I didn't know as much about him as I thought I did. "What's up, Greensleeves? Somebody's either been pulling your hair or pulling your leg—you look all in the air about something."

He evidently knew a good bit about *me*. I hesitated, then came out with it. "They've been pulling my hair—anyway, Mrs. Jackson has—because I cut Wynola's."

"You cut Wynola's hair? Well, I think that calls for a medal."

"Mrs. Jackson doesn't." I told him the story—an edited version, with my sleuthing activities omitted—adding my uncomfortable suspicion that Wynola was beginning to confuse me with Queen of the May.

"I don't doubt it, inviting her to tea and all. That was a real nice thing to do, Greensleeves."

That made me more uncomfortable, since I knew full well it hadn't been nice of me at all—my original purpose had been espionage, not kindness. "Well, I shouldn't have touched her hair. But, Sherry, it *did* do a lot for her morale." And there was a nice opening, which I seized. "That Mrs. Dunningham, the one who used to live in my room—she did a lot for Wynola's morale, too. Wynola was telling me."

At this point Helen belatedly sloped up to take Sherry's order. She'd been in the kitchen—very likely in front of a looking glass—and hadn't seen me come in. She stopped dramatically at sight of me and clapped a hand to her brow. "Heavens, if I'd *known*," she said in tragic tones. "That you were free this evening. That you could have traded days off with me. I could have been watching those fireworks right now!"

"Not right *now*, could you have, honey? It's not dark yet."

"I thought of course *everybody* would have plans for the Fourth," she went on, drowning me out. "Well, too late. Poor Vince. He was *so* disappointed. I'll have to make it up to him somehow."

"Give him a lock of your hair," I suggested.

Sherry said hastily, "Greensleeves isn't free. She's having dinner with me."

This struck Helen as a charming witticism; she laughed musically, fixed Sherry with a loving gaze, and even glanced my way so we could share our enjoyment of the joke. When I didn't respond noticeably, she managed to get her face straight and was at last persuaded to go fetch us some chicken.

"Gee, you really made her day," I commented, buttering a roll.

Sherry merely said, "Helen better watch out around you. You bite. Go on about Wynola."

Instead, I went on about Mrs. Dunningham, so that I could ask, presently, if he'd ever heard how she happened to come to College Street in the first place. "A taxi driver just *brought* her. Wasn't that lucky for Wynola? Brick Mulvaney, she said his name was. Said he lives around here."

"Next house to mine," Sherry informed me around a drumstick.

"Oh, do you know him?"

"Sure, everybody does. Big red-haired fellow. I'm surprised you haven't run into him. But then he works all day and half the night. Got to, with his setup."

"What setup is that?"

Sherry shrugged commiseratingly. "His wife's an invalid, he's got three children under twelve, and there's this no-good brother-in-law who's been camping on him for years. It's his wife's favorite brother. Pure parasite—but what can you do when your wife has a relapse every time you mention that maybe old Stanley could find himself a job?"

"But does this Mr. Mulvaney support the whole lot?"

"Yes, and it means a lot of taxi driving. He takes exactly three days off every year. Provided he can get free long enough to take them. Goes fishing, usually."

"He *does*," I breathed, trying busily to fit various pieces of jigsaw together. I must have sounded a bit too enthralled with what was, after all, a quite ordinary statement, because Sherry glanced at me in surprise. "I mean, just three days a year and he only goes fishing?" I explained quickly, if a bit lamely. "You'd think he'd want a little excitement."

"He wants a little peace. I guess his home life is exciting enough, what with old Stanley having an attack of the-world's-against-me every time he has to empty the garbage, and then Mrs. Mulvaney having an attack of hysterics for fear old Stanley's going round the bend, and the kids bickering or getting themselves lost or making Mama's headache worse—"

"Sounds to me like Mama ought to get lost. Poor man! Why doesn't he just walk out?"

"He's not the sort. Besides, I suppose he loves them all—except for old Stanley. He's a mighty patient guy." Sherry paused, fork halfway to his mouth, and looked as if he were remembering something interesting, so I said, "What?" and he said, "Oh, I was just thinking. Mrs. Dunningham told me once that everybody ought to get lost at some time in their lives—that it was the only way to find yourself."

I could almost have guessed who'd said that without being told. I was beginning to recognize the style of Mrs. Dunningham's pithy little utterances. "That reminds me! I hear you went all the way to England with her last summer. You might have told me."

"Well, it never came up, Greensleeves. What about it?"

"Well, gee, what was it like?"

"England? Oh, terrific. I really fell for the place, especially the south. And London, naturally. Who was it said that the man who is tired of London is tired of life? Dr. Johnson or somebody. We had a great time in our rented Volkswagen, Mrs. Dunningham and I—she was wonderful to travel with. She liked the south best, too."

"What's in the south?" I asked ignorantly, remembering Wynola's talk about Stonehenge.

Sherry told me Stonehenge was, and Bath, and Wells Cathedral, and Salisbury Plain. "Dartmoor, too—we both like moors. Mrs. Dunningham said every well-organized life ought to have a moor in it somewhere, just for breathing space. More moors and less people, then anybody could get free anytime, just by walking straight ahead."

"Free? I always thought Dartmoor was a prison," I remarked, pretending great interest in my salad.

"It is. That is, there *is* a Dartmoor Prison, a big one, right out in the middle of the moor. But you don't see anything of it from the road except a couple of radio towers and some distant roofs. They don't look like much out there. The moor's a vast place, Greensleeves. The very top of the world—at least, it feels that way—nothing but sky and clouds, closer than usual, and a lot of wild rolling hills with nothing taller than broom growing on them, and sheep and shaggy little ponies wandering around free. Even in the villages, when you happen onto one, the animals graze where they please. No fences. There's signs warning motorists to beware. One of those big black-faced sheep could be a nasty surprise for a Volkswagen, all right."

I decided I'd better go back and have another look at Dartmoor. There was a lot I'd missed. Maybe because I'd never crossed it in a Volkswagen.

"Still," Sherry said reminiscently, "the prison *is* there."

"And what did Mrs. Dunningham say about that?" I knew quite well she'd said something.

Sherry smiled. "That it was just like human beings to try to point out that freedom is an illusion. She didn't believe it was, though. She told me once she'd proved it was real—but you did have to reach out and take it."

You have to jolly well do more than that, I reflected, thinking of Mary's Creek and my erstwhile trap. I wasn't really free of it yet, only on holiday from it. I wondered what Mrs. Dunningham had meant, exactly. I pushed back my plate and said, "How come she took you, anyway?"

"Oh—she was getting on, you know. Her eyes had begun to fail her pretty badly. She needed a Boy Scout to help her across streets and so on."

"But why you? Hadn't she any children of her own? Or any grandchildren?"

Sherry looked faintly surprised. "I guess I don't know. She never mentioned any. Or maybe they weren't Elephant's Children."

Of course I got the allusion, but I said, "Weren't what?" and let Sherry lecture me about Kipling's *Just-So Stories* and especially the Elephant's Child who was so full of *'satiable curtiosity*. "You ought to read more," he said sternly. "Anyway—that's why Mrs. Dunningham *said* she took me, because we were both pure Elephant's Child and ought to get along fine together. We did, too. I wouldn't be surprised if she had me beat for curiosity. She even used to hire Brick Mulvaney to drive her around Portland—all day, just to explore, and find out where all the side streets went. Now, my curiosity stops short of Portland's side streets."

I thought College Street quite a fertile field but didn't say so. Instead, I followed the direction of Sherry's gaze, found my pushed-aside plate at the end of it, and said, "Help yourself." He grinned and started on my untouched drumstick, glancing at his watch at the same time. "You in a hurry or something?" I asked.

"Oh, no—I have to go to work sooner or later, but I've got all night to do that."

"Studying, you mean?"

"No, no. I've got a job. Such as it is."

This was news to me. I asked what kind, and he said purely lower-class menial. He swept out, scrubbed floors, and so on, at

Herndon's Bookstore, a place downtown that sold only paperback books. He went to work any time after the store closed for the night and got off whenever he'd finished. "I'm slow," he admitted. "I keep leaning on my mop looking through the books. They've got about a million I want to read, and I can't *buy* them all, not if I want to get through college. As it is, Herndon's might as well pay my tuition and then give me the rest in books—that's the way it works out. I even go back and hang around there in the daytime and buy some more—when I'm not hanging around *here*." He grinned, tossed the cleaned bone back on my plate, and signaled Helen to bring coffee.

I don't know why it surprised me to find Sherry had a job. I was glad to know it, though. It explained a lot more than those intellectual-looking paperbacks he was always reading—it explained, for instance, why he never asked me out. But imagine. Scrubbing floors half the night, as well as studying more than half the day. "You sure *must* want to get through college," I remarked.

"Well, naturally." Sherry glanced at me, then added lightly, "Might as well finish, now that I've started."

He didn't feel lightly about it, though; having seen our attitudes differed, he'd simply turned his own aside. Maybe it was his tact, but he had me suddenly wondering if I were the one out of step. What if there were something in college for me after all—only I just didn't know what it was yet? What if I never found out what it was until too late to get it? On the other hand, why go to college to get it until I found out what it was? . . . About then I decided my questions were becoming remarkably silly and so complicated that even I couldn't quite follow what I meant.

"Well, it takes all kinds," I said cheerfully, to dismiss the subject. But I didn't feel cheerful, or even triumphant about all the information I'd extracted in the last hour or so. By the time Sherry and I left the Rainbow and started slowly home, I was feeling restless and dislocated and irritable and as if there weren't much point in anything anyhow.

The evening had come really warm, with not a breeze stirring anywhere, and it was that exact time when you can't tell whether it's day or night—it's just an even mixture of the two, with the whole air colored a sort of smudged blue-gray. All down the street were little balls of golden light, and golden figure eights, and zigzags, where little children were waving their Fourth of July sparklers frenziedly around. You could hear the sputtering when another one was lighted, and the high voices of the children, and their dads and mothers telling them to be careful and not poke Jackie in the eye, and so on—the evening was that still.

Sherry and I walked along in silence, then sat on the cracked concrete steps in front of the boardinghouse and watched the infrequent lorries and cars go by, and the children with their sparklers.

"So what *do* you want out of college?" I asked. "Your dad said you had to want something."

"Information," Sherry said.

"No, come on—tell me."

"I did tell you. I want to find out things I might never find out otherwise. Reading books is all very well, but I could read twenty books about integral calculus, for instance, and still not learn much. Somebody's got to pound that sort of thing into me. I'm stupid about math."

"Then *why* do you take integral calculus?"

"That's what I'm telling you," Sherry said patiently. "Because I couldn't imagine what it was all about. Think of going all through life not even knowing what people *mean* when they say 'integral calculus.'"

I thought of it, and it didn't faze me at all, but it seemed to appall Sherry. Apparently, everything he didn't know appalled him until he'd got a few scraps of it for his own. He'd even taken a whole year of private work in Greek—the ancient kind—just to find out how people in those days *sounded when they talked.*

"Who'd you ever find to teach you Greek?" I asked moodily.

"Dr. Edmonds. He's good—a real teacher. Best I've had since I left my dad's English-grammar class. I wish he knew Sanskrit. I'd sure like to find out what Sanskrit sounds like. But nobody teaches that here. Or Anglo-Saxon, either."

"Would Russian be hard enough?" I asked. "But then, you could find out what that sounds like just by moving to Russia, couldn't you?"

"Yeah, I could," Sherry said in an interested tone. I just *looked* at him, and he grinned. "Well, anyway, I can't take it here, because of my major. Nuisance, but you've got to have a major if you want a degree, and you've got to have a degree if you want any postgrad work, and—"

"You mean to take postgrad work on *top* of all this?"

"Oh, that's where you can really browse around, in some good graduate school, like Columbia. They've got courses in everything you can imagine. Besides, I'd like to see what it's like to live in New York for a while. Or Oxford! I'd sure like to know what it's like to go to Oxford."

It sounded as if he meant to go to school all his life. "Are you really going to study at all those places?" I demanded.

He hesitated, then shrugged. "Probably not. Don't see how I can, unless I starve while I'm doing it." He thought a minute. "Oh, well—"

"I know. You'd like to find out how it feels to starve."

He smiled, turned in his lazy way, and studied me. "You think I'm crazy, don't you, Greensleeves?"

"Well—what *use* is all this going to be to you when you're—you know, out in the world and all?"

"Out in the world working on that cereal-box art? Oh, no use. No *practical* use. It's just that I don't want to limit my life to cereal boxes."

"But—" I said, and stopped. No practical use. Where had I heard something like that before, as if I didn't know? Sherry went on talking, but I'd quit listening; I was too busy adding twos and twos into nasty little fours and discovering with unpleasant ease where Mrs. Dunningham had got the idea for her dotty scholarship fund—and just how she'd happened to choose the first beneficiary of it—and how very convenient it was going to be for Sherry if the scheme went through—and a lot of other things I didn't want to discover. He was very persuasive, too—he'd even got me wondering if his kind of college-going might not be fun.

I stood up with a jerk and didn't even know I'd done it until Sherry stood up, too, saying, "What's the matter?"

The strange thing was that he looked just the same—just gentle and quizzical and nice, not mean and conniving at all. "Nothing," I snapped. "I've got to go in."

"OK, OK," he said mildly.

I didn't go, though. I just stood staring at him, getting angrier and angrier at him for not looking sneaky or at least a bit cynical, or *something* I could have disliked. I burst out, "Do you talk this way to everybody? Tell them about your poor life being limited to cereal boxes and so on?"

After a minute he said, "I didn't say my life was 'poor.'"

"All right, you didn't. But do you *talk* to people about it?"

"A few, I guess. If they're people I like to talk to anyway. Dr. Edmonds . . ."

"And the *so* understanding Mr. Bruce?"

He put his hands in his pockets and looked at me. I could feel the temperature drop. "What is all this?" he said indifferently—as if he didn't care whether he found out or not.

"Oh, nothing, nothing!" I said in a fury. "My head aches, that's all."

I whirled and started up the steps, fast. He started off down the sidewalk. Nobody said good-by.

I slammed into my room and threw my shoes at the wall, then stalked on into the bathroom and started a bath running. While I was soaking, I had plenty of time to calm down and ask myself what on earth that tantrum was in aid of, and why I was so excited about whether or not a boy I barely knew had helped to mulct an old lady I'd never known at all. What was it to me? Nothing whatever. I should be glad to have new information—and a deduction—for Uncle Frosty's case.

I wasn't glad. I climbed out of the tub, got dressed, and went out for a long walk to watch the sparklers. By the time I'd got home, I'd decided I didn't even have a good deduction. Sherry might have done nothing more than talk to Mr. Bruce or Dr. Edmonds or Mrs. Dunningham, the same as he'd been talking to me this evening, with no notion he was putting that scholarship-fund idea in their heads. Only what would Mr. Bruce or Dr. Edmonds stand to gain from such a notion? Well—the fat-salaried job of administering the fund. And the chance to siphon off bits of the principal in the course of that "wise investing." That was it. Sherry was merely the innocent source of an idea the other two had developed for their own benefit.

I'd got about this far when I found myself struggling to visualize Dr. Edmonds in the role of scheming financial manipulator. That nice, fast-walking, cheerful little man with the warm blue eyes? I did tell myself that scheming financial manipulators could have just as warm blue eyes as anybody else, but it didn't convince me.

Well, not Dr. Edmonds either, then. Mr. Bruce? Yes. He was the man in a domino—and there was a pickpocket underneath. Dave Kulka was in the plot with him—to a quite minor extent, evidently, since all he got out of it was a weed garden—and possibly Mrs. Jackson. But not Wynola, and surely not nice, timid little Miss Heater—

Miss Heater. My wrist shot out; my eyes flew to my watch. Five minutes of nine.

6

Right away, I began to suspect that Miss Heater had been regretting her invitation ever since she'd issued it. She opened her door rather as if she hoped I wasn't there after all, and when it turned out I was, she smiled more nervously than usual as she asked me in. She'd changed into house slippers, and I got the strong feeling she'd love to have climbed into an old dressing gown and watched her "Glorious Fourth" program in solitary peace. However, she fluttered around making me comfortable in the better of her two chairs, offered me a sweet out of a little glass bowl, and in general tried to convince herself she was glad to see me. I tried to convince myself that I was glad to be there, too, and stuck strictly to Georgetta-type conversation, to make her forget my lapse of the afternoon. We were both relieved when the program began and we could exclaim about the fireworks. During the commercials, though, we had to struggle through some small talk.

"My, TV sure is great, isn't it?" I said when the man began to extol razor blades instead of Independence. "Must be lots of company for you."

"Oh, yes, it is," Miss Heater said eagerly. "I used to sew, and—well, and do accounts, when I was in business, but my eyes are bad. I've had to give up my sewing. My sewing machine, too." She looked about the room with an odd, wistful expression. "I used to have a lovely Singer sewing machine. I've had to part with so many of my nice things. But I won't part with my TV, not unless matters—money matters—get a lot worse than they are."

"What kind of business were you in?"

"A knit shop. I had a nice little knit shop where I sold yarns and things and helped people with their instructions and blocked sweaters and so on. The Knitting Bag, I called it."

"That's a cute name. How come you don't have it any more?"

"Well, it got to be quite a burden," she said vaguely. "Oh—they're going to have some skyrockets now."

We dropped the talk and watched again, and I stole glances about the room. It did look as if Miss Heater lived in pretty straitened circumstances. The two chairs were shabby, there were worn spots on the curtains, and the rug was almost threadbare. The place had a stripped look, too, as if a lot of ornaments were missing. I wondered how she could have lent Mrs. Dunningham any money. Or was that why she was poor?

The second commercial was less successful, conversationally, than the first, and the third was worst of all. Miss Heater had withdrawn into her pained smiles and strained silences again, and all either of us wanted to say was "good-by." This we did as soon as possible.

I went back to my room feeling as disgruntled and discouraged as I had two other times this same stupid evening. Why had she drawn in her antennae like that? Maybe I'd slipped out of character again without knowing it. What's come over me? I thought. I've been popping in and out of this role like a jack-in-the-box all day. What's the matter?

I'm tired—that's what's the matter, I answered myself grumpily. When I examined this reply, I discovered it meant, "I'm tired of the role." I was. The fact, and I had to face it, was that I was very tired of Georgetta and her family and her flat vowels—tired of wearing *my* domino. There it always was, between me and people I wanted to talk to.

Very well, Shannon, I thought as I hung up my skirt. You're tired of Georgetta. You've got it all clear. So you go right on sticking with Georgetta anyway, my girl. You're *stuck* with Georgetta. So face *that* fact.

I got into my dressing gown, and since the cuckoo was announcing it was only ten-thirty, I sat down at my desk and began trying to put Georgetta on paper—a refresher course, so to speak. The thing that surprised me was that the longer I scribbled, the more fun I had. I was entranced, when I stopped an hour later to read the thing over, to find Georgetta herself flouncing across my page, patting her hairdo, big as life; I'd never dreamed I could do it. It made me think back to that period during grade school when I was always scribbling—as Uncle Frosty had said, I'd had my mind made up to win the Pulitzer Prize someday.

I stuffed my papers into a drawer and went over to take off the cuckoo's weights so he wouldn't yell at me all night, then leaned on the windowsill, breathing the mild, rose-scented air that drifted in from the dark garden and thinking about those naively sanguine days. I could still remember the plot of one of my numerous masterpieces. It was about an absolutely incredibly beautiful sixteen-year-old girl who was desperately in love with an absolutely incredibly handsome seventeen-year-old boy, and you'd never believe the trouble they had getting married. There was a flood and an earthquake, much parental opposition, and a shocking old party—a sinister Tibetan or somebody—who was always tripping them up for reasons of his own. On the last page, when they were about to be captured by Communist spies, here came this old Tibetan closing in from the other direction in a sort of pincers movement. But luckily a friend happened to have an airplane sitting about in his garage, and they climbed joyfully in and flew away into the sunset.

So much for my plotting ability. You can't say there wasn't *lots* of plot, but if quality counted, it would amount to a misdemeanor to loose me on the fiction-reading world.

So that old hope died a-borning. Its second death. Meanwhile, I was asleep on my feet, and Georgetta had to work tomorrow, and I still hadn't entered today's spate of information in my journal— and here I was depressed again. I dug out the journal and scrawled some hieroglyphs, then went bitterly to bed.

7

◇◇◇

Friday, 5th July . . . Woke up worrying about Mrs. J. and Wynola's hair, feeling dissatisfied about Miss Heater, and simply dreading to face Sherry. What excuse can you give for plain, offensive rudeness? Isn't any. He came in the Rainbow about noon. I smiled, rather tentatively, and when he smiled back—pretty tentatively, too—I went up to his end of the counter and braved it out. Just said please would he put my flight-off-the-handle down to nerves, Mrs. Jackson, and temporary insanity, because I didn't understand it myself.

Lame enough, but he accepted it with perfect calm. "Don't worry, Greensleeves. There's still a lot *I* don't understand about you, too. Such as why you say 'lorry' sometimes instead of 'truck.'" Then he smiled his gentle quizzical smile and tactfully drank some coffee while I went goose-bumpy and asked myself *when* I had said that and how often? He set down his cup and added, "Of course, it doesn't matter. If everybody understood everybody else, life might be real dull. Is Mrs. Jackson still mad at you this morning?"

She was (still is this evening), and I said so. No greeting when we met at the mail table, just a look from under those eyebrows that bracketed me with dog poisoners. Sherry said she was bound to get over it, probably as soon as Wynola gets a good haircut, and again told me not to worry. Yesterday Miss Heater kept telling me not to worry. This afternoon Wynola assured me, with a rather obviously stiffened upper lip, that Mom would like her hair once she got used to it, and anyway it was *done*—and not to worry. I'm still worrying.

Saturday, 6th July . . . Mrs. J. has begun speaking—but not to me, just to the air in my vicinity. She makes remarks about hair. I don't defend myself, because I keep feeling I deserve this—or at least that she deserves a chance to punish me, since she got none to prevent my ill-judged deed. But I'm beginning to feel like a barefoot penitent who'll never make it to the shrine. *Why* can't I learn not to follow impulses?

Sunday, 7th July . . . My flagellating arm is getting tired. So is my temper-holding mechanism. Really, you'd think I'd maimed Wynola instead of improving her! I spilled over to Rose about it today, and she said, "For heaven's sake, relax. The kid looks great. I've been noticing her."

No wonder. Wynola's become ever-present in the Rainbow. She keeps dropping in "on her way" to or from the grocer's or the cleaner's or the mailbox—which is in the opposite direction—to confide things in me or ask my advice or just keep a devoted eye on me in general.

Today she said, "Georgetta, do you think a person fifteen and a quarter years old is too young to wear eye shadow?" I said yes and nearly dropped a milk shake at the vision of Wynola daubed with Georgetta's irridescent blue. "Well," she said, "but I'm not too young for lipstick, am I? Look—I got the prettiest one yesterday, with my *own money*, and now Mom says I can't use it." She dug the lipstick out of her pocket, and to my relief it wasn't Passionate Pimento or anything, just a nice pale rose exactly matching that attractive flush along her cheekbones. But never mind. I said, "You better do what your mom says. Maybe she'll let you wear it just for dress-up."

WYNOLA (*darkly*): She won't. She won't let me have high heels, either. She won't let me do *anything*.

I told her quickly that I hardly ever wore high heels myself and that they didn't look right with ankle socks anyhow.

WYNOLA: But I want some nylons, too. And just some *little* high heels, to wear with my pink dress.

I remembered the big black oxfords and couldn't help agreeing, but I kept quiet. I'm through stirring hornets' nests. Then she began brooding about finances. "If I could buy my own clothes, she'd *have* to let me wear them. I wish I could get a job, for after school and weekends. Georgetta, where could I get a job?"

This sort of thing makes me feel exactly like Alice with the White Queen's chin resting heavily on her shoulder. Still, it's my own doing. I started the rebellion; Wynola now assumes she can count on me to stick by her through the hostilities, and I can't blame her, but my *word* how I would love to withdraw my fingers from this very sticky pie. On the other hand, *drat it*, here Wynola is showing signs of spunk at last, back on a slimming routine, and acting sort of generally alive. And every time I look at her hair—professionally trimmed yesterday and a big success—I ask myself if my sister Charmeen could have been wrong after all about my going into hairdressing as a career. Until the next time I see Mrs. J., who keeps right on making me feel like the only little skunk at the woodlands picnic. So I swing like a berserk pendulum between angry defensiveness and a sort of hunted guilt.

I could do with some support from the other lodgers, but Miss Heater's back in her shell, and Dr. Edmonds and Dave Kulka must have gone away for the weekend—haven't seen them since Wednesday. For all I know, my excommunication is complete, which will mean the end of Georgetta E. Smith, Girl Detective. It may anyway—I'm so on edge I'm ready to go off like a rocket if anybody looks sidewise at me.

9:30 a.m., *Monday, 8th July* . . . Well, half an hour ago Dave Kulka looked sidewise at me. Everything may be in smithereens.

I'd been over to the grocer's for oranges. Just as I was letting myself in the front door, Dave came down the stairs. "Oh, there you are," he said in his usual surly tone. Since I was feeling taut as a bowstring without any help from him, I just muttered, "Good morning," and made the jog around the staircase, heading for my room. To my absolute astonishment, he leaned over the banister and stretched out a long arm to bar my way. When I glared up at him, he merely looked contemptuous. "Why did you cut Wynola's hair?" he demanded.

"Oh, REALLY," I snapped. "Because she wanted me to—that's why."

"Well, you've ruined her. She was pure Gothic. That fright wig was just right."

My eyes and mouth both opened wide, but I couldn't say a word for a minute, I was too enraged.

With a shrug Dave added, "Artistically, she's all wrong now."

The rocket went off. I felt as if my whole head were full of sparks. "Why, you arrogant, *unmitigated* beastly blob of glup," I said. "Who do you think you are to talk that way about a human being? Of all the utterly sophomoric statements I ever heard, that wins the coconut, besides being none of your business in the . . ." And then I stopped, with the sparks burning out to little cold blue cinders. Dave's grin was slashing clear across his face, and those black Renaissance eyes of his were simply Machiavellian.

He said, "I thought so. Just wanted to be sure."

"Sure of what?" I gasped. My lungs couldn't decide whether to work overtime or not at all.

"Sure you were a fake. Where did you get that educated accent all of a sudden, Miss Greensleeves Smith?"

I began nasally, "I caaan't imaagine what you—"

"Oh, drop it. You know exactly what I mean. You should see your face right now." He propped both elbows on the banister, obviously enjoying the sight. "Don't worry. I'm not going to spoil your little game, whatever it is," he added, while I resolved that if anybody else told me not to worry, I would go straight downtown and jump off the Pacific Power Building. His eyes were running over me frankly and in minute detail, and under their heavy lids I'd swear there was a gleam of amused respect. "It's good," he said. "I've got to hand it to you—you're perfect. Just a little too perfect—that's the only flaw."

I attempted some withering remark beginning with "Gee" and was ordered to cut it out. "You're wasting your time—with me, anyhow. Just be yourself, whoever you are. Don't you want to know what tipped me off?"

I didn't answer, just stared up at him lounging there on the banister in his faded brown shirt, with the usual lock of hair falling over his forehead, and longed to slit his throat.

"Well, I'll tell you," he went on conversationally. "It was Wynola's haircut. Good job, even before she got it slicked up. Showed a real eye for form and composition." He smiled. "Yours doesn't. See? Dead giveaway."

His voice was casual—maybe disinterested is the word. But not *un*interested. He gave me another heavy-lidded appraisal, hairdo to shoe bows, before easing his shoulder off the newel post, remarking, "I'm not going to say a word," and ambling lazily down the last step and off toward the front door.

I walked rigidly to my room feeling as though I'd forgotten how to work my knees, set my bag of oranges down carefully on a drawer edge (they're still all over the floor), then made it here to my desk and sat. I continued to sit, like a stone image—with stone brains—until it occurred to me to try thinking it out on paper, in this journal. Not that it's helped much—though I do rather believe Dave meant what he said and actually intends to keep his large, revolting mouth closed.

Well it isn't really large and revolting. It's large and curiously attractive when it isn't twisting scornfully, as it usually is around me but certainly wasn't this morning. Not precisely large, either— wide. With a thin, curving upper lip and a very full lower one, cleft in the middle.

Anyway, *regardless* of Dave's mouth. Whether he mentions this to a soul or not, I'll bet he makes life difficult for me. Worse than Sherry ever did, because he hasn't Sherry's tact and Sherry's regard for people's feelings. Of course, he hasn't Sherry's devouring curiosity, either—I guess. I don't know. Neither do I know whether he keeps promises or ignores them. There's a lot I don't know about Dave Kulka, starting at A and going straight to Zed. All I'm sure of is that he (1) likes weeds, (2) dislikes people, and (3) is an artist—a jolly good one. And uncommonly perceptive. It never entered my head, that discrepancy between my tasteless hairdo and Wynola's tasteful one. Drat his artist's eye—and his quick mind that asked who was responsible for both coiffures. That's all it took to bring the unmistakable odor of fish and a chance to ruin my day by wafting it under my nose. He'd never forego that pleasure—but it just *may* be all he wants to do.

Evening . . . Today kept right on being eventful. I'd no sooner shut this journal this morning and headed for work than I encountered Dr. Edmonds, standing at the hall table. The mail had just come. I spotted something for me, disguised in one of Miss Jensen's discreet white envelopes. Dr. Edmonds had a book; he was struggling to free it from the corrugated paper and iron-clad staples Americans always use to wrap them. He said, "Good morning, Miss Greensleeves!"—cordial as ever—then paused in his struggles, glanced toward the kitchen, and lowered his voice. "I want to say right now—that was a real favor you did Wynola. She's amazingly improved. Remarkably. How did—it come about?"

I had a strong feeling he'd started to say, "How did *you* ever think of it?" His eyes had gone automatically to my tower, and they were blue and puzzled. I thought, Oh, my word, here's another one. Not artistic maybe, but frightfully intelligent. If he doesn't have the answer now, he'll have it in a minute.

Meanwhile, I was rapidly saying a lot of things intended to give the impression that *I* thought a coiffure more like *mine* would have been an even greater improvement, but that I just hadn't quite managed to—

Didn't work. Dr. Edmonds listened politely but couldn't quite hide the slight skepticism in his eyes. I could just see him thinking, "The lady doth protest too much." I quit overprotesting—too abruptly, and I saw him notice that, too—and switched to Mrs. Jackson. He commiserated and told me not to worry. Then he offered to try smoothing things over with her a bit. "She's difficult sometimes. I'll just have a word with her when an opportunity presents itself, Miss—er—Greensleeves."

His eyes went briefly to my hair again, then courteously back to his half-unwrapped book. One thing's certain: *he'll* not say a word, even to me. Too polite. He'd no more ask me why I'm in disguise than he'd ask me how often I wash my ears. To show my gratitude, I helped him wrestle his book free, and oh, what a book! Large and handsome and opulent-looking, with one of those fantastically beautiful archaic Greek horses on the dust jacket. The title was *Early Greek Sculpture.*

"Magnificent, isn't it?" Dr. Edmonds said softly. He was staring at the horse as if nothing else on earth had any importance. And I believe that for him, at that moment, nothing else had. He muttered something under his breath—in classical Greek, I was almost certain. I'm quite certain that what shone in his eyes as he thumbed reverently through the book was plain monomania. That man is madly in love; he just happens to have fastened on a dead civilization instead of a live human being as the object of his affections.

When I asked what he'd said, he repeated the phrase—gently and with love, not at all the way Nevin gobbles his occasional Greek tags. It sounded like a phrase of music. For a minute he even had *me* interested in how the old Greeks sounded when they talked.

"Is it poetry?" I asked him.

"No. It's the cornerstone of Greek philosophy and art and thought. 'Nothing in excess.' The line's inscribed on the temple of Apollo at Delphi—so I've heard."

So he'd heard. His voice had gone wistful as he turned back to his book. I thought of Delphi—that high, high, breathtaking place full of quiet and ivory-colored broken columns, with mountaintops down below you. That spring Dad and I were there, the little almond trees were blooming in the snow. Why haven't I *realized* what Mrs. Dunningham meant? She wanted him to see Delphi—and Mycenae and Thermopylae and Epidaurus, and the part of Athens on the hill, not around the Hilton. And suddenly, and very badly, I wanted him to see it, too.

Well, we talked a bit longer, chiefly about early Greek sculpture—he couldn't keep his eyes or his mind off his book, and I didn't blame him—and then about Sherry and the private lessons in Greek. Dr. Edmonds said he hoped Sherry would go on with the study, because the reward was well worth any labor. He added thoughtfully, "It's been far and away the most rewarding labor in *my* life."

"Isn't college teaching rewarding?" I asked.

He hesitated, rather bleakly. "At times. At least, there are some rewarding pupils—young Sherrill, for instance. A few more like him—students possessed of true intellectual curiosity—and I could feel it was all worth while. But there are discouragingly few." His voice thinned out a bit as he gazed through me. "One wonders sometimes if one has managed to teach a single person anything of any value."

"Why, Dr. Edmonds!" I said, then recovered Georgetta and added, "You kind of sound like you've got the blues."

He recovered himself, too, and gave me one of his usual brisk smiles, tinged with an unusual irony. "Oh, the blues are an occupational hazard in my profession—maybe because most teachers should have gone into a different profession in the first place. Now, I might have made an excellent plumber—my father was the best in town."

I said firmly, "Sherry told me you're the best teacher in this college—the best he ever had."

Dr. Edmonds dropped his irony and really smiled at me. "Thank you, Miss Greensleeves. But Sherry learns because he wants to, not because I want him to. I believe he learns because he must. He ought to go on and on, find out where it leads him. It will be a pity if he doesn't get—" I *know* he was going to say "that scholarship," but he caught himself and finished rather lamely, "—get to go farther. Into graduate school—where there aren't so many sheep to slow the others up."

"Sheep?" I repeated.

Dr. Edmonds smiled and shrugged. "It's a bit harsh, perhaps, but Ezra Pound once said, 'Real education must ultimately be limited to men who *insist* on knowing; the rest is mere sheepherding.' I think he was right. I seem to have spent my life with the sheep."

Again, that odd, bitter note in his voice; then he turned hastily—almost hungrily—back to his book, while I stood mulling all this over and watching his face relax and his expression turn worshipful again as he studied the pictures of the ancient sculptures.

"Dr. Edmonds," I ventured, "couldn't you go to Greece sometime?"

"I'd like it above all things," he said. He glanced up at me, then suddenly closed the book and returned to his everyday manner. He said a lot of hearty things about having to revise his physics textbook extensively this summer, teachers having no time to travel if they expected to publish, and besides there were always summer classes, and incidentally he was almost late for one—and the conversation was over.

Obviously, he doesn't want to talk or even *think* about a trip to Greece. Because he hates to admit he hasn't the money? I can't quite believe in that time-devouring textbook. Anybody could take three weeks off to do a thing he wants that badly to do.

My letter was from Franz. A good letter. It's made me homesick for him—for *anybody* I could be myself with for just five minutes. Good old Franz.

11th July (I think. Anyway, Thursday) . . . Day off. And I'm not going to do a solitary thing more energetic than wash some nylons and maybe file my nails. Nothing to report except that Dave seems to be keeping his word and my secret, and Mrs. Jackson is beginning, almost imperceptibly, to thaw. Maybe Dr. Edmonds did his promised bit of smoothing-over.

13th July . . . That Helen. My *word*, she's hard to believe in sometimes! When I got to work this morning, she was scooping ice cream—a job she loathes, so I wasn't surprised to be greeted with, "Dear, *could* you finish here? You manage this old scoop *so* much better than I can." She gave me the scoop and studied her undeniably slender hand with an expression intended to be rueful, though it turned out fond. "My hands are just too small to be very useful."

I wanted to tell her she should have lived in Old China, where they bound their feet to prove they weren't up to walking any farther than from this couch to the next one, but I didn't. I just closed my gross coal-heaver's paw over the scoop and started digging, while Helen happily relaxed and told me about her sufferings with geology, in which she had a quiz yesterday. "All those boring little minerals and things. Why do *I* have to know feldspar from quartz? I'll never need to."

I asked why she was taking it, and she said, well, you had to take *something*, and anyway it was required, and she'd be *so* glad when all those requirements were out of her way. I hooked the milk shake in and asked what she meant to take when they were. She said, "Oh, I don't know. Maybe education. I hear a lot of education courses are snaps. I *was* majoring in French, but it's too hard. Useless, too. I wish I'd taken Spanish. My roommate says Spanish is easy."

"Pig Latin is even easier," I said brightly, but of course too far under my breath to be heard over the milk shake mixer. Then I raised my voice and said what if she ever went to France?

"Oh, you don't need French to go to *France*, dear," Helen told me with a kindly smile. "Everybody in Europe speaks English now. They're glad to."

Oh, are they really, I thought. Funnily enough, I can't recall one single *enfant de la patrie* who'll speak anything but French unless he has to. I seem to remember that Austrians prefer German, too, and Italians Italian, etc., etc. However, I feel certain that even if Helen went to Outer Mongolia, she'd hunt up the Hilton—I assume there's an Outer Mongolian Hilton—where she'd be sure of air conditioning and Cokes, and everybody at a Hilton *would* speak English, so the whole thing would be as easy as taking a nap. Helen's always going to find the easy way—I feel one can rely on that absolutely. Well, it's her nap. Presumably, she doesn't even want to wake up. As Uncle Frosty would say, it's the shape her inner girl has been taking for eighteen years or so. Only thing is, I don't think she knows it.

I've been sitting here thinking, and I believe I'd rather be a mass of protoplasm like me, and *know* it, than be a sleepwalker like Helen and not be aware of reality at all. I wonder how *she* sees her inner girl—or her outer girl, for that matter. As a sort of youthful lady of the manor, maybe—maddeningly attractive, with tiny, fragile hands and an irresistible wit, but unspoiled despite countless suitors, and tremendously kind to noncollegiate peasants like me.

Well, *I* see a moderately pretty girl with an extraordinary lot of phoney affectations. And I've a notion most people see what I see.

It makes your skin crawl, rather. I mean, it's one thing to *write* fiction, or even put on a disguise and act it out. At least I jolly well know the difference between Georgetta and Shan Lightley. But Helen's mixing fiction up with life, and that strikes me as the road to utter confusion.

◇✕◇

14th July . . . Bastille Day, and I'm ready with several nominees for the tumbrills. Everybody's having quizzes—summer session's at the halfway point—so everybody's rushed and preoccupied and either waspish or glum, and it isn't even interesting to *overhear* conversations, which are chiefly about Part A under Question Six, or what's that element that sounds like manganese but isn't? Sherry didn't even come in, except to grab a fast hamburger during the noon rush when I couldn't stop to talk, and later Milton wittily sugared my cheese sandwich.

18th July . . . College, college, college. I promised Uncle Frosty not even to think about it, and here I am dunked right into the middle of it every day, like *Nockerl* in the soup. I can't *help* thinking about it. Even that letter from Franz was half about starting at the University of Vienna, long absorbed paragraphs describing Herr Doktor-Professors he'll study under, and lectures with names as long as my forearm that he's signed up for. Well, Franz has a real *reason* for going to college. When you're planning to be a surgeon, you can't find out what you need to know any other way.

I hope Dr. Edmonds doesn't have Helen in any of his classes. I can scarcely imagine a student less rewarding. I keep wondering why she bothers with college—she seems to loathe every course offered and doesn't mean to use any of them. Probably husband- or status-hunting. And I could point to half a dozen hamburger eaters in the Rainbow at any given moment who are in college merely because their parents decided they should be—the way Dad tried to decide for me. Charlie says frankly, "It beats working." I don't think much of any of those reasons. Seems to me Sherry has the only reason with any bite to it, anything to wake you up. Dr. Edmonds calls it intellectual curiosity; Sherry calls it "wanting information"—about what things like integral calculus are all about. A bit dotty, but a real reason, like Franz's, not just something he made up.

To tell the truth, Sherry's theory of higher education sort of sneakily appeals to me—maybe because it's the first argument for college I've ever heard that wasn't studded with "musts" and "shoulds" to get my back up.

Or maybe it's just that Sherry appeals to me.

I do like him; he's nothing like any other boy I've ever known. Not that I've known many very well—except Franz. Well, there was that brother of my roommate at Madame F.'s, but he scared me to death—madly good-looking and some kind of a count, besides, and always bowing from the hips. Fine to daydream about in study hall but no good to be with—he always made me feel my feet were too big. Then there were those two Principal Boy types Mother tried to pair me off with in London, but one was too old to be interesting and the other too fond of himself to be anything but nauseating, particularly when enacting the great lover, which was *every* time he could corner me alone. Of course, Mary-High was full of boys—two kinds: loud, boneheaded, and boring; and quiet, intelligent, and terrified of girls.

Anyway, Sherry's different from anybody. Special. Hard to say why—hard to put him into words, in fact. It would take a film with soundtrack to capture him, because one thing that makes him so *himself* is that inconspicuous, drifting way he moves, so that first he's here and then over there, and you never quite see him do it— and the other thing is his voice. It's light, never loud, a little gravelly, a little lazy, always with that faintly inquiring note. Everything about him is interrogative—eyebrows, smile, set of his head, the way he looks at people out of his narrow greenish-gray eyes, his entire personality. If you feel a kind of question-mark atmosphere coming into the room, you can look around, and there's Sherry.

Oh, well, I can't describe him. Maybe you can never explain what it is about one certain person that makes you feel there are a lot of little strings attached between you and him, all pulling. My problem is wondering whether the pull is all one way. I mean, a blind man could see that Sherry takes quite an interest in me—but a zoologist takes quite an interest in a brand-new bug, too. In my (admittedly limited) experience, when a boy feels those little strings pulling, he usually lets you know somehow, even if he only says your frock is pretty. And if the pull is very noticeable, drat it, he says *you're* pretty, whether you are or not. He doesn't talk about your sterling character, either—he makes *personal comments.* Enthusiastic ones.

Well, so far Sherry's personal comments have all managed to deflate me somehow. Look at his remark about my dimple—a subject I'd rather not have brought up at all. And the other day he said with an air of discovery that I had real bone structure—*good* bone structure, he added as an afterthought. I suppose that might have delighted some people—Wynola would probably have been flattered to death—but since I happen to be all too aware that I have bone structure, and that it's all too apparent in, for instance, a scoop-necked dress, I simply don't care to be reminded of it even if it *is* good. Sherry failed to improve matters by explaining that he was only speaking of the bones in my head—and then adding, in a fascinated voice, that he bet I was going to be a mighty good-looking old lady when I was about eighty-five. I told him, Gee, I could hardly wait, and all he did was insist he really meant it. As a pretty compliment, that leaves a lot to be desired.

I keep wishing he'd mention just *one* thing about me that's actually attractive. Not that I have a suggestion—except possibly my hair, and at the moment that's ruined by Georgetta's coiffure. He did once say he liked red hair, but he didn't add, "Especially on you"—he didn't add anything. So I said, "You'd be crazy about my dad; his is lots redder than mine," and that's where he left the subject flat and began to ask me about my dad, so I had to quick remember who Georgetta's dad is and think up a lot of convincing lies about him.

In a lot of ways, Sherry is impossible. I don't know why I keep on liking him so much.

8

Then one day about quitting time—it was July 25, I happen to remember—a taxi driver came into the Rainbow, a big taxi driver, whose hair was even redder than my dad's. I thought, *Brick Mulvaney, as I live and breathe*, and all but flung myself the length of the counter to wait on him. He was approachable enough, a friendly chap with a big homely blob of a nose and a round red face and blue eyes that looked innocent as a three-year-old's but a bit weary, too. Small wonder, considering old Stanley and Mama's hysterics. But he wanted coffee, not a chat—or else, logically enough, saw no special reason to chat with me.

I did my best, without eliciting any response beyond amiable monosyllables until I tried remarking that I'd sure rather be out fishing on a day like this instead of working. At that he perked up a bit. "Say, you and me both. What kind of fishing do you do, mostly?"

"Well—oh, *all* kinds," I said brightly, feeling myself falling head over coiffure into deep, deep waters. What I know about fishing is the following: it requires a hook and bait.

"Ever troll for swordfish?" he asked with interest.

"Swordfish. Well—" I pulled my cheek curl, trying to imagine what trolling was. "No, I never tried that. I'd like to. Is it fun?"

"I've never tried it either. A little too rich for my pocket-book." Mr. Mulvaney slapped his hip where I presume his wallet was and gave a wistful laugh. "I've trolled for pike, though, back in Minnesota when I was a youngster. And muskies. Those muskies are fighting fools, I *tell* you. Man, that's sport. But then you take these here Chinooks or steel-heads, they're not bad either. You've tried the Willamette down here, I s'pose?"

"Oh, sure, and the Clackamas and Santiam and Zigzag." At least I knew the names of some *rivers* in Oregon, if not the fish.

But Mr. Mulvaney was looking puzzled. "You trolled in the Zigzag?" he said slowly. "Now I'd have said that was a mite too fast to troll in. Whereabouts on the Zigzag?"

"Oh, I didn't *troll* there," I said hastily, wondering what to say I had done. "Just—you know, fished."

"Oh, yeah, I've cast in it, too, many's the time. This is really great fishing country. Well, thanks, young lady. I better be up and at we always just put 'em, I guess. So long."

He slid a dime under his saucer—which made me feel bad, because I suspected he needed it worse than I did—and gave me a sweet kind of smile and went to the cash register to pay. A minute later he was gone.

Well, better luck next time, I told myself glumly. It depressed me; I couldn't help it. Here I'd finally talked for five whole minutes to this elusive party, and what was the result? I knew all about muskies and not a thing about Mulvaney.

That evening, after an hour with Mrs. Dunningham's Stonehenge book and another with my journal, I was still brooding and decided to write the evening off and go to bed. Some detective I am, I thought as I climbed into my tub. Not one mingy bit of information have I dug out of anybody since way back early this month—in fact, since the Monday after the Fourth of July.

I got thinking about this, and it struck me as very odd. That whole Fourth of July weekend, fourth to eighth, I'd been inundated with information—it had come at me from all sides. Why *then*? And nothing since? It was ridiculous. Those were the very four days I'd been so up, down, and sidewise from one strong emotion after the other that I couldn't even hang onto my characterization, much less my wits.

I'd finished my tub and was belting my dressing gown before it dawned on me that I'd answered my own question. The *characterization* was in the way. The moments people had talked to me most freely were those when Georgetta had gone AWOL. As soon as I dragged her back, front-and-center, for instance when I went to Miss Heater's room, the confidences dried up.

Well, it was a truly nauseating little discovery. Just what *had* I accomplished with all my playacting and keeping tabs on Georgetta's relatives and squashing her vowels and struggling with her hairdo? Nothing. Which meant that Uncle Frosty's mistrust of the whole proceeding had been quite right. *Provoking* thought. No way to save face, either—Georgetta I was and had to stay.

But maybe if I just played Georgetta down a trifle? Backed her out of the spotlight? Kept her quiet about her relatives so somebody else could talk for a change? Would that work?

Maybe so, I told myself.

I couldn't wait to try. I leaped out of my dressing gown and into some clothes and in five minutes was dashing upstairs to Miss Heater's room. I'd already knocked before it occurred to me that it might be some ungodly late hour, and I jerked my wrist up so fast to look at my watch that I dealt it a nasty bang against the door jamb and scraped it raw. Only nine o'clock. I'd barely had time to feel relieved about this, and not enough time to stop dancing silently up and down grimacing over my banged wrist, when Miss Heater opened the door a cautious three inches and peered out. When she saw me, she gaped, not unnaturally. I hurriedly rearranged my face into a smile and said I hoped I hadn't got her out of bed.

"Oh, no," she said, and waited for me to say why I was there, which was a bit daunting.

"I—know it's late to come calling," I said, keeping the smile in place.

"Oh, that's all right—I mean it's not late, is it? I really don't— I was just reading." She still looked bewildered, but suddenly she remembered she was talking to me through a crack and opened the door, saying in a flustered voice, "Well, come in! My goodness."

So I went in. Then there was another very sticky patch because she didn't think to ask me to sit down, being still convinced I must have come on a specific errand and would explain it any minute. By now I was longing to be back in my room and out of this. Fortunately, I'd forgot to let go of my wrist. I was still clutching the skinned place—and considering my embarrassment, I wouldn't be surprised if I had an expression of acute pain on my face. Anyway, Miss Heater frowned and said, "Have you hurt yourself?"

I took my hand away, and we both looked at my wrist, which had obligingly turned red and angry-looking.

"Why, my dear! How did you do that? I'll get a Band-Aid," Miss Heater said, and began to bustle. I protested feebly, but she overrode me and found Band-Aids and iodine, with which she insisted on daubing my wound. This effectively took my mind off my other problems for a few excruciating moments; then she waved me to a chair and sat down herself, meanwhile telling me all about the first-aid course she'd taken during the war. After a moment she broke off, looking embarrassed. "My goodness, here I am chattering away, and you haven't even said what you came for." She smiled her flustered, nervous smile, but in the middle of it got to looking at me rather keenly and added, in quite a different tone, "Why *did* you come, my dear?"

I thought of telling her I'd just come to borrow a Band-Aid—it would have been so convenient and logical. Instead, I heard myself telling the truth. "I just wanted to talk to somebody. I guess I'm lonesome."

"*Are* you. Why—I'm so glad you came to *me*. I feel very flattered."

She meant it. She turned a faint pink—very becoming—and looked as if I'd given her an unexpected present, which perhaps I had.

I said, "You were so nice to me that time . . . I just thought—if you weren't doing anything special—"

"I'm almost never doing anything special," she said frankly.

That made us friends. We began to talk quite naturally—not about Georgetta's relatives—and within five or ten minutes she'd brought up that knit shop she'd had ten years before. "I just loved working. It didn't seem like work, you know—I suppose because it was *my* shop. Half mine, anyway."

"Oh. You had a partner?"

"Yes." She studied her hands, as if perhaps she didn't want to talk about *that*, then rather jerkily went on. "She—we went broke. The shop never made much money—we had the wrong location. It might have, in time, but . . . well, we couldn't save it. We'd borrowed money from the bank to start it—buy our yarns and furnishings, and take a five-year lease, and all that. And—when the end came, she just walked out. Went back to Chicago. I've had to pay the loan off all by myself."

"But—my word, how *could* she do that? Couldn't she be arrested or something?"

"She never signed the note," Miss Heater said bitterly. "*I* did. I never dreamed it would matter. She'd been my closest friend for years."

For a minute I felt so sorry for her that I couldn't find a word to say. It was a quite appalling story, I thought. I finally muttered, "That's a terrible thing."

Miss Heater smiled with an effort. "Yes. Yes, it was. I'd put all my savings into the business, besides, and lost it all. My brother warned me we were starting too ambitiously—investing too much. He was right. I guess I wasn't a very good businesswoman."

"How long did it take you to pay off the loan?"

"I'm still paying it." *Ten years later.* She explained: at first she'd done well to pay the interest; finally, she'd found part-time work; lately, her Social Security had helped. "My brother offered to help me, too, but that wouldn't be right. The debt is my responsibility. It was my mistake."

Something rang a bell in my mind. "How much is left to pay?" I asked cautiously.

"Just under four thousand dollars. It *was* seven."

Four thousand dollars. The light of intelligence belatedly dawned. Why had I thought Mrs. Dunningham owed *Miss Heater* money? Miss Heater owed the *bank*. The legacy was meant to pay off this debt for her. Now she wouldn't get it. Not if Uncle Frosty won his case, which I'd been trying all summer to help him do.

I must have looked a bit aghast, because Miss Heater sat up straight and said, "For goodness' sake! This is a fine way to cheer you up—tell you all *my* woes! Look here, I'll make us a cup of cocoa. Would you like that?"

She began to bustle around her little hot plate, while I tried for a suitably cheered-up expression. We exchanged small talk while the chocolate bubbled; then as she was bringing me my cup, she stopped to pull down the window blind and instead stood still a moment, looking out into the dark back garden and shaking her head a bit. I looked and saw the round beam of an electric torch moving here and there among the rosebushes.

"It's Mrs. Hockins," Miss Heater said, with a sad little "tsk-tsk" noise. "Now there's a woman with far worse trouble than mine. Talk about lonesome." She pulled down the blind, handed me my cup, and fetched her own as she went on. "That poor woman is utterly lonely. Lost her husband and her son on the same day—automobile accident. Twelve years ago, it was, but she's never got over it. She ought to move away, you know. Everyone tells her. But she won't—she lived all her married life in that house, and I guess the associations are all she has left. But that's exactly what makes it so hard. She can hardly bear to *be* in the house. Wanders around outdoors instead—if she didn't have her roses, I don't know what she'd do. Even in the winter rains she's out there walking around. She'll catch her death one of these times. It's really so sad."

So the plastic canopy was explained. And from Mrs. Hockins it was simple to get to Mrs. Dunningham.

"Oh, yes," Miss Heater said. "Mrs. Dunningham was wonderful to her. Mrs. Dunningham was wonderful to everybody. We all miss—" She stopped.

I smiled at her. "You aren't going to hurt my feelings, Miss Heater. She sounds wonderful. *She* wasn't sad about anything, was she?"

"Well—I don't know." Miss Heater stirred her chocolate thoughtfully. "There was a kind of look in her eyes. I think she'd seen plenty of unhappiness but just—put it behind her, you know. She was a *strong* person. But I don't think she'd had a very happy life—from a few things she said."

"Like what?"

"Oh—well, once she told me—we were talking about my debt, and security, and so on—and she said she thought security was too highly rated. Said she married to find security and get free of her early life—'Get out of my cage,' was the way she put it—but that she'd only got caught more firmly in another cage, and security wasn't worth it. She told me security wasn't what I wanted; it was freedom—freedom from the debt, you know. She said she understood *that*, all right, because when all was said and done, freedom was the only prize worth having."

And there was Mrs. Dunningham being pithy again, and talking about freedom again, too. I said, "Did *she* have any children? Or had they died, like Mrs. Hockins' son?"

Miss Heater blinked, frowned, and said finally, "You know, I'm just not sure. Odd. I knew her quite well, too. I don't think she ever *mentioned* any."

And there I was, with the same old answer. It depressed me so that Miss Heater started worrying about my wrist again.

It wasn't until I was back in my room, wearily undressing for the second time that evening, that I asked myself *why* I was so depressed by that same old answer when I should have felt delighted every time I got it. The more people who never heard Mrs. Dunningham mention her daughter, the stronger Uncle Frosty's case became.

The answer was easy. I didn't want it to be strong. I wanted it to fall flatter than a bad soufflé before it even started. At some moment in these last weeks, I'd moved over to the legatees' side, utterly and absolutely—anyway to Mrs. Dunningham's side. If she was a crazy old lady, then I was a crazy young lady, and wanted to stay that way. The more I heard of her, the saner she sounded. She'd even understood about traps; she'd been in one herself. She called them cages, but we meant the same thing. I'd have given anything to talk to her.

Too late for that now—but *not* too late, I told myself grimly, to help her do what she'd intended with her money. It was going to be a shock to Uncle Frosty to learn he'd been harboring a turncoat in his bosom, but I couldn't help it—I meant to scotch his case if I could. And—it dawned on me as I was pulling my pajama top over my head—I'd have to do it fast.

I yanked the pajama top down, to the ruination of my coiffure, and went over to look at my desk calendar. July 25—a Thursday— my usual day off, but I'd swapped with Rose, who was all but going steady with her dentist now. I'd be off Sunday, uncomfortably soon to go see Uncle Frosty; my case was far from complete, to say nothing of his. Yet also uncomfortably close was August 2, when he and Mona would leave for Mexico. On their return, the summer and my three-month Nirvana would be nearly over.

I dug my journal out from among my nylons and browsed through it to see what I actually had found out. Jolly little about Mr. Bruce and Dave Kulka. Nothing about Mrs. Dunningham's attitude toward money or Mr. Mulvaney's motives in bringing her to College Street. I flipped to a fresh page, rapidly noted down the information I'd gleaned from Miss Heater that evening, and finished the entry:

Above all, I must learn if Mrs. D. ever mentioned that daughter of hers—I've still several legatees to ask. If she did, to even one person, Uncle F.'s case loses its best legal leg, and mine (mine and the legatees') is practically won. So somehow, in the next six days, I must tackle Dave, Dr. Edmonds, Mrs. Hockins, Mr. Bruce, and Brick Mulvaney, even if all I do is ask them that one question.

As it turned out, that was the last entry I ever made.

◇◇◇◇◇◇◇◇ **4** ◇◇◇◇◇◇◇◇

Greensleeves

1

I woke up the next day still full of urgency and turncoat determination. And do you know, the entire day turned out to be perfectly blank—or it would have if I hadn't got desperate at the end of it.

Nobody came in the Rainbow in the morning—simply nobody. Well, Sherry, of course, but I'd already asked him my question. In the middle of the noon rush, Dr. Edmonds and Dave Kulka appeared, only I couldn't stop fetching and carrying long enough even to say hello, though I did overhear Dave say that he was off for the country at dawn tomorrow to gather weeds and wouldn't be home till late. That made me frantic because it meant I wouldn't get a chance at him until Sunday, if then.

The afternoon was devoid of spyees, information, and even hope.

It was about five o'clock when I got desperate and latched onto Mr. Bruce when he came to give me the new menus for dinner. I don't remember how I dragged Mrs. Dunningham into the conversation— by the scruff of the neck, I expect—but somehow I managed to start talking about her, and doggedly kept *on* talking about her, without results until I remarked that she took great pains to make friends with people.

"Yes, she did," Mr. Bruce said thoughtfully. "She was completely alone, you know. I think she needed friends."

"Oh. No family?" I asked, feeling as though I'd scaled Mount Everest hand over hand.

Mr. Bruce gazed at me in his courteous, unrevealing way and said, "Not that she ever mentioned."

"Well," I said, gazing back at him.

Then suddenly there was Helen, asking something about the new pink tablecloth, and there went my hard-won conversation. I wanted badly to push on with it, too, because even though I'd gotten the same old answer, when Mr. Bruce said it, it didn't *seem* quite the same old answer. It left me wondering if he suspected there was a family she *hadn't* mentioned. Mr. Bruce always left me wondering something.

Saturday was worse than Friday. Mr. Bruce took Saturdays off, and Dr. Edmonds, who usually showed up, didn't. I asked Sherry why not in an unintentionally exasperated voice that gained me a surprised look as well as the unwelcome information that Dr. Edmonds was spending the day at the library. Saturday evening brought nothing, not even Mrs. Hockins out into her rose beds, and I simply did not have sufficient brass to go knocking at her door.

Then came Sunday and my much-needed holiday. I felt like sleeping till noon, but prodded myself up at ten. As I was eating breakfast, I heard the back screen door bang, and Dave Kulka walked out across the yard. I left my toast in mid-bite and in ten seconds was out the door myself. I didn't plan any compaign at all, which was reckless of me, but I was *feeling* reckless. My sole thought was that Mr. Dave Kulka was going to talk to me whether he wanted to or not, and he was going to give me some information for a change. He'd vanished into the little shed behind Sherry's boardinghouse next door, presumably to get his gardening tools, and when he came out, there I was.

"Good morning," I said belligerently. No use being Georgetta with him any longer; he'd just tell me to come off it.

He seemed surprised, then amused. "Hi. What can I do for you?"

"You can answer some questions."

He looked me over, still amused—arrogant as ever—and propped himself comfortably on his spade handle. "OK. Shoot."

I drew a long breath and said, "Why are you so interested in *weeds*?"

I don't know what he'd expected, but not that. He actually forgot to act superior for a minute; he forgot to answer, too.

"Why are you?" I insisted.

"You really want to know?"

"Yes, I really want to know."

"All right," he said, straightening and tossing the spade aside. "Come on. I'll show you."

He took hold of my arm to turn me back toward the house. For some reason I recoiled as if he'd burned me, then felt perfectly idiotic because he stopped and looked me over again, one eyebrow raised above his black Italianate eye and that mouth of his with its cleft lower lip slowly curving at the corners.

"You hurt my wrist," I muttered, showing him the Band-Aid.

We both knew he hadn't touched my wrist, but he merely said, "I'm not going to eat you. I'm going to show you something in my room."

He pointed to the top of the house, and I nodded as carelessly as I could manage and started for the back door. Nothing whatever occurred to me to say on the way through the narrow little back hall or all the way up two flights of stairs, and he was not one to make chatty conversation, so we merely climbed in silence, arriving eventually in a very small, square hall leading into the only room on the third floor.

The room itself was huge, brownish, rambling, and dim, with

steeply sloping ceilings and several deep-set dormers. It was, in fact, the attic, with all the angles and complications of the whole roof defined in reverse, and a lot of cobwebby waste space under the farthest eaves where only a cat could have stood upright. Under the south dormer was a narrow camp bed, neatly made up with old army blankets, and near it a battered chest of drawers and a row of hooks from which a few nondescript garments hung. The remaining usable space was given over to artists' paraphernalia. The largest casement stood wide open to the back garden, and above it a skylight had been let into the ceiling, so that a fair-sized space was bathed in clear daylight. This space was littered with easels, drawing boards, an old paint-smeared table, Mason jars full of brushes and pens, some sheets of copper, and stacks and stacks of drawings. There were drawings tacked everywhere on the walls, too. All of weeds. All delicately and intricately drawn, yet with a crisp simplicity that reminded me a bit of Japanese prints. Many were duplicates, some only half finished, as if they were preliminary tries at something he was working to achieve. One rickety table held a conglomeration of jam pots, beer cans, and fruit tins all filled with earth and little transplanted weeds, carefully segregated as to kind.

"I collected those yesterday," said Dave's casual voice behind me. "I've only started to record them."

He pointed to a couple of sketches on the floor beside a table-top easel. A fresh sheet of drawing paper was fastened with drawing pins to the board; a glass of water containing one lone spray of tiny lavender flowers stood on the tall stool nearby. It was the spray in the sketches on the floor.

"Record?" I repeated. It seemed an unexpected word to use.

"Yeah. That's what I'm *doing*, recording them. Can't you see they're not just pretty pictures?"

Both his words and his tone were rude, but I thought I understood why. I said, "I can see they're a lot more than pretty. I think they're superb."

"They're accurate, too," Dave growled.

I faced him again and met a look like a blow from those black Renaissance eyes. Obviously, he was suddenly wishing me at the devil, instead of here in his private domain, seeing his private work in progress, his failures and first tries and repeated efforts—his private life. Thin-skinned, that's what he was. Sensitive and quick-reacting as something with antennae. He hadn't realized that showing me this room was going to mean showing me himself—and he was beginning to bristle all over.

"Yes, I can see they're accurate," I said.

"No you can't. You don't know anything about it."

"All right, I don't. But they *look* accurate, even to me. What I'd like to know—and I really would—is why it's so important that they be accurate."

He just stared hostilely at me a moment, no doubt trying to make up his mind whether to answer me or simply chuck me out. Then he said, "Ever hear of Audubon?"

"You mean that man who drew birds?"

"'That man who drew birds!'" Dave mocked. "He recorded— brilliantly—all the known birds of North America. Nobody's ever been able to touch him. There'll never be better paintings of birds—or more exact ones. There'd never been anything like them before, either. He put birds on the map. He made everybody see how beautiful they were. And just *as* they were, without any sentimentalizing or exaggerating."

"And you want to do the same with weeds." He didn't say yes or no, just stood there with his hackles up. "Well, I think you're doing it. Dr. Edmonds thinks so, too," I added before he could tell me I didn't know anything about it. "He once said you found a lot of hidden beauty in weeds. We were talking about those big drawings in the café."

Dave didn't bother to speak, just looked carelessly past me out of the window, but his hackles settled a bit, I thought. I asked, "Does Dr. Edmonds know about your idea?"

"Yes. I told him once."

"Does Mr. Bruce? Those drawings you gave him—"

Dave laughed shortly. "*They* don't mean anything. I swapped them for a couple of weeks' meals. I don't go talking to a lot of people about it. Why should I? They'd think I was nuts."

"I'll bet you talked to Mrs. Dunningham about it."

His eyes came back to me quickly. "She was different. She got what I was doing. She was the only other person I ever brought up here."

Something struck me as astonishing. "I wonder why you brought *me* up here."

"I don't know," Dave said, looking as if he wondered, too. He added roughly, "I can't imagine."

"All right, you needn't take it out on me. *I* didn't ask you to, so don't act as if I'm to blame."

"You started the prying. How else should I act?"

"Oh, just be your own sweet, surly self," I said exasperatedly.

Instead of barking back at me, he began to smile, just faintly, just at the corners of that wide, aggravatingly attractive mouth. He was looking straight down into my eyes.

"Why did you jump so when I touched you?" he said casually.

It was too unexpected a question to answer for a minute— besides, I didn't know the answer yet. It was something I meant to take up with myself later, when I had time to back and fill a bit. I did *not* mean to take it up with him. I said, "A goose walked over my grave."

"Funny. *I* jumped a little, too," he said.

"That's absolutely wildly interesting," I told him, having very little idea what I was saying.

He hadn't budged from his original position, which was an arm's length from me, but I suddenly felt suffocated with how close he was and had to work hard at controlling a powerful impulse to step away from him—or toward him. I couldn't tell which. Or rather, I could tell very well which and didn't care to admit it. I daren't shift my eyes, either, any more than I'd dare lower a pointed gun, though his were rapidly making me dizzy. And I was having a maddeningly difficult time breathing.

He muttered, "Potent stuff, isn't it? Like a lot of little electric charges. Shall we do anything about it?"

"I think not," I said as coolly as I could with my voice shaking.

"Maybe you're right. No future in it—we don't even like each other."

"Precisely," I said, deciding I must be imagining this entire conversation.

We said no more for a minute or two that seemed like an hour or two, though his eyes went right on sending disconcertingly blunt messages, and they were disconcertingly uninhibited. "You know," he remarked presently, "I think you're wrong. I don't think we ought to let this pass." His hand reached out, closed around my arm, and pulled. I set my feet and stayed exactly where I was. "Greensleeves," he said. "Listen. Things like this don't happen very often. Believe me."

I believed him—but I wasn't budging. This was potent stuff. I fully agreed with him. It was considerably more potent than any stuff I'd ever come across, and considerably deeper water than I'd ever tried flailing around in. My sole but fervent idea was to get to dry land if I could, and stay there.

He said, "Greensleeves, I'm going to kiss you."

"No you aren't," I told him. I jerked away.

I wasn't afraid of him—don't misunderstand. I was afraid of *me*. The plain fact is that I wanted to walk straight into his arms and hang on like a limpet, and for a split second it was perfectly clear to me that I didn't care a bean for anything else. I knew if I moved one inch toward him right then, I'd get so tangled up in his life that it would take ten years to dislodge me. And I had a vivid picture of what ten years with Dave Kulka would be like— the two of us fighting like wolverines but never able to get free of each other.

"You're a coward," he said. "But I won't insist—if you don't want me to."

"I don't want you to."

In a minute he said softly, "I don't believe you."

After a long time, during which I changed my mind fourteen times—I don't know what he was doing—he finally said, "However . . ." drew a reluctant long breath, and it became possible to look somewhere else. "I'll bet I regret this," he added.

"Mull it over and you won't," I quavered. I knew I had to get out of there, and I knew no way to leave except just to leave, so I said, "Good-by, I'm going," and started for the door.

He muttered, "So long."

I was walking past walls plastered with those painstaking, beautiful drawings. I stopped without turning and said, "Thanks for showing me these—and telling me what they're all about."

"Well, don't go blabbing it around," he said irritably.

I snapped, "Don't be silly," and started on. So there we were, *sounding* normal, anyway.

"No, I guess you won't," he admitted grudgingly, following me out through the little square hall. On the landing he caught my arm again. I jerked away again but didn't walk away. I didn't want to leave. I mean, my *feet* wouldn't go. He said, "I thought you had so many questions to ask me. You only asked one."

I blinked, slowly swam out of my deeps, and thanked heaven he'd reminded me. *Sometime* I'd care about knowing this—I knew I would. "Yes, well, here's another—I'll ask it if you won't ask why I want to know."

"What do I care why? Go ahead."

"Did Mrs. Dunningham have any children?"

He stared and gave a startled laugh, but didn't ask why I wanted to know, just stood and tried to remember. "No, I guess not," he said finally. "She never mentioned any."

"Thanks. Good-by," I said, and managed to start downstairs.

"Greensleeves!" he called after me, very low. I turned and looked up at him standing there in the brown dimness, leaning on the banister with that lock of hair falling over his eyes, smiling a little. "I'm regretting already—aren't you?"

I decided to treat that as a rhetorical question. I wrenched my eyes away and went on down the stairs. In a minute I heard him laugh again, but I'd a notion he was laughing at himself.

Easy enough, for him. After a mere—*could* it be only twenty minutes?—I knew he'd never permit a thing like whatever had happened up there to encroach on his one true, burning interest. He'd just hack it straight out of his life if it got distracting. And it would certainly get distracting, especially to me. *I* had no burning interest, not if I stayed away from Dave Kulka, which I'd been glad to learn I was just barely bright enough to do.

Besides, he was right—there was no future to it. We were as congenial as . . . well, as my mother and dad, whom I suddenly began to understand a trifle better.

I made it to my room without meeting anyone and fell into a chair beside my half-eaten breakfast, still feeling shaken up. I'd been there about three minutes when there was a tap at my door, and Wynola's voice said, "Georgetta? Are you there?"

"Hm? Oh. Yes, come on in," I said, hastily putting on my Georgetta face.

Wynola opened my door and put her head in. "Sherry said you were back. But I thought—"

"*Sherry?*"

"Yes, he's here. In the living room. He wants to see you."

Obviously, he'd already seen me—coming down the stairs. "OK," I said, with something less than eagerness. I'd sooner have confronted an X-ray camera at this particular moment. However, Wynola went away, mission accomplished, and I went to the living room to see what Sherry wanted.

2

I found him standing by the front window, moodily fiddling with the blind cord. He glanced around quickly, and it was a minute before he remembered to say "Hi."

"Hi," I said, and waited. It was certainly his move.

"Well. How are you?" he added about three minutes later, and smiled, but kept studying me sharply.

"Best of health." I decided I'd better move after all. "How come you're not teaching yourself Bantu or something over at the Rainbow?"

"Oh—it's Sunday."

"Gee, I never knew that to stop you before."

He fidgeted—I'd never known Sherry to fidget before, either—then, elaborately careless, said, "I thought you might like to go to the zoo."

Well, this was an unusual development. He'd never thought I might like to go anywhere before. "Why, sure," I told him when I'd got over being staggered. "That'd be nice. Can I just go as is?"

"You look mighty fine to me," he said without the glimmer of a smile.

Well, I looked mighty like I'd just got up and thrown on whatever came handiest, which was what I had done, but I decided the animals wouldn't care if Sherry didn't. I was delighted to get away from the house and hoped we stayed away for a long time.

"Do we walk or take the bus?" I asked as we went down the steps.

"We drive." Sherry bobbed his head toward an elderly but resolute-looking blue Volkswagen standing at the curb next door. "I borrowed my roommate's car."

"My, you *have* been busy this morning!" I said in astonishment.

He ignored that and helped me into the car, where I instantly almost disappeared into the upholstery. I guess there were a few token springs left in the bucket seats, but they'd collapsed so completely in the course of a hard life that a person was almost sitting on the floor. I attempted, without much success, to tug my skirt down over my knees, which were about level with my nose, as Sherry climbed into the driver's seat and folded up like a jackknife in his turn.

I sputtered, trying not to laugh, and asked, "Can you see out the windscreen?"

"Certainly," he replied with dignity, and started the car, repeating, "Windscreen?"

I dredged up some excuse for the Britishism and shouted it over the noise of the motor, but he'd already lost interest, which was totally unlike him. For a while, briskly shifting gears or staring in a preoccupied way at the traffic, he appeared to have forgotten I was there. But when we'd got well out on Jefferson and the Volkswagen had quit gnashing its teeth and settled down to sounding like a busy percolator, he glanced at me with an obviously forced smile and said in a voice intended to be casual, "Do you know Dave Kulka very well?"

"Not very," I answered, though I certainly knew him better than I had when I got up that morning.

"Wonder how old he is, anyhow?" Sherry went on.

"How *old* he is? No idea. In his twenties somewhere, I suppose."

"He may be older," Sherry said gloomily. "He may be darn near *thirty*. He was in the Marines four years."

I doubted if Dave was over twenty-five, Marines or no, but I didn't argue. "What's his age to do with anything?"

"Nothing, I just wondered." Sherry drove for a while. Then he added, "I'd have said you knew him pretty well."

"Now, why?"

"Well, you seemed mighty chummy with him out in the back yard this morning," Sherry burst out irritably.

So there it was; he'd seen us, probably from his window, when I bearded Dave outside the little tool shed. And I suppose he'd watched us talking in no very casual way, seen Dave take my arm, and me pull back, and Dave's raised eyebrow afterwards—then he'd seen Dave point toward his room and the two of us go in the house together. And twenty minutes later he had an outing all planned and a car all borrowed and was sitting in Mrs. Jackson's living room waiting for me to come downstairs. He *had* been busy. I couldn't help brightening as I contemplated this welcome picture.

Sherry's gloom had deepened—probably because I hadn't answered him. As I was wondering how I could explain a single thing without Blabbing It All Around, which I did not intend to do, Sherry said, "Don't I get an answer?"

I pointed out that he hadn't asked a question, adding, "Anyway, I can't think what you mean by 'chummy.' I don't even *like* Dave. Or he me. It's the one thing we agree on."

Sherry eyed me hopefully, then scowled. "Then how come you—"

He stopped because I stopped him, with a *look*. How come I'd gone upstairs with Dave was my own affair, after all. Whether I'd planned a whole campaign to hurl myself at his head or merely trotted up to borrow an egg, I failed to see that Sherry was due an explanation. I frosted up just enough to convey this sentiment.

"I'm sorry," Sherry muttered, and concentrated on the road. "I don't mean to grill you. I just don't like to see you get involved with Dave, that's all. He's out of your league, Greensleeves. He's too old for you."

"Heavens, yes," I said amiably, though I didn't think age had a thing to do with Dave's brand of high explosives. "Besides which he's got no manners. He's a jerk. So why not talk about something pleasant?"

"All right. I'll be glad to." Sherry grinned crookedly at me and relaxed a bit, presently asked me if I liked baby elephants, and by the time we turned into the zoo entrance, he was behaving almost like himself.

It turned out to be a good day, one of the best I can remember, in spite of the sticky start it had got off to. Sherry is the perfect companion at a zoo, and I was so glad of some nice low-voltage, unperturbing company that I managed to be good company myself. It's a charming zoo, anyway, not vast like the London one but large enough to do a lot of strolling around in, with a new cluster of cage buildings or pits always just down the next slope or around a bend in the path. Everything seems bright and fresh-painted and cheerful, and though the whole place is in full sunshine, it's ringed all about by soaring trees. Sherry and I just dawdled along, exactly the way I like to do at a zoo, standing hypnotized for quite a while beside the pool with the Emperor Penguins, who were also standing hypnotized in little rows on their cement island, staring back at us, while they enjoyed the clouds of fine spray that shot up all around to keep them nice and wet. An object lesson, Sherry remarked, in the *laissez-faire* theory of philosophy: you just stand there, and eventually everything turns out all right.

"If you're a penguin," I added. "A zoo penguin. The wild ones *must* have to hump themselves a bit just to keep the food coming."

"Well, I guess so, but I'll bet they do an awful lot of just standing around in rows, contemplating—even in the wild. You always see pictures of them doing that. It's not a bad life, come to think of it."

"Oh, come off it. You'd be bored stiff unless you were charging around seeing what it was like to live in Timbuktu or someplace."

Sherry grinned but looked thoughtful as we walked on. "I'm not so sure. Maybe all I want to do is just stand around *wondering* what Timbuktu is like. I haven't done much charging so far."

"You went to England."

"I was taken."

"Well, my word, be patient. You're not even out of school. Oh, look—bears."

There was a whole row of pits, full of bears of assorted flavors, but I was inattentive at first because I was thinking about what Sherry had said. It struck me forcibly, and for the first time, that he might have hit himself off quite well at that. Of course, it was early to pass judgment. But already it was clear he was no man of action. Look what it had taken to galvanize him into merely asking me out. His *mind* was a dynamo, but he even walked in a drifting, contemplative way—he even played *tennis* that way—and as long as things were jogging along well enough, he let them jog. And he'd planned his whole life along those lines. Cereal boxes from nine to five—because he could do it, not because he particularly liked to. That would supply necessities and leave his mind free to go on finding out about things he'd no need to know and never meant to use, and wondering how it felt to live in places he might never bother to go to.

Well, all right, what's wrong with that? I thought. Nothing. But it had never occurred to me before.

"Which one do you like best?" said Sherry, who was still on the subject of bears.

"The Kodiak."

"You *do*?"

"You bet your life." I want my bears big and dangerous and awesome—real honest-to-gosh *bears*, and the Kodiak was the biggest and awesomest of the lot.

"I like these little black fellows," Sherry said, gazing fascinated into the honey bears' pit—I think they were the honey bears. "Look, it says people sometimes make pets of them. I wonder what it would be like to have a bear for a pet."

"Nerve-wracking. They might want to sleep on the foot of your bed."

"At least they'd keep your feet warm."

We grinned and went on toward the monkey and reptile house, and I gave over analyzing him. It was too pleasant a day; I was all for *laissez-faire* myself. It was wonderful just to stroll about in the sunshine with Sherry and let my mind drift. We began to agree about everything—that the iguanas looked like Javanese dancers wearing those slit-eyed, stylized masks and scalloped headdresses, and the giraffes precisely like Parisian fashion models, right down to their sweeping eyelashes and studied walk, and that there seemed no excuse at all for Bactrian camels. Sherry's favorites of the lot were the two baby elephants, and I even pretended to agree on that, though my own choice was the Barred Bandicoot—a very small, appealing monkey-creature sitting in a small, tucked-away cage all by himself. He looked much more babyish than the baby elephants—though I guess he was a full-grown bandicoot—but what really gripped me was reading on his cage that "expert dodging" was his only defense. That seemed so frightfully pathetic, somehow.

About midafternoon it dawned on us that we were starving, so we toiled up the various little hills to the canteen and ate hot dogs at a little table in the shade, then toiled downhill again to finish our walking tour. We were slowing by this time and tending to lean against guard rails whenever the opportunity arose, and finally sat down to rest in the shade of a minute oak sapling planted beside the American Bison's enclosure—only we couldn't locate any American Bison, merely a long-legged crane standing on one foot taking a siesta.

"Oh, well, you can't expect *everything* in life to be logical," Sherry said after we'd peered around in vain for the bison.

"I don't see why not," I remarked.

"Well, it wouldn't have any charm. It'd be out of character."

I was reflecting that I'd been out of character myself, all afternoon. I'd only bothered to be Georgetta in snatches, when I happened to think of it, the rest of the time just being any old person who happened along. It seemed not to matter, not today. I didn't even argue with Sherry about life's being logical, which I usually think it should be; I just nodded lazily and sat listening to some assorted bird twitterings from a row of cages on the next rise, and looking out over the canyon and the treetops just beyond us, and feeling the breeze on my face, and hearing the shrill voices of children in the middle distance and the murmur of their parents. I knew quite well I ought to be back on College Street asking Mrs. Hockins and Dr. Edmonds my question. I knew I ought to be worrying about Brick Mulvaney. But I wasn't worrying about anything at all.

Sherry said, "I don't want this day to end."

"Me, either."

"Why don't we stretch it out a little? We could find some nice quiet place and have a long, slow dinner."

"Don't you have to go to work?"

"I worked last night. I only clean once on weekends."

"Oh. But I'd have to go home and change."

"What for? I don't care how you look."

I gave him a Speaking Glance and remarked, "Now that's what I call a really thrilling thing to say to a girl."

I thought he'd laugh, but he looked discomfited instead and turned to frown out over the canyon. In a minute he said, "Sorry. I guess I'm not a very thrilling type."

This discomfited *me*, and I couldn't think what to say except that I hadn't meant it like that. I added, with some feeling, that I didn't think I cared for thrilling types anyhow—which made him turn back and study me carefully a moment. He reached for my hand on the bench between us and gave it a preoccupied squeeze, then rose and pulled me up by it. "Come on, we've rested enough—let's go find that bison."

The bison turned out to be in the next cage south, which *said* it was the Sarus Crane's, so either they'd swapped, or the bison had flown over the fence in search of company. A second crane was at home entertaining him, and a third was visiting in the cage of the Agile Wallaby next door, along with two or three of those odd-looking chickens who always turn up in other animals' bailiwicks in zoos. All this illogical charm cheered Sherry enormously, and when he casually repeated his invitation to dinner, I just casually accepted it without mentioning changing clothes. I don't know why I'd been resisting, anyhow—maybe I didn't believe our mood would hold, once we left the zoo.

It did, though. We folded ourselves back into the Volkswagen and percolated out Sunset Highway while the sun sank and a bank of clouds arose. After they'd collided in a Hollywood technicolor production of reds and golds, we turned around and headed back toward Portland. Somewhere along the way we found Sherry's nice quiet place, which was also so nice and dimly lighted that nobody would have noticed if I'd come in my bathing suit. And it was still a wonderful day, and I still wasn't worrying, and Sherry was as perfect a companion facing me across a red-checkered tablecloth as he was strolling around a zoo. We had veal scallopini and salad and crusty bread, which was an exhilarating change from Mr. Ansley's shrimp, chicken, or steak at the Rainbow. We ate slowly and luxuriously, holding our forks poised while we talked—about animals and people and electric toothbrushes and Oxford and muscles and fossils and dill pickles and Oxford and folk music and postgraduate courses and Oxford and harpsichords and Oxford . . .

"You'd really like to go to Oxford, wouldn't you?" I remarked.

"Well—there or somewhere. Sure I would."

"Still just for information? To find out what things like integral calculus are all about?"

"Sure. And at Oxford you'd learn so much on the side. You'd have a course in British manners and customs built right into your life—probably one in international relations, too," Sherry added with a grin.

"But why do you *want* to know all about British manners and customs?"

He shrugged. "Why do I want to know all about anything?"

"I wish you'd answer that very question," I told him.

Sherry took a meditative bite of salad and considered while he chewed. "OK, listen," he said finally. "Suppose you'd always lived in one room—a room about six-by-eight, bare walls, low ceiling, no windows. There's one bed, one chair, and for entertainment a radio that plays the same tune on all the stations and a copy of *Reader's Digest* for March, 1937. This is home—the only one you've got. You try to get out, but the front door opens onto an empty place lined with mirrors. The back door's locked."

"You're ruining my appetite!" I protested.

"Well, I'll restore it. Suppose one morning you find a key to the back door. You open it and find it leads into a big comfortable room with other doors all around the walls. One by one you open the other doors with your key. You find a huge library, with all the books you can read. Then a laboratory with all sorts of test tubes to play with, then a fully equipped art studio, then rooms full of games and musical instruments, and a concert hall with a symphony orchestra ready to play anything you choose, and a planetarium with a lecturer, and a place full of maps and globes, with windows looking out on every country in the world, and a theater where you can watch the Battle of Hastings being fought or the pyramids being built or Rome falling. You find a zoo, and a room where people are putting a rocket ship together—and in every room you find more doors, more than you'll ever be able to open. That six-by-eight room where you've been living is only the front-hall closet of a *mansion*—and it's all yours. All you have to do is open doors." Sherry smiled. "Of course, I'll never get around to all of them, or even half. But I just can't see a keyhole without getting itchy fingers. Does that answer your question, Greensleeves?"

It did indeed. "No wonder Dr. Edmonds said you ought to have your graduate school," I said. No wonder, either, that Mrs. Dunningham had wanted to give it to him. "Sherry, do you think you will have it?"

"There's a chance. A sort of scholarship I might get."

"Tell me about it."

Sherry hesitated, then shook his head. "I'm scared even to think about it until I'm sure."

So we didn't talk about that, but I didn't care, so long as we went on talking and I could go on watching Sherry's smile come and go, and his long greenish eyes turn greener when he was especially interested, and feeling the little strings between us pulling. It wasn't until we were on our second cups of coffee that I realized he was holding my hand across the table—and I hadn't even noticed. No little electric charges. I hadn't even noticed when he picked it up.

It bothered me just enough to make me lose the thread of what he was saying. I caught up in a minute, but the mood that had held all day was gone. Everything was subtly different, as if a thin bubble had burst. Sherry felt it, too; he broke off whatever he was talking about and said, "What's wrong?"

"Do you know it's nine o'clock?"

"What's the difference if it's midnight?"

"No, Sherry. It's time to go. I've got to work tomorrow."

He studied me curiously a moment, still half smiling. Then he shrugged and said, "Whatever you say," and reached for the check.

I couldn't get the mood back, even on the long drive home. I don't remember what we talked about, just that I felt vaguely mournful, and I'd started worrying again—not about anything special, just things in general. Maybe just because we were headed back toward College Street. About halfway there I suddenly said, to my own surprise, "Sherry, what does your room at Mrs. Moore's look like?"

He was surprised, too, not unnaturally. "Like a mess most of the time, I guess."

"No, describe it."

"Well, let's see. It's second floor back, fairly big, two windows, and it's got an old dresser, and a highboy, and a bed—"

"What kind of bed?"

"*I* don't know, a boardinghouse bed. Why do you want to know all this? What's on your mind?"

I didn't answer because what was on my mind, vividly, was Dave Kulka's narrow, monkish little camp bed with the army blankets, and the battered chest and row of hooks—all crowded into a small, unimportant corner to make way for that one burning interest that occupied all the rest of the attic and all but a small, unimportant corner of his life. He was building *his* mansion himself, brick on brick, with a kind of furious patience, and it was going to be just one vast room. It would be a beautiful one, though, and one was all he wanted.

It dawned on me that I was *comparing* Dave and Sherry—which was idiotic, because you simply couldn't do it. Yet I'd been doing it all day—at the penguins' pool, while we were looking at the bears, especially when Sherry was holding my hand in the restaurant. I'd been odiously, if unconsciously, measuring one against the other.

Well, then *stop* it, I ordered myself, aghast. They're utterly different, and isn't that fortunate! Two of Dave Kulka would be a lot too many, and, in fact, who wants two of anybody?

I can't tell you how this little monologue relieved me.

"Greensleeves?" Sherry said presently. "Anything wrong?"

"Not a thing!" I said, and meant it.

He peered at me a moment in the light of a passing streetlamp, then settled back with a patient-sounding sigh. "I wonder what it would be like to be a mind reader?" he said reflectively.

There was certainly only one of *him*.

"Sherry, I've had a wonderful time today," I said. I had. And all the rest of the way home the little strings had never pulled harder.

3

The next morning I turned into Georgetta again, took a firm resolve to put Dave Kulka and his monkish life and his very unmonkish effect on me right out of my mind, and turned my whole attention to my sleuthing. From the grocer's phone I rang Miss Jensen to say I'd come in Thursday, August 1; then I rang the Poudre Puff to make a hair appointment for Thursday afternoon. Then I went back to the boardinghouse and straight through it to the rose garden and Mrs. Hockins, and with absolutely miraculous adroitness managed to start out talking about fungicides and end up talking about Mrs. Dunningham, and asked my all-important question. Before noon I'd cornered Dr. Edmonds and asked him, too. Both of them gave me the same old answer, practically word for word.

That left Brick Mulvaney the only piece of the jigsaw not in place. And for two whole days Brick Mulvaney didn't set foot in the Rainbow. It left me plenty of time to gnaw my fingernails and wonder how I was going to pop my question when—if ever—he did come in.

About four Wednesday afternoon, at the very end of the slack hour and my hope, in he walked. By then I was under far too much pressure to fool around with nonessentials like adroitness. I nearly knocked Rose down getting to him first and ignored two students and a hungry van driver while I started a conversation. Within three minutes it was clear that I'd get no results with any old pussy-footing, roundabout tactics. So all at once I just came right out and asked him how he happened to bring Mrs. Dunningham to the boardinghouse that day four years before.

And he just came right out and told me.

4

Thursday morning I washed my hair completely free of Georgetta's glue, toweled it dry, and piled it all on top of my head with a scarf to hide it, pulling out bangs and cheek curls to re-create the Georgetta look and adding the earrings and blue eyelids. Then I assembled eye shadow and journal, my white pumps and my yellow linen, which I'd never worn on College Street because it rather spells out Paris, and packed the lot in a roomy basket affair I'd got recently to double as a handbag. Then I put on my forgettable gray and took a bus to town. I walked into the nearest ladies' room as Georgetta, emerged as Shannon Lightley, and went on to Uncle Frosty's office.

I hadn't set eyes on him since June, and he did look jolly good to me—comfortable and unproblematic and known and tried and true. Evidently, I looked good to him, too, because he got up quickly from his desk when I came in and hugged me hard.

"Well, Shan. I must say I'm glad to see you." He held me off and looked me over carefully. "Everything OK?"

"You mean about the case?"

"I mean with *you*."

"Oh. Well, yes. As OK as can be expected."

He peered at me a moment longer, then said, "As can be expected by whom under what circumstances?"

"Oh, *really*." I gave up and laughed at him, and he joined me rather half-heartedly.

"Well, anyway, sit down. What've you got in your basket, bread for Grandma?"

"Georgetta," I told him. "I'll add the hairdo when I leave here."

"How did she work out?" Uncle Frosty asked with real curiosity.

"Just fine," I told him firmly. I never think it's really good for a person to be told he was quite right in the beginning and you were quite wrong. Anyway, I hadn't been *all* wrong.

"Well." Uncle Frosty sat down, poked the intercom to tell Miss Jensen we weren't to be disturbed, then settled back. "I can't wait. Begin."

I began by informing him stiffly that he probably wouldn't like anything I had to tell him. Then I got my journal from Grandma's basket and started talking—using the entries just to remind me in three or four words of things I wanted to say three or four hundred about. Such as how wonderful Mrs. Dunningham had been to Wynola. And how entirely likely it was that Sherry had originated the scholarship idea without the slightest conscious intention of doing any such thing. And how tragic Mrs. Hockins seemed to me now, out in the rain with her roses—and how pathetic Miss Heater, still paying for her friend's treachery after ten long years. And how *important* it was for Dr. Edmonds to see Delphi, and for Sherry to go to Oxford, and for Dave Kulka to push on with his work—maybe as important as it had been for Audubon to. How did anybody know? "Because in spite of the fact that he has the manners of a barracuda and all the lovable charm of a sore-headed grizzly bear, plus more arrogance than the whole House of *Lords*"—I took a deep breath and restrained myself—"he *is* a real artist, possibly a great one."

I caught Uncle Frosty's startled and curious eye on me and, to my intense annoyance, felt my cheeks heat up.

"You seem to feel rather strongly about Mr. Kulka," he observed.

I looked carelessly out of the window and said, "Oh, no," and found my mind full of detailed pictures of Dave's dim attic room, and his lower lip with the cleft in it, and his brown, strong throat.

"How old is this man?" Uncle Frosty asked with dawning suspicion.

"No idea," I said, then suddenly met his eyes and the issue. "Too old for me, and I can't bear him, and he's interested in nothing whatever but drawing weeds. So relax."

"I doubt if I relax about you until you're ninety-nine," Uncle Frosty muttered. "However, go on. What about Mulvaney? Henry Bruce?"

"Mr. Henry Bruce," I announced oratorically, "is the most impenetrable man I have ever come across. I don't know a beastly *thing* about him. I like him, though. Don't ask why, I just do—and Rose said once she'd never work for anybody else if she could help it. And he can just smile a bit at Milton in passing, and Milton stops being obnoxious and turns into a fairly nice youngster—and Sherry once said he probably had me figured out. I don't know whether it's true or not." I consulted my notes and added glumly, "And his feet hurt." Then I brightened because I had real news about Brick Mulvaney.

Here's what Mr. Mulvaney had told me the afternoon before and what I started telling Uncle Frosty right then. On a June morning four years back, a little old lady had come out of the Heathman Hotel carrying a folded section of a newspaper, walked straight to the first taxi in the rank—Mr. Mulvaney's—and asked if she could hire it for the day. Mr. Mulvaney said yes, helped her in, and stood studying her while she explained what she wanted to do. He described her as "a spunky little lady" with ideas "all her own." She'd arrived in Portland the day before, she told him; she knew nobody and was unfamiliar with the city—but she'd come here to live. She wanted him to drive her around so she could look Portland over and decide where to settle. She had studied the classified sections of the papers and had them with her, but she doubted if she'd find what she wanted the very first day. It must be furnished, but the landlord must let her gradually refurnish it with pieces she'd choose herself; it must be quiet and a bit old-fashioned—"because *I* am," she explained firmly—it must have pleasant people around and roses somewhere. Now he could start the tour, please, and would he tell her about everything they passed.

Well, Mr. Mulvaney took a shine to her right off, as he put it, and said he enjoyed that tour of Portland as much as she did, partly because he hadn't really looked at the place in years, partly because her questions, which I gather were both penetrating and original, made him see everything a bit differently, anyway. They were comfortably acquainted before the day was over, Mr. Mulvaney being a warmhearted, chatty man and Mrs. Dunningham as full of curiosity as Sherry. They stopped occasionally at some apartment for rent, but she always emerged shaking her head, and from her comments afterward on what she hadn't liked, Mr. Mulvaney began to have a fair notion of what she *would* like. At noon of their second day of touring, he took her to the Rainbow for her lunch, confiding that this was *his* neighborhood, and after lunch asked if she'd consider just a single big room and bath overlooking a rose garden. She was dubious at first at the idea of a boardinghouse, remarking that she knew she'd said she wanted people around, but she didn't want them very *close* around, and asked him straight out if he thought they'd try to take care of her. He just laughed and said, "Not Mrs. Jackson!"—a remark I understand well—so Mrs. Dunningham agreed to have a look at the place. Ten minutes later they were off to fetch her luggage. She had one small suitcase—that was all.

"And that's all the conniving there was to it," I told Uncle Frosty triumphantly. "Mr. Mulvaney was just plotting to find her the place she wanted, nothing more. He said he knew she'd like College Street because she liked *him*—he could feel it. He said he'd never talked so much about himself in his life as he did driving her around, but that a person couldn't help it—she was *interested*. I think he just needed someone to talk to. He's *such* a nice, sweet, patient man, Uncle Frosty, and wait till you *hear* what he has to cope with—"

Uncle Frosty waited, and he heard, in my most passionately indignant accents. Then as I paused for breath, he infuriated me by remarking in very dispassionate accents, "You've got quite emotionally involved with these people, haven't you?"

"Of course I'm emotionally involved with them!" I exploded. "I *know* them. And they're no more conniving than I am, in fact, *less* so—and I might as well say right now that I've not found out one thing to indicate they unduly influenced *any*body, and—"

"Shannon, calm down. I never wanted to find out anything but the truth. I admit that what you've told me so far is not what I expected to hear," he added.

"Well, the rest is even less so. Uncle Frosty—I guess I shouldn't ask, but—well, won't you just drop the case?"

"My client would only get another lawyer, old dear. Unless your information proves that the case won't hold water, legally."

"Well, it proves no such thing." I sighed. I went on with the rest of what I'd noted in the journal, including the fairly cryptic clues I'd gleaned concerning what Mrs. Dunningham had really been like. It was during this part, I think, that Uncle Frosty murmured, "This is as good as a novel. A mystery novel," he added with a grin.

And you know, he was right. I stopped talking, I was so struck by it, and began working out how the novel would begin (with Mrs. Dunningham emerging from the Heathman Hotel with those newspapers in her hand) and how the plot would thicken and the suspense grow as you showed this mysterious little lady influencing all those people's lives . . .

Uncle Frosty brought me out of my momentary trance by saying, "Is that all you have in that journal?"

"Jolly near all. A few more bits and pieces of remarks Mrs. Dunningham made to people—completely irrelevant, for all I know. She seemed to have freedom on her mind a lot, if that means anything. I did find out she never mentioned her daughter to a soul. Don't know why, and I can't understand it. In fact, there're *masses* I don't know or understand about the whole thing."

I tossed my journal onto the desk and sat staring dejectedly at it while Uncle Frosty stared out of the window and thought. Presently, he poked the intercom and asked it for two cups of coffee and the file on Lorna Dunningham Watson.

"Mrs. Dunningham lived with the Watsons for a year after her husband died," he remarked as we waited.

"She did? You mean just before she came here? Well—maybe they were mean to her. Maybe that's why—"

Uncle Frosty was shaking his head. "According to Lorna Watson, her mother seemed perfectly happy with them—'just like always,' she said."

"But she wasn't perfectly happy always. Miss Heater said she had a look in her eye—as if she'd seen plenty of unhappiness but just put it behind her."

"Well—after all, she'd lost her husband not long before."

"I don't think that was it," I said stubbornly. "She told Miss Heater her marriage was a cage." I grabbed the journal again and found the exact quotation. "She said she married to find security and to get free of her early life. 'Get out of my cage,' was the way she put it. But said she only got caught more firmly in another trap and that security wasn't worth it." I tossed the journal aside. "There. She didn't *like* her husband."

"Oh—that may be jumping to conclusions. She stayed with him forty-nine years."

"Maybe he wouldn't let her leave. Wonder what her early life was like?"

"She was an orphan. Grew up with foster parents, in Sacramento. Went briefly to business college there, but quit at eighteen to marry a man ten years older than herself."

"Well, where did you get all *this* information!" I exclaimed.

"From Lorna Watson, of course. I haven't been just sitting here, Shan. I had to go to Medford a while back, so I nipped on down to San Francisco, too, and came back with more notes than you have there. That's what I've sent for."

Miss Jensen appeared then with the file and coffee, and after she'd gone, Uncle Frosty sat up and began to go through his papers with a good deal more interest than he'd betrayed so far. "Let's have a look at those bits and pieces of yours, Shan," he murmured. "I've a notion, if we fitted them in with this stuff . . ."

I got excited, too. And the most remarkable thing began to happen as Uncle Frosty read things Lorna Watson had said about her mother, and I chimed in with her mother's quoted remarks. It all began to make a sort of sense—at least, we began to get a picture of Mrs. Dunningham's married life. The vividest touch was a snapshot Uncle Frosty had in the file—Mr. and Mrs. Dunningham and Lorna standing in front of their Sacramento home about fifteen years before. One glance explained why Lorna had been late to marry. The snapshot showed a large, stolid woman with implacably crimped dark hair, staring the camera down. Everything about her looked humorless, unimaginative, conventional. I asked

Uncle Frosty about her personality, and he said, "Rather oppressive. She's a good, forcible organizer, but hard to deflect when she's once launched on a course—such as this lawsuit."

That fitted her appearance. Even more interesting, she was a near duplicate of her father. He, too, was large, stolid, humorless, unimaginative, and conventional. The difference was that he also had a kind of wistfulness about him, and his arm curved around Mrs. Dunningham's shoulders in what seemed a very gentle way.

Mrs. Dunningham, standing between the two of them, looked a creature from some other world—leprechaun land, maybe. A tiny little lady, as Wynola had said, with white hair drawn back into a bun high on her crown, where a child might wear a ponytail; a still, almost placid face; deep-set eyes turned into black caverns by the too-harsh light; a plain dark dress: she seemed a quite unremarkable frail little lady. Yet it was there, all the same. Was it the slight tilt to her chin? The fact that you *couldn't* read her eyes?

"I'll bet he just adored her," I murmured, staring fascinated. "And I'll bet he never once bought her a present she really liked or understood the least bit how she really felt about anything. I'll bet she never blamed him for it, either—but what a lonesome forty-nine years that must have been, Uncle Frosty!"

"For him, too," Uncle Frosty said.

"*He* had Lorna. No wonder she never got to go clear to England just to see Stonehenge. Can't you see their reaction? I'll bet Mr. Dunningham took her on his next business trip to Fresno, instead."

"No, he took her to Victoria, B.C.," Uncle Frosty said, smiling.

"Of course! 'Just the *same* as England, and so much closer!'"

"And more practical," Uncle Frosty added. He thumbed through his papers and selected one. "Lorna reports that her mother was always terribly impractical. 'Always wanting to spend money on useless things.' Wanting to only, I gather. Mr. Dunningham apparently kept the purse strings in his own hands."

"So she wouldn't go buying things like cuckoo clocks to keep her reminded of the ridiculousness of the human race," I said reminiscently.

"Come again?"

I explained, and Uncle Frosty looked enlightened and shuffled his papers again. "There was something about a cuckoo clock she'd had for years—wedding present, I think. Here it is—according to Lorna, she was 'plain silly' over it, and when Lorna dropped it one day during a housecleaning, she 'took on something terrible.' It couldn't be fixed, to Lorna's relief because it was a dust-catcher and so old-fashioned, but she gave her mother a nice new electric clock the next Christmas."

"Oh, dear," I said.

"Lorna told me forcefully several times that she was always good to her mother, never let her lift a finger about the housework, never let her go into town alone for fear a big place like San Francisco would confuse her. She thinks her mother abominably ungrateful just to walk out like that, because she took the very best care of her."

No doubt Mr. Dunningham had taken frightfully good care of her, too, but for those forty-nine years she'd at least had her own house to occupy her and make her feel useful. It was becoming very clear what her year with the Watsons had been like. Worse than a cage—it must have been a prison. Small wonder that she had waked up one morning, thought, "What am I *doing* here? Why don't I just *go*?", and instantly packed that one little bag and headed north, leaving her whole life behind.

I remarked, "She actually told Sherry once that everybody ought to get lost at some time in their lives—that it was the only way to find yourself. That's exactly what she did, wasn't it? Then afterward I suppose she didn't want to risk what she'd found by even mentioning Lorna's name."

"Superstition," Uncle Frosty muttered.

Maybe so—but I understood how she'd felt.

Uncle Frosty closed his file at last and said slowly, "To me, the basic idea behind that will of hers is still unclear. I feel there was one, but I don't get it. I do think the idea was her own—and I think she was in possession of all her faculties when she had the will drawn up. But, Shan, I still can't absolutely prove it. The thing might not stand up in court."

It was maddening, having to be legal about all this when the situation was plain as the nose on my dad's face, and that's remarkably plain. I asked Uncle Frosty what would happen now, and he said all he could do was talk to Lorna Watson, explain things, and advise her strongly not to contest the will—to respect her mother's wishes, though they were hard to accept.

"Talk to her when?"

"We're planning to stop over in San Francisco tomorrow on our way to Mexico City. I can see her then."

"Will she listen to you?"

"I don't know. I'm wondering whether she's—well—*generous* enough to step aside for these strangers, whether they were her mother's friends or not. Seems to me, if she were that kind of person, her mother never would have felt as she did about her."

"That makes sense," I said moodily. "But you *will* try?"

"Oh, I'll try my derndest. Really, I will, Shan. And I may succeed. But if she insists on going ahead with the suit, I'm obligated to conduct it."

"How soon do you think we'll know?"

"Depends on her. But if she decides to sue, I suspect she'll do it right away."

"She can't, until you get back!"

"Oh, yes—young Turnbull can start the first wheels turning. So if it's thumbs down, you may know soon." Uncle Frosty took a last swallow of his cold coffee, made a face, and added, "In any case, you can quit behaving like a detective. Your job's done. Mighty well done, too."

"Done?" I said blankly. "You mean it's—over?"

"Sure. I've got all the information I need to make up my own mind, and that's what you were after."

"But—" I swallowed, trying to fight down a sudden panic. "What'll I do now?"

Uncle Frosty shrugged and smiled. "Come with Mona and me to Mexico, why not? Rainy season, but we're ignoring that. It's the only month I can get away."

"But I don't—I mean, it's frightfully nice of you, but—" But I didn't want to go to Mexico, rain or shine. I could think of scarcely anything I wanted less. Besides, Mona and I never seemed to jell; I'd spoil the trip for everybody. "If I don't do that, must I go back to Mary's Creek?" I asked warily.

"Nope. You've got a whole month to go yet on our bargain. What you do depends entirely on how you feel about things by now."

Well, the way I felt was that I belonged right on College Street, in the Rainbow. It was the only place I *had* belonged, for years and years. "Could I—just stay put?" I said slowly. "I can live on my waitress salary, you know—I've been doing it. Your checks are just piling up in the bank."

"That's what you *want* to do? Sure? Our plane leaves early tomorrow, and then it'll be too late to change your mind."

"I'm not going to be changing it. This is what I want."

"Fair enough. I see nothing against it." He pawed briefly in a drawer and handed me a thin typed sheet of paper. "Here's our itinerary. It's vague—we're after ruins, not tourist centers. But our dates at a couple of hotels are firm if you want to get in touch. We'll be home the thirty-first. Give me a ring the next day, will you?"

– 215 –

I promised and got up feeling oddly happy and light on my feet. I kissed him good-by, told him to have a lovely time splashing about in his ruins, and went out reflecting for the hundredth time that Uncle Frosty must be the fairest man alive. We both knew that when I rang him on September 1, his part of our bargain would be complete; it would then be time for mine. But he'd said not a word to spoil my last month of being left alone.

Cautiously, as I reached the street and headed toward the Poudre Puff, I let myself wonder—just testing—if my attitude toward college had changed at all. I found I still shied away, though my reasons weren't quite the same. Sherry had punctured my theory that college was "just more school." I knew I might even like it—if I could be somebody besides myself. But my imagination still boggled at the picture of Shan Lightley diving gracefully into a whole freshman class of Americans and doing anything but sink like a stone.

Well, then, I thought, stopping automatically at a "wait" light, what *shall* I do next year? Go back to Europe? No, blind alley. I've got to start doing something besides tag people about. If I don't enter the university, I'd better get a job.

The next minute I was thinking, "But I've *got* a job!"

People began to brush past me and detour around me, and I realized I'd had a "walk" light for several seconds. I started across the street, still carrying on my silent monologue. Why get a new job when I had an old one I liked already? I'd stay at the Rainbow. I'd go right on living in Mrs. Dunningham's room and winding her cuckoo and watching Mrs. Hockins prune roses and Wynola grow up—without spying on anybody. No reason I couldn't stay several years. Maybe I'd just stay and stay, until I got married or something.

The more I thought of it, the more exhilarated I felt and the faster I walked. Somehow, the decision put everything in a new light. I was all but hugging the basket with my domino in it and wishing the hairdo were over so I could renew my eye shadow and slip back into character.

I turned a corner, met a gust of wind that made me duck and not look where I was going, and ran slap into somebody coming out of a book shop. The person grabbed my elbow to steady me, I looked up to say "pardon"—and it was Sherry.

5

Fortunately, I was simply frozen from the shock—too much to betray myself in those first few seconds. In the next few, praying that my stunned expression would pass as blank nonrecognition, I twittered in my strongest British accent, "Teddibly soddy. Ohl my fohlt." I then turned away casually and started on. The temptation was to run like a stag, but I managed to hang onto myself when I realized Sherry wasn't following. I think that's all that got me to the next corner without a collapse or a sudden uncontrollable sprint.

Once around it, I moved so fast that several people turned in a bemused manner to blink after me. Within three minutes I was in a ladies' room turning myself back into Georgetta and hiding my hair in the scarf. No sign of Sherry when I ventured cautiously onto the street. Five minutes later I was thankfully giving myself over to Opyl.

He couldn't have been *sure* it was me, I told myself. When I turn up tomorrow acting perfectly normal, he'll decide he made a mistake. He's got to. Sure to. Anybody would.

None of these assurances served to calm me. Throughout the entire hair operation, I sat chewing my lipstick off, going over and over that unlucky encounter, wondering where on earth Sherry had

sprung from, why on earth he'd had to materialize on just that corner at just that moment. It seemed *cosmically* unfair. It wasn't until
my coiffure was receiving its final cloud of glue that my memory
offered me a snapshot of the bookstore window behind him—filled
with paperbacks. Herndon's. Merely the place he worked—that's
all. He'd *told* me he hung around there when he wasn't working. If
only I'd listened, if only I'd located the place and made a rule to
avoid it . . . If only, if only . . .

I paid my bill and left, reflecting that my best course would be
pure, unadulterated bluff. Tomorrow I'd simply deny the whole
thing, lie like a pitchman, and invent an airtight story proving that
I was nowhere near that corner all day. Just now, I was so demoral-
ized that I could barely work out how to get home without appear-
ing to have come from town. I did accomplish that, taking two
buses and ending by cutting through Mrs. Hockins' rose garden to
our back door. I encountered nobody but a cat during this maneu-
ver, and once safe in my room, I stayed, eating an egg for dinner so
as not to risk meeting Sherry at the Rainbow. None of this did any
good. Sherry merely presented himself at the boardinghouse that
evening and asked Mrs. Jackson to fetch me. If he'd sent Wynola,
I could have sent her right back to say I had a headache or a nervous
breakdown. As it was, I went myself to tell him something—I
couldn't think what.

He was waiting just inside the front door. He turned and smiled
at me and without preliminaries asked gently if I'd go for a walk.
"And, Greensleeves, please don't tell me you've got a headache."

"Oh. Why, no, I wasn't going to," I said guiltily. "But—that
is—what about your job?"

"I've got all night to do that. Come on."

He took my elbow and led me firmly out of the door. I came quietly, feeling fatalistic, and began rapidly inventing and rejecting airtight stories. We walked in silence over to the park near the college,

found a bench near the statue and not too near a streetlamp, and sat down. It was a beautiful evening, clear and gray-blue, with a bit of sunset color left in part of the sky and the trees as still as if they'd been etched against it. I'd roughed out a fairly decent story and was filling some airholes when Sherry took my hand, smiled, and said calmly, "OK, Greensleeves, what are you up to?"

"Up to? What do you mean? I—"

"Don't waste time. I want to know the name of the girl I met on the street today. I want to know when she lived in England. I want to know all about her."

I feigned astonishment, fighting down rising panic. "Well, my word. How do *I* know who you met on the street today?"

Sherry sighed. "I met a girl on the street today," he began patiently, "with wonderful red hair, and big black eyes like yours, and a mole on her left earlobe like yours, and a little hollow in her upper lip like yours . . . and the funny thing was that she had your voice—with a different accent—and she was wearing your watch and your white shoes with the scuffed place on the right heel, and she walked away from me with your walk, which isn't like anybody else's, anywhere. She could think mighty fast—like you—but she didn't fool me for a minute." He looked down at me a moment, smiling faintly. "Greensleeves, did you really think I wouldn't know you?"

My panic had long since collapsed for lack of employment. Obviously, the crisis was all over; my team had lost the match several hours before. The finality of it left me stunned and without the haziest notion of what to say now. I just gazed at Sherry and said nothing.

He said gently, "You put an awful lot of faith in a hairdo and a funny name."

"They worked—for a while," I got out finally.

"Yes, with people like Helen, maybe others. I was pretty sure from the beginning that you were somebody else. You just had to be."

"It was because I said 'white coffee' and mentioned Brünnhilde and wore my watch," I said bitterly.

"No it wasn't. Listen, Greensleeves, don't be ridiculous. You can dye an Easter egg bright purple with green polka dots, but it's still quite clear that it's an *egg*."

"Gee, thanks," I muttered.

Sherry grinned briefly but, being Sherry, added, "Actually an egg's a beautiful object, when you study it. You've just got to study it."

"You certainly seem to have studied me."

"I certainly have," Sherry said. He added pointedly, "I still don't know who that girl on the street was."

"And I'm not going to tell you," I said slowly. I was beginning to emerge from my daze and *feel* the situation I was in, and I didn't like it. It gave me claustrophobia.

"You mean not ever? Or just—not yet?"

"I mean not ever."

Sherry frowned down at me, then let go my hand and faced me, resting his arm along the back of the bench. "But, Greensleeves, why not?"

Because you wouldn't like that girl. Because I'm scared silly you'd go away and never come back. "I can't—that's all," I said.

"Can't? You can tell me anything; it'd never go any farther."

"That's not the point."

"What is the point?"

I squirmed claustrophobically and said nothing.

Sherry's usual easy calm had gone. So had the usual humor in his eyes. "You don't trust me, is that it? You don't want me to know you. I can go hang for all you—"

"Sherry, it's *not* that. It's not anything *like* that."

"What is it, then?" He didn't relax. "Listen, by any chance does Dave Kulka know that girl? Did he know her before she was Georgetta?"

"Not by any chance at all," I said wearily. "Sherry, you're nagging. Quit it. Can't we just—"

"No, we can't. Greensleeves, I *care* about this. If you trusted me, you'd tell me what it's all about. I got only a glimpse of that girl on the street, but I want to know her."

"No, you don't!" I said, feeling absolutely cornered. "*That's* the point, if you must have it. You don't want to know her at all. You wouldn't *like* her—nobody does. Sherry, please believe me. I know what I'm saying."

"I'll be the judge of that."

"No, I won't let you. It wouldn't work."

"Well, this won't work *either*." Sherry clawed a hand through his hair and sighed explosively. I'd never seen him so upset, so nearly angry—and so blind to the fact that I was upset, too. "Be sensible, Greensleeves! You can't go on acting like Georgetta Smith any longer—not with me, not now."

"I know, I know."

"And if you won't tell me who you really are—not even your name—"

I shook my head hard, feeling suddenly as if I wanted to cry. If once I told him I was Shan Lightley, I'd begin *being* Shan Lightley, because all the old tiresome problems and confusions and rootlessness and boredom and indecision and hopelessness that belonged to Shan Lightley would come right home to roost—and if anything could be more fatal to absolutely everything—! "Do I have to have a real name?" I said desperately. "Can't I just go on being Greensleeves?"

Sherry was silent so long that I turned to look at him and found him staring at me with a stricken expression on his face and all the anger gone. "Yes. Of course you can," he said huskily. His arm came off the back of the bench and swept me close against him. "Greensleeves, you're crying."

"No, I'm not."

"Well, almost." His other arm came around me, tight. "Oh, darling, I'm *sorry*. What the heck have I been *doing*? This is important, isn't it? Really private and really important."

"Yes, really."

"I must have holes in my head. Be anybody you darn well please. I'll never mention it again."

"You will, though."

He drew his head back long enough to look straight down into my face. "I won't. I may want to, but I won't. I promise."

"Well—thank you, Sherry," I said, a bit distracted because he was holding me so tensely, and had called me darling, and acted very much as if he meant it. He looked very much as if he meant to kiss me, too, and presently he did, in an intent, experimental way as if he were afraid I'd run—which I didn't dream of doing.

" 'Thank you' nothing," he murmured. "I've given you a bad time, haven't I? From the beginning. Nagging you, trying to find things out . . . senseless." He moved one hand to run his fingers gently up the nape of my neck. "Simply senseless. Doesn't matter who you are. I'm a goner anyway." He interrupted himself to kiss me again, this time with a single-minded concentration that left me dizzy, and perhaps him, too, because afterward he drew a long, shaky breath against my ear. "Greensleeves, or whatever your name is," he whispered. "I've got something to tell you, as if you didn't know. I'm in love with you. I've been in love with you for weeks."

"You—have?"

"I have. I am. I think you're the most wonderful, fascinating, contradictory, unexpected, upsetting, maddening, I don't know what all girl on earth, and when I'm not thinking about you, I'm asleep dreaming about you. I can't get my mind on anything else, and I'm probably going to flunk all my courses. I don't care, either. I don't want to get my mind on anything else. I don't want to do anything else but kiss you. I'm in a complete rut."

I was half laughing, half tearful. "You might have told me."

"You really didn't know it?"

"Of course I didn't."

"Neither did I, I guess—until I got so jealous that day and found out I couldn't stand for anybody else to even look at you." Sherry's arms tightened fiercely. "Greensleeves, tell me the honest truth, or so help me I'll hit you. Do you really think Dave Kulka is a jerk?"

"Not—really," I puffed. Sherry loosened the vise a trifle but still glowered as if he might hit me, so I hurried on. "You know he isn't. Not a *jerk*. Be fair."

"I don't want to be fair. I want you to say you loathe the ground he walks on. Then I want you to stay a mile away from him."

"Well, that's different. I do loathe the ground he walks on, and I intend to stay as far from him as I can get. That's the honest truth."

I thought it was, too. I immediately had my breath cut off again by Sherry's excess of relief. After a moment he drew away and silently memorized my face, then kissed me once more and took his time about it. He could have taken the rest of the evening. I was filled with a sort of happy disbelief and was in no hurry to discover that this was all a mirage or something.

That part ended soon enough. For a few minutes Sherry went on telling me lovely but fairly idiotic things that don't sound right when they're repeated. Then he reluctantly unwrapped his arms a trifle and peered at me. "Greensleeves, you haven't said a word."

"How could I?"

"I mean—about how you feel about *me*. If any way. Come on—and it better be the honest truth again."

"Well, I—love you, too, I think," I told him nervously.

"You think."

"You *said* the honest truth. Sherry, it's—well, all been a bit quick, hasn't it? It's rather soon to *know* exactly how I feel."

"Is it? Not for me. I know the real thing when I find it." Sherry suddenly let go of me and turned away. "And now that I've found it, I can't do a thing about it," he added. "I didn't mean to say any of this yet. It was because of what happened today—running into that other girl on the street—I got stampeded. It seemed as if you were just going to vanish or something, get away from me altogether. Scared me to death. I didn't mean to say a word until I could say everything—make it definite and permanent."

"Permanent?" I felt a sudden, alarmed urge to tramp on the brakes. "Are you talking about—getting married?" I asked uneasily.

"Of course I'm talking about getting married." He gave me an odd, inquiring glance. "That hadn't occurred to you?"

"Well, no—I mean, not yet."

"I know. I'm rushing everything." Sherry was leaning forward with his elbows on his knees, talking to the air in front of him. "Don't worry. I can't do anything but talk. I've got to graduate next spring. Then I've got to get a job drawing cereal boxes—if I can. Then I've got to get a raise over beginner's pay . . . It's going to be quite a spell before I can support a wife on anything but roots and berries. Maybe two years."

"Longer," I said quickly. "Remember Oxford and all that."

"I'll skip all that. Two years is bad enough." He turned to frown at me earnestly in the dimness. "Greensleeves, have I got a right to ask you to wait that long?"

"Oh, my word, I'm only eighteen. That's not very long. I mean, I probably wouldn't be doing anything else, anyway." This new trend the conversation had taken was putting me into a kind of queer panic. "You mustn't skip anything, Sherry. That'd be—all wrong. To cheat you out of something you want so much—and *I'd* be responsible."

"No, you wouldn't."

"I would. Sooner or later you'd hate me for it, too."

"*Hate* you? Listen, I couldn't hate you even if you—"

"Resent me, then. You would, Sherry. Maybe later instead of sooner, but you'd resent me, because there I'd *be*, in your way. And too late to do anything about it."

"It may not be possible to do anything about the other. Listen to me a minute, Greensleeves. You've got the idea that just because I keep talking about Oxford, I'm all set up to go there. That's wrong. It's all just talk."

"But you said—you mentioned some scholarship or something," I said warily.

"Some miracle, you mean. Just count that out."

There, I thought. That's how much he wants it. I said, "Couldn't you save up the money?"

"Oh, I've had a fund going for quite a while, though lately it's not going anywhere very fast. I keep buying records and things with my dough instead of socking it away."

He didn't sound as concerned as he did ruefully amused. It bothered me. "But, Sherry!"

"Will you quit worrying? I don't need to go to Oxford or any place else."

"But you've been perishing to for years. Dr. Edmonds said you *ought* to."

"Oh—'ought to,'" Sherry said disparagingly. He looked away. "Of course I'd *like* to—it'd be great."

If somebody dropped the money in your lap? I asked silently. The way you went to England when you were *taken*? Is it true what you said about yourself, that maybe all you want is to stand around *wondering* what it's like in Timbuktu? "Sherry, that's just being a penguin!" I burst out. "If you want something, go after it! You've got to quit buying records! You ought to put every spare penny in that fund!"

"Well, for the love of Mike," he said mildly.

"I'm sorry. I guess it's none of my affair, but—"

He smiled and reached for my hand. "I did do that for quite a while, Greensleeves—squirreled away every acorn I could get my paws on. Then a few months ago I thought—well, I sort of slacked off."

I relaxed, feeling disproportionately relieved. A few months ago he *had* begun counting on the scholarship, whether he'd admit it or not. He might still get it, too—Uncle Frosty had said so. I said, "Well, slack right on again. You're not skipping anything, not on my account."

"You know what?" Sherry said slowly, staring past my right ear at an idea. "I might not have to. If that miracle should actually work out. Or if I could save enough more. Maybe it wouldn't be two years, only one. Maybe next *spring* . . ."

"Sherry, wait!" I begged. "Are you actually thinking you could go to Oxford and take me along? That's the most impractical—"

"How do you know? I'll do it that way or not at all—that's sure."

"No, it's not sure, nothing is! I'm not even—I'm not really—" I stopped.

"You're not even sure you love me. Is that what you mean?"

Is that what I mean? I asked myself. Then I looked at Sherry sitting there waiting, with his long, interrogative face turned to me, and his questioning eyes and his gentle mouth, and I thought, Oh, no, I can't mean that. I must love Sherry—there was never anybody so lovable. Suddenly, I felt the most peaceful sensation, a kind of dizzy happiness. What was I dragging my feet about? This was what I'd *said* I'd do, wasn't it? Just stay right on College Street until I got married? Maybe this was my new life showing up. Why not? If I grabbed it, I'd never have to decide about college or Europe. I could forget all that, forget everything, and start my life fresh from tonight.

Forget *everything*? I thought. And just as suddenly, Aunt Doris and Dad and Jeanne and London and Harlan Manning and Tivoli and the Pension Algère and Franz and Vienna and the Lausanne airport and Uncle Frosty and my bargain all came crowding in on me, and I was confused and panicky again. How *could* I forget all that? It was all I had to remember.

"Don't you know what you mean, Greensleeves?" Sherry said.

"No. That is, yes, but— Oh, Sherry, I mean I just don't want to talk about it any more right now. Please."

He was silent for a moment, studying me. "*I* don't want to talk about anything else, for some reason."

"Well," I said breathlessly, "that works out, because actually we've got to quit talking, anyway. You have to sweep floors, and I have to go home." I stood up. "Don't bother to walk back with me. I'll just—"

"You trying to get rid of me?" Sherry asked, standing up, too.

I took a long breath. "I guess so—right at the moment. I sort of want to—think, or something."

Sherry smiled, then put his arms around me tight and kissed me, and that beat back Europe and my panic to a comfortable distance again. "OK, Greensleeves," he said. "Just so you think about me."

I told him, with feeling, not to worry.

He struck off through the park in the direction of town, and I walked slowly back toward College Street in the dim blue evening, feeling weightless and unreal. What Sherry had told me changed all sorts of things; having someone in love with you simply puts a new complexion on the world. What I wished I knew for sure was *which* things were changed, and how, and what they would mean to me in specific terms. All I knew was that life was now a different shape and could never go back to the way it had been that morning.

Well, who wants it to go back? I asked myself.

But there seemed so much unfinished business back there—
way back before this morning. And my very hypothetical wedding
"or something" had been scheduled for some very vague future, not
in two short years. Two *very* short years. Long to Sherry, maybe,
but they cut off my breath whenever I thought of them. Now why?
I asked myself. Why do I keep shying off, not wanting to think
about it? Don't I love Sherry after all? Of course I do—that's what
all those little tugging strings are in aid of. But then why am I not
more—well, overwhelmed or something?

I pondered this point uneasily. Surely being in love was supposed to overwhelm a girl, carry her far past doubts of any kind? I'd
always thought so—I wanted it so. I like my emotions big and powerful, same as I like my bears. And it was jolly confusing to feel so
excited and happy, then so alarmed whenever I thought of those two
years. It *isn't* a short time, I told myself impatiently. Twenty-four
months—that's *long*. In Mary's Creek it would be interminable.

When I finally gave up and went to bed, I was still feeling
happy, excited, and confused, in about equal proportions, and still
conducting jumpy dialogues with myself when I fell asleep.

6

The next few days were downright strange. So much had happened to me on the first of August that I thought the entire world must be different and could scarcely believe that everybody else hadn't noticed it, too. Actually, nobody even noticed that *I* was different. I tried to behave naturally, but I was astonished that I could bring it off. Even Sherry's first appearance in the Rainbow the next morning went without a hitch, thanks chiefly to his placid lack of nerves. He accepted Georgetta as if he'd never dreamed I was anybody else, and aside from one private, special smile when nobody was looking, acted as if I meant little more to him than Rose. I wondered how he could do it, then realized he'd been doing it right along. If he'd always disbelieved my act and known he was in love since that day he saw me with Dave, he'd had good practice concealing his emotions. It helped me conceal my own and slip back into character. By day.

Evenings were something else. Every night now Sherry and I walked to the park or along the dusky streets, and with him I never bothered to be Georgetta. The peculiar thing was that I was never Shannon, either. I couldn't tell who I was, if anybody. Sherry seemed not to notice, but it bothered me, and the more I tried to ignore it, the worse it got. I felt just a nameless, faceless Something floating around with no identity to live in. It was a situation I'd insisted on myself, but now I didn't like it. Sherry didn't know *me* at all; he only knew Georgetta—that small fact I mentioned earlier.

Well, the large headaches had begun—chiefly the impossibility of visualizing Sherry or *anybody* married to a Miss Smith whose entire background was a blank. Oh, maybe if Miss Smith had amnesia—but I didn't. I had eighteen years' worth of memories and mental pictures and relatives and oddly assorted friends . . . So did I intend never to see Uncle Frosty again? Or Aunt Doris, or Dad and Jeanne? Ridiculous. I meant to see them again frequently and all my life. I meant to see Mother and Nevin—sometimes anyway—and Franz and Harlan Manning and even Ann and Kingsley Benton-Jones if I ever went mad and wanted to. I couldn't cut myself off from everything—the notion was insane. Imagine never going back to Vienna or London—or going as a tourist, scared to admit I'd ever been there before. Imagine never again walking down that little street with all the button shops, in Athens, to eat *souvlaki* for lunch. I wondered if Sherry would like *souvlaki*. I wondered if he'd like Dad and Jeanne—what he'd make of Mother, and of the staggering racket of polite screaming that hits you over the head when you step into her dressing room after a performance. He'd be entranced, if I knew Sherry. He'd be entranced by Dad and Jeanne, too, and, for all I knew, by the Mary-High drama club and learning to say "scram" in fourteen languages, and—well, by everything. He'd want to know every one of those worlds I'd lived in and never really belonged to.

And if he never knew anything about them, he'd never know anything about me.

It was odd, but thinking about them from a distance and from Sherry's point of view, I began to find those worlds fairly interesting myself and forgot for the moment how extremely uncomfortable some of them had been to live through. Just before I slept that night, I even indulged in a bout of homesickness—as well as I could for tripping over what I meant by "home"—and caught myself reflecting that those years weren't altogether bad—now that they were over—and might have been wonderful if I hadn't been flung into the middle of them so young and green. Even so, I'd picked up a job lot of odd experience and found I wouldn't want to give any of it up. Still, I daren't tell Sherry about it, because that might mean giving *him* up . . .

Nobody seemed to realize that I was so preoccupied, I was virtually sleepwalking. The everyday world kept prodding me inconsiderately awake to fry hamburgers or make change or take my uniforms to the laundromat or react to Wynola's announcement that she'd lost three pounds or to chat with Miss Heater at the mail table.

Dave Kulka kept interrupting my meditations, too. He simply hadn't received the news that I was putting him straight out of my mind, and went on being as disturbing as ever, without doing anything but exist. I can't explain this, and it was no part of my plans, but there it was. I kept finding my eyes following him—and I had to mind what I was about or my feet would start drifting his way, too. Often enough, they did. I'd see him from my window, working in the garden, and decide instantaneously that I needed fresh air—so instantaneously that it always seemed I'd had the idea *before* I saw him. Then I'd decide there was no reason to change my plans just because *he* happened to be around, and I'd defiantly go out and walk about, or sit in the sun on the back steps, careful to snub him if he noticed me. He always noticed me, all right. Occasionally, he'd even stop work, lean on his spade, and give me his undivided attention, which always made me decide that what I really wanted was a cup of tea in the privacy of my room.

He must have noticed me in the Rainbow, too; I felt outlined in neon, head to toe, whenever his eyes were on me—which they more frequently and lingeringly were, the more often he caught mine on him. Once or twice, exasperated with the way I was feeling, I started a casual conversation with him, just to prove I *was* casual. It didn't work. One day I thought he was doing the same thing. I'd been making a circuit of the booths, filling water glasses; he'd watched me all the way. When I got to him, he said, "Were you ever a dancer?"

I said blankly, "No. I studied ballet for a while." He didn't comment. Wishing I hadn't answered him, I picked up his plate and said, "You want something else?"

With complete and unmistakable candor, he said, "Yes."

That put an end to the small talk. Ordinarily, we seldom exchanged a word, beyond those needed to order and produce a cup of coffee—and when we did, we clashed as we always had done. One day, just before quitting time, he wandered in for coffee and caught me studying a sketch of Georgetta that Sherry had drawn at lunch to amuse himself. It was one of those utterly Sherry-like wavery-line cartoons, and it managed to imbue even Georgetta's ridiculous hairdo with a touch of pathos. I was wondering how he could make those few little queer lines say so much when Dave's hand suddenly reached into my line of vision and plucked the paper from the counter. For once I hadn't noticed him come in, and it threw me so off balance that I just stood stupidly while he examined my private property.

"Not bad," he said.

"Not *bad*? It's good!"

"What do you know about it? Who did this, anyway?"

Without answering I snatched at the paper, which he handed to me in the most deflating way, saying, "All right, don't tell me. Coffee. Black." He turned away indifferently, then gave me a sardonic glance as I sloshed a cup down in front of him and stalked away. A few minutes later, as I was hooking in a milk shake, I checked on him in the long mirror behind the counter—the way your tongue goes to a sore tooth. He was lighting a cigarette, and as I watched absently, he shook out the match, glanced into the mirror himself—and there we were, staring directly into each other's eyes. Not glaring for once, just—I don't know—plain staring. It was odd. After I'd taken the milk shake to whoever wanted it, I went to the kitchen to shed my pinafore and go home. When I came out, I knew very well Dave was still there, but as usual I made sure—and as usual he saw me do it. Immediately, he tossed a dime on the counter and slid off his stool; by the time I'd passed the front window, he'd overtaken me.

"Look, Greensleeves," he said without preliminary. "In case you're having second thoughts about our unfinished business, I'm available. Any time."

"I couldn't be less interested," I told him—after I'd got my breath.

"Seems to me you couldn't be more so."

"I don't care how it seems to you, and I don't want to discuss it."

"Discussion's not what I had in mind."

I regarded him glacially a second—without effect—and said I wished we could drop the subject for good and all.

"We tried that, didn't we? It didn't stay dropped. You don't 'wish' it, anyway. You ought to level with yourself for once. You'd find out a lot of things."

I whirled and started along the sidewalk—conscious, a second later, of his footsteps behind me. Conscious? If I'd had one of those big Kodiak bears on my heels, I could hardly have been more conscious of it. I whirled back. "Will you quit following me!"

He said scornfully, "I'm not following you—I'm merely going home. I live here, too, remember?"

He walked straight past me and up the steps, leaving me no choice but to follow *him*, which I did, asking myself furiously why I'd spoken to him at all, why I *ever* did.

However, the situation didn't change much. He continued to go his careless, arrogant way, and I went my seething one, while I waited for the whole distracting thing to pass, as I could only hope it would. We reminded me of two hostile cats unable to control a slight bristling and arching of the back at merest sight of each other—and there were moments when if anybody had stroked our fur, it would have crackled.

I found it bitterly hard to understand how this could be when I was so busy thinking of Sherry every minute.

7

My interlude of somnambulance received a rude jar late in the afternoon of August 12, a Monday, and came to an end that night.

Half an hour or so before I got off work, I saw Mr. Bruce come in from the kitchen, where he'd been called to the phone a few minutes before. I can't say he looked any different, but something about him made me quit thinking about myself for a minute to watch him. He paused by the service cupboard, not even noticing he was in Helen's way, spotted Sherry in one of the back booths, and walked directly to him and said something. Sherry looked mildly surprised, but pushed back his plate at once, thrust some money at Rose as she passed, and told her to skip the pie—I could read his lips across the room. Then he followed Mr. Bruce out the street door, flashing me a quick smile just as he left. A second later I saw them pass the front window.

Rose came back to the cash register, her eyes still following them, too. "Well! Wonder what their hurry was."

I wondered, too.

Seven o'clock and quitting time rolled around, and Sherry

hadn't come back, so I said good night to Mr. Ansley, who'd taken to nodding cautiously to me lately, and walked home alone.

As I was climbing the last steps to the boardinghouse porch, I saw Mr. Bruce through one of the beveled-glass panels flanking the front door, standing in the hall talking to Dr. Edmonds. As soon as I walked into the house, I saw practically everybody else I knew. Miss Heater was climbing the stairs toward her room; Mrs. Jackson and Mrs. Hockins were retreating down the little passage that led to the back door. Dave Kulka lounged near the mail table muttering to Wynola—who looked a bit tight-faced and strange—and Brick Mulvaney and Sherry were just emerging from the living room. They all looked a bit strange, preoccupied, and overly calm.

Naturally, I'd stopped in surprise at sight of all this traffic. By then everybody'd seen me, too, and abandoned their private conversations. Mr. Bruce and Dr. Edmonds greeted me and separated, one heading upstairs and one for the door. Wynola drifted down the passage. Mr. Mulvaney went out quickly after Mr. Bruce, smiling at me vaguely as he passed. Sherry came directly to me, of course, gave me a loving pat on the cheek, and said, "See you in about half an hour, OK?"—and Dave, who had started for the stairs, saw the by-play and stopped dead. I said, "OK," to Sherry, so conscious of Dave in the background that I couldn't help glancing at him the instant Sherry turned away. As I expected, I encountered a pair of alert and intensely irked black eyes. Dave had leaped to all the correct conclusions and was reacting like a bull to the first flutter of the cape. He glanced measuringly at Sherry's retreating back, then sauntered toward me.

"I want to see you, Greensleeves," he informed me.

Sherry's footsteps hesitated. I could *feel* him standing there with his hand on the doorknob. Everybody else had gone. I snapped, "Some other time," and started quickly toward the passage. I heard the front door slam—behind Sherry, I hoped. An instant later Dave had stepped directly into my path.

"If you don't *mind*," I said furiously.

"Oh, don't be so jumpy," he told me in such casual, scornful tones that I felt an absolute fool and was conscious of heat creeping up my neck and into my cheeks. Dave just stood there unhelpfully and watched me blush. "I merely want to ask you something. You still want to know if Mrs. Dunningham had any children?"

"What's *that* to do with anything?"

"I don't know what it's got to do with you. But I can answer you now. She did."

"Oh," I said. Next instant my wits came back, interpreted the unusual traffic in the hall, and I began adding various twos into fours with dazzling rapidity.

Dave was observing my face closely. "I had a notion you'd be interested. Well, so long."

"Wait a minute!" I gasped.

"What for?"

"You didn't even—explain what you—"

"I don't need to. You knew all about that will, didn't you? From Sherry, I suppose. Too bad about his scholarship now. It's blown sky-high."

He started past me. "Dave, *wait!*" I said frantically, and caught his arm.

Instantly, he clapped it against his side, trapping my hand and pulling me off balance. "All right. What for?"

"Quit saying 'what for'!" I wriggled my hand free, with some difficulty. "Tell me how you know this."

"Didn't you see that powwow breaking up? Some lawyer telephoned Bruce this afternoon. There's a daughter, and she wants the dough."

I swallowed, wishing I could make my mind work. It just kept rushing madly in all directions. I hadn't stepped back away from Dave when I freed my hand—maybe because I was too distracted. Maybe. Standing so close to him was part of what was distracting me. So was his tautness—a kind of slow smoldering underneath the surface.

"So that's the end of the bequests," he finished. "She gets the works."

"But she can't! She mustn't!"

"It's all settled. She can have it, for all of me. I don't want it. I don't think any of us did."

"Oh, don't be idiotic!" I choked.

"Who's idiotic?" Dave's hackles had inexplicably risen. "I'll get where I'm going without help from anybody, now or ever. I don't want handouts from my friends."

"Oh, *you*. You don't even want friends—just plenty of enemies," I snapped, wondering if anybody had ever talked to Dave ten seconds without being goaded beyond endurance.

"Right. With enemies you know where you stand." Again he turned to go—and before I could stop it, my hand was reaching for his sleeve. I snatched it back, but not quickly enough. In a flash he'd swung around to block the passage again, remarking, "Whatever you say, Greensleeves. I've got all evening."

"Oh, *really*. I was only—I've got to go change. Get out of my way."

"I'm not in your way. You can get past."

I stared coldly at his shoulder—feeling my usual treacherous desire to touch it, plus a flick of panic. Its hard curve, molding the old brown shirt, looked implacable, in spite of his casual air. There was room to pass him—just. To brush against him. Well, I wasn't going to. I wondered what I was going to do. I felt a strong suspicion that I wasn't handling this at all well. I burst out, "What do you want with me, anyway?" Then, realizing he might just tell me, in words of one syllable, I added, "Quit acting childish!"

"You know, it's the last time I'm going to," Dave said. Abruptly, he stepped aside and past me. "You're going to be late for that date," he added. He walked without haste along the hall and out of the door.

I stood immobilized, torn between wishing him at the devil and agonizing about the will. I was frantic with questions, permeated by sinking guilt. I'd spared scarcely a thought for my cherished legatees since the day I collided with Sherry on the street—having been richly absorbed of late in contemplating my navel. Now suddenly everything had blown sky-high—so Dave said—but it couldn't be "all settled"! *Infuriating* man. Why on earth had I clutched his arm that way? Why did I always challenge him to duels when he always won? I should have walked straight past him and got my information from somebody else. Wynola . . . there wasn't *time* to find Wynola; Sherry would be back soon. But what if I should be *doing* something to stop this happening?

I sagged against the staircase and held my head a minute. My brain refused to do anything more useful than conjure up heart-rending visions of my legatees reaching bleak old age with debts still unpaid, Greece still unvisited, hearts' desires still unattained, hope proved a liar. Dave might talk contemptuously about nobody wanting the bequests, but Mr. Mulvaney must have been counting the days until that money would substitute for some of the long hours in his taxi, free him to have some life of his own—"go fishing." No more days to count now; he was probably driving along this minute facing the fact that nothing was going to be any different for the rest of his life. And Dave—contemptuous or not, he needed paints and litho stones and expensive brushes and free time. And Sherry needed Oxford . . . I woke up, remembering I was concerned in that bit, too, and suddenly found my central worry sprouting as many heads as a hydra.

The thought unglued me at last from my spot in the passage and sent me rushing toward my room. I still had twenty minutes. If I dressed fast, then found Wynola . . . I found her coming out of the kitchen just as I reached my door.

"Oh, there you are, Georgetta!" she exclaimed. "I wanted to talk to you, but—"

"It's mutual! Come on in." I flung open the door and pulled her through it despite her protests that she had to get to the store before it closed. "You'll make it. Talk. I know part of what it's all about—Dave told me about the meeting."

Wynola nodded unhappily. "I'm not going to get my sky-diving lessons. Of course, I always knew I shouldn't count on it."

"Don't give up yet. It's not certain—"

"Oh, yes it is."

"But I mean—" I floundered a second, remembering Georgetta wasn't supposed to know as much about this as I did. "I mean there's sure to be a lawsuit or something."

"No, we all decided against it."

"You all—you *what*?"

"Decided we shouldn't. You see, she had a daughter. None of us knew that. It wouldn't be right to take the money from a person's very own daughter."

Slowly, it dawned on me what Dave had meant by "settled." "You mean—you're not even going to fight this?" I said blankly.

"No. Mr. Bruce wrote on a piece of paper that we hereby renounced our claims or something, and we all signed it."

"But he can't make you do that!"

"He didn't make us. We wanted to," Wynola said simply. "We all felt the same, when we heard about the daughter. Even me."

It was a denouement that had never once occurred to me—though I might have expected it. Now what could I do? No more than a fireman poking around some dying embers.

Wynola, one eye on the cuckoo clock, assured me that nobody minded, really. "Miss Heater said it wouldn't be right for somebody else to pay her debt. And Mrs. Hockins said she's never bothered by a little rain."

"What did Dave say?" I asked, knowing full well he'd said something idiotically high-handed.

"He said he'd rather fight his own wars in his own way."

"Just so he gets to fight," I muttered. He made jolly sure he did, too, keeping a chip like a badge on his shoulder, going around alienating people and provoking them and trying their patience— besides living from hand to mouth and scorning the world and wearing every other kind of hair shirt he could think of. He could scorn anything—except a challenge—he *wanted* things hard and hostile. It was all of a piece, right down to the life work he'd chosen—one so quixotic and near impossible that it kept him belligerent about it every minute. It struck me that belligerence might quite simply be what held Dave together, same as it holds a revolution. He acted as if he *needed* to fight—against odds just barely superable . . . But if that were true, the bequest wouldn't have been good for him at all. It might have ruined him—just made him disintegrate for lack of inner glue.

It shook me a bit, seeing that so clearly. It was the first hint I'd had that Mrs. Dunningham could be anything but right. Then I thought—but Dave's different. I asked Wynola what the others had said.

Well, they'd all said something unconvincingly gallant— except for Mr. Bruce, who'd kept his reactions to himself, as usual. Dr. Edmonds had remarked that he hadn't time for travel, what with the new revisions on his textbook. Sherry had smiled and said it had been a nice pipe dream while it lasted—which first made me vexed with him because it didn't seem belligerent *enough*, then vexed with myself because there I went again, comparing him and

Dave. Mr. Mulvaney had said that knowing the little lady in her lifetime was legacy enough.

Mrs. Jackson, predictably, had found a good deal to say on the I-told-you-so order—but Wynola, quite unpredictably, informed me that she meant to have those sky-diving lessons anyway; she meant to earn the money for them herself, just to *show* her mother.

"That's what I wanted to talk to you about. I've just *got* to get a job. But I don't even know how to look for one, or . . . Oh, I *have* to go get that milk! Could we talk tomorrow?"

I said yes, closed the door after her, and stood hatching one frantic scheme after another, discarding them as fast as they were hatched. It was too late for schemes, for anything. They'd already signed that paper. Still . . . nobody *knew* they'd signed it—no lawyers—and wouldn't until office hours in the morning. The waiver was probably still in Mr. Bruce's pocket. For an instant I longed for proximity and light fingers. But if I nabbed that paper, he'd just write another, and they'd all sign it again, like sheep—like lambs. I had to convince him they were being fleeced—that's what. Go talk to him. Right now.

I glanced at my watch and began tearing off my uniform. Ten minutes—to dress, streak to the Rainbow, convince Mr. Bruce, and streak back before Sherry discovered where I'd gone and began to wonder why. I'd never make it. No matter, I'd think of something to tell Sherry—anything but the truth, as usual. Right now nothing mattered but to tell Mr. Bruce a thing or two.

A thing or two? I zipped my skirt and groped for my other shoes, feeling those little prickles along the cheeks and jawbone that come when the curtain's going up and you're not ready. I'd have to tell him *everything*. He'd never believe me until he knew all about Lorna Watson—by then he'd know all about Uncle Frosty, and me, and what I'd been up to on College Street and in his restaurant. Well, he'd just have to know. Let him sack me. Maybe I'd feel better if he did. I grabbed a cardigan and ran, six minutes before Sherry was due.

I ran all the way to the Rainbow, burst in, saw nobody but some late customers and Helen, whom I confronted. "Where's Mr. Bruce?"

"Hmm? Oh, he's gone. Dear, as long as you're here, I wonder if you could—"

"No, I couldn't. Gone where? Home?"

"Well, really, dear! I don't know. He sent me out to mail that thing, then—"

"Mail what thing?" I said, feeling my heart drop like a yoyo, pause, shuddering, then begin the long climb back.

"I don't know. Some paper he had," Helen told me with great patience and a reproving look. "Addressed to an attorney's office, so definitely none of *our* business, dear."

Oh, no, not much, I thought. My heart gave up the climb and fell back, leaden, to the bottom of the string. Helen walked past me, saying something Helenish about where Mr. Bruce might be, but I didn't listen. It didn't matter where Mr. Bruce was now.

8

I left the café and started home. All I could think of was the ghastly, *preventable* futility of everything. People tried to help each other, went at it wrong, and ended by delivering each other mortal blows. Mrs. Dunningham should never have concealed her daughter's existence—certainly not from the lawyer who wrote the will. He knew about "testamentary capacity" even if she didn't; he could have worded the will to stand up in court. But she'd kept quiet, and see the result: bitter disappointment for the very people she'd wanted to make happy. It wasn't fair. It was *never* fair to hide the truth—not when it affected other people's lives. I hoped I'd remember that, I hoped I'd never, never be guilty of any such . . . then I saw Sherry, just starting up the steps of the boardinghouse, and my spirits took a final sickening plunge as I realized why I was feeling so guilty already. What had *I* been doing, right along, but hide the truth—most especially from Sherry, whose life it had been affecting more and more since the first of August? That wasn't fair either—to put it mildly.

He spotted me and came back down to the sidewalk, looking confused. "Hey, I was just coming to get you."

"Well, I—had to go back to my locker. Forgot something."

A feeble excuse, but it scarcely mattered. He said, "Want to walk over to the park?" and I just nodded and fell in beside him, absolutely miserable. I don't think he noticed, at first; he seemed subdued himself, and I knew why. He was absorbing the blow of that scholarship turning to fairy gold and vanishing forever.

"Quite a mob scene when I came home," I ventured, watching him sidewise as we walked along.

"Yes. It was—oh, sort of a meeting." Sherry smiled down at me. "A piece of unfinished business got finished. That's all."

"Sherry—I know about it . . . Wynola told me," I added hurriedly, dodging the issue one last time. "I'm sorry. You'll not get the scholarship, will you?"

"No matter," Sherry said. "I won't have time to fool around with that sort of thing anyway—I hope."

He glanced at me again, and I quickly glanced away—dodging that issue, too. But I knew I couldn't keep it up. How could Sherry be sure he wanted to marry me until he knew which me I was? I didn't know myself—part Georgetta, part Shannon, and Shan was nobody but part Dad and part Aunt Doris, part Mother and Uncle Frosty . . . We reached our bench by the statue, and I sat down as if my knees had given out on me. It's really quite a ghastly experience, to feel your sense of identity slipping right away, leaving nothing but a sort of uninspired casserole of other people.

"Greensleeves, what's the matter?" Sherry said in alarm.

"Nothing," I said distractedly; then all of a sudden I gave up. "No, everything! Sherry, I've been lying to you. All summer long."

Sherry blinked, then said reasonably, "Well, I know. But I wouldn't exactly call it lying, just—"

"I would. I've got to quit it. It's not right, it's not even *safe*. I've got to tell you all about that girl you met on the street whether I want to or not!" Before he could be noble and talk me out of it, I plunged desperately into the middle.

The next few minutes were pure farce, though I certainly didn't see it that way then. I was trying to tell everything at once, that was the trouble—and the result, for Sherry, was total confusion. I don't know what he expected to hear. Surely not a garbled outpouring about somebody named Shannon Kathleen Lightley who didn't come from Idaho at all, but from Dublin, Ireland, or maybe Mary's Creek, Oregon, except she didn't live either of those places, didn't really live anywhere or come from anywhere. She was about as close to a complete stray as you could find, which was part of the problem, only it was no excuse, I realized that quite well, and I wasn't trying to—

"You mean you're an orphan?" Sherry asked, trying to grab a fact as it went by.

"My word, no! I've more parents than fingers. Anyway, it seems so. Actually, seven."

"Greensleeves, you can't have seven. I mean, there must be two principal ones."

"Well, there aren't. They're *each* principal while I'm with them, which means nobody is, really. *That's* the trouble—well, no, I guess it was mostly living all those different places and not actually belonging in any of them or wanting to go back to any of them. Though I do love London, if only it weren't for Mother and that lot—"

"There! You said 'Mother,'" Sherry said, faint but pursuing.

"Rosaleen O'Leary. She's another part of my trouble. I don't suppose she can help it, but—"

"Wait, who are we talking about now? Rosaleen O'Leary the British actress? The movie star? Why is *she* part of your trouble?"

"Because she's my mother! I just told you."

"Rosaleen O'Leary is your *mother*?" Sherry repeated in astonishment. "But you said your name was—"

I finally got everybody's name and relationship unscrambled and explained about Dad's work. "But that's not the worst. It's *me*. What I am. What I've been *doing*. Sherry, you won't like me any more when you know!" I warned him wildly.

"Quit that. Just go ahead and tell me."

"All right. Sherry, I'm a spy."

There was a dead silence for about five seconds. Then Sherry said, in a firmly dispassionate voice, "Greensleeves, don't you think you'd better stick to facts, now that you're started on this? The more fiction you drag in—who are you a spy for? The Mary's Creek Acme Detective Agency or somebody?"

"No, for Uncle Frosty, and it's not fiction." I clasped my hands together tightly. "I've been spying on *you*. I knew all about that will before I came here. I know a lot you still don't. I've known all along about the daughter—and that you probably weren't going to get to go to Oxford—and what *you* don't know is that it's probably my fault because of my spying!"

Sherry regarded me in utter amazement. "The will has something to do with Shannon Kathleen Lightley?"

"It has everything to do with her!"

"Well, then go on. But before I lose control and shake you, will you *please* start making a little sense? For instance, could we take these things in some kind of order? Alphabetically, if you want to. But begin at the beginning, and go slow! Better start when you were born."

Since my birth did seem the real source of all the trouble, I said glumly, "All right. I was born."

"Where?" Sherry demanded.

"Dublin. In a taxi on the way from my Aunt Kathleen's flat to— my word, I was even *born* traveling. It's just now struck me."

"Don't get off the subject. Who's your Aunt Kathleen?"

I told him Mother's sister, and just went on from that moment, chronologically—which on the whole seemed clearer than alphabetically. Sherry interrupted me frequently to ask questions—nervous ones, at first, then when he realized I wasn't going to go skipping around confusing him, more and more interested ones, and once a sharp one.

"Wait a minute. Who is this Franz?"

I told him who this Franz was, and, in response to other sharp questions, what this Franz looked like, when I'd known him, where he was now, how I knew where he was now, and that I jolly well did mean to answer his letter and any others because I liked Franz.

"I can tell you do. What I can't quite tell is whether I ought to be jealous."

"Oh, don't be silly."

"Did he ever kiss you?"

"Yes, but it didn't take, and we just dropped it. Sherry—Franz would be my brother, if I had one. Does that clear things up?"

Sherry muttered, and I went on, feeling obscurely comforted. I'd no right to—I was convinced that when I'd finished, Sherry wouldn't care *what* Franz was to me, if anything. But I suspect it was along in here that I gradually forgot this was a confession and began to make a good narrative of it. It started with audience stimulation, which I'll doubtless react to on my deathbed. Sherry *was* fascinated, as I'd foreseen, and I got fascinated making him know the people I knew, even throwing in anecdotes not necessary to the plot, just to entertain him. Yes, and I found myself thinking of it as a plot, too, same as in Uncle Frosty's office that day—though I didn't think much of the central character of *this* novel. Still—I caught myself reflecting—if one wrote it, one could fix all that.

Well, that woke me up. I wasn't writing a novel, I was trying to tell the truth. And I was editing. Whitewashing. Embroidering. I was *making* it fascinating. It shocked me so that I quit talking.

Sherry waited a minute, then said, "Go on."

"I will," I told him grimly. "I'll go back, too. I've been lying again. I haven't told you what that girl is really like." Scrupulously, I told him, sticking to bare, unwelcome facts. It was worse than a session with the dentist, but when I finished, there was Shan—the perennial malcontent, cross-grained, sharp-tongued, short-tempered, unliked and unlikeable, a stiff-necked American to Europeans, a snobby European to Mary's Creek, a trial to Aunt Doris, a problem to Uncle Frosty, and to Dad an unreasonable, impossible teen-ager who fought tirelessly all his efforts to educate her and give her something she could keep. I quoted a few of Dad's more astringent remarks about my character, winding up with my own version of it as all thorns outside and protoplasm within. Then, sulkily, because I was entirely miserable by now, I explained about Georgetta and confessed my treachery. "So, do you see? Not only is it my doing you've missed that scholarship, but I'm nobody you even want to know, much less be in love with. I release you from everything. You don't even have to walk home with me. I'll understand perfectly, and I don't blame you at all." I stood up.

Sherry pulled me right back down. "Don't talk foolishness."

"I'm *not* talking foolishness!"

"You're talking like a perfect idiot, and you are one, if you think any of this is going to make the slightest difference in the way I feel about you."

"But, *Sherry*! Oh, how discouraging! Didn't you listen to anything I *said*? Will I have to say it all *over* again?"

"I heard everything you said. I'm beginning to understand you a little for the first time, and that's great! Why should it put me off?"

"For all sorts of reasons! Your bequest—"

"Oh, forget that. I don't think you had a thing to do with it."

"Well—maybe not. I do think that daughter would have fought the will regardless. But that's only the—"

"You know, there's something you haven't explained," said Sherry. "Why don't you like your dimple?"

After a moment's blankness at the abrupt change of subject, I told him why I didn't like my dimple. He listened thoughtfully, then shook his head. "Not a good reason—just because it looks better on your mother."

"*That's* not what I said."

"Yes, it is, in effect. Naturally, I've only seen your mother in the movies. But I never even noticed she had dimples. They don't do the same thing for her at all." While I was still open-mouthed at this heresy, he calmly added another. "I know she's supposed to be a famous beauty. Frankly, I never liked her type, if you don't mind my saying so. Too perfect."

I said finally, "Well, that's *one* thing that isn't wrong with me."

Sherry smiled, then reached out and took me in his arms, very tenderly. "I can't find anything wrong with you," he said.

"Sherry, I don't see *how* you can sit there and say that! I've told you what I'm like."

"Phooey. I knew already. Greensleeves, I'll swear you're not very bright sometimes. You're not anything like that girl you've been describing."

I pulled away in dismay. "But I *am*. Sherry, you're just blind, and you mustn't be. I *am* that girl. I've just been acting."

"Playing Georgetta, you mean? Oh, sure—when you thought of it. But she was a phoney. I saw that, didn't I?"

"Yes, but you liked her anyway. I did, too. But nobody likes Shan. *I* don't. You don't really know Shan yet, and—"

He effectively shut me up by kissing me hard, then giving me an exasperated little shake. "Will you get it through your head," he said very distinctly, "that none of this matters? What the heck difference do names make? It's you I'm in love with. *Greensleeves.*"

"But that's only another name. An alias for what I am when I'm not being Georgetta *or* Shannon."

"All right, that's what I mean. That's you."

I stared at him. "You mean my—inner girl is somebody else? I'm *three* people now?"

Sherry let go of me and burst out laughing.

"I fail to see what's funny," I told him resentfully.

"*You* are! Don't you know you're Greensleeves and not any of these other characters?"

"Sherry, that's easy for you to say, but *I* don't know how Greensleeves is different from those others. I don't know what she's like at all. Besides, you probably mean I'm some certain way with you—and I'm different with you from the way I am with anybody else."

"Well, a little, but not much. All the other people around here like Greensleeves, too. They discovered you under that hairdo same as I did."

"Well, fine," I said bitterly. "Now all I have to do is discover myself."

Sherry started to answer, then didn't; he took my hand and started playing thoughtfully with my fingers instead. After a minute he said slowly, "That shouldn't be hard. Why not give it a try?"

I eyed him suspiciously and said, "How?"

"Come to a picnic with me next Sunday. Dress like that girl on the street, let me introduce you around as Shannon Lightley, but act like Greensleeves—and see what happens."

There was a challenge in his voice, but I didn't care a pin for that. "Certainly not!" I said instantly. "You can't fool me. There'll be a lot of people there. Students—Americans."

"American students don't bite."

"They're the very ones who do," I muttered. "I'd be an unassimilated lump and have to start that *smiling*, and—it'd be the whole Mary-High routine all over again. Besides, they'd all know me from the Rainbow. Know Georgetta."

"No, this is a different crowd—the Listener's Club. I've never seen one of them at the Rainbow; they're usually over at the Union, where the phonograph is."

"What's a listener's club?"

"Just people who like listening to music and each other's opinions. You'd like them. There aren't so many—thirty-five or forty."

I shuddered. Forty sharp-eyed critics all at once. "I couldn't, Sherry."

"I'd be there. I'll stay right beside you."

I felt absolutely worn out suddenly. I patted his cheek and tried for a smile, but it wasn't a very good one. "You're sweet, Sherry," I told him. "But don't ask me to do something I can't do."

We left it at that. At least, after studying me rather unhappily a moment, Sherry abandoned the subject and seemed to go off into a silent debate of his own. I hung my cardigan over my shoulders and huddled into it. I knew he was disappointed in me, and it made the night chilly. Both brooding, we started home and were nearly there when Sherry picked up the conversation where we'd dropped it.

"Greensleeves—I've already asked you to do something you can't do, haven't I? I've heard no news yet on the subject of—getting married." He turned to look down at me rather bleakly in the light of a streetlamp. "Seems as if I would have if you felt you could make up your mind."

"Yes," I admitted, feeling guiltier than ever. "I've thought about it ever so much, Sherry. But I just—"

"Does it have anything to do with Dave?"

"Dave? Dave Kulka? My word, no!" I said quickly—maybe too emphatically, but he'd startled me.

"Sure, Greensleeves?" he said, with a look so thoughtful that I wondered if he'd noticed me watching Dave and heard the fur crackling.

"Sherry, it's not Dave or anybody else. It's just that—that I'm not sure yet." I paused, then returned stubbornly to my refrain of the evening. "Besides, it wouldn't be fair if I decided now. You still don't know Shannon."

"If I ever saw a one-track mind," Sherry muttered. "Will you tell me how I'm going to *get* to know her if you just keep on looking like Georgetta and acting like Greensleeves? If you won't be Shannon even at one picnic?"

"Well, you—well, I don't know." I was feeling tireder by the minute.

"I don't either, and it doesn't worry me a bit. It's all foolishness anyway."

That tired me most of all, because it wasn't, but there seemed no way to convince him. Anyway, he'd returned to *his* refrain. "Greensleeves, you said you weren't sure 'yet.' Do you think you will be, later?"

"Sure to be sometime, I should think."

"Well, listen. Are you going to do what your dad wants? Go to college?"

"I haven't decided. I'm not even supposed to decide yet—I've got another whole . . ." I swallowed. "Not quite two weeks."

"Greensleeves, do it. Stay here and go to Fremont with me—for just a couple of years. I could take a *little* graduate work . . . Wouldn't you be sure by then?"

"Sherry, I don't know. Two years is such a long time ahead. Only somehow I feel it isn't long enough. I know that doesn't make much sense," I added fretfully. "But—well, I don't actually know how I feel about getting married—to anybody. I may be scared of it."

"Oh." Sherry sounded as if he were restraining a sudden grin. "When are you going to decide whether you're scared of it or not?" he asked patiently.

"Oh, Sherry, why do you want to keep on trying to cope with me anyhow? I'm really just impossible. I can see it myself."

"No, you're not." He reached for my hand and held it tightly as we climbed the long flight of steps up to the boardinghouse. "Most of this is my fault. I shouldn't even have brought it up until I could say, 'Marry me tomorrow.' All I meant to do was just—let you know I loved you. And see if you might have anything to say about it. About me."

He stopped as we reached the porch and looked down at me in the dim reflected light that came from the city to mix with the fragile white moonlight. It touched his cheekbone and the rim of one ear. The rest of him was a silhouette—but such a Sherry-like silhouette, with the head tilted at that quizzical angle, and the old windbreak jacket clinging at the shoulders and sagging at the pockets, with the collar carelessly turned up, that I found myself practically in sentimental tears. I knew I'd never, never been so fond of anybody in all my life.

"Sherry," I said. "I can tell you one thing I *think* I'm sure of. I think I'm sure I'm in love with you, too."

The light on his cheekbone moved as he smiled; then he pulled me into his arms, sighing. "You'll be the death of me, Shannon Kathleen Lightley," he murmured. "Don't you know you can't just *think* you're sure of something? You either are or you aren't. But never mind—I'm sure. And you're trying. That's good enough for now." He kissed me briefly, then drew a long breath and stepped away. "Go get some sleep—you're pooped. And I've got to work. I'll see you tomorrow."

He ran quickly down the steps. I watched until his jacket turned into a pale blur moving along the sidewalk, then drew a long breath myself and started for the door.

That's when I smelled the cigarette smoke. Possibly, I'd been smelling it before, unaware of it—now I was aware of nothing else but that faint, ominous fragrance. I turned and saw the glowing tip, not fifteen feet from me. Dave was lounging on the porch railing, his shoulders dark against a moonlit pillar, one knee cocked—and he hadn't just arrived.

He saw I'd discovered him and shrugged. "Sorry. But as it happens, I was here first."

If I'd turned my back right then, walked straight into the house . . . I didn't. I walked straight toward Dave, feeling anger rise in me like lava in a volcano.

He flipped his cigarette away—it traced a thin, bright arc against the night. "Quite a touching little love scene. Now you've got us both eating out of your hand, haven't you?"

"You watched? You *listened*?"

"With great interest."

He reeled out of focus as the volcano erupted. "Well, you utter *pig*," I said, and slapped him as hard as I could.

It wasn't very hard, because his hand flashed up and caught mine before its force was half expended. He kept hold of it, tight, at the wrist, and slowly got to his feet. "Pig, am I?" he said, ignoring my efforts to get my wrist free. "All right, that's done it. I'll tell *you* something now. I don't eat out of anybody's hand. What's more, you're beginning to bother me too much for comfort. Put up or shut up."

"What does *that* mean?" I demanded.

"Oh, quit lying to yourself. You know you're bothering me. You're trying your best to bother me."

"I'm not! If you'd leave me alone—"

"You won't let me. You don't want me to."

"Why, I've told you in so many words—"

"Oh, sure. 'Get out of here' every time you open your mouth—and 'Come on' with every move you make. You think I don't get the message? . . . Hold still! You're going to hear this." He yanked me closer, effectively immobilizing my wrist and dislodging my cardigan, which slid to the floor. He smiled, half perplexed, down into my face. "What are you scared of, anyhow? Your own feelings? Facts? Not of Sherry finding out—he never will, because you'll see to it. 'I think I'm sure!' You've got him blindfolded, and you know it."

My heart was behaving like a Cadillac motor in a Volkswagen. I felt shaken to bits by it. "I don't know anything of the kind!" I choked.

"You mean you just won't look," Dave said. He let that sink in, then added, "Who do you think you're fooling, anyway? You've been daring me to kiss you ever since that day in my room—we both know that. It's time I did it and got it off our minds."

I said desperately, "That won't *get* it off our minds, you idiot!"

"Well, I didn't know the truth was in you! And why do you suppose it won't? I'll bet Sherry'd be interested in the answer to that."

"It's got nothing to do with Sherry—"

"No? Hadn't you better find out? Or are you scared to? You're scared of everything, aren't you? Scared to be yourself, scared to feel, scared to live, scared to face a fact, scared to tell the truth, scared to answer a simple question . . . Let's try you. Do you want me to kiss you, or don't you?"

I didn't answer. I didn't want to hear the question, but I'd heard it. Both of us listened to my silence and to my heart thudding. We stood just not touching, except for Dave's grip on my wrist—I leaning as far away as he'd allow. Still keeping that tantalizing inch between us, he leaned a trifle farther, eyes half closing, and brushed warm, parted lips across my forehead, then down my cheek, then back and forth, slowly and lingeringly, across my mouth.

"Make up your mind," he whispered.

Mind? I'd lost track of everything but those moving lips, and his breath on my face, and the fireworks going off around my head. I felt the pressure on my wrist change and knew it was because I wasn't tugging any longer. Far from it, I was straining toward him, trying to close that inch—and couldn't—and knew he was deliberately holding me away. Then I realized this might be his exact and whole intention and went all to pieces. I thought, If he doesn't kiss me soon, I'll die.

Dave muttered something, twisted me hard against him, and took possession of my mouth.

No use pretending I thought about anything after that. I wasn't thinking, I was drowning—in pure unadulterated, irresistible sensation, compounded by demoralizing weakness. If Dave hadn't been holding me up bodily, I don't think my knees would have. The crude fact is, I forgot who was holding me up and didn't care. Discrimination vanished among the skyrockets. All along, it had been me I'd been afraid of—and all along I'd been right.

I don't know how long this went on—it was a savagely rough and thorough kiss. Even so, I was fathoms deep with no desire for rescue when Dave dragged his mouth away from mine long enough to catch his breath. It was a tactical mistake. Mainly because I wanted him back, I opened my eyes, and—I can't explain this—suddenly saw him plain: that Medici-eyed gardener, a stranger, just somebody I didn't know, holding me plastered against him in a hard, harsh grip, and breathing raggedly, and turning down to me a hard, dark face I didn't love. I stared up into it, and the fireworks spun away, and I came to. There wasn't one little string pulling anywhere—never had been, never would be. I'd always *known* that.

Abruptly, the whole thing became insane. What was I *doing* here in the arms of this man I didn't even like? He was going to kiss me again, too. Swiftly, he was kissing me again, avidly, with shaking mouth—and this time I felt nothing but revulsion. I fought so bitterly that I ruined even Dave's notion of exhilarating battle. I made it imposssible for him to go on kissing me; he had to resort to brute force just to hold onto me, and after an astonished moment he simply let me go.

I staggered, regained my balance, and rounded on him—then saw there was no need for heroics and sagged against the railing to try to stop the trembling of my knees. For a moment we measured each other. Dave straightened slowly, got control of his breathing, and clawed back that lock of hair which promptly fell over his forehead again. There was a touch of chagrined amusement in his expression.

"Well," he said matter-of-factly enough. "I see that's the end of that."

"Yes. It is," I said with immeasurable relief.

Dave shrugged. "OK, now we know." We went on staring at each other. "Queer," he added after a minute, then with real curiosity, "What happened?"

"I don't know. You just—"

"I just quit acting childish. Like you said."

"All right. It worked. Got you off my mind."

"Clear off?"

"Yes." For a while, anyway, I thought. Forever if I'm lucky.

"Well, I'm glad one of us is comfortable," Dave remarked. He moved closer and stood looking down at me hard. "It can't be. Just like that. Come back."

"I won't. I do not want to," I said distinctly.

There was a pause. In the cold light of the moon, I thought I saw a faint sting of color along Dave's cheekbones, but his eyes told me no more than two scraps of black velvet. He said indifferently, "Some other night." His amusement returned when I stiffened. "Oh, don't panic," he told me. "I'm not going to pursue you. I know when I'm not wanted—if I'm not. I know the difference, too."

"All *right*. You've already made that point."

"It's time somebody did, if you're going to keep playing with matches. Men are combustible, and you'd better keep it in mind." He added caustically, "For that matter, you're pretty combustible yourself."

I thought, *I want out of here*, and wondered if my knees would work yet. They felt untrustworthy, and I decidedly didn't want them making a fool of me halfway to the door.

Dave said, "What really happened was that I let you get away the day all this started. I knew I'd regret that."

"Oh, come off it. It's not in you to regret a thing." I relinquished the support of the railing and cautiously tried my legs.

"Isn't it?"

"No, it isn't!" I said bitterly. "Not even eavesdropping on my private conversations."

"And handing you those home truths. That's what rankles, isn't it?" Dave caught my chin and turned my face to him. "Isn't it? If I had just shut up—just scared you and kissed you and made you like it—"

"*Like* it?"

"—don't lie, you loved it—and never called your bluff or mentioned Sherry—"

"Never *mind* Sherry! Will you please leave Sherry out of this?"

"I might as well—you did. Out of sight, out of mind. He never entered your head, once I took hold of you. You call that true love? Or even fair fighting?" Dave's voice became casual. "By the way, are you going to mention this little interlude to him? . . . No, I can see you won't feel that's necessary. It won't be cheating—much. Well, that's your affair."

"Dave, *stop!*" I choked. I tore free and started blindly across the porch away from him—found a door, stumbled through it, and went on—anywhere, just so it was away from him. The big, dim, shabby hall seemed unfamiliar suddenly, unbelievable, a place in somebody else's dream. Dave came in carrying my cardigan, strode after me, caught my arm not ungently, and turned me in the opposite direction.

"Enough's enough, is it? All right. Come on, your room's this way."

I actually let him lead me across the hall and around the stair. Then I shook off his hand and said, "I'll go alone!"

"Relax, I had nothing else in mind." He stopped, though, and stood looking at me, faintly scornful, in the feeble yellow light of the wall sconce above us. "So I played a little rough. You had it coming. You ought to thank me for the education."

I felt perfectly exhausted. Almost with detachment I said, "I think I literally hate you."

"No doubt. But you certainly didn't hate being kissed—and kissed for keeps—by somebody who wasn't bothering about your delicate sensibilities. In fact, by *me*. Did you? *Admit* it." He held my eyes relentlessly a moment, found what must have been there, and relaxed. "There, now did that hurt you?"

I said bitterly, "That's all you wanted, wasn't it? Your ego salved."

I'll never understand Dave Kulka. He gave one of those brief, ambiguous laughs—I never knew whether they mocked me or himself. "No, you little fool. Oh well, you can't learn everything in one night. Go on to bed."

"I'll be so glad to."

"You can dream of murdering me," he suggested helpfully. He put both hands in his pockets and leaned against the wall to watch me go, his face half shadowed, his voice musing. "Ballet dancing, was it?" he said softly. In silence I snatched my cardigan from the crook of his arm. "It's too bad," he said. "I suppose you'll always remember me as a pig." He was still smiling a little as I turned away. "But I'll bet you remember me," he added.

I walked on down the passage to my room, managed to restrain myself from slamming the door hard enough to wake everybody in the house, and went straight to my dresser drawer to find a handkerchief and scrub my mouth so hard it hurt. It already hurt a bit from Dave's bruising attentions. So did my wrist. So did my self-esteem. So did something else inside me that I hoped would get well pretty soon if I didn't look at it. I found I was shaking with reaction, so I went over and curled up in my big chair and hugged my knees tight, calling Dave Kulka everything I could think of in three languages, including a lot worse things than "pig." That helped the shaking, but it didn't do a thing for my smarting pride or for the other thing inside that I could see right now wasn't going to get well at all until I looked at it good and hard.

It turned out to be fear—as usual. I'd found one more thing to be scared of, besides that list Dave had named over. I was scared he was absolutely right—about absolutely everything he'd said.

One thing you had to concede about Dave Kulka, and I sat there conceding it, I can't tell you how reluctantly. He saw things straight, and he was bluntly honest. Brutally so—but never mind. That was better than being so dishonest you could even lie to yourself. I wondered if I had any integrity at all. I wondered what I could be made of, to walk straight from Sherry's arms into Dave's, as recklessly as if I'd been longing to for weeks—well, I *had* (quit lying!)—and without any idea of the outcome. I hadn't even found it in me to admit I had to know the outcome—Dave had told me. I'd never thought of Sherry—Dave had done that. I hadn't known or cared whether it was matches or TNT I was playing with, and Sherry, who wasn't playing and who knew nothing about any of this, was trusting me right this minute as if I deserved it. Blindfolded—by me. I'd *told* him he didn't know Shannon.

I leaned my head on both hands and held on tight while I reached an unnerving conclusion. *I* didn't know Shannon either—not if she was a hypocrite and a cheat. I wondered if anybody did, besides that gimlet-eyed, thrice-blasted Dave. He'd seen right through her weeks ago. And tonight he'd tired of her minuet, decided the ball was over, and torn away her mask.

Worst of all, this was a mask I hadn't known I was wearing. It raised the question of how many more masks there might be underneath. It raised another question, too, one I didn't even want to formulate yet and couldn't answer.

A difficult half hour later I'd decided to take first things first. It was high time Sherry and I both got acquainted with this tricky masquerader, *sans* domino. There was at least one thing I wouldn't stoop to do, and that was to walk straight from Dave's arms back into Sherry's—not until I'd faced that other question—certainly not until Sherry knew just whom he was holding. This time I wouldn't cheat, I wouldn't lie, and I wouldn't just *talk* about Shan—I'd show her to him. First thing tomorrow I'd give my word to go with him to that picnic or whatever it was, and he could see the whole girl for himself. After the picnic I'd tell him about Dave. Then let the heavens fall.

◇◇◇◇◇◇◇◇ **5** ◇◇◇◇◇◇◇◇

The End of August

1

The heavens did fall as a result of that picnic, but in a way I could never have foreseen—though I foresaw every other dire eventuality in nearly a week of nervous brooding.

Ideally—say, in a well-written play—that week would not have existed. The picnic would have followed immediately on my decision to go to it, and I would have gone, head up, on a high, keen note of sheer nobility and at the highest pitch of my resolve. But I've often noticed how widely fiction differs from real life in this sort of thing. During five real days that must be worried through, not only can a person's high resolve work itself down into a crumbling ruin, but also the pattern of everything can shift.

Unfortunately, I *had* given my word to Sherry, first thing Tuesday morning, while my nobility still had the upper hand, and had arranged with Rose to trade days off. So there I was, caught, while the practical aspects of keeping up my courage began a rapid decline. Sherry wasn't around much to sustain me. Park-strolling weather ended Tuesday afternoon when Oregon gave up and lapsed into its normal chilly drizzle. At the time I welcomed this. The picnic might be canceled; meanwhile, rain ruled out *tête-à-têtes* with

Sherry, and therefore kissing—which I meant to rule out anyway until a few things were straighter in both our minds. He did walk home with me Tuesday evening—*run* home with me, through a downpour—and come hopefully into the living room, but Miss Heater and Dr. Edmonds were there, too, so though the evening was sociable, it was a mile from being intimate. My sleep that night was a mile from being restful, too. Wednesday evening was worse, because as we were climbing the porch steps, we met Dave coming down. Sherry gave him a curt nod. Dave responded with an amiable one, accompanied by a casually penetrating glance—then turned a velvet eye on me that said, "Still our secret, is it?" as plainly as words could.

After that I was too afraid the living room might be intimately empty even to risk finding out. I stopped on the porch and told Sherry I had a headache—truthful enough because I could feel one rapidly coming on—and that I wanted to go right to bed.

He stood looking down at me a minute, then turned to stare thoughtfully after Dave. "I wonder why I don't like that guy any more?" he remarked. Then he looked back at me.

"I can't think why you ever liked him in the first place," I said hurriedly. "Well, good night, Sherry. I'd better go get these wet shoes off."

"Good night," he said, even more thoughtfully, but he let me go.

It was *not* a good night. I was out of bed as much as I was in, padding about because I couldn't lie still, or leaning beside the rain-dark window because I was too tired to pad any longer. I did not see how I could tell Sherry what had happened five minutes after I left him Monday night. I did not see how I could *not* tell him. I could not forget, ignore, or explain away anything Dave had said, though I'd been trying hard for two days now. Worse, I could not explain or even want to forget the way I'd felt when Dave first kissed me. That had been a real honest-to-gosh emotion, right enough—big and dangerous and about as disturbing as anybody could feel. But the trouble was . . .

The trouble was that the question I hadn't wanted to formulate had relentlessly formed itself, had matured into a full-grown paradox, and was now coming at me head-on. It had the devastating simplicity of a homemade bomb: Dave, whom I didn't even like, had turned loose in me the biggest emotion I'd ever felt; Sherry, whom I thought I loved, had not yet tapped it. I didn't know whether he could or not. I only knew he never had.

Well, that's explainable, surely, I thought, padding back to the window for the fiftieth time. He's never kissed me the way Dave did.

The real difference might be that I'd never kissed *him* as I had Dave—submitting absolutely, drowning and forgetting where I was and who he was and all the rest of it. Never. I always held back, just as I'd always held back so much else from Sherry, right down to what my name was. I always drew an inward line and never stepped over it. Did I call that true love? Maybe it was exactly that. On the other hand, maybe it was cheating. This was one thing Dave hadn't straightened me out on—he'd simply yanked me over the line, willy-nilly. But Sherry would never grab more than I was ready to give. He didn't force things out of a person, not even information, much less emotions too powerful to control.

I didn't know whether to be glad or not. I'd finally told him my name and what I'd thought was the whole truth, but truth seemed to have as many layers as an onion, and until Sherry and I got to the real middle of it, *I'd* never step over that line—I'd as soon step off the Eiffel Tower. Scared to commit myself, scared of being hurt. Just a natural coward, I thought bitterly. Scared to feel, scared to live—and maybe plain scared (or unable?) to be in love with anybody, ever . . .

And though it seems silly to be frightened by a metaphor, I grew more and more scared to peel any more layers of the truth away for fear I'd end the way you end up with an onion—by finding there isn't anything there in the middle at all.

Well, by the time I finally got to sleep, I felt as if *that* night had lasted twenty years. I guess my battle scars were beginning to show. Thursday morning Rose asked if I were catching cold, and Helen said, "You know, dear, I think you ought to change your shade of makeup. That one makes you look kind of sallow." Mr. Bruce said nothing until the morning coffee hour was over, but I caught his eye on me several times. When the place thinned out, he came over to the table I was clearing and began to help.

"We been working you too hard, Miss Smith?" he asked. "Take off a little early this afternoon. We can manage."

"Oh, gee, no. I'm fine." I looked up and met his eyes. They were gray and patient and a bit mournful, and looked as if they knew everything about anything you cared to name, and had known it for a long, long time.

"I wish you wouldn't worry so," he said. "Things'll probably come out all right, you know—just take your time." While I was wondering if a remark could possibly be so apt without being clairvoyant, he glanced toward the front of the counter, murmured, "What's keeping Sherry today? He'd cheer you up," and went off toward the kitchen with his load.

That gave me something fresh to think about, right enough.

As for what was keeping Sherry, he had an exam, like everybody else. The rest of the week would be full of exams and the Rainbow full of morose, preoccupied faces, and nobody would be in any shape to cheer me up before Saturday, when summer school ended. After that, everybody would be so cheerful I wouldn't be able to bear them. On Monday grades would appear, and the exodus would begin; by that evening everybody in sight would have packed and gone home. Then we really would have a morgue around here—a decor with which my frame of mind by then would blend beautifully, no doubt.

I went on putting scoop after scoop of ice cream in a milkshake container until Helen sighed long-sufferingly and said the noon rush *was* beginning, dear, and if I *could* move faster, she knew the students would appreciate it, because they *did* have a lot on their minds.

I said, gee, I was sure lucky to be carefree, and drifted away, reminding myself that by Monday Helen, too, would have gone home. We were training her replacement. In every cloud, I reflected, there is a slightly tarnished silver lining.

Sherry turned up at quitting time, but only to take me for a very short prowl around the block—a thoroughly unsatisfactory one, hampered by gusty winds and an umbrella—to say he had to study the rest of the evening. "It's my calculus—I told you I was no good at it. Once that exam's over tomorrow, I'll be OK. Oh—and did I mention I'm going home Monday morning, to Bell Landing?"

"No," I said in a voice of doom.

He eyed me around the umbrella handle in mild surprise, which changed to gratification. "Well, don't look like that. I'll only be gone a week. I got a letter from my mother yesterday—she has this idea she ought to see me once in a while, and she's a fierce woman when roused. I haven't been home since Easter."

"Of course, Sherry, don't mind me. I think you ought to go."

"Well, I do, too. But you won't be rid of me for long. I've landed a second job. Got to be back to start it on the twenty-sixth."

"What kind of job?"

"Oh, something clerkish in the administration office. Just mornings. Then I'll turn back into Herndon's mop-leaner every night, like Cinderella. It's only till fall term begins, but it'll add to the fund."

I felt a prickle of hope. "Then you've changed your mind about skipping graduate school?"

"Oh, no."

"But that's what your fund is for!"

He said gently, "That was the original idea. I've got a better motive now—at least I hope I will have, soon." He stopped and faced me, standing very close and holding the umbrella like a little dripping tent over our heads. "You think I will have?"

I said, "Sherry, it's beginning to pour," and edged away.

He caught my elbow and held me. "Maybe you'll think so once Sunday is over."

I didn't answer. I thought once Sunday was over, he was more likely to have every motive for going back to his original idea. And after last night's vigil, I was further than ever from sorting out *my* motives for anything. But obviously Sherry was counting on that picnic to solve all problems, sweep away my last resistance, and end like a Grade B film with a fade-out kiss against the sunset . . . and here came my paradox again.

When he splashed in Friday noon for a quick hamburger before his exam, I said, "Look here—we'd better skip our walk tonight, and tomorrow night, too. You've got to study, and there's all this rain—"

"Oh, the rain's going to stop this afternoon, right after my exam, and Saturday everything's going to dry out, and Sunday's going to be hot and clear. Perfect picnic weather." He smiled. "Anyway, that's my plan. Unless it's really cloud-bursting, see you tonight."

I picked up my tray and my Georgetta accent and went back to work, praying for a monsoon. I was beginning to feel exactly like the Barred Bandicoot, with expert dodging my only defense.

The heavens favored me with a perfect torrent Friday night, but it was their final effort. Before I went to sleep, I saw a star, and by

Saturday morning Sherry's weather forecast had won the vote. I got into my green uniform wishing I never had to take it off again, wishing I'd never met Sherry or heard of the truth, wishing a car would run over me before I had to peel off more layers of it tomorrow. Why had I ever thought I was tired of my domino—lovely, protecting green thing? It was the only safe place to be, and Monday morning I'd dive back into it and stay. All I asked was to work at the Rainbow and be Georgetta E. Smith until I was ninety-five. So I told myself, until it struck me that Sherry's continued presence around the neighborhood, after he'd learned to loathe me tomorrow, might detract a trifle from my comfort. So would Dave's . . . Maybe I'd better just find a deep, deep hole and crawl in.

I braced myself for the callously cheery mood I'd find at the Rainbow today and started for work wondering if life in a nice, peaceful deep, deep hole didn't sound just the thing at that. On my way out—like an answer—I found one of Miss Jensen's envelopes on the mail table; inside was a postcard from Franz, with a picture of a Vienna street and the little *Konditorei* he and I had haunted one Christmas holiday, spending whole mornings over one cup apiece of *kaffee mit schlagobers* and endless games of tick-tack-toe. He'd written, "Remember this place? I lodge in the next street now. I think of you." Remember it? I wished I were there this minute.

That's what gave me the idea, I suppose. I began wondering why I shouldn't go there—if not this minute, then in early fall. Franz had as reasonable a facsimile of a deep, deep hole as I'd ever find. He lodged obscurely in the Praterstrasse, probably lived on pastries and *mocha* at that little *Konditorei*, and trudged daily to the university to attend his round of lectures. When he thought he could pass an exam, he'd arrange to take one; after several years of this he'd have a degree. No coping with personal relationships or dormitories full of other students. No campus activities or picnics. You could go to school at a place like the University of Vienna for years and never even get acquainted with your professors. So why not write off this year as lost, accept my fate, crawl on back to Europe, and hole up in the University of Vienna? Or the Sorbonne. A degree from the Sorbonne should certainly ease Dad's pain. And if things got rough, I could go over to the Pension Algère and talk to Auguste.

I can't say I was staggered with delight at this solution to all my troubles, but it was a solution, and I knew it. By the time I'd changed the tablecloths for dinner, I was treading the old familiar mental paths of passports, airplane tickets, and hotels.

At seven o'clock Sherry stood up from his end of the counter, where he'd been keeping an unblinking eye on me, and told me to come along. "It's not raining, I'm all through with exams, and if you tell me you've got a headache, I won't believe you. Tonight we're going to walk in the park whether you want to or not."

"Oh, why sure, Sherry, I want to. What makes you think I don't want to?" I said feebly.

"Every move you've made since Monday night," Sherry answered. "I'll wait five minutes exactly for you to change out of that uniform. Take any longer, and I'm coming in to get you, ready or not."

Five minutes later, as we started for the park, he said, "Now, tell me what's the matter."

"Nothing, Sherry. Beyond being nervous about tomorrow."

He turned a disbelieving eye on me. "You can't be that nervous over just a picnic!"

"Yes I can, too. I'll be more nervous than this before I'm done."

Sherry's face relaxed a bit. "Greensleeves, this is all in your mind. These people aren't werewolves or anything; they're a real nice bunch. I *know* them."

"All forty?" The sheer number still made me shy like a filly.

"Sure, at least by sight. It's a club. I told you, just a lot of people who like music and swapping records and getting together to listen to them, and squabbling about inane things like whether Bartok's better in his way than Bikel is in his. The whole thing began with half a dozen music-happy paupers who didn't even own a turntable—so they formed a club and asked somebody with a good record player to join." Sherry grinned. "We're respectable now—even got a couple of faculty members, one actually from the music department."

"I don't know anything about music. I don't even like it. I mean I'm tone-deaf. I—"

"Well, relax, you won't be asked to sing a solo. Actually, this thing tomorrow is purely social, very little music involved."

I wasn't reassured in the least. "How long will it last?"

"Well, all afternoon and part of the evening, anyway."

"*That* long?"

"Greensleeves," Sherry said patiently, reaching for my hand and patting it. "It'll take us an hour or so just to *get* to this place. I'm going to borrow my roommate's car—if you don't mind sitting on the floorboards again."

"What place is it?"

"Big hunk of mountainside about forty miles east, in the Columbia River Gorge. Overlooking it, that is. One of the trustees owns the property. It's got a big rustic sort of cabin and a tennis court and picnic tables, and a creek with a waterfall, and lower down a pool where you can swim if you don't freeze easily, and—well, it's a swell place."

"I haven't a bathing suit. Not with me."

"That's all right—not many people swim. The creek's pure ice water. Fine for chilling the watermelons."

"I haven't any picnicky clothes, either. Just an old skirt and blouse, or—"

"Wear your old skirt and blouse, then. And a warmish jacket."

"I don't have a—"

"Warm *sweater*, then," Sherry said, raising his voice. "Will you stop thinking up excuses?"

"Let's just stop talking about it," I said gloomily.

"OK." Sherry tucked my hand through his arm and smiled to himself. "You're going to feel awfully silly about all this tomorrow."

I didn't answer. We found our bench near the statue and sat down, and I stared reproachfully at the cloudless sky. It was slowly turning bright apricot, with a star showing above the statue.

"Greensleeves," Sherry began in that tell-me-what's-wrong voice.

I said quickly—feeling the complete bandicoot—"Sherry, what courses will you take this fall?"

After a moment Sherry sighed and quit studying my profile and said, "Spinach, mostly," and told me what courses he'd take that fall. Then he dug the new Fremont catalogue out of his jacket pocket and began thumbing through it, warming to his favorite topic as he described all the nice useless, flavorful non-spinach he wished he could take—things like Ethnomusicology and Case Studies in Dissent. Most were graduate level, I noticed. I wandered off on some lonesome mental side tracks of my own as the park grew dusky, and ended back where I'd been at dinnertime, trying to remember when my passport would expire.

"Getting dark earlier these days," Sherry said. He'd been watching me, apparently for some time. I nodded. Summer was nearly over—and I didn't want to talk about it. Sherry asked suddenly, "What does Shannon look like?"

"Look like? Sorry, but a lot like me, in general."

"I don't mean in general. I mean without all the eye-gunk and—" Sherry waved a hand vaguely.

"Sherry, you saw me that day. On the street."

"Only for ten seconds."

"Well, tomorrow you'll have all day to memorize me—and without any of the eye-gunk and—" I waved my hand, too.

"And with your hair—down, or whatever the word is?"

"With my hair down." In more ways than one, I thought.

Sherry drew a long, happy breath. "I can hardly wait."

"Can you possibly mean there's some trifling thing you don't like about *this* hairdo?" I demanded.

He smiled, but the conversation did not progress into a lighter vein. He said, "I like everything about you, and I don't care which one of you you are, and someday, sooner or later, I'm going to marry you."

We were silent a moment.

"Greensleeves—" Sherry began.

"Sherry—" I luckily happened to say at the same moment, and he let me go first. "Sherry, I want you to promise me something. I want *your solemn word* you'll fatten up that fund and go to Oxford or somewhere on it. Whatever happens."

"What do you mean, whatever happens?"

"Whatever happens tomorrow."

"I'm not going to promise any such thing. We'll *see* what happens tomorrow—then we'll talk about promises afterward."

"We might not be seeing much of each other afterward," I said desperately.

"Why not?"

I muttered, "Well, you said you were going right home Monday."

"I'm coming right back, too, don't forget. And a week in Bell Landing isn't going to cool me off a bit, if that's what you had in mind."

It wasn't what I had in mind.

"Why are you so interested in packing me off to Oxford, anyway?"

"I think you ought to do what you set out to do. What you—talk about doing. Not just talk."

After a minute Sherry said, "I'm not sure I follow that, but isn't it irrelevant? I've changed my interests."

"No you haven't. You can't help wanting to browse in those nice graduate courses any more than you can help having curly hair! It's the shape your inner man has been taking for twenty-one years, or however old you are. It's your—your burning interest."

"Well, I've got a new one, and it's more important."

"No, just conflicting. Just in your *way*. It is, Sherry. You *know* if I weren't available, weren't anywhere around—"

Swiftly, he caught my chin, turning my face so he could subject it to a slow, grim scrutiny. "Don't get any ideas," he said.

"I'm not. I mean I was only trying to—"

His hand dropped. "Greensleeves, what are you driving at? Can't you just up and tell me?"

"No," I said wearily. "What time is it? I can't see my watch."

"I can't either, so it's finally dark enough to kiss you. I thought it never would be."

He reached for me, and I jumped up as if the bench had ejected me, saying something breathless about its certainly being time to go.

Sherry sat very still a moment, then slowly rose and stood beside me. "Greensleeves, don't you want me to kiss you?" he said quietly.

"Not—just now," I answered with much difficulty.

"Not all this past week, either. Not since Monday night. You were perfectly willing then. Have I done something?"

"No, Sherry! Truly not." I met his eyes, silently pleading for understanding of something I wasn't going to explain—an unreasonable plea if I ever heard of one. "Sherry, wait till tomorrow's over. Then you won't even want to."

"How can you be so ridiculous," he murmured, more or less to himself, but he smiled, if a bit unhappily. "I hope that's all it is," he added.

I did, too, but didn't say so. My emotions seemed to have got as incredibly complicated as only my emotions can get. Sherry took my hand, and we started slowly across the park. "OK, Greensleeves," he said gently. "We'll wait till tomorrow's over, if you must have things all proved and cut and dried. You'll see. After tomorrow everything's going to be just fine."

But I had a strong feeling his interests might change again. By now I almost hoped they would—that he'd lose all interest in me within the next twenty-four hours. At least it would spare me trying to resolve my paradox or peel any further into that treacherous onion. It would also render quite irrelevant the matter of whether or not to tell him about Dave.

2

Somebody had been living right—though not I—because Sunday, August 18, turned out to be the most beautiful day for a picnic anybody could have ordered custom-made. Things glittered and shone, and birds behaved like coloratura sopranos, and sounds reverberated from far off, as if the world were new and larger. The air was like a length of silk, the temperature precisely seventy.

I got up to all this glory, feeling as if I were going to the guillotine, and washed my hair.

By the time Sherry came for me about one-thirty, I'd piled it under the scarf the way I'd worn it to Uncle Frosty's office that day that seemed a hundred years ago, and added earrings and blue eyelids. It was well I did, because we encountered Wynola and Dr. Edmonds and Dave before we folded ourselves into the Volkswagen.

"How do you feel?" Sherry shouted sympathetically as we percolated noisily across town. "Still nervous?"

"No, I'm perfectly calm," I said. Numb might have been a better word—it was that flat fatalism you feel when they actually wheel you into the operating room, and you know you can't do a thing about it now.

We stopped at a petrol station before crossing the river, and Sherry, murmuring, "Well, so long, Georgetta," had the Volkswagen's tank filled while I went into the rest room to perform my transformation. After I'd finished, I stood a moment before the looking glass, knowing Sherry expected to see some stranger. Well, that's who *I* saw—a stranger. For better or worse, I couldn't tell. All the emphasis was different—or lack of emphasis. I'd got so used to blue eyelids and bangs and side curls that the effect without them seemed unfinished, as if I hadn't tried hard enough—and my hair swinging loose about my shoulders felt queer, besides elongating my face into a now unfamiliar shape. I wasn't at home with Shan any more. Thoughtfully, I hung my cardigan around my shoulders and went out to join Sherry, whose eyes riveted on me. He helped me into the car and stood leaning on the open door, frankly staring.

"Let's go, before I lose my nerve," I muttered.

"I've got to look at you a minute. You know, this is real strange. I feel as if I were only just now *seeing* you."

"That's what I'm afraid of."

Sherry reached out tentatively and took a handful of my hair, lifting it, then letting it slither gradually through his fingers. "Rapunzel, Rapunzel," he murmured. It had certainly grown too long. I tried to push it around to the back of my neck and hold the bounce down, but Sherry took my hand away and kept hold of it. "And your *eyebrows*—"

"Mother's eyebrows," I said crossly. It was beginning—the same old flicks on the same old raw spots.

Sherry said, "They're *your* eyebrows—whether she's got some like them or not. You know, I begin to see why those Mary-High girls found you hard to take. You're so much *yourself*. You'd make them all look like dittos of each other. That'd put any girl's back up. And the boys'd be scared of you." He looked amused suddenly, closed the door, and came around to get in beside me. "I'm kind of scared of you myself," he added as he started the motor.

"Why?" I asked incredulously.

"I don't know yet. Oh, I don't mean scared, exactly. What do I mean, anyhow?" He gave me a considering glance. "It's astonishing. You're not even *pretty*."

I took a deep breath of self-control and said, "You're making me feel lots better."

Sherry grinned, but went on analyzing. "Now if I were a Mary-High boy . . . well, I know. It's just a 'Now there comes somebody' sort of feeling—that's what I mean by scared. A boy doesn't just walk right up to somebodies. He needs to circle around them a little first and work a few things out."

"I can't follow this," I said irritably.

"I mean you're an unknown quantity. Can't you see that? The girls would close ranks, and the boys would go all over cautious. High-school boys are a pretty scary bunch. Real rabbity at heart."

"Rabbity? Those bugle-voiced lords of creation in football sweaters?"

"The louder, the scareder. Don't contradict me about high-school boys. I've been one."

"Well, they weren't scared of me. They just ignored me. I don't think the *boys* even noticed me, actually."

Sherry threw me a glance of mingled amusement and impatience. "They may have ignored you, Shannon Kathleen Lightley, but I can tell you right now they *noticed* you. And don't contradict me about that, either." He turned onto the Steel Bridge and added thoughtfully, "Of course, they'd have noticed Georgetta, too. But for some reason, the effect shoots up about 500 percent the minute you unfurl that hair."

I clasped my hands tight and tried to concentrate on the beautiful Willamette River we were crossing, which was impossible because bridge railings are always placed at the precise eye level of people in cars, besides which I didn't have my mind on it.

"What's wrong now?" Sherry asked.

"Well, you're making me feel *conspicuous*! How am I *ever* going to get through today if I can't sort of blend into the crowd?"

"The day you blend into a crowd, I want to see the rest of the crowd," Sherry said with a grin. "Your reactions are cockeyed, Greensleeves. Most girls'll go to any lengths short of wearing a ring in their nose just to stand *out* in a crowd. You can't help doing it—but what's wrong with that?"

"Everything! It'll make the girls close ranks and the boys go cautious! You said so yourself. And if people are thrown off right away just by my *looks*—"

"I didn't say this bunch would act like that. I said a high-school bunch probably would."

"College freshmen are just high-school seniors one year older."

"Unless they've worked for a couple of years in between, or been in the army a couple—my roommate was in for three—or got married and had kids and *then* decided they'd better get an education. Or came from Saudi Arabia or Kenya or Tokyo in the first place and haven't any clearer idea of an American high-school senior than you seem to have of an American college."

"Oh," I said, blinking.

Sherry eased the Volkswagen onto the freeway east and settled back. "Greensleeves, you don't seem to know much about colleges, if you don't mind my saying so. You're kind of ignorant."

"Well, I know it. But—"

"They're not anything like high schools. High schools are homogeneous, especially the small-town ones. If you don't blend with the crowd—and run with the pack—and try to look and talk and dress and think just like everybody else, you're sunk. The great unloved. You're either In or Out, and no climbing around between pigeonholes, either. Have I hit off Mary's Creek High pretty well?"

"To perfection," I said bitterly.

"Bell Landing, too." Sherry mused a moment. "It's a kind of feudal system, with the May Queen and the football captain on top, and the people like me on the bottom."

I turned slowly to look at him. "People like you?"

"Certainly." Sherry smiled at the windscreen—or maybe at my tone. "I never found a pigeonhole in high school any more than you did."

"And you have found one in college?"

"There aren't any. That's the difference. People come from all over, and they can't bring along their little feudal systems—or anyway make them stick—because everyone else has one, too, and besides, the May Queen got married and the football captain is running a filling station, and there's nobody to regroup around. Before they can locate some new grooves, they're all cramming for midterms, and they just never get back around to it. So there won't be any entrance examination for you today, because there aren't any rules."

I thought this over and very cautiously let myself feel a small ray of hope. "You mean the girls *won't* get their backs up, and the boys won't circle, and—"

"Well, I didn't say that. But it'll be on an individual, not a group, basis. Once you get acquainted with a few people—"

"How will I do that? You'll introduce me?"

"You bet I will." Sherry smiled, reached for my hand, and squeezed it hard. "Introduce you! I'm going to wave you like a flag."

I clung to his hand, feeling warmed and grateful, and a bit more hopeful in spite of everything. It made the rest of the hour's drive almost enjoyable. Sherry watched the road and I watched the Columbia, flowing broad and deep and dark beside the highway, with the sun flashing on its surface and the steep sides of the gorge thrusting up on either side. Once a car passed, hands waved, and Sherry tooted and waved back, saying that was some of our bunch. The waving hands, at least, looked gay and friendly. Maybe Sherry was right, and college students were nothing to be scared of—all the boys like Vince and Charlie, the girls like Rose. But Rose wasn't a college student—Helen was.

"Will there be anybody there like Helen?" I asked nervously.

"If there is, we'll leave. What does that sign say? Kendrick? That's our turnoff."

We took a small bumpy road that climbed through woods and patches of deep forest and a few nearly perpendicular meadows that looked more suitable for goats than cows. Then quite abruptly we went through some wrought-iron gates, and the road leveled off as if it had reached the top of something. It had. We came around a last wooded curve, and there we were looking over the gorge, with several miles of the Columbia in sight below, and beyond it, across a lot of space, the state of Washington.

Sherry maneuvered the Volkswagen into the parking area, saying, "The view's a lot better from down yonder."

"Down yonder" was a big, low, rustic house set among tall trees, with a green lawn that ran right down to a final fringe of rhododendrons and the view. Beyond the house, picnic tables stood here and there among the firs. In a clearing, a fire built in a huge old iron pot sent up streamers of transparent smoke into the sunshine. There were knots of students everywhere, the largest group around the fire. I caught a glimpse of tennis courts behind the house.

"Now, listen, don't go stiffening up like that," Sherry said as we started across the lawn. "It's a simple social occasion. Not a hanging."

"I can't help it, Sherry. I *won't* start that awful *smiling*."

"Scowl, then. Tell you what, I'll converse casually with you, and you converse back, OK? It'll relax you. You like to play tennis?"

"Don't know how," I muttered.

Sherry took my hand firmly. "No tennis? What did you do for exercise in that Swiss school you went to all those years?"

"Rode. Swam. Sailed. Skied."

"Well, that sounds adequate. Ever ski around here? Up at Mount Hood, for example?"

I didn't answer. Sherry had steered me on a supposedly absent-minded course that was taking us directly past a bench on which sat two blond crew cuts and a tanned girl in blue shorts. I felt a battery of eyes upon me—two pairs blue, one brown.

"Hi, Sherry," said a crew cut genially, staring at me.

"Hi, Steve," Sherry said. "Hi, Mary, Roger." His hand tightened like a hand on the reins. We stopped. "Shan, this is Mary Warneke. Mary, Shan Lightley."

"How do you do?" I said tonelessly.

"Hi, Shan," Mary Warneke said with a bright smile and a measuring glance.

"Steve and Roger Miller, Shan."

Two large forms arose from the bench. One seemed to keep on arising for an unconscionable length of time. Two pairs of blue eyes questioned me; two grins spread over two homely faces.

"How do you do?" I repeated. I had to tip my head back to meet one pair of blue eyes for an instant; then I concentrated on feet. My own, in Georgetta's familiar and rather worn-out flats (sans ornaments). The Miller brothers' enormous sneakers. Mary Warneke's trim dark sandals on smooth tanned feet.

Sherry's hand was still tight on the curb rein, his voice casual. "Mr. Fairly here yet?"

"Over by the fire. With Sue and that bunch—see? Red plaid shirt. They'll hit you for dues as soon as you show up, I warn you."

"Can't hurt me. I'm broke," Sherry said, raising a small responsive laugh—all male.

Mary Warneke's bright, cool voice said, "Are you a transfer, Shan? Or will you be a freshman this fall?"

I said, "Neither one, actually," tried to think of something to add, failed, and studied a nearby tree trunk.

"Shan's new in Portland. She's still window-shopping," Sherry put in.

"Oh, that's it," one of the crew cuts said affably. "Canadian, aren't you?"

Here it came—the accent routine. Stiffly, I said, "No. I'm—" I'm what? I thought. Irish? Only by birth. American? Only by passport. British? European? Mongrel. "I'm—not," I said, looking somewhere else.

There was a small silence, during which I could feel myself being dismissed as hopeless from three minds.

Mary Warneke's voice, sounding warmer and easier, said, "Say, Sherry, that foreign exchange student arrived yesterday after all, and Bob's bringing him. I'm supposed to tell everybody to be real nice to him, because he'll be kind of—you know."

"Oh, sure, I'll make a point of it."

"And if you want to play tennis, Woody Marshall has charge of the rackets. End of announcements." She laughed, a pleasant, ringing laugh.

"I'm more interested in coffee than tennis at the moment," Sherry said, to my overwhelming, intense, abject relief. "Guess we'll go find some. See you later."

"Sure. Glad to have met you, Shan," one of the crew cuts said respectfully.

There were three other muttered, formal, glad-to-have-met-yous, one of them mine, and we strolled on across the lawn. I found I'd been holding my breath, as usual, and now I felt giddy and a little blind—but not too blind to see that there were at least ten people clustered around the coffee table under the trees ahead.

"Oh, please. Not yet," I gasped.

"I never did show you the view, did I?" Sherry remarked in a voice loud enough to carry back to the three we'd just left. We swerved toward the rhododendrons, followed an unexpected little path through them, and arrived at a piece of cliff edge with a bench on it and an iron rail around it and the whole gorge in front. I stared miserably upriver, feeling as if I could never face Sherry again.

"It really is bad, isn't it?" he said. "I always thought you must be exaggerating, but I see you weren't."

Well, that's that, I thought. I knew it. I said, "We can go home now, can't we? Or I could just jump off right here."

"Now, calm down."

"You said yourself it was bad—"

"I didn't mean the way you acted. I meant the way you suffered. I even thought you looked kind of faint for a minute."

"Oh, that's only because I forget to breathe."

"To *breathe*?"

"Yes, breathe! I do the same thing at the dentist's, when he's putting in Novocain. It's just one of my stupid—Sherry, let's not talk about it. Give up and take me to a bus or something. Then you can come back."

After a minute Sherry said, "Shannon Kathleen, look at me." With enormous reluctance I dragged my eyes away from the distant curve of the river and forced them to meet his for a bare instant, then frowned down at my hands.

"No, keep *on* looking at me," Sherry insisted. "Don't glare. Just plain look at me, as if I were an ordinary human being, and tell me why it's so hard."

"Because I've humiliated you before your friends, Sherry! You wanted to show me off, and I acted like a complete—complete—"

"Aaah, no you didn't. You build these things *up* so. No, never mind the view right now . . . Things are always easier when you *look* at people, Greensleeves." He held my eyes, smiling into them, and the clenched fist inside my chest began to loosen a bit. "You hardly glanced at Mary and the Miller twins. I bet you didn't even notice those skyscrapers were twins."

"No. I noticed one was more of a skyscraper than the other."

"That's Steve. Nice guy."

The one who'd asked—civilly enough—if I were Canadian. "They probably thought I was stuck-up. Insufferable. They probably thought—"

"They thought you were reserved, and slightly baffling, and had the most dramatic hair they ever laid eyes on. They don't have any idea what you're like yet. You've got the twins beginning to circle."

"How can you possibly know all that?"

"I was *looking*," Sherry said pointedly.

"I know I put Mary's back up. I didn't need to look."

"Well, she's engaged to Roger. She relaxed when she decided you weren't going to eat him. She won't let *him* circle far. But Steve'll be back around. Of course, he's going to find me more or less in his way." Sherry grinned, and I felt the fist unclench a bit more. I glanced back at the view and decided I wouldn't jump off into it just yet, after all. I'd have one more shot at this. Just one. "Come on," Sherry added, pulling me to my feet. "This time, look at people. And for gosh sakes, remember to breathe."

The place seemed fuller of activity and voices. Several newly arrived groups were walking down from the parking area, there were people on the long porch of the house, and several dripping-wet hardy souls in swimsuits were streaking out of the lower woods toward the fire, amid a lot of exaggerated tooth-chattering. The coffeepot was doing a thriving business. Sherry walked right into the thick of the crowd around it, taking me along. "Hi, Sue. Got any of that for us?" he said.

"Sherrreee! I thought you were never *com*ing! Now you can pay your dues and be on the Mustard-Slathering Committee and make Tim Stiles behave himself. He keeps telling me I *must* run away with him tomorrow, I must, I must—he can't live without me, and I drive him mad."

"Well, you drive me mad, too, sort of," Sherry said with a grin, while my tentatively budding new notion of myself as a mysteriously fascinating though tongue-tied creature withered up and died on the spot. Nothing mysterious about this girl's charm; she was the prettiest thing I ever laid eyes on, blond and wide-eyed, with a laugh like a bell and blue-white teeth. She seemed to know Sherry very well indeed.

I said, "How do you do," without hearing her last name and might have cut and run that minute if I hadn't immediately had to say "how do you do" to a lot of other people, including Mr. Fairly, who had a thin, dark moustache and was something called a faculty adviser. I couldn't keep track of anybody's name after this, but I must have been looking at people because there was a kaleidoscopic procession of faces flashing past my eyes—all smiling when they turned toward Sherry or each other, all arrested in curious or polite or startled or noncommittal expressions when they turned to me.

Well, back to Mary-High, I thought. Nothing's changed, nobody's different, I haven't learned a thing all summer, Shannon's still Shannon, and there goes your popularity contest, college level.

Sherry reached out casually, pried one of my hands loose from my coffee cup, and led me toward the fire, saying "Breathe!" out of the corner of his mouth. I let the air out of my lungs, dragged some more in, and after a moment took a shaky swallow of coffee, scalding my tongue in the process. Things began to look less kaleidoscopic, and I relaxed infinitesimally. One thing was different, after all—I hadn't had Sherry beside me at Mary-High.

"Ordeal by introduction," he observed sympathetically. "I know that was a little rough, but I had to check you in with Mr. Fairly. We'll just take them as they come after this, one or two at a time."

Three of the dripping-wet tooth-chatterers were still clustered around the fire, and though my every instinct voted nay, we joined them.

"Hi, Sherry," said two of them, male and female. The other girl just watched Sherry and waited, smiling. In the midst of introducing me to Ginny Somebody and Bill Somebody else, Sherry seemed to focus on her for the first time, and stared.

"Well, I'll be darned," he said with one of his nicest grins, and took the hand she extended, laughing. "And this," he said to me, "is little Betty Patros, of all people."

"The Nuisance," Betty Patros said, dimpling roguishly. I suddenly felt lonesome. Ginny said, "You mean you know each other?" and they explained in chorus that they'd been next-door neighbors all through grade school.

"Ginny, I poisoned Sherry's life for years before it finally got through to me that big boys don't like babies tagging along everywhere they go. How's Bell Landing, Sherry?"

"Oh, it's transformed. New addition on the high school, and the feed store's repainted. Listen, what are you doing here? I thought it was Medford you moved to. Are you *old* enough for college?"

"I will be by fall. I'm staying with Ginny all year, poor her. She's my cousin."

"Small world," Bill observed, grinning amiably at me. "I didn't happen to live next door to you at any time, did I?"

The invitation was wide open for me to dimple roguishly in my turn and try my hand at the type of banter that seemed to be the *lingua franca* in these parts. That beautiful Sue was a past master at it, Betty Patros was a confident beginner, Bill and even Sherry seemed idly proficient. Ginny, having barely opened her mouth so far, was an unknown quantity, but could doubtless hold her own if she tried. I suddenly decided I couldn't and that the fact might as well be established right away. I merely smiled at Bill—or tried to—and shook my head.

"I was afraid of that," Bill murmured. "Where do you live? Portland?"

I said, "At the moment," and drank some coffee.

Sherry and Betty Patros had been working out exactly when they'd last seen each other and had just turned back to the rest of us. "At the moment, what?" Sherry inquired.

"At the moment she lives in Portland," Bill said, studying me. "That's all I can get out of her."

"Maybe that's all she wants you to know," Ginny remarked. She huddled into her beach towel, a friendly gray eye on me, and added, "Don't tell him a thing. Betty, I'm *freezing*. Let's go get dressed."

"Well—but, Sherry, I'll see you later, won't I? So much to catch up on! Now don't *move*. I'll be back."

She hurried off after Ginny toward the house, and after a moment during which we all watched her retreating figure—and a very good figure it was—Bill turned to Sherry and laughed.

"Far as I'm concerned, she's still a nuisance to the big boys. You going to obey orders?"

"I think not," Sherry said mildly.

"I hoped you'd say that. In fact, sort of vanish, will you? I'd like to keep her mind on me this afternoon—if I can." He grinned at me and loped off toward the house.

"Still breathing?" Sherry asked me.

I said abruptly, "Sherry, I can't do this."

"Do what?"

I waved my hands incoherently. "All this. Be like—these people. I don't speak the language."

"Who wants you to? Be like yourself."

"That's what I've been doing," I said bitterly.

"No, you haven't. Not one person we've talked to has the slightest idea what you're really like. It doesn't matter—take your time. Maybe none of these people have appealed to you."

I remembered a friendly gray eye and said, "Ginny—seemed nice."

"Well, she is. We'll hunt her up later if you want to."

"Actually, Bill was, too," I admitted. I glanced at Sherry. "Queer, your running into that girl you used to live next door to."

Sherry met my eye and smiled, and I suddenly quit minding about Betty Patros. He said, "Come on, let's oblige Bill and vanish. Here, I'll get rid of our cups."

He moved away toward the coffee table with that lazy, lounging grace that was as much a part of him as his wiry hair. I waited nervously, feeling unprotected, then found myself listening in astonishment to a conversation going on in the middle distance somewhere behind my left shoulder. When Sherry came back, I said, "Who's the Viennese?"

"Who's the what?"

"Listen!"

We both listened, I with a mixture of nostalgia and amusement. A diffident male voice was explaining all about having seen wonderful mountains from the air yesterday—explaining rapidly and eagerly in a soft, singsong, cadenced German. It announced his birthplace and background with every rolled r and hissing s, but so distorted regulation *Hochdeutsch* that only another working-class Viennese (or Franz, who has more than a touch of it himself) could have followed all he was saying. Unfortunately, he wasn't talking to another working-class Viennese, but to several German-speaking students with strong American accents who, understandably, were finding even *ich habe gesehen* unrecognizable when pronounced "i' hawp ksehn" and were busy interrupting him with "*Bitte?*" and asking each other, "Did you get all that?" and laughing helplessly at themselves.

I glanced over my shoulder and spotted the group at once because nobody could have missed the Viennese. He was carefully bareheaded, carefully sloppy in an open-necked shirt and slightly too-new American windbreaker, but in spirit he was still wearing one of those stiff blue suits and a tie, and obviously stood ready to click the heels of his new sneakers at any moment. He was neither as tall nor as good-looking as most of the Americans around him, but the girls were reacting like bees around a honeypot.

Sherry said, "I'll bet it's that exchange student we're supposed to be nice to. Doesn't look as if he needs it. How can you tell he's Viennese?"

"The accent. His is really a thick one. It's like spotting a Cockney . . . Why aren't they speaking English? They'd get along better."

They didn't though. Having bogged down in the visitor's language, they gave it up amid general laughter—rather anxious laughter on the Austrian's part—and switched to American. That turned out about as similar to the Austrian's book-learned English as his Viennese was to the Americans' book-learned German. Now it was he who was muttering "Please?" every other minute and looking a bit wild-eyed at such phrases as, "I'm sure gonna hafta bone up," and "Did-nigh *tell* y' I was flunking German?"

"Even I can see they'll never get anywhere that way," Sherry said. "You want to go help him out?"

"No! Too many people around." I did feel for the Austrian, though; his smile was growing more and more strained, and he'd begun just limply saying "yes" to everything.

"There aren't many now," Sherry pointed out as several students peeled off and headed for the coffeepot. "Come on, that's only Bob Peters—he's the guy's roommate—and Bob's girl, and she's nice."

I'd rather have got the Austrian alone, but of course nobody was going to leave him alone at his first American picnic—certainly not his roommate, who was already looking dutifully about for somebody else to introduce him to, and appeared happy to see us coming. The Austrian didn't; he braced himself and eyed us fearfully, and when the complex machinery of double introductions had got around to him, he clicked his sneakers, bowed jerkily from the hips, smiled miserably, and said, "Heinrich Wenzl. I must apologize myself that I do not speak English very well."

I said, "You speak good enough British English; it's American that's giving you trouble."

Relief sprang into his eyes. "You are English, Fräulein?—Miss?"

"No—only half." I was using the broad a and the British r, though, because obviously his teachers had. I glanced quickly at Bob Peters and his girl, but found them walking away toward Mr. Fairly, and Sherry was asking Heinrich when he'd arrived in Portland.

"The forenoon yesterday, with the airplane," Heinrich said carefully. "And before, I have come with—on—the ship from Bremerhaven, but it was a Netherlands ship, and I have not enough possibility to speak English and make myself more practical." His syntax suddenly collapsed in a rush of confiding. "Perhaps that is because I am so stupid now. I am not understanding almost everybody. It is a great embarrassment."

"Don't let it bother you," Sherry advised him. "I noticed the snafu was mutual."

"Please?" said Heinrich, beginning to look hunted again.

I said in Franz's Viennese German, "He means the students of German could not understand your German either."

"*Ah, so! Ja-ja, tatsächlich! Aber ich—*" He stopped and stared happily at me. "*Mein Gott! Sie sprechen Wiener Deutsch!*"

"*Ja-ja. Ich habe von einem Wiener gelernt,*" I told him.

I thought for a minute he was going to kiss me on both cheeks, and I understood exactly how he felt. There were a dozen mysteries worrying him—American expressions, American customs and attitudes, American college routines. He implored me to explain—in German, *bitte!*—and I did my best, applying to Sherry for answers I didn't know. Then Bob Peters and his girl came back with Mr. Fairly, and presently Sherry and I drifted away.

"There now. You talked to *him*," Sherry said.

"Oh, I can talk to Europeans."

"You can talk to Americans, too. Anybody who comes in the Rainbow. Students, and taxi drivers, and that dentist with the moustache, and Dr. Edmonds, and—"

"Well—Georgetta can," I said uncertainly.

"Greensleeves can, too. Does it all the time."

"Oh, really!" I was confused enough already. The fact is, I told myself, you've just made up all this confusion, so you can hide behind it. "Sherry, forget all those names. They don't change anything at all. I'm still nobody but me."

"Well, *finally!*" Sherry ejaculated, stopping in his tracks. "You have stated a simple truth—without intending to, naturally." He grinned down at me. "Welcome to the party, Nobody But Me. Now if you'll just start talking to these harmless students the way Nobody But You talks to people in the Rainbow, pretty soon you'll know who I mean by Greensleeves. And so will everybody else."

"It's not that simple," I said crossly.

"Isn't it? You know, you've got quite a taste for the complicated, Greensleeves. I don't think you *like* things to be simple. Has this picnic really been like Mary-High so far?"

I had to admit it hadn't, really—except for my behavior. "*I* haven't improved any, Sherry; it's just that—that college students are easier to . . ." The rest trailed off as I realized that was exactly what everybody had been trying to convince me of all this time. That Mary-High wasn't the U.S.A., that college might be easier, that I needn't cram myself into unnatural molds. Clearly, I wouldn't stick out as European with people like Heinrich around—anyway, these Americans had *liked* him. Hope burgeoned. Maybe if I'd just defrost a little . . . Then I remembered. "That's not all there is to it. There's Dad. That whole routine. And somebody'll find out sooner or later that I'm related to *Mother*."

"Greensleeves, you don't have to live up to them. Just be you! It's a long time since you were anybody else, with me."

Or with Dave, either. With a sinking in the pit of my stomach, I reflected that nothing was as simple as Sherry thought.

Still, the day began to change. Maybe Sherry's simple truth got through to me; maybe lesser bugaboos dwindled once I'd thought of Dave. Maybe Ginny was responsible; she emerged from the house just then, dressed now in slacks and pullover, toweling her hair, and stopped by the bottom step, where we were sitting, to ask if we'd seen Betty.

"Not since she left us—with Bill in pursuit," Sherry said.

"Um-hmm. Well, I wasn't a bit worried anyhow. If ever I saw a girl less likely to be lonesome, it's my little cousin." The frank gray eye came to rest on me. "You know, you've got the prettiest hair I ever saw. Is it naturally curly, *too*?"

I lost my breath for a minute—but in an extremely pleasurable way—and stammered, "My word—thanks! Yes, it is, just a bit."

"Just about the way a nasty old fifty-dollar permanent would curl it. Oh, well, my character's lovely, and someday I'll buy a wig."

Sherry smiled down at me and started to say something, then stopped, an odd expression coming over his face. He turned to Ginny. "Shan's dad has red hair, too," he said. "You've probably seen him, if you watch the six o'clock news. Or seen his byline on AP stories. Gregory Lightley—he's one of those far-flung reporters." He met my stricken look with a calm one and went on, "Her mother is Rosaleen O'Leary, the British actress. Can you believe that?"

"Ye gods," Ginny said in startled tones. "What a *pair*. It must be—very exciting." I turned, feeling absolutely numb, to meet a penetrating gray glance. "Or is it gruesome?" she added baldly.

Our eyes held; I heard myself saying, "Gruesome."

Then I heard *Sherry* saying, incredibly, "Excuse me a minute, will you?" and saw him bounding up the steps to the house. Appalled, I stared after him, but Ginny calmly sat down in the place he'd vacated and asked if I were entering Fremont in the fall.

"I don't—know," I said, paralyzed by Sherry's abrupt desertion—by his apparent temporary insanity.

"You don't? How come?" Ginny asked.

"Well, I—" I turned and looked at her. And all at once I told myself to come off it—she was no more frightening than Rose. I said, "I may not go to college. I've been trying to make up my mind all summer. I think I'd like to. Well, I know I would. But the stupid fact is, I'm scared."

"What of?"

"Americans," I said bluntly.

Ginny regarded me with interest but without surprise. "I suppose you've lived abroad a lot . . . Say, by any chance are you well acquainted with London?"

"Yes, I—yes."

"Well, for heaven's sake tell me what Mayfair is! I've never been able to pin it down. Is it a place, or an accent, or just a state of mind, or *what?*"

I blinked, laughed, then got to thinking about it. "All three, actually. It is an area of London—roughly West 1, though it'd end at about Oxford Street. But you're right. It's mainly just a short way of saying very swish or smart."

"Where'd the name come from, then?"

"Oh, they used to hold a real fair there, ages ago. Every May, I suppose. I think Shepherd's Market was about the dead center of it.

But it got so scandalous they shut it down, way back in the eighteenth century or sometime."

"Scandalous? A *fair*? What did they do to be scandalous?"

"No idea. Cheated the customers, maybe?"

"Oh, it must have been worse than that."

We began to hazard guesses about it, which grew increasingly original and struck us as increasingly humorous. Then Ginny started telling me about a term paper she'd done on the Common Market, and presently, to my disappointment, some people came to collect her for a tennis match. When she was gone, I sat musing a moment, rather happily, then looked at my watch and found that a whole half hour had evaporated, and Sherry *still* hadn't come back.

I stood up, feeling panicky, and was wondering whether to stay where I was so he'd be sure to find me, or start searching the house for him, when I heard music start up from somewhere in the distance—recorders, I thought, maybe a trio of them, their reedy, flutelike harmonies almost lost in the bigness of the outdoors. People were drifting toward the sound, but I paid scant attention until it dawned on me that the tune was "Greensleeves." Then I moved free of the angle of the house and spotted the players—not such a distance away after all—grouped around the end of one of the picnic tables, sharing a music book lying flat between them. The one half sitting on the edge of the table was Sherry.

Greensleeves was all my joy, Greensleeves was my delight . . . . A likely story. Why, I thought indignantly, he must have sneaked out the back door. He's just ditched me, that's what he's done, he's—

Right then Sherry, still playing, spotted me and took the recorder away from his lips—then grinned, replaced it, and serenely turned back to his music book. I was in the process of swelling with wrath when a diffident bass voice at my side said, "Looks like Sherry sort of got shanghaied for a while. Must be the only alto player who showed up today."

I looked around, then up—way up—into the engaging, homely face of one of the skyscraping Millers. The taller one. His name eluded me.

"Steve," he supplied helpfully. "That alto recorder's unpopular, you know. Tuned to G instead of C like the others. So alto players get kind of in demand at times." He eyed me hopefully. "Now, I'm perfectly free. I don't play any musical instrument."

I told him I didn't either, and added in astringent tones that I hadn't known before that Sherry did.

"Well, I don't think he intended to today. That's not even his own instrument—it's a spare Jack Lincoln had along. You'd better forgive him. I heard him sort of arguing about it—in the house a while back—and then the sounds of a body being dragged away. I thought it might be just the time to come out and hunt you up."

Steve smiled happily and with perfect candor. I considered him in silence a moment. Circling back around, that's what he was doing. And Sherry, having looked up from his music and seen his prediction coming true, had blandly abandoned me to this—this giant.

"How tall *are* you, anyway?" I was surprised to hear myself saying.

"Six-five in my stocking feet," Steve said, giving me another choir-boy's smile. In a voice to match, he added, "Want to walk up to the waterfall and make Sherry feel real bad?"

So that's how I spent a second quite painless thirty or forty or fifty minutes without Sherry even in sight. Steve and I headed for the woods without a glance at the recorder trio, who were now piping "Sumer is icumen in, Merrie sing cuccu—" and started up the little sloping path that ran along the edge of the stream.

That path must be one of the prettiest places in the world. What with the creek bubbling away as background music, and Steve's shy bass rumbling genially at my side, and occasionally his huge hand diffident as a butterfly's wing on my elbow to help me over a tangle of roots, it was impossible to find him hard to talk to. We kept encountering other people on their way up or down, and when we reached the top—a big fir-fringed pool with the waterfall plunging noisily into it—we stood about quite a while shouting companionably over the racket to some other nature lovers. I was forced to conclude that I could do this sort of thing as well as I'd any need to. And I began to form a tentative picture of this Greensleeves person Sherry said was me. She was part Georgetta—minus the bogus accent—and part the same old Shan I'd known all my life, and part somebody new that I was just beginning to get a grip on.

Just which part was responsible for last Monday's episode with Dave I didn't know, and it did occur to me—dimly, in the back of my mind—that maybe I'd better find out. I'd discovered myself to be far from impervious to Steve's wide-eyed and purportedly ingenuous charm—in fact, I enjoyed it thoroughly—and something was telling me (though not very loudly) that if I kept on with this sort of thing, reacting more or less combustibly to every male in sight, I was a long mile from having a reliable answer to Sherry's question or any of my own.

We finally came back to the clearing to find Sherry sitting on the nearest picnic table looking as if he'd been there for some time. He lounged to his feet when he saw us, strolled over, and gave Steve a limpid glance. Steve smiled angelically, said, "Well, so long. I guess I have an urgent appointment," and conjured himself into a receding figure in the middle distance. At least, I never saw him go. I was savoring the lovely homecoming sensation that had filled me at sight of Sherry. I thought, Oh, maybe I'm worrying for nothing.

"Well, that's *my* last good deed for the day," Sherry remarked with asperity.

"*Good* deed? Why, you just pulled the rug out from under me and then went off and *left* me, to sink or swim—"

"Entirely for your own welfare. Like the Indians used to throw their babies into the river or whatever it was."

"You might have let me know where you'd got to."

"I *did*. Why do you think we started off with 'Greensleeves' on those blasted recorders?"

I hooked my arm into his nice, comfortable, familiar one in the old saggy white windbreak and said mildly, "Well, never mind, I didn't sink, I swam. Dog-paddled, anyway."

"Looked to me mighty like you were training for the high dive," Sherry muttered. He studied me sidewise as we walked toward the fire, though, and smiled, and presently added in a mollified tone, "You see? Now aren't you glad you came?"

3

No need to go into detail about the rest of that afternoon—we listened to records a while on the big porch of the house, and watched a madly disorganized tennis game, and eventually ate quantities of food, and watched the sun drop low and the shadows gather under the fir trees. Afterward somebody built up the fire and a girl produced a guitar, and everybody sat around on the ground or tables and sang—loudly, cheerfully, and for the most part, off-key—with now and then a cozily whispering twosome drifting off beyond the edge of the firelight. It was deep, soft dusk when Sherry muttered suddenly, "All right, I'm good and tired of all these people. I want you by yourself and no argument. Come on, let's fade out."

"Go home, you mean?" I inquired as we picked our way over sprawled-out legs and feet.

"Eventually. I've got something to say to you first, and I don't want to say it in a Volkswagen—or in that Grand Central of Mrs. Jackson's, either."

I guess it was the sudden mental picture of the boardinghouse that woke me up—or maybe something about Sherry's tone and the unhumorous look of his profile as we left the firelight. All I know is that by the time my eyes adjusted to the dark, my memory had joltingly adjusted to what this day was all about and what was unfailingly coming next. I walked in silence beside Sherry across the dusky lawn toward the rhododendrons, feeling those little prickles of dread again along my jawbone. I'd never expected this drama to get as far as the last act—now, abruptly, the curtain had rung up, and I didn't know my lines.

The last of the sunset light still lingered on the cliff edge near our bench and dimly defined the shape of the river far below, turning it into a sweep of pewter alongside which headlights raced like tiny sparks. Sherry wasn't looking at the view—he pulled me down onto the bench and faced me.

"I've got two questions to ask you, Shannon Kathleen. Just two. They ought to be easy to answer now."

"Don't count on it." I sighed.

"Well—all right, I won't. But let me ask them anyway. I want to know . . . I want to know if you have any clearer idea how you feel about me, now that today's turned out the way it has." I opened my mouth, then hesitated, watching the little racing sparks below, and he went on quickly, "I mean—I've seen Shan now, and I get what you've been talking about all this time, and I still feel exactly the same. Anyway, you've started to get over all that—you *are* over the worst of it. You're out of your chrysalis or whatever the word is, and all those dire problems you kept putting in our way are gone."

"All *those* are," I mumbled. I knew of others—worse ones. I said a bit pleadingly, "I haven't been out of my chrysalis very long, Sherry. Couldn't I just sit right here on this leaf a few days and get my wings dry?"

Sherry grinned briefly and relaxed a bit. "I'm not going to rush you—you'll see. But I hope my point's clear? I feel just the same about you—only more so."

"It's clear," I said. It was *my* feelings that weren't clear; they were still roiled and muddied by Monday-night undercurrents, especially Dave's taunting, "Do you want me to kiss you or don't you?"—and his incontestible proof two minutes later that I emphatically *did*. How was I supposed to fit that in?

"Greensleeves?" Sherry said. "You can answer my question now."

I took a long breath and said, "Sherry, I love you—now, tonight. I know I do. What I don't know is whether I'm *in love with you*. For keeps, I mean. I mean getting married. I daren't make a mistake—I'm only going to get married *once*, and my children are only going to have *two* parents, if I can possibly, possibly arrange it. And so far I—oh, I *know* I ought to know by now, but I just—"

"No, wait a minute—it's all right." Sherry took my hand quickly. "That's all I want right now in the way of an answer. It's more than I thought I'd get. OK—question number two. Has today made any difference in your feeling about college? Are you going?"

Visions of catalogues, the Sorbonne, the Oregon campus, Fremont revolved in my head. "I—think so. Somewhere, anyway."

"All right." Sherry drew an enormous breath of his own and settled back. "Now I'm going to make a speech, and I want you to listen. I may never get it so well organized again."

Rapidly, as fast as I'd ever heard him talk, he made his speech, frowning out over the darkening gorge. All this had been his fault, he said. He'd put too much pressure on me—that's why I'd panicked. Now he had a sensible plan, been thinking of it all day—all week. He wanted me to enter Fremont, so I could be near him all the coming year. Next spring, he would graduate, and immediately go out and worm his way into a job. We could forget the graduate-school notion—Oxford and all the rest of it. He was ready, able,

and anxious to quit being a penguin, to become sensible and practical. He saw perfectly well now that life should be logical, and he
meant to make it be that way. He completely understood why I'd
hesitated to rely on somebody as vague and impractical as he'd
been, but he meant to quit being so—in fact, he had quit. By the
end of the year, I'd see for myself how firmly he meant this; then
maybe I'd be willing to go back to Fremont for my sophomore year
while he began to earn enough for us to get married on, in case I
decided to marry him. Please—would I *please* trust him and follow
his plan, at least to the extent of enrolling in Fremont this fall.
Would I just try it. *Please.*

He fell silent and, after a moment, turned slowly and looked at
me. He was gripping my hand so tight that it was getting numb. I
sat with my brain spinning futilely for another minute; then I had
to say *something.* I said, "Sherry, I don't know—Fremont, all this
today, it's *your* world. I was trying to find *mine.*"

"Make this one yours. Just let me be in it with you—for this
one year."

What's wrong with that? I asked myself distractedly. Why *not,*
for pity's sake? I've got to make some decision about *something*—
and this way I needn't decide about Sherry until I'm really ready—
besides, if I'm going to some college, why not Fremont? Why can't
I just say yes? Isn't it perfectly simple?

"Greensleeves, maybe I've thrown it at you in too big a lump.
Could you think about it this next week while I'm at Bell Landing,
then tell me for sure when I come back? Could you do that?"

"Oh, yes. I can do that. I *will* do that, Sherry. I'll probably do
everything you want me to. I honestly can't find any reason why I
shouldn't—it's just that—"

It was just that something about all he'd said and the way he'd
said it was dismaying me. Something was telling me I liked him
better as a penguin—impractical and illogical and curious and just

Sherry. Some dim conviction had got hold of me that we were both starting to compromise, starting to run counter to our natures—and that nobody can do that for long. I didn't know whether to pay any attention to all this or not.

"It's just that you like to worry," Sherry finished for me, in a voice once more teasing and relaxed and like his own. "Well, save it for next week, when I'm gone. I have now waited exactly as long as I'm going to wait to kiss you."

I'd just time to ask myself frantically if there was still some reason why he shouldn't—but not enough time to answer, because he was already kissing me. And immediately I knew there was no reason at all why he shouldn't, and every reason why he should. He loved me, I loved him, and people who loved each other kissed each other. What's more they didn't hold out on each other, either, or draw inward lines. I must *not* hold back from Sherry any longer—it wasn't fair. I suddenly decided that the moment had come to find out whether I was playing for keeps.

In the middle of his kiss, I acted on my decision and obliterated my inward line. I can't say precisely how I did this; probably I don't need to. Anybody knows. It's instinct or something; it's what you're usually fighting *not* to do—release your hold on caution, turn over all responsibility to somebody else, abandon yourself completely to one person and one moment in time. I simply let my body dissolve against Sherry and my brain go ahead and whirl and with the best of intentions *tried* to drown.

Well, I found out one thing, right away and without the slightest doubt. Sherry was as combustible as anybody else, and fully as able as Dave to ignite emotions in me too powerful to control. It was all too easy, and it happened all too swiftly, and the conflagration soon rose high and bright enough to scare us both. It was Sherry who abruptly, even roughly, thrust us apart and sprang up from the bench to put the width of the tiny clearing between us. There he stood for a moment, rigid, looking down into the vast blue-gray spaces of the gorge, while I sat slowly filling with the suspicion that the one decision I'd managed to make all summer had been disastrously wrong. When he turned to meet my eyes, I knew it for a fact.

He said, "Greensleeves, that wasn't a bit smart—do you realize that?"

I realized it. In the space of a kiss, our whole relationship had changed. That line we'd crossed was behind us for good. We couldn't go back now—and it had been nice and safe back there, and it was quicksand here. Moreover, I hadn't proved a thing. Those fireworks had no real value as a proof of love—as I'd already learned from Dave, they could exist in a vacuum of dislike. My sole accomplishment in this last five minutes had been to make things a lot more complicated than they'd ever been before.

"I'm sorry, Sherry," I whispered, and I was—very, very sorry, now that it was too late to do a thing about it.

"Never mind, we'll handle it."

Would we? Following that good "sensible" plan of his—seeing each other every day and every evening for the next twelve months? It was going to be a long, long year—and the pressure we felt now was nothing to the pressure we were going to feel. We wouldn't be able to keep sensible plans or even clear heads; we'd probably wind up married before the year was out, ready or not, mistake or not, with all possibilities of free choice right out the window forever.

"Sherry—!" I said.

"Now, calm down. I said we'd handle it." He came back and sat down beside me and took both my hands. "*I'll* handle it, Greensleeves. Just trust me." I sat in silent foreboding, frowning down at our hands. In a moment he added, in what I realized was rather a strange voice, "What I don't understand—" and stopped.

I glanced up to find that the look he was giving me was a strange one, too—a very still and very searching one. I could almost hear his thoughts: until Monday night you kissed me just like always; after Monday night you stopped kissing me at all; now suddenly you kiss me like this. What happened Monday night? . . . I had a notion he was making some quite elementary deductions, too.

"Sherry," I said unsteadily. "Sherry, I want to tell you something—about Dave." His face changed—something flashed across it and was gone, wiping out all expression. He straightened, leaned back against the bench. I faltered, "I've been meaning to say this—"

"Wait!" he interrupted, with a fierce pressure on my hand. In a moment he added in a calm voice, "You don't have to, Greensleeves."

"But I really want to." I was suddenly eager, anxious to. "I want to tell you everything about Monday night. It was—"

"Greensleeves, listen to me!" Sherry turned his face to me, waited a second as if he hoped I could read it without his speaking, then said gently, "Greensleeves, do you love me? You said you did."

"Yes, Sherry, I *do*. Only—"

"Then don't tell me anything about Monday night. I don't want to hear it."

"But, Sherry—" I said, and stopped, because something in his eyes finally got through to me and stopped me. I don't want you to hurt me, they said. What good would that do?

I said, "But, Sherry—you'll think it's worse than it was!"

"No, I won't."

But I've been so *burdened* by it! I thought frantically—then realized that what I really wanted was to pass the burden on to Sherry, thus getting rid of it myself. And why should he let me do that, after all? It was my burden. When all was said and done, it had nothing much to do with him—only with my discovery of myself, which was far, far from complete yet, as this latest foray into the jungle of my motives showed all over again.

I silently accepted sole custodianship of the burden of Monday night and nodded. Sherry kissed me briefly—careful to keep it light—then stood up, saying it was time to go home now. That was the last we ever said on the subject.

We said little on any subject, all the long drive home. Not that there was any stiffness between us—on the contrary, there was such closeness that we felt no need to underscore it with words, and were free to be alone with each other, and let our minds drift and rest, and our emotions, too. Mine felt exhausted—it had been an eventful day, emotionally. I was too tired to sort it out, maybe too close to it. I simply let it go and thought about something else.

It was about half-past ten when we reached College Street. Sherry cut off the motor and lights and sat looking at me, while the night's quiet and the paler, dimmer light from an old moon slowly crept in around us.

"This is the last I'll see of you for a week," he said.

"Yes . . . What time does your bus leave?"

"Early. I'll be halfway home before you're up." He reached out for a handful of my hair, twining his fingers through it where it lay thickest on my neck. "And back before you know it, Rapunzel," he added.

"Of course. A week's nothing."

"All the same, I wish I weren't going." His hand closed around the back of my neck and pulled me to him; he held me tight. "I'm scared to leave you. Greensleeves, come with me. Would you?"

"No, Sherry. You know that's—"

"I know. Impractical, illogical, there'll be another time. But I wish I could leave part of me here to keep an eye on you. I wish I could tuck you in my wallet with my other valuables and just touch you sometimes, to be sure you were still there. I wish it weren't so many days and nights and hours until next Monday. Where's your face? Turn it up here."

He kissed me—like always—then slowly his hand twisted hard into my hair and it wasn't like always—it was like that conflagration out on the cliff edge, it was like it was always going to be now whether we wanted it to or not. I fought free, and that hurt, because I didn't want to fight Sherry, ever. But I knew right then I'd be fighting him for the next year, two years—or else surrendering—all because I'd done in a moment what he'd been very careful all these weeks not to do.

He got out of the car quickly and came around to open my door, standing there with the moonlight on his shoulders and his face in shadow. He said in a low, rapid voice, "Darling, I'm sorry. I said I'd handle it and I didn't. I—"

"Never mind, Sherry," I said as I got out. "Maybe we'll learn how—in a year."

He caught both of my elbows and held them tensely. "We could get married earlier. Lots of students do. They manage somehow."

I said, "Let's talk about it later—next time we see each other. Please, Sherry? Today's over."

After a moment he nodded, and his hands dropped. We walked the few yards along the sidewalk to the familiar cracked cement steps and started the long climb.

"I'll tell you one thing—I'm in no proper mood for scrubbing floors," Sherry muttered.

"You have to go to Herndon's yet tonight?" I asked in dismay.

He gave me a faint sidewise grin. "Don't worry. It's not going to hurt me a bit to sweat at something for a while . . . I'm going clear into the house with you, if you don't mind."

I didn't mind, though I didn't know what he was up to until we stepped inside and I saw the swift but thorough glance he swept about the hall. It was quite empty. Upstairs, some faint voices on Miss Heater's television were emoting throatily.

"All clear," I said. It was the nearest we ever came to mentioning Dave.

Sherry turned back to me and smiled, the old gentle, quizzical, Sherryish smile with his greenish eyes questioning me above it.

"Well—so long, Rapunzel. I love you. Don't vanish in a cloud of pink smoke or anything while I'm gone, will you?"

"Sherry, I'm glad I went to your picnic," I said. "I'll always be glad."

He grinned and said, "I told you so." At the door he lifted my hand to his cheek for a second, then muttered, "I'll see you in a week," and ran rapidly down the steps. I stood on the edge of the porch and watched until I couldn't tell his jacket from the moonlight—and kept on watching until some time after I was sure there was nothing but moonlight there. I think I must have known even then what I was going to do, though I didn't yet know I knew it.

I went back into the house, and across the big dim hall and down the passage to my room, and kicked off my shoes and shed my clothes, intending to go right to bed. In fact, I was about to relieve the cuckoo of his weights for the night when my eye started hovering speculatively about my desk. First thing I knew, I was sitting at it, writing. Not in the journal. I wrote a story. It had nothing to do with Sherry, or me, or Dave, or a college picnic, or a cliff edge, or anything else that was supposed to be on my mind. It was a story about a young poorly born Viennese with a dreadful accent who comes to America and has a frightful time getting used to it and catching onto things and finding work. I'd liked that boy today; in the story I gave him a beautiful, gay girl named Sue to fall in love with him, and after fifteen or twenty pages of difficulties, I let them get married and go back in triumph to Vienna and live blissfully on the Ring-strasse for ever and ever.

It was nearly three o'clock before I finished.

A demented reaction, anybody will agree, to one of the most complicated days of my life. Only it didn't feel demented. It felt like the sanest and truest reaction I'd had so far, and the most direct— right straight from the inner girl.

I came out of it gradually—like ether—and read over what I had done, and blinked about the room and, incredulously, at the clock. Then I got up stiffly, wandered over to the window still clutching my story like a talisman, and stood a few minutes looking out. It wasn't even a very good story, I was aware of that; I didn't know how to write a good story. But that didn't mean I never would. The pages in my hand felt thick and comfortable. I had a world of my own, after all, right inside my head—a whole Wild West waiting to be tamed and made into a place to live. It was a bit like Dave's world, come to think of it.

The moonlight had grown white and strong; it lay like snow on Mrs. Hockins' rose garden and the lawn—Mrs. Jackson's lawn, Dave's lawn. I turned away from it and found my shaded desk lamp—no, not mine—throwing a single pool of light in a dim room full of somebody else's furniture. It was somebody else's room. I looked around it—at Georgetta's white flats pigeon-toed in a corner, and Georgetta's can of hair spray holding court on the dresser among her scattered hairpins and eye shadow box and shoe ornaments—and realized that the emotion I was feeling, with growing discomfort, was claustrophobia. Whatever my world was, this wasn't it; this was Georgetta's world, and sometime during my absence today Georgetta had departed, with a snap of her gum, and she'd left me in another trap.

I think it was right then that what I'd already known, as I stood watching Sherry from the porch, rose to the surface to where I knew I knew it. I had to get out of here. I'd never find out who I was or what I felt about anything while my mind and every hour of the day were full of Sherry, and cliff hanging, and tangled-up emotions. I'd never have a chance to make a decision about him, either; it would just go by default, and we'd have to find out afterward whether it was right or wrong for us. Well, I wanted to know beforehand. I wanted out of the tangle for just long enough to *think* a minute. Detachment—that's what I needed, and above all, distance. All I could accomplish here was to make this into a trap for two.

But where to go? How long to stay away? How soon to leave? The last question was easy; everything in me said *immediately*. The minute I could quit my job, wind things up—absolutely before Sherry came back, or I'd never be able to do it. But where? Uncle Frosty wouldn't be home for another fortnight. Mary's Creek? No detachment there. Well, *someplace*. Go someplace for a fortnight, and after that—well, that might be long enough. Mightn't it? If not, then Oregon University and that sea of Americans. I had to take the plunge sometime; it might as well be while I was young and would still bounce, instead of really shattering to bits. But . . . maybe a fortnight would be enough.

I tossed my story onto the dresser and wavered over to the bed, swaying a bit from weariness and cerebration. *Everybody ought to get lost once in their lives—it's the only way to find yourself. Freedom is real, if you'll just reach out and take it.* I hoped Mrs. Dunningham was right.

I heard a familiar rasping, and the cuckoo popped out—rather draggily—to announce in progressively discouraged and reedy tones that the time was one—two—th-ree o'clock. He couldn't even make it to the final syllable, just gasped out "cuck—" and expired with his beak open, still hanging out of his little door. No need to take his weights off tonight—he'd completely run down.

By the time my head hit the pillow thirty seconds later, so had I.

4

I woke up, lonesome, to a Portland with no Sherry in it—and to a relentlessly clear memory of everything I'd made up my mind to last night. My mind was still made up, though I lay about in bed several minutes trying my best to poke holes in all that depressing logic. No use—my subconscious had even added a few items to it while I slept, besides supplying me with a perfectly obvious destination.

I climbed out of bed, wound the cuckoo so he could finish last night's "—oo" and get started on today, then sluggishly began to dress. I was reaching for my green uniform when I was suddenly sickened by the idea of trying to be Georgetta for even one more day. I dropped into a chair to think about this and to come to grips with some of the immediate, practical aspects of my decision. I had to go to work; Mr. Bruce expected me. He might need me for several days or let me quit at once; either way I must show up this morning. As Shannon, then? *Sans* accent, *sans* eyes shadow, hair down, the whole works at once—just start this minute being old Nobody But Me? Well, why not? I thought. All I have to do is use my new secret weapon and be honest. I can't go through my whole life dodging the issue, I might live to be ninety-nine—unless I bored myself to death years before.

Suddenly I was ready—I couldn't wait to shed my domino and be free of it forever. And I must say I was delighted to be quit of the gluey morning ritual of Georgetta's coiffure. I threw her hair spray into the wastebasket—and on second thought her hairpins and shoe bows and eye shadow and earrings. Then, feeling as if I'd just shed a particularly outgrown snakeskin, I brushed my hair and again reached for my uniform—at which point my memory presented me with a brilliant solution to the whole problem of my job. I put on my yellow linen instead, bundled all three uniforms under my arm, and started for the Rainbow.

Dave was trimming the grass edge in front of the hydrangea bushes as I started down the steps. His head turned casually, then stayed turned. I could feel him staring, but he didn't speak and I didn't stop. It was a morning like yesterday, big and shining, and well along by now, since I'd wakened late. I was due behind that counter in fifteen minutes.

Helen's replacement, a cheerful sophomore, was behind it when I came in. I doubt if she recognized me as her banana-split teacher of Saturday, but Mr. Bruce's eye fastened on me at once, alert but as usual unsurprised. When I asked if I could talk to him privately a few minutes, he simply nodded and led the way into his little office off the kitchen.

I slid into the chair he offered, wondering how to begin. I murmured, "I haven't been in here since the day you hired me."

"And this is the day you're quitting, isn't it?" Mr. Bruce said calmly, sitting down with a creak in his swivel chair.

"How did you know?"

"I've seen it coming for quite a while. It's all right, Miss Sm—Miss—Greensleeves."

"Lightley is the name," I said dryly. "Did you know that, too?"

"No, I only knew it must be something different from the one you chose to go by here. That was all right, too. Perfectly all right. Entirely your own business."

"Well, not—" I took a long breath, looking into those patient, unsurprisable, faintly mournful gray eyes. "—not entirely, Mr. Bruce." His expression didn't change; he merely nodded gravely. I said, "I think I want to tell you about it—if you want to listen."

"I'd be interested."

I think he was, too—but not in quite the way I'd expected. He wasn't at all indignant at being spied on, or being thought the mastermind, and he hardly seemed regretful enough at the way it had all turned out. I made up for it. By the time I'd recounted—and relived—the whole frustrating, sorry outcome again, telling him how I'd tried to find him and been just too late, I was feeling as bitter and futile about everything as I had that day.

"I just don't understand Mrs. Dunningham," I finished unhappily. "She wasn't crazy, so why did she make the will sound crazy? If she hadn't, it might never have been questioned. If she'd just listed sums of money for certain people, never mind what for—"

"Ah, but 'what for' was the point. She wanted to open people's cages for them. That's what she was trying to do with those bequests."

I looked up, feeling as if I'd heard an echo. Mr. Bruce smiled and went on quite gently, "It was a fine thought, but foolish of her. That sort of thing never works. People have to open their own cages before they're actually free. She really should have known that. She got out of hers by herself—that's what made her aware of other people's. But she couldn't have done it for anybody else even if the will had been allowed." He sighed and creaked back in the swivel chair. "I never approved of that will," he added thoughtfully.

I was too astonished to be anything but blunt. "Then why did she make you executor?"

"Same reason she made the bequests. She was trying to open my cage."

"Yours? Is the Rainbow a cage to you, Mr. Bruce?"

"It's a nice little business." He paused; the patient, perceptive eyes considered me a moment; then he seemed to reach a decision. He leaned forward and folded his arms on his desk. "But the business I like—and was trained for—is banking. I started out in that business, started well. I was a teller by the time I was twenty-four. Then I took some money." He said this quite calmly and without emphasis and went right on. "I took a lot. Later I gave it back, gave myself up, paid my debt to society with several years of my life. I was supposed to be square with the world when I came out. But I have never since dared to put myself in a position that required handling someone else's money. You see, I don't know whether I can be trusted or not."

I swallowed. "Mrs. Dunningham thought you could?" I asked.

"Yes—she was trying to force open the cage. It wouldn't have worked. Oh, I would have handled *her* funds honestly. But in other circumstances—not a test situation with someone's eye on me to see if I passed or failed—well, I don't know. I never will know. I'm never going to take the chance. This is a nice little business."

We sat in silence while I mulled this over. "What is Dr. Edmonds' trap?" I asked at last, quite humbly. I had a notion he was trying to teach me something—and I had a notion I was learning it.

"His is fear, too—a little like mine. Well, not really. It's his reluctance, his *unexamined* reluctance, to let go of the one task—that physics textbook of his—which seems to him worth the time he puts in on it. It fills a hole in his life that he doesn't want to know is there. If he ever finished that book, he'd have to face the possibility that his years of teaching have netted nobody anything."

"But they have! That's not true!"

"Oh, no, it's not true. But he won't look to see, for fear it might be—because if it were, he's not sure whether he could face it. He clings to his busywork to put off the evil day. Forever, if he can."

"But Mr. Bruce, he's looked—peeked, anyhow. He told me once he sometimes wondered if he'd ever taught one person anything of value."

"Then he's beginning to pry away at the cage door."

"So is Wynola," I said after a moment.

"Oh, yes—the diet," Mr. Bruce said, smiling.

"And she wants a job. Oh—and I thought—if you've no objections—she could have mine. At least until you found someone else."

"I've no objection—tell her to come and see me."

So my solution had worked out fine. That was good—I supposed. I said unhappily, "Then I can quit today?"

"Right now, if you like."

Reluctantly, I stood up. Mr. Bruce remained seated, watching me. He seemed not at all surprised when I didn't go. I said, "Is *everybody* in some trap or other?"

He said, "I think it likely. We move from one cage to the next one, don't we?"

"But people don't always *cling* to them—they don't always make them *themselves*! Look at Mr. Mulvaney."

Mr. Bruce didn't answer. I sat down again and had a look at Mr. Mulvaney myself. Surely his trap was imposed on him by other people? But on second thought . . . he did cling to it a bit, didn't he? He refused to get rid of old Stanley. Yet wouldn't that be an obvious first step in relieving his financial situation?—and a firm hand might get his wife's tyranny under control, too. But he wouldn't take those steps. Maybe, like Dave, he needed to drag the heaviest possible burden—to reassure himself incessantly that he was a good man, that his life was worth something, that he was needed, that he was creditor and not debtor to the human race.

I said in a rather subdued tone, "Miss Heater?"

"Hers is purely financial. She'll get out. All she needs is time—and to be allowed to do it by herself, so she can have her pride back. Now Dave's a different proposition altogether. He needs his trap, and he's careful to preserve it. He's right. It brings out the best in him."

And the worst in other people, I thought. I already knew all I wanted to about Dave. I said, almost pleadingly, "Surely Mrs. Hockins could have used the money?"

"It would have been irrelevant," Mr. Bruce said gently. "She refuses to live anywhere but the past—she clings to her grief. A plastic canopy wouldn't have done a thing about that." He paused, then added thoughtfully, "She and I won't get out of our traps. She's too old, and I find I'm—comfortable enough."

"Mr. Bruce, are you telling me—that people can't *ever* help each other?"

"I expect I am."

It's not true, I thought. Sherry helped me yesterday—he opened at least one cage door and shoved me right through. Or did I walk through? Or *am I still inside* and just don't know it? In other circumstances, with nobody's eye on me to see if I passed or failed . . .

Clairvoyantly, as usual, Mr. Bruce added, "Often, with the best of intentions, people just get in each other's way."

"I suppose so," I mumbled. I felt a great disinclination to ask any more questions. Abruptly, I stood up. "Well—I'd better go."

He stood up, too, this time, and held out his hand to me. "You've been a valuable employee, Miss Lightley," he said gravely.

"Thank you. I've—liked it."

"Will you be back in this neighborhood at some time?" he asked in a casual tone that didn't fool me at all. "Or is this more or less permanent?"

"It's beginning to look more or less permanent, isn't it?" I muttered. I dropped his hand and stood looking him in the eye for a moment. "How do you know so much about people?" I asked bitterly.

He only smiled. "I pay a lot of attention to them. I'm very fond of people . . . By the way, I owe you for a week, don't I? We'll stop by the cash register."

We stopped by the cash register, and he gave me some money and another smile, and I went home and rang up Western Airlines, then found Mrs. Jackson and told her I'd be leaving before night, and took an astounded Wynola aside for a little farewell talk that sent her flying toward the Rainbow to start my job.

Then I went into my room and slammed the door and sat and held my head a few minutes, thinking over all Mr. Bruce had said. I hadn't dared mention Sherry—not that I needed to. I wondered what Mrs. Dunningham had thought his trap was. His plans to draw refrigerators and design cereal boxes instead of finding out where those little wavery lines might lead him? An omniverous mind caught in a spinachy world? . . . Well, probably that's what his trap had been—then. I knew what it was now. Me.

So my vanishing act couldn't be for just a fortnight after all; it had to be for a lot longer. More or less permanent. But did it really have to start *today*? . . . I was still sitting there, trying to persuade myself that I could stay just long enough to see Sherry again, that I ought at least to talk it over with him (so he could talk me right out of it) when the cuckoo slammed out to tell me twelve shrill times exactly what he thought of me.

I found my handbag and left the house to catch a bus to town.

I was just starting down the long concrete steps when I saw Dave starting up them, hands in his pockets and a loaf of bread tucked under his arm. We met in the middle of the flight. He stopped me—unceremoniously—by thrusting an elbow in my way and saying, "Wait a minute."

I waited. For a moment he just studied me—my hair, especially—with the sort of impersonal, careful attention he might bring to a new sort of weed. "So that's what you look like," he remarked.

"Yes. Whether you approve artistically or not."

Lazily, but for once with no mockery in his eyes, which remained heavy-lidded and somber, he focused on me personally. "Oh, I approve, Greensleeves." A slight pause. "I ran into Wynola over at the café. She says you're leaving."

"Yes."

"How soon?"

"Today. As soon as I finish a couple of errands and pack."

He acknowledged this with a raised eyebrow. After a minute he said quietly, "Did I scare you that bad?"

I hesitated, then let my guard down, and said, "Yes. You did."

There was an odd silence, during which we came so near to making real contact—I thought—that it rather rattled me. I said, "But don't apologize—it'd be out of character."

He looked faintly surprised—very much *in* character—and said, "I wasn't going to apologize. Why should I?"

"No reason at all." I drew a long breath, thinking, Will I ever learn?

"Still feeling put upon, are you?" The customary hard little mocking devil was creeping back into his eyes. "Well, I expect you'll get over it."

"Dave," I said wearily, "did you ever try being nice to anybody for just five minutes?"

"Yes. I've tried it. I found out it didn't pay off."

"Well, does *this*?"

"Oh—sometimes." He smiled slowly down at me.

How true. I looked at him standing there, the hard bulge of his shoulder shaping the faded old shirt, his brown throat thrusting up out of it, and wondered how it could be that even right now, when I was weariest of his perversity, readiest to say good-by, while my mind was rejecting and disowning him, I knew quite well that the whole thing could very easily start all over again, any time he cared to start it. I thought, This man can play me like a trout—reel me in, throw me back, just as he chooses. It might go on forever.

He was saying, "The fact is, I'm glad you're leaving. I don't have time to fool around educating infants. I lost close to two weeks' work on you as it was." His eyes flicked to my hair again, curiously. "Who are you, anyway?" he asked.

That was the big question, all right, but I felt no need or desire to explain a thing to him. He didn't really want to know, anyhow. I said, "Does it matter?"

"No, not a bit. Well, so long, Greensleeves. It's been interesting."

He smiled, hitched his loaf of bread more firmly under his arm, and climbed on up the steps and out of my life. On his way I saw him stop, lean down, and carefully uproot a small sprig of something growing in a crack between the squares of concrete. He took it with him into the house.

I ran down the rest of the steps feeling that I couldn't start vanishing too soon.

I caught the next bus to town. Since a sort of gone feeling in my middle was reminding me that I'd forgotten all about breakfast, I went first to a drugstore and fortified myself with one of those flannel-and-tunafish sandwiches—it didn't matter; I didn't know what I was eating anyway—before going on to the bank to close out Georgetta's account. There was quite a lot there; all my detective pay, intact. Half an hour later I'd spent a good chunk of it for space on a flight to Mexico City, leaving at eight-thirty the next morning. Uncle Frosty and Mona weren't in Mexico City; I knew they wouldn't be for another ten days, when they got back from whatever ancient ruins they were poking about in; but the typed schedule he'd given me promised they'd turn up sooner or later at the Hotel Del Prado before catching their plane back home. If they didn't, I could always fly back later by myself; meanwhile, it seemed an eminently likely place to get lost.

I arranged for the airport limousine to collect me at the Heathman Hotel at some ungodly morning hour, then went by taxi to Uncle Frosty's house, where I pried the spare key out of its crack under the front steps and went in to burgle my camel-bag. By midafternoon I was back in College Street packing.

It wasn't much of a job. About halfway through I remembered I had a skirt at the cleaner's and had to leave things scattered while I fetched it, but that was the only delay. Within half an hour, everything I meant to take was in—except some notepaper and a pen. There remained the wastebasket full of Georgetta, and a pile of her movie magazines, which I stacked on the dresser with a scrap of paper labeled "Wynola" propped against them. Then I took the rest of my marmalade up to Miss Heater, and my new can of Earl Grey tea to Mrs. Jackson. I hesitated briefly over a folder on Greece I'd picked up at the airlines offices, then—Mr. Bruce or no Mr. Bruce—went upstairs and slipped it under Dr. Edmonds' door. Nothing else in the room was mine to give away, though I sort of gave my silent blessing to the next person to sleep in that dark, carved bed and wake up to the sight of sunny yellow walls and the voice of the cuckoo.

At last, when I couldn't put it off any longer, I sat down at the desk and stared at a sheet of notepaper for quite a while, and finally wrote what I had to write:

"Sherry dear: Please forgive me. I've gone to get lost. We're badly in each other's way, and you know it. I told you the truth, I love you—now. Enough to marry you. But I've got to get a firmer grip on the person you'd wind up married to. I'm changing too fast—I don't even know who I'll be tomorrow, because today I'm not who I thought I was yesterday. In two years we could be strangers—married or not, Sherry! We've got to give ourselves a chance to jell a bit before we start changing each other's lives. *You too.* Promise me you'll do something with that fund. Please, Sherry. Go find out what it's like to live in Timbuktu. Then let me know you've done it. Here's an address that will always reach me, but I won't be there. Good-by for quite a while—S.K.L."

I added the address of Uncle Frosty's office, then sealed the envelope, put Sherry's name on it, and went quickly down the street to Mrs. Moore's. Nobody was there, but they had a mail table, too, and I left my letter where Sherry would see it the minute he came back. Then I walked quickly home, trying not to think about how he'd look when he opened it, or what he'd think of me, or how he'd feel.

When I reached my room, I found that in my absence something had been slipped under *my* door—a rather grubby manila envelope that looked as if it had spent weeks knocking about behind a radiator or somewhere. Completely baffled, I opened it, and from between two pieces of laundry-box cardboard extracted one of Dave's drawings.

It was a beauty—a tall, spiky sort of weed vigorously captured in pen and ink over a wash of watercolor. On the margin were several quick, exquisite sketches of details: the curling tip of the leaf, a section of branching stem done once, then again, minutely altered; three gradually improving studies of a seed cluster. Obviously, this was one of those work-in-progress versions of something not yet perfected for the etching press and the outsider's eye—perhaps one I'd seen tacked to the attic wall. It was like a glimpse into the center of Dave's mind—a snapshot of his furiously patient hand at work. Across the bottom, in a bold, half-printed script, he'd scrawled, "Something else to remember me by."

I'd stood for some minutes, admiring the crisp, tense grace of stalk and leaf, before it dawned on me that it was pigweed.

Feeling as though I were packing my Dior hair shirt, I eased the drawing in flat on the bottom of the camel-bag—on top of Sherry's wavery-line sketch of Georgetta—and buckled the bag shut.

I caught a bus to town, checked in at the Heathman, and went to bed at eight-thirty. By eight-thirty the next morning, I was airborne, staring at a bald man's head in front of me, wondering what Sherry was doing right this minute, and clinging hard to the hope that what *I* was doing wasn't something I'd regret for the rest of my life.

Nine days later—August 30—Uncle Frosty was sitting in my room at the Hotel Del Prado, looking around him in a dazed manner at the paper-strewn room, the desk buried under a drift of manuscript, the two short stories he'd just moved in order to sit down—and I was saying nervously, "My inner girl, I think," and wondering how on earth to begin my account of the last three weeks.

He nodded, and his eyes returned to me. "Shan, stop pacing and start explaining. What's happened?"

"A lot. So much that—" I gave up trying to find a place to start. "Oh, Uncle Frosty—I'm in love, and I wanted so terribly badly to get married that I just ran away."

Uncle Frosty drew a long breath and settled back slowly in his chair. Presently, he began to smile a little. "That's your kind of logic, all right. I'd recognize it anywhere."

"Well, it is logical. I've just skipped some bits."

"Old dear, please go back and put them in."

So I dropped into the other chair and started on the story—reserving some bits that belonged to my new private life, but telling all I could about the picnic, my conversation with Mr. Bruce, my final decision, and my flight. And about Sherry. "Uncle Frosty, he's somebody you'd like, you'd like him enormously . . ." I began pouring out words to demonstrate this truth, and though I never came close to an adequate description of Sherry, I had Uncle Frosty's absolute attention. I think he was listening to much more than words, and his eyes had a peaceful expression when I finished.

"And does Sherry concur in this—this postponement of the whole matter? He agreed you ought to come down here?"

"Oh, he doesn't know where I am. Or even that I was going. I just went—while he was in Bell Landing." I saw Uncle Frosty's face and suddenly felt hollow. "What's the matter?"

"Matter? Holy smoke, Shan! Unless he has exceptionally steady nerves—"

"I left him a note. I *tried* to explain—oh, was it so treacherous? I gave him your office address . . . But he mustn't have any other— don't you see? He—"

"He *has* the note by now? He's back in Portland?"

"Oh, yes. He got back last Monday."

Uncle Frosty looked at me helplessly a moment. "That's rather left Miss Jensen with a handful, hasn't it?"

"What? Sherry wouldn't *go* to the office! Whatever for?"

"To wrest your real address out of my embattled secretary—if I've still got one. It's what I'd do."

This had never occurred to me. "But she doesn't know where I am either," I confessed. I was beginning to feel appalled—and I knew I mustn't feel anything but resolute. "I *had* to do it this way, Uncle Frosty. You ought to understand that—it's nothing but your own idea, extended a bit."

"*I'm* responsible?"

"You and Mrs. Dunningham. Didn't I go to that boardinghouse in the first place—incommunicado—so I could clear my mind about college? Well, now I'm going to college, to clear my mind about Sherry. It's got to work. It will."

"I see," Uncle Frosty said slowly. He fell silent, his eyes again moving about the room. They came to rest on Sherry's cartoon of Georgetta, pinned above the desk. "The Sorcerer's Apprentice. Who drew that?"

"Sherry. Isn't it—odd and wonderful? *That's* what he's like." We both sat gazing at the sketch a moment.

Uncle Frosty said, "I think I'm going to be very interested to meet that young man. And I'll bet I won't have long to wait, either."

"Do you really think he'll have gone to your office? That he'll—be all upset and everything?"

"Shannon, use your head. I think he's probably been battering down the walls."

"Oh, no . . . oh, I *hope* he'll understand. I think he will."

"Well, you know him—and I don't, yet. Though I've an idea I'll have ample opportunity this coming year."

"Well, you'll enjoy every minute of it," I said miserably.

Uncle Frosty smiled. "Yes. I'm looking forward to some good, satisfying, masculine discussions—about women."

The next morning we flew back to Portland. I felt as if I'd been gone for years—and as if I'd never left. I was almost afraid to walk into Uncle Frosty's office, but it was all right—Sherry wasn't there. He'd been there, though. Miss Jensen told us about it right away, rolling her eyes in a reproachful way at me. I guess Sherry was beside himself. "A bit distraught," was the way she put it. Uncle Frosty explained that I'd been a bit distraught myself and hadn't had time to inform her of my movements, and she forgave me, said he certainly seemed a *nice* young man, and that she'd felt awfully sorry for him. "Oh, and a letter came yesterday," she added. "I put it on Mr. Frost's desk."

I moved toward Uncle Frosty's private office as if pulled by magnets, and they started talking business.

The letter was fat and bumpy-looking, as if something too big for the envelope had been stuffed in anyhow, after complicated foldings. Of course it was from Sherry—addressed in the same tall, thin handwriting I'd seen, upside down, a hundred times as I set a coffee cup down beside his notebook. I picked it up and stood holding it, then finally got my courage to the sticking point and opened the envelope.

It wasn't a letter at all. It was music—two pages torn from a large songbook, maybe the very one I'd seen open on the picnic table that day. The music of "Greensleeves"—nothing else. It was quite enough. I swallowed, and in my mind the melody began to play itself—on three recorders—as I read the words through. *Alas, my love, you do me wrong, to cast me off discourteously—and I have lovèd you so long, delighting in your company! Greensleeves was all my joy, Greensleeves was my delight—Greensleeves was my heart of gold, and who but my lady Greensleeves? . . .*

I blinked hard as the blurring lines ran out, blinked some more, and managed to focus on the next verses. *I have been ready at your hand to grant whatever you would crave, I have both wagered life and land, your love and good will thought to have . . . Greensleeves was all my joy, Greensleeves was my delight . . . Well, I will pray to God on high that thou my constancy may esteem. For I am still thy lover true— come once again and love me! . . . Greensleeves was all my joy, Greensleeves was my delight—Greensleeves was my heart of gold . . .*

The page blurred again. I stood blinking out the window, seeing nothing. I can scarcely remember five minutes that hurt so bad.

At last, when I'd begun to see the window frame again, I refolded the music sheets into their crazy halves and thirds and sevenths, and put them back in the envelope. I was fairly composed when Uncle Frosty came in a few minutes later, after a tap at the door. He looked at me, and at the letter in my hand, and said, "Bad? Or reasonably OK?"

"Reasonably OK," I told him shakily.

"Any small thing I can do for—anybody?"

"Yes—you can lock me in your guest room for the next couple of weeks, so I can't get away and run right back to College Street."

"I'll do better than that. I'll take you to Mary's Creek and your Aunt Doris. That's the place for you now—and it won't be long until the university is keeping you too busy to look back. You'll make it, Shan."

And of course, I did. It was in Mary's Creek that I realized how far I'd come, got a little perspective, and began to feel I really could stick it out and not miss Sherry more than I could actually bear to. At least, after a couple of weeks there in the old house, with Aunt Doris and Uncle Syd, I gradually wore the thing down until I knew it was only a normal pain of parting that I was suffering, not downright medieval torture. And by the time I'd been at the university a month or two, I'd learned to live with it.

5

Looking back now, it seems a long time since all that happened, though as I've said, it'll only be two years this coming summer. It's May now, my second one at the university in this sea of Americans, and I'm still afloat. Actually, I've found college less abrasive than College Street—I suppose I've toughened a bit—and it's been just as engrossing, in a totally different way. A big part of that has been the writing. Oh, I'm still at it. You'd think I'd been under a vow of silence all my life until I hit this campus. Ever since, I've been trying to say everything I've had stored up. In view of this unending stream, I'm glad to report that my plots have improved since the days of the impossibly beautiful girl and boy and the sinister Manchurian or whatever he was. In fact, I had two stories published in the college magazine last term, which filled me with such confidence that I impulsively sent them off to a national magazine. The editor impulsively sent them right back, bringing me down to earth with a fairly painful thud. It doesn't matter—all I ask is to keep on trying.

I've done some theater work, too, and made some friends—though none as close as I suspect Ginny might have been—and opened enough doors to leave my front-hall closet behind forever.

I haven't found out what truth is yet, but I've found out it's quite all right not to know. If I'm reading my current philosophy course correctly, *nobody* knows for certain—and people have been peeling away at that onion for about five thousand years now. If there's no middle, it's at least reassuring to realize that there are probably a lot of layers yet to go. The real trick seems to lie in asking the right questions, and never mind if the answers are slow in coming, or never come at all.

About a fortnight ago I got a letter from Wynola, who at first wrote madly every day, then tapered off to every month, and now sends me a news bulletin when she thinks of it. That's still pretty faithful, all things considered. She says she's lost fifteen pounds but has gained some of it back, is taking a secretarial course and likes it fine, works afternoons in the Rainbow, and still wears her hair the way I cut it. Dr. Edmonds is going to Greece next month. Rose is getting married and moving to Seattle. Dave's already gone—he headed south, hitchhiking, just before Christmas, having evidently exhausted the Oregon weeds, and nobody's heard from him since. Sherry has been at Oxford since late last August.

Wynola needn't have told me that—I already knew it. For a whole year I heard nothing about Sherry and nothing from him—and Uncle Frosty never got those nice masculine discussions, either. Then one day last September I got a postcard from Devonshire, with a picture of a couple of those black-faced sheep standing on a patch of Dartmoor. There were two lines of tall, thin handwriting: "It's been 381 days, 6 hours, and 32 minutes since I said, 'I'll see you in a week.' Just shows how wrong a person can be." No signature, but I didn't need one. No address, either.

Months later, in mid-January, came an envelope postmarked Oxford containing three cartoons—apparently clipped from some sort of local publication. They were Sherry's unmistakable wavery-line sort, all featuring the same puppet stage, with a highly individualized Punch and Judy exchanging comments. Punch looked a bit like Sherry; Judy had Georgetta's hairdo. The captions sailed right over my head, since they dealt with Oxford current events; one of them was in Greek. There was a return address this time. After some painstaking thought, I sent my two published stories to it (mailed via Uncle Frosty from Portland) after trimming off the university magazine's name.

Sometime after Easter another postcard came, from some little village in the Basque country—apparently right on top of the Pyrenees, from the quite breathtaking picture. But Sherry datelined it "Timbuktu," adding only, "Here I am, Greensleeves, and I've got to admit it's wonderful. But where are *you*?"

Just last Thursday came another card—I suspect the last I'll get. It said, "I'll be home in Bell Landing the fifth of June. Greensleeves, I've been *awfully* patient. It's time to tell me where you are."

But is it? I've wondered so often if we'd both wish later that I'd just stayed lost. Everything is so changed—Sherry in England busy unlocking doors, I here in Eugene, Oregon, up to my ears in amateur fiction. Are we the same two people? I've been dating a boy who reminds me of that tallest Miller skyscraper—I met him in a play I stage-managed last fall. He's very nice. So, I suppose, is the film editor of the student news sheet here, though he spends most of our occasional evenings together talking earnestly about my mother. Oh, neither of them can touch Sherry. They're just men— the moment I really think about it, I know that. But I've been training myself so long not to really think about it. And, in fact, there are times when College Street and even Sherry recede into a sort of dream memory that's growing hard to believe.

I spent last August with Dad and Jeanne, much of it in England—I must have just left when Sherry arrived. I didn't know, of course; so we crossed like letters in the mail. It's just the way our lives crossed on College Street, really. Three months out of twenty years—it's no more than a fingertip touch. I realize it's superstitious to regard that near miss last August as an omen. Omens are medieval. But—so are masks and dominos, and a merrie singing cuckoo and a song called "Greensleeves" that may haunt me all my life. To me that whole fading summer has rather the flavor of medieval music. It had the shifting key changes, the gay, skipping rhythm and minor melody, and that unresolved, inconclusive end. I've kept telling myself, of course, that Sherry and I will never change, that we'll never be strangers, that we couldn't be. The fact is, I know we might well be already—and if so, how can we bear to find it out? Still, fair's fair. It's time for me to keep my part of that hard bargain I drove.

The truth is, I've done it, scared or not. Last night I wrote a note to Sherry. It's still here on my desk; I mean to wait for June and then send it to Bell Landing. It doesn't say very much about—anything. But it does tell where I am.

About the Author

Eloise Jarvis McGraw was the author of many novels for children and young adults, including *Mara, Daughter of the Nile*; *Moccasin Trail*; *The Golden Goblet*; and *The Moorchild*. She also wrote several books in the Oz series started by L. Frank Baum, including *Merry-Go-Round in Oz* and *The Forbidden Fountain of Oz*, both of which she wrote with her daughter, Lauren Lynn McGraw. *Greensleeves*, first published in 1968, marked a departure from her earlier fiction, which had been largely historical. In a 1982 letter to her friend David Maxine of the International Wizard of Oz Club, she wrote: "It was the most difficult thing I ever did to shift gears, get into the present and come to the party. *Greensleeves* was the product of that wrench, and it took me years to write . . ." During her lifetime, her writing won numerous awards, including two for lifetime achievement. She was a longtime resident of the Portland, Oregon, area. She passed away in 2000, but her works remain popular to this day.

Discussion Questions for *Greensleeves*

By Nancy Pearl

1. Considering that both cell phones and social media are now so prevalent in the lives of teens in America, do you think Shannon could "disappear" these days?

2. What is the significance of the song "Greensleeves" to the plot of the novel? Why does Sherry call Shannon Greensleeves?

3. What examples of humor do you find in the novel? Why would the author include these?

4. Why do the beneficiaries of Mrs. Dunningham's will decide not to fight to get their bequests?

5. Did you find any of the characters in the novel unsympathetic? Which ones, and why?

6. What are Sherry's reasons for going to college? What do you think of them?

7. Why or why not did you find this novel realistic?

8. Shannon has to choose between Sherry and David Kulka—what do you think of her choice? Why do you suppose she chooses the way she does?

9. Do you think Henry Bruce knows that Shannon is pretending to be someone she isn't when he first interviews her for the waitressing job?

10. How are Shannon's experiences in high school in Mary's Creek typical or not?

Further Reading: Realistic Teen Fiction

By Nancy Pearl

Laurie Halse Anderson, *Speak*

Judy Blume, *Forever*

Beverly Cleary, *The Luckiest Girl*

Maureen Daly, *Seventeenth Summer*

Sarah Dessen, *Along for the Ride*

John Green, *The Fault in Our Stars*

Daniel Handler, *Why We Broke Up*

E. Lockhart, *The Disreputable History of Frankie Landau-Banks*

Carolyn Mackler, *The Earth, My Butt, and Other Big Round Things*

Rainbow Rowell, *Eleanor & Park*

Mary Stolz, *In a Mirror*

Made in the USA
Charleston, SC
22 November 2015